EARLY PRA.
THE LAST HOBO

"*THE LAST HOBO* IS A LONG OVERDUE BOOK. Like the works of Kerouac and Steinbeck, it takes us on a thrilling journey through the heart of America. Although it takes place in 1979, the book offers a snapshot of who we are right now in the twenty-first century.

"As readers enjoy its breezy spirit and its sharp, often bemused observation, they will be challenged to consider with fresh eyes the current wrestling match for America's soul. Those on all sides of the political divide—even those with the "sex, drugs, and rock 'n' roll" mentality—are not judged but treated with compassion. Most significant of all, the author presents everyone as yearning for the same thing: something deeper and richer beyond the shenanigans."

— Louis Markos, author of 7 books including *On the Shoulders of Hobbits: The Road to Virtue with Tolkien and Lewis*

"A FUN, ENTERTAINING STORY about life on the road —the life of a true-hearted hobo—when America felt itself toppling into decline. This book gives you a keen sense of the soul-searching quests many went on during the tail end of the so-called 'Me Decade.'"

— Kevin Mattson, author of 8 books including *What the Heck Are You Up To, Mr. President?* A much-sought-after contemporary historian on radio and TV.

"A combination of F. Scott Fitzgerald and James Patterson. Brilliant use of Americana. A quick read on a lazy afternoon."

— Jan Speck, avid reader, Assistant Principal of Crestwood High School in Dearborn Heights, Michigan

Dan Grajek

The Last Hobo

A clueless Detroit kid hitchhikes
across America the summer
the seventies ran out of gas

Dearborn, Michigan 2016

*THE LAST HOBO: A clueless Detroit kid hitchhikes across America
the summer the seventies ran out of gas*

Copyright © 2016 by Dan Grajek

Published by Round Barn Media, LLC
P.O. Box 2333
Dearborn, Michigan 48124
(313)806-0937
RoundBarnMedia.com

Cover design and illustrations by Tim Grajek
Internal design by Dan Grajek
Edited by Joan Kettel
Printed in the United States of America

U.S. Library of Congress Control Number: 2016938423

ISBN: 978-0-9973247-0-9

Contents

AUTHOR'S NOTE

*"There was things which he stretched,
but mainly he told the truth."*

– Mark Twain, *The Adventures of Huckleberry Finn*

Kerouac wrote *On the Road* in three weeks. This book took 35 years. It began as my travel journal, but over time, it grew into a story that will take three books to tell.

As much as possible, I tried to preserve and stay true to what really happened. In addition to using the journal as my primary source, painstaking research allowed me to more accurately depict actual places, persons, and ideas. In some cases, I conducted interviews and used Google Earth.

Though facts received preferential treatment, most of the the names have been changed to protect the guilty. Creative license was used to help the reader to grasp the real story more fully. To this end, establishing simplicity, continuity, and dramatic flow was the priority. Fictional elements and characters helped clarify, illuminate, and explain things that would have otherwise been too difficult to get across.

Should this book be labeled fiction or non-fiction? Good question. *The Last Hobo* is probably about 80% true in the strictest sense.

I would advise the curious reader to keep in mind the old adage "truth is stranger than fiction." Expect the most outlandish, fantastic and unbelievable elements of this story to be true, and the more low-key elements to be fudged. I tried my best to stick to this formula while writing this book.

THE LAST HOBO trilogy by Dan Grajek

THE LAST HOBO: *A clueless Detroit kid hitchhikes across America the summer the seventies ran out of gas*

THE LAST HOBO'S QUEST: *A Dearborn student searches America for life's meaning the summer disco died**

THE LAST HOBO FINDS PARADISE: *A Motor City hitchhiker stumbles on the perfect world, but is it too good to be true?**

(*As of 7/4/2016, not yet available)

THE LAST HOBO

A clueless Detroit kid hitchhikes across America
the summer the seventies ran out of gas

Book I of THE LAST HOBO trilogy

Dedicated to my parents
Arthur and Theresa Grajek

PART I:

POVERTY GULCH

CHAPTER 1

THE UNICORN

Friday, June 29, 1979

I T WAS THE SUMMER OF MALAISE. As the Fourth-of-July holiday drew near, America had become thoroughly unhinged. We were engaging in "The Grand Experiment" when something strange happened from out of the blue: Heaven seemed to touch earth like a tornado.

Was I delusional or what?

Along Highway 14, we were coming out of the bustling college town of Madison, Wisconsin.

My traveling partner Pete LeBlanc and I stood on the shoulder of the road when the sun, reflecting off the chrome of a passing vehicle, briefly blinded me. As my eyes regained sight a second later, we spotted a moving figure on the other side of an overpass. It was brilliant white. It rolled like an imperial flag with the rhythm of the wind.

What... no... *who* is that?

The sight made my insides flutter.

As we approached, the form took the shape of a woman in a flowing dress. She reminded me of images of the Virgin Mary with her garment bathed in celestial light. However, her arms flailing in the air evoked a very different mental picture: Lucille Ball in *I Love Lucy*. The way she jumped around and waved at traffic cracked us up.

"Wow! She looks pretty crazy," Pete remarked.

"Does she really expect drivers to stop at her command?" I wondered aloud.

When we got even closer, "the apparition" was transfigured into "the girl next door" in her early twenties. She was petite with ample curves. She fermented a cloud of road dust with her quick, bold, confident steps. Her upper extremities were out and open as if ready to shake your hand or slap you. She wore woven leather sandals and a white cotton sundress with skinny straps that tied at the shoulders. The skirt part went down below her knees when it wasn't blowing.

Hunched over like Neanderthals due to our backpacks, we made our way toward the attractive stranger through the exhaust-filled underpass. The donut shop she was standing in front of came into full view.

She noticed us emerging from the shade into sunlight.

"HEY, GUYS, HOW'S IT GOIN'?!" she yelled.

Up close, we beheld the roadside diva in full splendor. She had tanned skin and short auburn hair. She sported Indian jewelry: a jade stone necklace, silver bracelets, and turquoise beaded dream-catcher earrings dangling from her dainty ears.

She greeted us warmly like we were her long lost chums.

"My name's Rosalynn, but my friends call me Rosie. I probably have the most uncommon last name in the world— *Smith*," she wisecracked.

Pete and I introduced ourselves.

Rosie Smith's very presence exuded something mysterious like laughter that catches you by surprise. Her wild green eyes, turned-up nose, and full lips constituted a face of unusual radiance. Her biggest asset was her immense smile, which reminded me of the Cheshire Cat from *Alice in Wonderland*. Her laugh was easy and deep. The way she beamed and crinkled her brow to punctuate her words made my heart flutter. It projected both sincerity and jocularity.

"Where are you guys headed?"

"San Francisco."

"The greatest city *in* the world! I'm in, man. Can I come with you?" she kidded. "I have a few friends out there."

Our mutual stories burst forth. Pete and I told Rosie we were from Detroit. She said she'd grown up in a suburb of Milwaukee. We recounted information about Point A, Point B, and everywhere in between.

At first, we'd thought Rosie was stranded on the highway due to car troubles, but we soon found out otherwise. She happened to be hitchhiking like us. She said she'd just visited a guy friend in Madison and was now returning home to a village called Liberty Pole.

"Do you guys have any idea what time it is? I've been out here awhile."

"Oh, it's 9:37," I replied staring at my watch.

"Actually," Pete chimed in, "I don't wear a watch. To me, the concept of time is pointless. People are always running around here and there, staring at their watches, freaking out when they're late. Me, I don't really care. I just take things as they come."

Rosie's face lit up with a dazzling display of teeth. She bobbled up and down. "Yeah, yeah, you're right! I agree totally! Time is just a man-made thing that puts people in chains."

"You know," Pete continued, "I was thinking about this the other day: Animals don't carry watches. They're different from us because they don't worry about anything. They're happy just doing what they feel like doing. You know, following their natural instincts. I believe humans should be more like the other animals."

"I say *amen* to that!"

LeBlanc's know-it-all demeanor irritated me, as it often did, but it was particularly galling to see him use it to impress a girl. Though he'd hardly whispered two words to me all day, insightful, illustrious words now flowed from his lips like a river. I may have slipped in a point or two, but I was, in effect, washed out of the conversation.

After animals, the topic finally shifted to the all-important topic of rock & roll. The fact that Rosie's musical tastes matched my own impressed me. She, too, was a huge fan of Bob Dylan, Bruce Springsteen, and The Beatles. To my mind, things-shared-in-common, especially being fans of a particular artist or band, signaled a mystical connection.

Was this chance meeting *meant to be*? Written in the stars, as they say?

I thought I could score a few points with Rosie with my knowledge of the rock stars who count. I'd read about them all in *Rolling Stone* magazine. The trouble was Pete also liked Rosie's music. He employed his rarely used gift-of-gab to impress her with all kinds of rock trivia, just as I ran out of stuff to talk about.

I felt humiliated.

"The Blockhead"

Pete LeBlanc had a stringy frame, a high forehead, and straight blond hair like Tom Petty. I'd met him nine months before. Our first meeting was pure serendipity, just like our chance encounter with Rosie. It happened on a chilly September night in the seminary parking lot. I was sitting with my best friend Randal Stark in his light blue Ford Pinto, talking and drinking beer when we spotted two young men next to a van. They were apparently smoking a joint.

Hoping to escalate our good time, we decided to walk over to them and introduce ourselves. The initiative paid off. Randal and I shared our beer; our new acquaintances, Pete LeBlanc and his pal Wally shared their weed.

Pete and I found out we had a lot in common. We were both huge Bob Dylan fans, a rare species in those days, at least in our age group. This made me think we were meant to be friends. At the same time, there was something about Pete that made me cringe. Maybe it was his awkward appearance, his hard-to-hear voice, or the way he laughed at his own jokes which I didn't get.

When it came up that Dylan was coming to town, we resolved to get together to buy tickets. Pete and I exchanged phone numbers and, a week later, we partnered up to wait in line all night in front of the Olympia Stadium box office.

This experience helped quell my initial apprehension about LeBlanc. In fact, over the next few months, we became close buddies. Observing how inseparable we were, Pete's sister once noted that we were like brothers. In a way, she was right. For a time, we were on the same page on practically everything: progressive opinions; taste in movies, books, and music—and most notably a desire to flee Detroit and never come back. Some folks even suspected us of being gay lovers, especially when they found out we were going on a long road trip together.

In some ways, I regarded Pete and myself as equal partners. But, in other ways, I felt superior to him. First, he was eighteen and I was nineteen, a huge chasm in those days. Second, the fact that he was a gawky-looking late bloomer made me shutter. His head was out of proportion with his body, his nose and eyes with the rest of his face. A few zits marred his fair complexion. His hair style didn't flatter him at all (though I was pretty gangly myself).

A dreamy loner type, Pete was hard to peg. On one hand, he came across quite unsophisticated. Early in our friendship, I learned not to share what my college professors taught me in class. Pete just blew it off as crap. Needless to say, he had no interest in higher education.

On the other hand, Pete seemed to be wise beyond his years. He frequently rambled about his views regarding "deep things" (spirituality, philosophy, and such) referring to the views of the "enlightened" rock stars. He was also into the transcendental poets Thoreau, Emerson, and Whitman.

Socially, LeBlanc was either inept or lackadaisical or both. He rarely smiled. He had an icy demeanor and a cryptic way of talking that came across uncouth, weird, and even rude. Much of this I think was because he refused to engage in small talk with people he deemed as "shallow." Even when he let down his guard with a selected few, his listeners seemed mystified by his outrageous opinions.

Pete simply didn't care about what people thought of him. He liked being the bohemian provocateur like Bob Dylan, or the potty-mouthed comedian like Lenny Bruce, or the wise-guy cynic like Holden Caufield in *The Catcher on the Rye*.

Like any friend would, I defended Pete behind his back, but I must admit that I was more than a little embarrassed by him. Family members and other friends wondered what I saw in him. Randal detested him. My mother hated his guts.

Mom dismissed Pete as a "lazy, good-for-nothing loafer." Her nickname for him was "The Blockhead." His detached manner and the way he didn't look her in the eye made her think he was up to no good. LeBlanc was the devil incarnate in my mom's eyes. He was the lowest of the low in the procession of bad influences on me.

She was probably right about that.

But that was all in the past. Far from home in Wisconsin, "The Blockhead" was now the formidable lady-killer!

Chucking It All

The subject of Rosie's destination—ninety miles northwest of us—came up.

"Say, if you guys are interested," she put forth, "We're having a big bash on my friends' property tomorrow. There's going to be a band and everything. Would you like to come?"

LeBlanc and I looked at each other and smiled broadly. Silly question! We would go to the ends of the earth with the likes of *her*. Besides, we loved a good party.

So off to Liberty Pole, Wisconsin it was! Rosie, our vivacious guide, claimed it would be a breeze to get there before nightfall.

To say that the three of us "joined forces" hitchhiking would be a misnomer of the highest degree. Rosie Smith was the only "force" in our midst. The snappy succession of rides came from mostly males driving alone, obviously enchanted with Rosie's bright, toothy smile, as well as the sublime sway of her voluptuous body. She was like one of the sirens from Homer's *Odyssey*.

We strategically positioned ourselves along the road—with Rosie the most visible, displaying her best hitchhiker's pose. Pete and I stood inconspicuously in the background, maybe a little off to the side.

Beholding Rosie's luminous presence, numerous motorists took the bait and stopped. After her brief introduction, Rosie would say to the driver with her hand on her chin, a contrived expression of afterthought, "Hey, any room for my friends too?"

After getting picked up by a Mitch, a Ken, and a Mike, it was clear that Pete and I weren't the only guys under Rosie's spell. This was a bitter pill to swallow. We wanted this woman all to ourselves. The odds of winning her love must have been a million to one.

But that realization would not stop us from trying. It was as if we'd encountered a unicorn, a one-of-a-kind woman in every conceivable way. Rosie was like our dream girl "Breezy," the free-spirit hitchhiker chick in the movie of the same name—wide-eyed and gushing with childlike innocence and joy, beatific like the Wisconsin landscape around us.

Rosie loved to jabber with the male drivers about everything under the sun: children, music, hunting and fishing, healthy diets, relationships, psychic energy, holy books of the East, etc. Even Pete had a hard time getting in a word edgewise. I got a smug satisfaction seeing him get a taste of his own medicine.

Nevertheless, I thought that he—and even I—had the edge over the competition. She was a hardcore hitchhiker. That meant she was a kindred spirit, a female version of us!

As we got to know Rosie, her smart, serious side emerged. More things-in-common surfaced, most notably her philosophy of life. It not only matched ours, but she had surpassed us, living it out completely, consistently and fearlessly. She raised the bar, as we'd soon learn.

"What are your plans for the future?" I asked her as we waited for rides next to a weather-beaten fence along a cow pasture.

"I stopped making plans," Rosie replied.

"What do you mean?"

"I learned that planning and scheduling and preparing for things is a waste of time. They suck the life right out of you. In my opinion, if you know what you're doing tomorrow— you're not fully alive!"

"How'd you come to *that* conclusion?"

"I used to plan everything out—school, work, marriage, family, whatever else. I got up in the morning each day and did what I was supposed to do. Eventually, the whole thing left me uninspired and drained. And, at one point, I just snapped.

Something inside of me told me I'm losing touch with what's meaningful in my life. I wasn't happy. I felt like nothing more than a cog in a machine. I realized I had to either surrender to it, or *chuck it all*."

Pete and I knew exactly what Rosie meant by "the machine." It was a metaphor for society-at-large.

"Yeah," Rosie continued. "I quit my job and everything, and just sort of disappeared. Everybody thought I was nuts but I'm so glad I did. I used to be a prisoner of the rat race. Now I'm out *here*, content, free as a bird."

"Living for the moment," added Pete.

"Exactly! Being *spontaneous*. Yeah, yeah, living moment to moment... in the present. Existing *now*, not in the past or the future. Each day is an exciting adventure. I never know what's going to happen next. And, isn't it funny? I can't stay in one place too long!"

Pete and I could relate completely to what Rosie was saying about "chucking it all."

Both of us had gone through a similar process of soul-searching (each of us separately). We agreed that our lives were miserable back home in the Motor City for a number of reasons. Number one, we were bored being there. Number two, we were sick of the racial tensions, crime, and blight. Number three and most importantly, we were tired of people telling us what to do. We wanted to come and go as we please. We wanted to be *free*.

We set out to experience freedom in its purest form...

That's "The Grand Experiment" in a nutshell.

A cross-country road trip seemed to fit the bill. Ironically, the place we were "escaping" from—Detroit, Michigan—was also the architect of the dream. Our hometown sold to the world something much greater than the automobile. It was the fantasy of jumping into your car, going to exotic places and enjoying the sights along the way. Detroit taught the world that freedom and happiness are all about *mobility*, driving where you want, going sixty with the wind blowing in your face, car radio blasting, and a McDonald's shake in hand. This formula was the perfect tonic for a restless young soul like me.

The only trouble was I had to rely on other people's cars for that freedom.

The Adventures of Rosie

Our lucky streak in getting rides came to an end when Rosie, Pete, and I went through more thinly populated areas. We didn't mind though. The long waits amidst rolling hills, cow pastures, and farmland revived the spirit. And they gave us a lot of time to talk.

Rosie went on to recount her experiences as we listened often with raised eyebrows and mouths agape.

She didn't tell us much about her life before hitting the road, except that she'd been raised in a well-to-do family, her parents were divorced, and she had taught Special Education.

Since Rosie had chucked it all, she bummed rides all over the continental U.S., mainly in the West. She'd visited Canada a couple of times and Massachusetts once. Then there was the "big Alaska adventure." She said she typically drifted back and forth along a triangle of favorite spots in Colorado, Oregon, and her beloved home state Wisconsin.

How she managed to fit everything in a span of a year-and-a-half boggled the imagination. When she wasn't moving from place to place, or attending parties, she worked temporary jobs, mostly waitressing at places like Denny's.

Her modus operandi was quite simple: She'd "experience" a place as long as it remained interesting and then she'd move on to another desired location. Like the wind constantly changing directions, Rosie simply followed her own whims.

Sometimes she'd relish a setting for a few hours and move on; other times she'd end up somewhere for a month or two, particularly when she needed to hunker down to earn funds for her free-wheeling lifestyle.

Rosie said she preferred to live in towns off the beaten path like Jackass Meadows, Idaho, because she liked the "small town experience." She also enjoyed being in enclaves of liberal people like her, particularly college towns like Madison, Wisconsin; Boulder, Colorado; and Eugene, Oregon. Since she was a die-hard nature lover, the ideal destination had to have natural wonders close by, such as mountains, ocean, or desert.

At one point, Rosie made an interesting remark: "It's weird, I got my teaching degree so I can help people, but I found out I can help more people *on the road*."

What did she mean exactly?

As much as she loved carousing with friends and taking nature walks, Rosie seemed to get the most kick out of playing guardian angel to strangers—old people, children, poor folks. For example, one time she stayed for five weeks in Jackass Meadows to take care of an ailing elderly fellow named Norman whom she'd befriended in a laundromat. Another time, she served as a nanny for a struggling family in Compton, California. Most important of all, she did humanitarian relief work—transporting supplies and helping build homes—for dislocated villagers in Alaska.

When Rosie said she hitchhiked all over the country for a full *eighteen months*, I wondered: What about safety?

How did Rosie—an attractive young woman—get away with it? How could she have all these adventures and not once be assaulted by some scum bag? In my mind, females seemed to be ten times more vulnerable to predators than males.

"Isn't it dangerous?" I asked flat out.

"Dangerous?" Rosie laughed. "*Of course* it's dangerous. But isn't all of life dangerous? Hell, breathing is dangerous. The only time you're safe and secure is when you're *dead.*"

Hmmm.

A Glimpse of Heaven

Our longest wait outside of a dairy farm ended when a guy named Steve picked us up. A blond-haired fellow wearing a black cap, he fit the driver profile: a young male driving alone. We had to squeeze like sardines into the back seat of his red '76 Dodge Dart, but who was complaining? We were just grateful for the ride.

A few miles out of farm country into underdeveloped territory, we were in for the shock of our lives. Rosie suddenly shouted out at the top of her lungs.

"STOP HERE! Do you hear me?! *STOP!*"

Startled, Steve slammed on the brakes. The inertia sent our bodies flying forward, along with numerous other objects—maps, travel mug, lunch box.

"What's *wrong*?!" Steve exclaimed dumbfounded. Pete and I were wondering that ourselves.

Rosie didn't say anything. She just bolted out of the car as if some extraterrestrial force took control over her. She ran into a resplendent green meadow saturated with purple wild flowers, and twirled herself around with her arms up like Julie Andrews in *The Sound of Music.*

"Oh God! This is *beautiful!*" she exclaimed.

Rosie had the look of ecstasy. She rolled her eyes into her head and smiled like the Cheshire Cat.

True, the meadow was pretty, but we men were more astonished by the sight of *her.* Steve reacted with a pensive gaze as he leaned back against the car. Pete and I burst out laughing.

I think everyone experienced something like a vision of heaven at that moment. For Rosie, it was the joy evoked by the beauty of nature. For us men, it was through watching this maniacal woman dance around in a state of utter bliss. She was like St. Teresa of Ávila, the saint who was pierced in the heart with God's golden lance—except Rosie was much better looking.

Lunch at Denny's

At one point, hunger brought us back to earth, so we stopped at the Denny's in Readtown. As we waited for our order, Steve seemed like just another guy competing for Rosie's attention. However, he had something else in mind.

"I used to be like you—into the whole hippy thing—but I turned my life over to Jesus."

Our first response was stunned silence like when your TV goes on the fritz in the middle of a good movie. Pete, Rosie, and I studied each other's faces.

"Oh, really?... Well, thanks but no thanks." LeBlanc finally blurted out as his burger and fries arrived.

"Have you ever read the Bible?" Steve asked.

"Oh yeah, I read it all the time. It's a good source for metaphors." Pete replied.

"Metaphors?"

"Yeah, I write poetry."

Rosie jumped in: "Oh you write *poetry*? I love poetry!"

LeBlanc was ready to respond. He whipped out a notebook from his backpack like lightning and handed it to her. Rosie examined his verses with an abounding interest.

After reading a couple of them silently, she quivered with delight. "Wow! This one really flips me out!"

Pete had found the express lane to Rosie's heart. He scooted closer to her.

Steve looked agitated that he couldn't get through to us.

As for me, I was mortified. Jealous anger poured into my heart like the grease in the kitchen and settled there simmering. I felt like lunging across the table and strangling LeBlanc on the spot. In the competition for her affections, he'd drawn the final trump card and won. I imagined Rosie putty in his hands from then on.

This turn of events put me in a sulky mood all the way to the day's destination.

Liberty Pole

LeBlanc, Rosie, and I arrived at Liberty Pole an hour or so later. A local farmer in a yellow Chevy pickup dropped us off in front of an inconspicuous Cape Cod-style house across the street from the general store.

The tiny town's main street consisted only of the store, maybe seven or eight houses, and a United Methodist Church.

The store appeared to be the village's center of gravity. The place looked like the recreated 19th century dry goods shop at Greenfield Village, Henry Ford's tourist attraction in Dearborn, Michigan.

The sign attached to the store's facade, just above the overhanging roof, read LIBERTY POLE STORE EST. 1845. A picture of an American flag appeared under those words and occupied two thirds of the sign.

Rosie had said the town was named after an actual flag pole in front of a local resident's house. During the mid-1800s, the home was supposedly a stop along the Underground Railroad. A banner was raised to communicate to fugitive slaves that "the coast is clear, it's safe to run here for sanctuary."

We sauntered into the overgrown backyard of the Cape Cod house to the garage.

SSSSSSSCCCCRRRRREEEEEECH!

Rosie lifted the weather-beaten garage door revealing a shiny orange '73 Datson 240Z. It was rusty in spots, but in good condition. Out of her suede shoulder bag, she whipped out a set of car keys.

This prompted the Question of the Day...

"Rosie, *why* did you have to *hitchhike*?"

"I really didn't have to," she replied with a shrug. "Well, don't just stand there. Get in."

So we did. She revved up the engine, backed it out of the driveway, and drove off.

Rosie turned left at the church and peeled down the dirt road with a trail of dust. Fifteen minutes later, we came to a hand-painted sign that read, "POVERTY GULCH."

CHAPTER 2

THE ARRIVAL

AHHH, THIS MUST BE PARADISE! I thought to myself in a serene valley deep in the woods.

I was all alone on the back porch of a log cabin. Surrounded by maple, spruce, and cedar trees, I sat basking in the lacy waves of sunlight on a bench with my feet up on the guard rail. A black Labrador retriever was next to me. The lazy dog rested its lower jaw and belly on the newly-laid pine plank floor. Its name was Choo-choo Charlie.

The aroma of freshly cut wood filled the balmy summer air. I felt extremely light-headed, relaxed, and euphoric as I listened to the delicate forest movements, the robin song, the rushing waters of the nearby stream. A faint breeze stroked my face. Above me, the sun and woolly clouds in the majestic blue sky peeked through gently swaying foliage.

It was like I'd gone back in time. This must've been what America was like two hundred years ago! The pristine scene and my sense of equilibrium with nature was *it*.

I had finally arrived!

Only hours before, it was Rosie fawning over nature in the wild meadow along the roadside. Now it was me. As weird as it sounds, it was like I was possessed by Rosie's spirit. The uncultivated surroundings, saturated with color and light, sent my emotions soaring like a glider. And, the half-hour absence of Pete and Rosie did me good. It allowed my addled feelings to stabilize somewhat.

I must admit, my sense of well-being was also chemically-induced. My new acquaintances at Poverty Gulch had kindly passed around a pipe of homegrown marijuana.

The moment of tranquility did not last long. The baby in the cabin started wailing. The talking and pounding from the house resumed.

A short bare-chested guy came plodding down the dirt path leading to the house. He had straight brown hair going down to his shoulder blades. His shirt was tied around his waist. With one hand, the young fellow managed to grip a knapsack over his shoulder—and a portable audio system. With the other hand, he held the apple he was munching on. The boom box blasted a tune by blues singer Taj Mahal...

> *Champagne don't drive me crazy*
> *Cocaine don't make me lazy*
> *Ain't nobody's business but my own*
>
> *Candy is dandy and liquor is quicker*
> *You can drink all the liquor down at Costa Rica*
> *Ain't nobody's business but my own*

After that, another song came on...

> *Sugar magnolia, blossoms blooming,*
> *Heads all empty and I don't care,*
> *Saw my baby down by the river,*
> *knew she'd have to come up soon for air.*

A male voice from the cabin yelled, "Turn it up! It's the Dead! The Dead!"

So the fellow cranked up the volume full blast as he walked up to me on the porch. It was a song by The Grateful Dead. Just then, Glenn Erikson, the owner of the property, came running out of his house. He was holding a hammer.

"Hey Roy! How's it going? Long time no see! Whatchaya been doin' with yourself?"

Roy had to turn down the music or force Glenn to strain his vocal cords. The two men gave each other an Indian handshake and embraced each other.

Glenn pointed to me.

"Roy, I'd like you to meet our new friend Ted Granger. Ted, this is my *old* friend Roy. We go back a long ways." He said they met in some bistro in El Paso, Texas, of all places.

"Where are you from, Roy?" I asked as I scratched the dog behind its ears.

"I live in my tent."

"C'mon. Where are you from originally?"

"Oh, it doesn't matter. That's a *past thing*."

His glib response struck me as funny. With one master stroke, he willed his personal history out of existence.

Glenn Erikson lived in the log cabin with his wife Emily and two children. Glenn was a good-looking guy with wavy, red hair flowing down over his shoulders. He also sported an untrimmed beard. Of Swedish decent, he wore tight faded blue jeans and an orange "Riders of the Purple Sage" t-shirt. Sweat covered his face and muscular upper torso. He also had on a tool belt that sagged below his waist.

Along with Emily, Glenn was the perfect host. Though he was occupied with many chores, he found time to make sure everyone was comfortable and properly introduced. Mostly notably, he made sure the weed was shared by all.

"Ted here is from *Detroit*," Glenn said to Roy putting his hand on my shoulder.

When Glenn uttered the word "Detroit," I noticed a slight kick-back in Roy's body language. By now, I was used to people having that reaction.

"Whoa. Pretty rough neighborhood, huh?" he replied with a mouth full of apple.

I thought *I* was cool hitchhiking across the U.S., but I'd learn later that he had done so *six times*! But he didn't brag about it. He had an unassuming quiet nature that I liked. I'd soon discover how popular Roy was around here, a reassuring fact because I happened to be shy. I'd long associated shyness with being an outcast.

"Hey Marcus, did you see Hooter around here somewhere?" Glenn called over to an older guy named Marcus next to a pile of plywood on two sawhorses. The man was wearing overalls with no shirt and a gray Stetson hat.

"No, haven't seen him."

"Where can he be? We haven't seen that devil in days, since he drifted off somewhere."

"He's out drinking again," Marcus said with a concerned voice. "One of these days we're gonna find that man dead."

"Don't worry. He's disappeared like this before."

"For *this* long? What's he doin'? Surviving on nuts and berries in the woods? Pretty soon, we'll have to send out the posse to look for him."

"He might be over at the Love's house."

"Or else, at the Finch's."

"No, not likely at the Finch's place. Remember, Blissful got disgusted with him and threw him out."

"Oh, yeah."

"I betcha Hooter shows up tomorrow at the bash at just the right time."

"*Of course* he will. That's the thing about Hooter. He's like a homing pigeon. You always wonder where he's at, but he always manages to find his way home."

"Yeah, home for him is where *the party* is."

Wild laughter ensued, not only from our circle, but from five or six people within earshot. Obviously, they were all in on the joke. It revolved around this guy named Hooter. I surmised from the banter that he was a very colorful character. There was a long litany of "Hooter stories."

O Pioneers!

The fact that Glenn and Emily Erikson had built the house from scratch blew me away. I was impressed, not only by their work ethic, but their competence in doing so many different things. I found out they'd grown most of their vegetarian diet. They'd made "junk" useful like a cable spool converted into a dining room table. And they'd generated beautiful paintings and other works of art.

The most interesting thing was Glenn and Emily cast themselves as pioneers. I mean real 19th-century American pioneers who trekked west in covered wagons to create homesteads and live off the land. It was so Jeffersonian. When Rosie first told us about this, I immediately thought of the Ingalls family in the book and TV series *Little House on the Prairie*. I imagined Glenn being Charles Ingalls in a flannel shirt and suspenders chopping wood; Emily as Carrie Ingalls, in a bonnet, stirring a pot of stew over a fire in a stone hearth.

When I actually met them, Glenn and Emily did fit the description. For instance, Emily hung stuff to dry on a clothes line, and wore a lacy pioneer blouse and her hair combed back into a bun late-1800s style. Glenn cut firewood in the backyard like Pa Ingalls.

Nevertheless, the log cabin and its solar panels on the roof were a sign of old and new things reconciled. The Eriksons were "pioneers" in more ways than one.

My talk with Emily started when she made her rounds and handed Roy, me and the others a plate of carrot sticks.

She was a pretty petite blonde with a distinctive gap in her front teeth. She, her sister Kay, and her girlfriends had been busy for hours preparing healthy snacks for the big party the next day. However, for some reason, Emily decided to take a break to give me a tour of the log cabin.

The house, spacious for pioneers, had four rooms: two small bedrooms, family room, kitchen and dining area. The stone hearth, just as I'd visualized it, resided there. Though most everybody used the outhouses in back, the cabin actually had a flush toilet and a real bathroom. A large picture window helped illuminate the interior. The whole place was decorated to celebrate everything down-home, rustic, and natural—antique furniture, old lanterns, paintings of fowl. Patchwork quilts thrown over furniture, an Indian rug, and a collage of rainbows and sunsets over the fireplace; added color amidst the backdrop of pine surfaces. There were half a dozen potted plants on shelves and hanging from the ceiling.

A number of people dashed in and out of the cabin to get stuff. The main focus was the kitchen area, of course, where the food was. Leafy things—jars of herbs, spices and other edibles—cluttered every inch of counter space.

I wasn't drawn to the food as much as the books. They were arranged on a shelf in the other side of the big room.

There it was: Glenn and Emily's family bookshelf!

To me, books are like an attractive woman. When you notice them, your eyes become fixated on them. You want to get to know them. You like the way they look, smell and feel.

While book collections are cool in and of themselves, they also serve as a kind of window into who their owners are. The number of "self-help," "how-to," and "do-it-yourself" volumes, confirmed my hunch that the Eriksons were utterly independent, self-reliant, and self-made. A well-worn copy of *The Farmer's Almanac* showed their practical, down-to-earth side. Titles on different philosophies and religions from Alchemy to Zen, revealed their owners' intelligence, creativity, and open-mindedness. Time-worn copies of classics like *Moby Dick*, *The Great Gatsby*, and *Huckleberry Finn* brought to light their affection for old things.

A dilapidated, but comfortable-looking brown couch stood next to the bookshelf. On it was a little girl and a young blonde woman sitting cuddled next to each other, sharing an ancient-looking book. The girl "Molly" was identified as Emily and Glenn's daughter.

Home School

Today, most people associate "homeschooling" with the religious right. But I first found out about it at Poverty Gulch.

The woman next to Molly had a very interesting name—Galaxy. She was a family friend. She wore a flowery blouse, stylish at the time, and faded blue jeans.

Molly, a russet-haired girl, probably about six years old, had on a long cotton dress with a floral pattern. She looked like the daughter of pioneers.

"What are they reading?"

"A McGuffey reader," Emily replied.

"McGruffy..."

"No, it's *McGuffey*. There is no 'r.' M-c-G-u-f-f-e-y. Here I'll show you one, Ted." She pulled out a volume—obviously from the same book series—from the shelf and handed it to me. It looked like some kind of school textbook from the early 1800s.

"Oh, she's doing homework?" I queried.

"Well, no, it's just... learning," answered Emily cryptically.

"Where do kids go to school around here?"

"Where? Why right *here*. This is school."

Galaxy and Emily looked each other and giggled.

"Ted, we teach Molly ourselves, right here at home. We *homeschool* her."

This was the first time I'd ever heard of homeschooling. Still largely unknown to the public that year—the idea of educating your own children without government supervision—seemed quite out-of-the-mainstream. It seemed radical.

"Isn't that against the law?" I asked hesitantly.

Emily turned to Galaxy and asked with a subversive grin. "Oh, *is it*?"

"I'm not sure. Yeah, I think so."

"I'll have to ask Glenn... Even if it's illegal, that's okay," Emily said with a shrug. "Laws are meant to broken."

"What are they gonna do? *Arrest* us?" Galaxy laughed.

"We teach Molly at home, because we believe public schools do more harm than good to children," Emily opined. "They're all about rules, rules, rules. And punishment! Oh God, Ted! Children are supposed to be free and happy, and schools fill their heads with nothing but negativity."

Galaxy sounded out: "What are government schools all about? Crushing independent thinkers who ask too many questions. Those who question authority!"

"*Outlaws*," Emily blurted out. "That's what *we* are!" It must've been the effects of the pot, but the idea of these women being outlaws in the mold of "Mrs. Sundance"—the character played by Elizabeth Montgomery on ABC-TV's *Movie of the Week*—made me laugh.

"Is there a better school than Poverty Gulch?" Galaxy posed rhetorically as her face shone. "In a public school, kids are forced to hear boring stuff in a stuffy room all day. Here at the Gulch we're always doing stuff hands-on—building and fixing things, farming, cooking, fishing, hiking, camping, creating art, shooting, swimming, climbing trees, exploring, experimenting, partying with friends, enjoying our beautiful land!"

I must say, the Erikson's innovative child-raising practices really inspired me. I knew right then and there that—when I have my own kids—I'll be as parentally-involved as these trail-blazers. It seemed heroic.

As the adults conversed, Molly sat quietly with the book on her lap, looking positively bored.

"May I go outside and play now?" she requested with a delicate and sweet voice.

"Oh yes, darling, of course you may."

At these words, the young girl jubilantly leaped off the couch and dashed out of the back door into the fresh open air.

Later, Molly Erikson would be seen resting on her daddy's lap on the back porch.

I must admit that I was a deeply troubled: The six year old girl was right smack in the middle of several people in a circle *smoking pot*. She wasn't taking part, but the grownups didn't seem to mind her being exposed to the activity.

Where I came from, taking mind-altering drugs in front of children would be considered very irresponsible (except if that drug happened to be alcohol, of course).

The Hobo Thing

Come to find out, the people at Poverty Gulch were very idealistic about "the individual." The term was constantly used. As odd as it sounds, they venerated *"you."* In overt and subtle ways, they seemed mindful about "your personal space" and letting you express and be yourself. I felt embarrassed when they'd say stuff like "Ted, what do *you* think?"

"Hey, maybe *you* can sit in that quiet place, so *you* can have *your* solitude," and "That's alright. That's *your* thing."

They really tried to zero-in on who *I* was, something I wasn't used to in the outside world (at least not to that extreme). This gave me the strong sense that Poverty Gulch was a very special place.

Back outside on the porch. Roy asked me the question of all questions...

"Ted, what inspired you to travel the country?"

"I suppose it started when I wanted to *hop a train*."

Roy's face beamed. "Oh yeah. Just like Woody Guthrie!"

"That's right!" I replied impressed that he knew where I was coming from. "As a matter of fact, a couple years ago I was inspired by the movie *Bound for Glory* where David Carradine plays Woody Guthrie. Did you see that one, Roy?"

"Of course."

I was referring to the '76 film about the legendary folk singer who wrote the song "This Land is Your Land." and "Tom Joad." Guthrie was a self-styled "hobo." This quintessential free-spirit stowed away in empty boxcars with other hobos during Dust Bowl days of the Great Depression. The movie poster with the image of Carradine as Guthrie strumming his guitar on top of a boxcar had left a lasting impression on me.

"I saw that flick for the first time with my mother at an afternoon matinée," I continued. "Mom and I left the theatre completely divided: I admired the way Guthrie did his own thing. Mom couldn't see past Guthrie walking out on his family to do so. She called him an irresponsible dead beat."

Roy smiled broadly as he shook his head.

"I swear, that movie knocked me out, man." I further explained. "After seeing it, I knew what I wanted to be when I grow up. Not a doctor... not a lawyer... not an airline pilot... I wanted to be a *hobo*."

"I love it! Hobo-ing—your chosen professional career!"

"Absolutely, just like Woody," I said enthusiastically. "He rode the rails whenever he felt like it. He did whatever he wanted to do, *when* he wanted to do it."

"No attachments at all."

"That's right. He just went around playing his guitar and helping people. Woody would get a job here and there, make a little money, and then move somewhere else. That's the life!"

"So where did *you* hop a train to?" Roy asked.

"*Nowhere.* I never got the chance to hop a train," I replied with sigh.

There was a trace of disappointment in his face.

"Here's the story," I began. "My best friend Randal Stark and I were walking along the railroad tracks bored out of our minds. Randal kept whining like a broken record about how he missed a girl named Constance. The trouble was he (as did I) lived in Detroit and she lived in New York. Suddenly a train comes by. After it passes and the noise fades, I look at Randal and he looks at me. One of us says to the other, 'Are you thinking what I'm thinking?'"

"You were considering hopping a train."

"Yeah."

"But you and your friend didn't hop the train to New York after all."

"Yeah, we thought better of it. We figured stowing away in a boxcar would be too much of a hassle. Trains always stop and go in order to load and hook up with cars. They can change directions unexpectedly and maybe end up in the wrong place. And you always have to worry about railroad cops and dangerous situations. So instead of riding the rails, Randal and I decided to play it safe—to *hitchhike* instead."

"That's cool. Definitely much safer! Y'know, in *Bound for Glory*, Guthrie hitchhiked too." Roy smiled, reaching out his hand and shaking mine. "So you're *still* following in the footsteps of your hero."

"I guess I never thought about it that way."

"How long was your trip? I mean that trip to New York."

"Only two weeks... but in a way..." I reflected, "It never ended. This trip to California is like an extension of that trip."

"So the guy you're traveling with is this Randal guy."

"No, that's Pete. Pete LeBlanc."

At one point, Glenn chimed into the conversation. He told me he'd done a lot of thumbing with Roy and on his own. Of course, that was before Glenn got married and started his own family.

A bond formed between us. We laughed at each other's stories of absurd discoveries and secret treasures that can only be found "on the road." As we talked, us three—Glenn, Roy and me—made even the simple and mundane things about our trips sound larger than life. My heart quivered as I chatted with these kindred spirits.

Down by the River

Getting acquainted with the Poverty Gulch gang temporarily got my mind off of Rosie. It's amazing what a difference it made. Being in Rosie's presence reminds me of what someone said about Teddy Roosevelt: When you parted with him, you had to "wring the personality out of your clothes." She was like TR that way.

I knew for sure I was in love with her.

In spite of my brief time-out, all the emotional stress came crashing back: Pete and Rosie had returned! They'd been wandering in the woods for a while. They were holding hands! Seeing them together felt like a corkscrew to the heart, as Bob Dylan would say.

In addition to that, I observed something quite remarkable: a change in Pete's appearance. For as long I as I'd known him, Pete looked stiff and cool like a sphinx, and, at the same time, awkward as the late-bloomer he was. Now, like Moses coming down from Mt. Sinai, his face lit up. He was animated, smiling, and comfortable in his own skin.

That's what a walk alone with Rosie Smith does to you!

"Hey Ted, you got to check out the river down there. It's great!" he exclaimed.

"Sounds cool," I replied trying to not to reveal my wounded heart. Glenn then asked Pete and Rosie, "Have you guys seen Hooter?"

"No, we haven't."

Suffering from the mother of all mood swings, I decided to blow off steam and to see for myself the creek everyone was talking about.

A short jaunt down a trail, its rushing waters could be heard from the house. Like the sacred Om reverberating from the river in Hermann Hesse's novel *Siddhartha*, the sound had contributed to my sense of calm and contentment on the porch before Pete and Rosie reappeared.

So I ambled down the well-trod path until I reached a steady flowing stream about twenty yards wide. Crystal clear waters rushed against the emerald moss-covered rocks and downed birch branches. A jumble of light and color pulsated on the water's mirror-like surface from the sparkling reflection of trees, clouds, and sky. It was picture perfect.

After taking a deep breath, I stood there on a rock buried in thought for what seemed like an hour, staring into the flickering water playing havoc with my image.

I contemplated dark thoughts, not only regarding LeBlanc winning over Rosie, but ones I kept suppressed for a while—

such as anxiety over what could go wrong on this trip, guilt over my estrangement from my parents, and even worries of how my rigid, oppressive Catholic upbringing may have permanently messed me up for life.

I envisioned myself as Siddhartha on the water's edge pining to drown himself!

I tried to pull myself together, to psyche myself up to be positive again, and return to the heavenly bliss I'd shared with Choo-Choo Charlie, just a short time ago. But it was no use. I couldn't control the negative feelings eating away at my spirit like a slow-acting lye.

The Old Trailer

Rosie showed LeBlanc and me our designated sleeping quarters—a trailer.

It was an old Serro Scotty camping trailer, perched on a clearing on a hill, a quarter of a mile from Glenn and Emily's cabin. The thing looked as though it had been to every campground in the world. The top half was white and the bottom was teal green. A third color, that of rust, hopelessly spotted the aluminum exterior like leprosy. Countless nicks, scrapes, and dents also marred its appearance. The only new feature appeared to be a decal of a leprechaun on the door.

When we got inside, we rolled out our sleeping bags on a king size mattress on the floor. The trailer's interior was a little grungy, but clean. You could tell Rosie took great care to make it her home away from home. (This was one of the many places she had lived from time to time.) She displayed plants, and pictures of animals and scenic landscapes. Light streaming through the picture window illuminated water bottles and jars of herbs on the shelves.

A sign that read, "DON'T WORRY BE HAPPY" caught my eye. So did a bookshelf that was filled with captivating titles on herbal remedies, pop psychology, and Eastern philosophy.

Pete and Rosie had planned another nature walk together, leaving me behind of course. Rosie said I could hang out in the trailer for as long as I wanted. This was actually a good idea after being on the highway all day. I could rest and even take a nap.

Observing me mentally salivating over her books, Rosie pulled out a paperback and handed it to me.

"Here you go, Ted. This book changed my life. Feel free to check it out."

My weary, bloodshot eyes examined the front cover. It read *Ecstasy: the Forgotten Language* by author Bhagwan Shree Rajneesh. It showed an Indian or Pakistani man, middle-aged with a long white peppery beard, bald head, and an effervescent smile.

After Pete and Rosie left, I eagerly flipped through the pages. The chapter titles really caught my attention. For example: Chapter one: "Now or Never"... Chapter two: "The Radical Revolution"... Chapter three: "Natural, Spontaneous, Aware," etc.

As I did so, it dawned on me: This is the stuff Rosie kept talking about all afternoon. In fact, it seemed to exactly fit her personal code.

This book may well be the one-stop source of Rosie's thoughts, ideas, and things that make her tick. Her gospel, so to speak. Perhaps I held in my trembling fingers the *key* to Rosie Smith!

As I read *Ecstasy* more out-and-out, I could see why Rosie liked this book so much. In fact, it swept me away like the perfect storm. One ah-ha, eureka, and amen after another. I devoured it like a hungry man in a smörgåsbord. I even scribbled much of it down in my notepad so I could remember it.

One particular passage leapt off the page:

> *"It is not that the intellect sometimes errs;*
> *it is that the intellect is the error. It always errs.*
> *Ecstasy is freedom. Joy is mad...*
> *The mind is ambitious, lives in the future;*
> *the mind is egotistical, stupid..."*

As I said before, a dark cloud, so to speak, had descended over me since Pete and Rosie returned from their first nature walk. I wished I could shake off my depression.

The above Rajneesh quote planted the idea: Maybe I'm *thinking too much!* My mind is like a spider, working itself into a frenzy, spinning a web of distressing notions, contributing its own entrapment. Why do I always have to hyper-analyze everything? Why do I dwell on the bad instead of the good? Why can't I just relax and enjoy Poverty Gulch?

The solution? *Insanity!* Abandon intellect and become crazy, suggested Rajneesh. As the author said, "The intellect always errs." Reason and logic blind the eyes of the spirit. Inner peace can only be achieved when one realizes the "madman" within himself, delighting in what the world calls... nonsense.

I imagined Rosie as a role model of this ideal. She was extremely happy in her "insanity." I wanted to be deranged and authentic like her! She seemed so content rambling around everywhere without worrying about consequences. She didn't rationalize everything like me. As Rajneesh advised, "Madmen who love life don't trust reason."

The Mormons claim you get a "burning in your bosom" when you encounter a major truth. That's how I felt when I read this!

★ ★ ★

Speaking of madmen, after a couple of hours of solitude in the trailer, I decided I needed to get up and walk around. I eventually rejoined Glenn, Emily and the gang at the log cabin. After talking for an hour or two, I made my way back to the trailer shortly after midnight to turn in.

There, the glow of starlight and a waxing crescent moon revealed the forms of LeBlanc and Rosie already asleep on the mattress (in separate sleeping bags). Crawling into my bed roll, I heard strange sounds.

At first, I thought it was Pete or Rosie stirring in their sleep, but it was coming from the outside. I heard grass rustling, heavy breathing, and grunts like some wild animal approaching the trailer. I laid there with my eyes open as, whatever it was, played with the door latch and tried to enter.

The door flung open.

A silhouette of a fat dude with a hairy body stumbled in awkwardly. He was stark naked! The burly beast-man found its way to the bed, flopped down its bulky flesh onto the mattress, and fell asleep right between Pete and Rosie! A funny smell invaded the room.

Hooter, I presume?

CHAPTER 3

UNDER THE STARS

Saturday, June 30, 1979

I WAS BOWLED OVER BY THE NUMBER of party attendees entering Poverty Gulch during the wee morning hours. All night long, crickets competed with the sound of engines and voices. One after another—cars, vans, campers, motorcycles, and other vehicles—proceeded down the private dirt road that stretched about a quarter of a mile from the main drag.

Party planners were obviously prepared for the massive invasion. Three teenagers wearing reflective tape on their clothes, stayed up all night to direct traffic. With flashlights in hand, they skillfully led drivers to designated spots where the new arrivals could park and pitch tents. But some guests would snooze in their vehicles. Others would sleep under the stars. Still others would continue their all-night binge into the daylight, drinking and smoking, walking around or sitting in lawn chairs. Occasionally, gales of raucous laughter and loud talking erupted.

It was fascinating and a bit bizarre when I first got up. Two or three o'clock in morning is always a strange time to be awake. The mind plays tricks as it mulls over, amplifies, and twists random thoughts and feelings that are normally kept in check during the day.

That night I had a hard time falling asleep next to Hooter.

Hooter! There he was: the man, the legend, and a large naked, stinky, mound of flesh rolled up into one person. His heavy breathing sounded bear-like. I found myself burying my nose in my sleeping bag to filter out the subtle garbage juice smell. It was horrendous.

The moment of truth came when I realized I had to leave the trailer to pee. I got up, left the trailer, and relieved myself under a big pine tree a few yards away. I'd decided against going back to bed because of Hooter. And, besides, the faint sound of merriment and motors in the distance piqued my curiosity. I was determined to make my way toward it like a moth to a flame.

The Welcome Center

The dying glow of my Bic disposable flashlight guided my steps. When it finally expired, I stumbled through thick, country-style darkness, tripping and bumping into trees, until I came to a clearing where I beheld lights streaming from a big canopy. As I approached it, I discovered I was at a vantage point where I could see everything.

The sight of steady incoming traffic and the gathering crowd made my spine tingle like that of a child on Christmas morning.

The herd of people, mostly in their twenties and early thirties, came and went under the navy blue 20 x 20 canopy they called "The Welcome Center." Red, blue, green, orange white, and yellow Chinese lanterns outlined the parameter of the tent. Three strategically-placed kerosene lamps cast a soft glow on the sea of faces.

The family friend I'd met earlier in the log cabin, Galaxy, was apparently the official greeter, directing folks to the water source—a rusty hand pump a few yards away—and the near-by outhouse. The spirited young woman also showed people where the organic garbage bags and other necessary items were, such as jumper cables, first aid, and bushels of fruit for those famished from the journey. Tables and folding chairs were set up for late-night conversation.

"What's your sign?" asked Galaxy.

"It's up *there*," I responded with a smile, pointing to the hand-lettered banner hanging from the canopy ceiling.

> WELCOME TO POVERTY GULCH
> WE'LL KEEP IT SIMPLE. NO FIRES.
> USE OUTHOUSE.
>
> – THANK YOU!

Galaxy looked up at the sign and then to me with a baffled look. "No, that's *not* what I meant."

"Sorry, just pulling your leg, Galaxy. I am Taurus the Bull-sh**ter," I said with a grin.

She was feistier and more wound up than before (and that's saying a lot). I think talking nonstop was part of her high-strung personality type. The flickering glow of the candle enhanced the beautiful features of her face. It added warmth to her otherwise pale complexion. There was something about her high cheek bones and her blue penetrating eyes that made her look exotic like she was from Paris.

Under the bug-infested tent, Galaxy brought up various interesting things to talk about.

Galaxy, who fit the profile of a "hippy chick," considered it cool to talk about "deep things" —usually spiritual and philosophical stuff. I found this refreshing. I was sick and tired of people's shallowness back home. Thankfully, up to now, friends like Pete LeBlanc and Randal Stark had rescued me from drowning in pointless chatter. We'd talk for hours about stuff like black holes in space, extra-sensory perception, and the meaning of life.

Most notably, we'd tackle the touchiest subject of all— religion. Our theological ramblings were often insightful, pretentious, and occasionally chemically-induced.

The discussion began when Galaxy, a self-described pagan, commented about the "mystical force" behind the chirping crickets. Two new arrivals, a Buddhist guy and a self-described "white witch," joined us at the round table. I felt comfortable enough with these strangers to discuss God, the soul, karma, and so on. I appreciated their feedback regarding Rosie's Bhagwan Rajneesh book.

Unfortunately, forces from without rudely interrupted our sublime exchange of ideas—two angry middle-aged women in polyester.

"This is *outrageous*! Definitely not what I signed up for!" the tall one blurted out.

"Yup, I'm definitely calling the sheriff!" yelled the short, heavy-set one.

A red-hot controversy, I found out, had been simmering throughout the night and finally exploded. The nearby Liberty Pole United Methodist Church had graciously donated the canopy, chairs, and church picnic supplies. And members of the congregation even volunteered to help out in the all-night vigil. However, it gradually dawned on these kindly churchgoers that they'd been "used as pawns," unwittingly aiding and abetting in activities they strongly disapproved of—heavy drinking, illegal drug use, and non-stop carousing.

Ill feelings escalated into fury. Fury gave way to an outburst of harsh words like "sin," "scandal," and even "hell."

As Marcus and others took measures to quell the dispute, Galaxy made the snide comment: "These religious fundamentalists are so judgmental and intolerant!"

I felt bad about the situation. And I found out later that this was only the tip of the iceberg. It would take a full three hours to hammer out a tentative truce. The meeting in the Erikson's house was a big deal, like the last emergency summit on the Titanic. I witnessed it first-hand. The inner circle huddled around the kitchen table as Glenn Erikson and Gunner Larson, the church elder, tried to work something out before someone called the cops. When it was determined the police would probably find out anyway, Gunner phoned Sheriff Haney, who was Gunner's (and Glenn's deceased grandfather's) fishing buddy.

To make a long story short, the Eriksons had to return only the "high-profile" items like the canopy, but at least there would be no major drug bust. A contrite Glenn took responsibility over the whole sorry affair. He apologized profusely to Gunner, an old family friend, who had to wake up and drive twenty miles to the cabin in the middle-of-the-night.

The Age of Aquarius

Galaxy, the Buddhist, the White Witch, and others went on blasting the Methodists.

"If you ask me," the White Witch said, "Religion is behind all the wars in the world. I saw the perfect bumper sticker one time that read, 'There will be peace on earth when there is peace among the world religions.'"

"Ahhh, *world peace!*" Galaxy uttered wistfully. A flash of inspiration seemed to light up her face as she peered at the crowd. Wheels of thought turned as she popped a few grapes into her mouth.

"Maybe... this is *the beginning*," she said dramatically.

"Beginning of what?" asked the Buddhist.

"The revolution! The children of Gaia, the Earth Mother, rising up and coming together... *here* at Poverty Gulch."

"Whoa, that's deep!"

I'm telling you, something wonderfully weird is going on here...We're entering the *Age of Aquarius!*"

Hmmm, the Age of Aquarius.

For years I'd known the Age of Aquarius to be the subject of a hit song in 1969 by a popular vocal group called the Fifth Dimension. However, the concept was fully explained a week before by our good friends Dave and Mary Zarret.

It was the very first night of our trip in Leslie, Michigan.

The Zarrets had claimed each Zodiac sign (Cancer, Virgo, Aries, etc.) has its own two-thousand year reign, and we're moving from the Age of Pisces to the Age of Aquarius. In the Aquarian Age—unlike the preceding historical periods—peace, unity, and love will rule mankind. Walls separating folks will be broken down. Bridges of understanding will be built. Each person will be able to tap into his or her own "inner power." There will be an outburst of spiritual awareness.

Was Galaxy kidding around, or was she serious in claiming that this sudden, unexpected change-for-the-better was happening at Poverty Gulch? It was hard to tell.

Maybe I was a naive college student, but I had dreamed of being an agent of change in a dying world. Inspired by the sixties, I fancied the notion of joining some movement to help save the planet. But I was discouraged by the heavy lifting that radicalism required, such as door-to-door canvassing, picketing, and blowing up buildings.

Perhaps the White Witch had slipped some strange brew in my drink, but it was now conceivable that the Zarrets were right: World peace was coming sooner than we think. It was going to happen naturally, without the messy Marxist class war thing, without me getting too involved. Maybe, *now* was the time.

Was Poverty Gulch ground-zero for the long-awaited outbreak of the new consciousness?!

In the Tree House

Yes, believe it or not, the next sequence of events occurred in a tree house. At a certain point, Galaxy wanted to take a break from her role as host of the Welcome Center. When there was a lull in traffic, another wonderful idea seemed to transform her round face from that of a woman into an innocent little girl.

"Hey, do you guys wanna to go up the tree house?"

The few souls present, including me, expressed ambivalence, not knowing what this "tree house" was. But Galaxy persuaded us to follow her lead.

So, with the light of a white candle in a mason jar, our host took our little entourage a few hundred yards to a huge oak tree dubbed "Methuselah" because of its age. The flickering light revealed something as magnificent as the tree dwelling in *Swiss Family Robinson*. It had crude spiral-staircase steps and, once you got to the top, you could stand on soundly-secured floor boards.

The view of the night sky above rendered everyone there speechless. The mood shifted from gleeful to pensive.

When the candle was placed on the tree house floor, it irradiated the five people in our midst: the resplendent Galaxy; Livgren, a college professor; a tall, big-boned manly-looking woman named Beth; and a young couple named Jeb and Dottie who seemed more interested in making out than saying anything.

"Have you ever seen so many stars in your life?!" I cried, leaning on the railing of the tree house. "I could stare at this for hours."

"I'm trying to figure out the group of stars over there. Does anyone know the constellations?"

"Oh yeah," replied Galaxy. "See the Big Dipper up there?"

"Ahhh, yeah… That's the scooper and that's the handle."

"Follow the handle away from scooper until you get to the next brightest star. That's Arcturus, the key part of the constellation Boötes."

"Boötes the Herdsman."

"That's right," affirmed Galaxy. "He's also known as the Plowman who drives the two bears—Ursa Major and Minor— over there. And those three over there are his faithful hounds. Together they make up Canes Venatici."

"Think about it," Livgren reflected. "How our Sun, let alone Earth, is the size of a sawdust speck in comparison to just one of those stars." His thoughtful gaze made him appear as the professor he was. At the same time, he looked more like a hippy, with his shoulder-length hair, wire-rimmed glasses, and Yosemite Sam mustache.

"That really cuts us humans down to size, doesn't it?" Beth remarked.

"Yeah, we're less than the size of microbes compared to even our tiny Sun," I injected.

"So much for mankind's inflated ego," Galaxy said.

The subject of the infinitesimal smallness of humankind in comparison to the scale of a gazillion galaxies depressed me. It reminded me of a gloomy conversation I once had with Randal Stark back home. Randal said he worked himself into a clinical depression pondering his own insignificance in the Universe. I think he wanted me to remind him that we humans were special in the eyes of God in spite of our puny size. However, sad to say, I could not comfort him with these thoughts. For the past several months, I had experienced "enlightenment" as a college freshman and had consequently abandoned my former religious beliefs.

"Where do you think the Universe came from?" I asked.

Livgren thought about it for a minute.

"Who knows?" he responded reflectively. "I do believe it all started with the Big Bang."

"Did *God* start the Big Bang?"

The professor chuckled, shook his head, and sighed, "I'm afraid not, Ted. All this came about entirely on its own. No supernatural guiding hand."

God does not exist. Period. End of story. That's basically the gist of what Livgren was saying. His words stabbed me in the heart like a dagger. Ironically, only a few months back, I was the smug village atheist going around campus challenging people's faith. That was before my new friend—none other than Pete LeBlanc—had persuaded me that this wasn't cool.

Beth jumped in. "You can believe in that stuff if you want, Professor, but personally, I believe God spoke it into existence, just as the Bible says." It was apparent she was one of the leftover Methodists.

"No, the *Goddess* created it!" Galaxy inserted with spunk. "Yeah, I think God is a 'she.' The Universal Mother!"

Whoa! This exchange was beginning to make me feel uptight. Even Jeb and Dottie, who were busy kissing the whole time, stopped and stared at the rest us. This was a telltale sign that our talk had gotten way too heavy. Discussing religion, I learned, is risky business like playing with matches in a dry woodland.

A raging forest fire could spoil a perfect romantic evening under the stars.

CHAPTER 4

DEJA VU

I'VE BEEN HERE BEFORE—but not necessarily in another lifetime. I'm talking about the Eriksons' living room. I slept about three hours on the sofa, in spite of the high-stakes drama going on in the kitchen—namely, the deliberations between Glenn and the church elder.

A warm, wet sensation jolted me awake. It was my ol' friend Choo-Choo Charlie licking me in the face! Wagging its tail, the clueless-looking mutt watched me launch to my feet to wipe off the disgusting layer of slime with my sleeve. Who knows where that tongue had been?

There was no one else in the room but the friendly canine and me. Again, the room followed the pioneer theme like the rest of the house. It had a charming natural and rustic decor, and, of course, an enticing book shelf. A medley of aromas from burnt wood, musty antiques and coffee coming from the kitchen delighted my nose. Still, the commotion from outside annoyed me because I wanted to wake up slowly. Through the opaque cotton drapes over the picture window, I could make out human forms roving around in the morning sun.

I'd failed to mention before that the log cabin's living room had a Marantz stereo system, complete with receiver, speakers, and turntable. On a shelf next to the turntable was the record collection. There, I found one of my all-time favorite rock & roll albums, *Déjà vu* by the band Crosby, Stills, Nash, and Young (CSN&Y).

I pulled out the album and examined the cover. I always got a kick out of how the rock group posed like a bunch of obstinate Civil War rebels, with pacifist David Crosby shown sitting stone-faced with a rifle in his hands.

"Good morning, Ted!" greeted Emily as she walked into the room.

Emily, a petite blonde wore her tie-die party dress with a turquoise-color sash. Her hair ran down her shoulders, no longer in a bun like Ma Ingalls. Though I'd only known her for a short time, I felt a strong bond with her. The fact that she had taken so much of her time to show me around meant a lot. She treated me like her younger brother.

"Would you like something to eat?"

"...Uh, yeah, sure, if I'm not..."

"No trouble at all, Ted. I'll have it ready for you in a little while. Would you like to listen to that?" Emily asked me referring to the *Déjà vu* album I was holding.

"Yeah, sure!"

So I put the record on the turntable and gave it a spin.

Breakfast with the Eriksons

As a festive pandemonium mounted outside, I mentally prepared myself to encounter hundreds of party guests. For now, I had the unique privilege of having the Eriksons all to myself, if only for a short time.

Glenn and Emily Erikson had not been part of the all-night contingency greeting and assisting incoming guests at the Welcome Center. Their leadership role qualified them to get a good night's sleep in their own bed. At least that was the plan. Unfortunately, the dutiful Marcus had to rouse them from a deep slumber at around 4 a.m.. By that time, it became apparent that Glenn and Emily were the only ones who could avert the crisis. They were qualified to prevent a strident church lady named Mabel Bergstrom from calling the cops.

Once the Eriksons were awake, the log cabin became a public place like the local post office. People invited themselves in for some reason or other. This allowed me to hang out, have a midnight snack, and eventually occupy the brown couch in the family room.

A patchwork quilt covered up the furniture piece, notably its worn-out spots. Its cushions contained lumps, dust, and animal hair. It smelled from dog dander, but it was a welcome alternative to the odor Hooter had emitted in the trailer.

Listening to the *Déjà vu* album was a pure delight. To me, the song "Helpless" captured the gist of Poverty Gulch— organic, beautiful, and wistful. Another song "Our House" seemed to fit the sweet and earnest Eriksons. (I'm not sure if they had "two cats in the yard," but they had a dog and a turtle.) Glenn and Emily made a cute couple. Emily frequently bragged about Glenn's accomplishments, making him act sheepish. This smart and able-bodied jack-of-all-trades was also very modest.

The Eriksons were "laid-back" to the extreme (or, in modern jargon, "chill"). They always seemed to be above the fray, figuring nothing—absolutely nothing—in this world is worth fretting over, whether it's slow supermarket lines, screaming babies, or even the roof caving in. I had to marvel at the Erikson's superhuman ability to deal with the hysterical Mabel before dawn. In the face of her most insulting, holier-than-thou, road-rage level rants, they managed to keep their cool, nodding and interjecting in the calmest way possible, the words "I hear you."

After I heard Side One of *Déjà vu*, Emily invited me to the breakfast table. I found myself face-to-face with the whole family—Glenn and Emily, the masterminds behind Poverty Gulch, along with their adorable little daughter Molly, and their baby boy Casey in a high chair. The dog was there too begging for scraps.

It wasn't a meal that I'd write home about: a bowl of oatmeal, toast, and black coffee, but it was all they had ready for now. An industrial-sized drum of chili was being prepared for the big meal later on.

Molly said grace. Then the Eriksons answered some of my burning questions about last night. After they explained the Methodist flap in detail, I asked, "Why did so many folks show up after midnight?" Answer: Most of them came straight from work—all the way from *Missouri*. "Who is Livgrin?" One of Glenn's college professors. "How is it possible to have so many friends?" You have a friend like Rosie Smith who has a gazillion friends.

Most of all, I was dying to know: Who is our mysterious midnight visitor named Hooter?

"Oh, he's just some guy we just kind of adopted," replied Emily. She admitted that she forgot where they'd met him. Apparently, Hooter came in and out of their lives on his run-down Harley-Davidson like some stray dog, *usually* as a guest with the good sense to not wear out his welcome.

The lawmen in the county, I was told, didn't know what to make of Hooter. The derelict biker seemed harmless enough, but he had a criminal record as long as your arm. For starters, he was a former member of the notorious motorcycle gang

Hell's Angels (known for its top-shelf criminal activity) out in California. For this reason, the police kept a close watch on him like antibodies on a virus.

The cops must have scratched their heads in bafflement: How did this sort of dude get mixed up with the enterprising, peace-loving Erikson family?

The common thread of breakfast time was story-telling. I told Glenn and Emily about me being inspired by Woody Guthrie, trains, and hobos as well as my most recent hitchhiking experiences. The Eriksons, in turn, went way back into their family history.

Glenn had deep roots in the area. His Swedish clan had been around these parts for four generations. Interestingly enough, his great-great grandfather, named Amos Erikson, had helped establish the Liberty Pole Methodist Church.

Emily was a "city girl" from Chicago. The couple met at the University of Wisconsin in Madison where they crossed paths with Rosie Smith and her circle of friends. After graduation, Glenn decided to hitchhike around the United States a couple of times. Somewhere along the line, he married Emily and persuaded a half-dozen friends to move to the Liberty Pole area to help start an organic vegetable farm. (Glenn and his brother Ray had recently inherited a few acres of land.) As the enterprise grew, the number of Glenn and Emily's friends employed there increased. The local old-timers initially had their misgivings about their new hippie neighbors. But they seemed to accept them after a while. Last night proved, however, that the reservoir of tolerance had reached its limit.

At around 9 a.m., the family soap opera flared up again. Sadly, phone calls regarding the Methodist crisis constantly interrupted our conversation. The pain of having "to patch things up" with kin folks living close-by was written all over

Glenn's face. However, Emily just seemed to shrug off the whole affair, smiling and acting like it was no big deal. In spite of her wavering husband, she remained the Rock of Gibraltar of laid-back.

"I probably appreciate the Liberty Pole folks a lot more than Glenn," she reflected, "because in Chicago everybody has to lock their doors. Your next door neighbors are perfect strangers. Here, everyone's like family." What she said about Chicago reminded me of Detroit.

"Not *like* family, babe. They *are* family—literally," Glenn quipped with a deadpan face.

There was a pause. Then the couple laughed heartily. He was alluding to the fact that his blood relatives comprised about three-fifths of the local population.

"The people around here are pretty tight-knit."

"Yeah, tight-knit... and *uptight*."

"Another Woodstock"

After Emily gave me the grand tour of the root cellar, I was anxious to go outside to see what was going on. I thanked Glenn and Emily copiously and left the cabin. As I walked from the back of the house to the front, I felt the cool fresh oxygen of the forest fill my chest and the morning sun caress my face. At the same time, I encountered exhaust fumes and crowd sounds.

The sensory experience was beyond description. The light of day exposed everything that was once shrouded in darkness. And there it was: the multitude—throngs of people before the glorious backdrop of lush green forest and rolling hills, surrounded by motor vehicles, and a chaotic array of blankets and camping gear. Folks were walking, talking, and giggling. Many had already started throwing around balls and Frisbees as I rubbed the sleep out of my eyes.

"*YYYYYYEEEEEEEEEEEE-HHHAAA!*" let out some guy at the top of his lungs. It sounded like the ecstatic scream of a cowboy riding his horse across the plain.

I interpreted the high-pitched shout as the official sign that the party had commenced.

The first people I recognized were the Missourians I'd met the night before. The White Witch could be spotted in the distance, as well as Jeb and Dottie.

After using the porta-john, I made my way back to the trailer to reunite with my toothbrush and other toiletries in my backpack. Along the main trail, I finally caught up with Pete LeBlanc. It felt like we hadn't been in touch for a month. Pete was wearing a slightly too-big green polo shirt and the grey denim slacks that his mom got him for Christmas. His unraveled navy blue sleeping bag hung draped over his right shoulder like a tunic.

My traveling partner looked rather perturbed.

"All night long Hooter had his fat ass on my sleeping bag," Pete barked, "Now I have to wash it!"

Once he got this off his chest, we turned to lighter topics, such as my all-night vigil at the Welcome Center. But Pete was only half-listening, preoccupied by the blithesome mayhem surrounding us. His face suddenly brightened.

"I can't believe it! It's like *another* Woodstock!" LeBlanc exclaimed sounding utterly mystified.

Exactly how big would the party end up being at Poverty Gulch? LeBlanc's off-the-cuff comparison to the famous Woodstock Music Festival in 1969 was obviously hyperbolic, but, then again, somehow the word "party" did not quite suit this gathering. Perhaps "bash" or "blow out" would be better. On seeing how things were shaping up, the word "festival" may have been an even better word. During a cursory walk through the parking area, I noticed license plates from as far as California, Oregon, and Massachusetts!

Besides crowd size, there was another obvious point of comparison with Woodstock. Quite a few of the gatherers dressed like they'd just come from the renowned musical event, via time machine.

One fact deserves pause: This was 1979... the Disco Era. It seemed like these people had missed the memo that the sixties were over.

They were out-of-style, or at least on the verge of it. The common denominator was "the natural look." First, it was the hair. Long flowing heads of hair, facial hair, even arm pit hair. Then there were tattered, faded blue jeans, and t-shirts. The most distinguishable clothing articles were bandanas (wrapped around heads or necks), and tie-die clothes that blasted swirls and patterns of vivid colors. Natural fabrics seemed to be standard, along with prints with flowers, lots and lots of flowers.

After the "back-to-nature" theme came the "exotic," seen in gypsy-style head scarves along with loose-fitting peasant blouses, dresses with Sanskrit lettering along the hem, ponchos, East and West Indian jewelry. Next, there was the "mythical past" motif: 1940s Stetson hats, buckskin, and the aforementioned *Little House on the Prairie* look, anything related to cowboys or Indians. And, finally, there were the stubborn "in-your-face" elements from the sixties: army surpus attire, misused American flags, and so on. One guy was even dressed like Uncle Sam!

While it might seem like an all-out hippy blow-out, to suggest that everyone was a "hippy" would be a stretch. True, many of the people were bona-fide hippies *philosophically*, but believe it or not, a few devout Methodists still lurked (though a good number of them went home). Some locals showed up, farmers, red-neck types, and such. There were a few bikers like Hooter mixed in. Many of the Eriksons' college friends and professors had stopped by. All said, the party was a mixed stew of hippies, intellectual-types, zoned-out party animals, and common everyday folks.

Another observation: The label of "hippy" was not used at Poverty Gulch. People couldn't stand being categorized as such, or anything else for that matter. One long-haired fellow, who donned hippy clothes from head to toe, said to me "Man, once you label me, you *negate* me."

Northern Comfort

The *Déjà vu* album continued to play in my head. One of the CSN&Y songs, "Woodstock," would take on major significance for me at Poverty Gulch for obvious reasons. But it was also *prophetic*: Who was the "child of God... walking along the road" in the song lyrics? None other than Rosie Smith!

The song had also mentioned that this "child of God" was going to farm country to "join in a rock & roll band." What did Pete and I encounter? A *rock & roll band.*

The band was called "Northern Comfort." Of course, this was a play on the name of the popular brand of whiskey, *Southern* Comfort.

We walked up to the scruffy musicians and introduced ourselves. Eyeing their guitars on the stage, Pete acted like a kid in a candy store, wanting to pick one up and start jamming right then and there. A roadie, noticing his intentions, politely discouraged him.

Northern Comfort came from Madison. Members of the band and roadies scrambled to set up for their long-awaited performance. They were all male except for a female fiddle player. Most of them wore the hippy uniform. One guy looked like a caveman minus the fur shoulder wrap, another like Robin Hood with his Van Dyke beard and a pheasant feather in his hat. The distinctive characteristic of the only girl in the group was her tall, lanky frame, long red hair, and calico cowboy boots.

I watched the crew work slavishly to somehow transform a jumbled up pile of instruments, cables, and wires into some semblance of order. They set up a five-piece drum set and energetically plugged everything into a mysterious black box connected to a thick cable going into the house, including the guitars with their respective amplifiers and speaker cabinets. The cave man hauled out the keyboard to the stage and hooked it up.

As Robin Hood mobilized the mics, the redhead checked the sound with a hearty "GOOOOD MOORNIN', POVERTY GULCH!" I felt my internal organs quake at the loudness of her voice. The crew made sure even fish and fowl in the valley (and my intestines) would feel the vibrations of the music.

Two vans of PA equipment indicated to me that Northern Comfort was not your typical weekend rock band. Two folks confirmed this notion—Roy and Marci.

"I got to tell ya, Northern Comfort are kind of a legend around here," Roy had explained. "I listened to some of their tapes. They sound really good... a little bit like the Allman Brothers, but bluesier."

"I think they have a good shot at hitting the big time. They have an agent in L.A. and everything," contended a sanguine young woman named Marci. A friend of one of the band member's wives, she was really pulling for the group. She described the sacrifices made by "Randy and the boys" to achieve that dream of stardom. While juggling jobs and relationships, they still found time to rehearse and record.

I must admit, I felt envious. Where I came from, it was every young man's fantasy to be touring in a rock group like The Band in the movie *The Last Waltz*. All you did was jam with buddies, party, and have women chase you all the time. That's the life for me!

Blaise and His Library on Wheels

During the Poverty Gulch bash, LeBlanc and I were like childhood friends who grew apart. I don't know about Pete, but I didn't want to hang out with him anymore. The main reason: I didn't want to see him with Rosie all day. But, as it turned out, Pete and Rosie were hardly together. Rosie was too busy socializing with her friends from all over the planet. The last I saw of Pete in the daylight was when he was improvising on a guitar and talking music with fellow musicians. I tried to stick around, but I got bored and set off on my own.

It was a fateful move. Another perfect stranger would come into my life and leave an indelible mark on me, as did Rosie, the Eriksons, and the Zarrets.

His name was Blaise.

I met him as I was aimlessly wandering around the parking lot. I was partly daydreaming and partly trying out a mental exercise prescribed by Mary Zarret. She'd claimed you can cause things to miraculously materialize by visualizing them first in your imagination. I was using this technique to meet girls. Well, it seemed to work—in a sense: I found someone willing to share his "Mary Jane." That's slang for marijuana.

"You look kind of lost, my friend," said a man in his late twenties. "Are you lookin' for somebody?" He was alone, leaning on the side of a blue '75 Chevy van.

"No, I'm just taking in the sights," I replied.

"*Oh-wee!* I know what you mean. There are quite a few hot mamas around here," Blaise declared with verve.

The man had average physical features, but he stood out in terms of fashion. Unlike many of the party guests who were stuck in the time warp of 1969, he looked "alternative" 1979 with his straight-legged black jeans and vintage black vest over a white t-shirt. His craggy appearance resulted from a ruddy complexion, coarse beard stumble, and unruly gray hair. Chains dangled from his belt. He wore Western-style tan boots. His blood red eyes must have been from either driving all night or smoking too much pot, or both.

We introduced each other. Blaise said he came from Boise, Idaho with his friends. He claimed he was "named after Blaise Pascal, the French philosopher." I had no idea who Blaise Pascal was at the time, though it impressed me that he did.

But that wasn't the thing that won me over.

It was the *books*.

Looking through the open side door, I could see that his van was chock full of them. In fact, the interior was like the town library with a makeshift bookshelf bolted to the wall. A middle seat had to be removed to accommodate it. Tattered paperbacks littered the floor of the van with covers faded by the sun. When I surveyed Blaise's collection, I spotted familiar titles, most notably *Damien* and *Siddhartha* by Hermann Hesse (LeBlanc's favorites, the ones he'd recently turned me on to). And there was also *Catcher in the Rye*, *The Grapes of Wrath*, *One Flew over the Cuckoo's Nest*, *Atlas Shrugged*, and the Mark Twain books. Many of these were essential titles, ones that had impacted me in the past like Sacred Scripture. I was amazed seeing them all under one roof.

The burning in my bosom flared up.

Blaise invited me inside the van for a closer look. As I excitedly browsed through the titles in the back, he sat in the driver's seat.

"Ever read *Jack Kerouac*?" he asked me.

I thought about it for a second. "No, I can't say I have... Jack *who*?"

"Aw, man, you haven't heard of Jack Kerouac?" Blaise said, making me feel like I was from the planet Venus. "He wrote *On the Road*."

He picked up a worn-out copy of the book from the floor and handed it to me. I examined it front and back.

"*On the Road*," Blaise continued, "inspired me, and a lot of other folks around here, to bum across America—just like what you and your friend are doing."

"You mean hitchhiking around?"

"Yeah, or driving or walking or doing whatever, man. It's about a writer and his buddy raising hell across country—partying, meeting people, doing weird random stuff."

"Free as a bird, spontaneous," I added with a wistful pride. It occurred to me I was channeling Rosie.

"Right on!" Blaise responded adamantly. "With Kerouac, it's all about *wonder*, man. There's something about random experiences. They stir up a certain... *consciousness*... you know, at the wonder of it all."

Consciousness. That was a word used a lot. It was usually preceded with the adjectives "higher," "deeper," or "new." Its meaning was not easy to grasp, sort of like "you will know it when you *feel* it." It implied a state of being when you're at the finish line of human evolution. You're fully alive, flat out enlightened. In this condition, a clear understanding of the profundity and meaning of the universe sweeps over you like the waves of the sea.

At one point, Blaise opened the glove compartment and pulled out a plastic bag of dried-up leaves—his "stash." The bag also contained some previously rolled marijuana cigarettes, maybe five or six of them. He pulled out one of the joints, placed it between his thin lips, and lit it with his shiny silver butane lighter. He took a long protracted puff, held in the smoke for a few seconds and blew it out of the open window like an exhaust pipe.

"Awe... amazement... wonder... at the world around you," he cried rolling his eyes in deep contemplation. "Each breath you take, each person you meet. As you behold the beauty of it all, man ! Yes, that's it—*beauty*! Inexpressible, inexhaustible beauty in its highest and purest form, the kind that makes you tremble and cry amen, man. amen!"

With rapture radiating from his face, Blaise handed me the smoldering doobie for a toke. His hand was shaking.

"Ted, you know, Kerouac came up with this word 'beat,'" he continued, "It's the state when you're so *beat down* that you're looking *up* into heaven. It's also short for 'beatific' which means beautiful or rapturous or heavenly."

Beat. I remembered hearing that word used in different contexts throughout the sixties. Rock & roll, of course, had a *beat*. There were The *Beat*les. Sonny and Cher sang "The *beat* goes on."

*Beat*ific—a very Catholic word... The beatific vision... Hmmm... Renaissance paintings depicting hosts of cherubs adoring the face of God. The Shekinah Glory: the physical manifestation of the Lord's presence such as the pillar of fire and the Eucharist.

Plato also used the term "beatific vision" for what you experience when you first emerge out of the dark cave into the brilliant light.

Oh yeah... the *beat*niks! I suddenly recalled.

This Kerouac guy was the founder of the beatniks—or simply "the Beats"—a group of wild-eyed eggheads who'd hung out in coffee shops, listened to jazz, and roamed across the continent for thrills. They wrote the finest prose and verse you'll ever read and liked to get high. I had read about them in *Rolling Stone* magazine. They reached their zenith in the mid- to late-1950s, but their popularity had started to wane by 1960, the year I was born.

Kerouac, their leader, was an adventurer, sort of an adult Huckleberry Finn.

Once this and other connections were made, I soaked up Blaise's words like a sponge. I now made it my mission to read

On the Road sometime soon. And Kerouac was only the tip of the iceberg. I was anxious to survey all the other books Blaise had, one by one.

Blaise and I ended up talking for nearly an hour. The man from Idaho seemed to have all the answers. It's like he had a clean, crisp copy of the road map to salvation.

CHAPTER 5

THE WALLFLOWER

S PIKE THE BALL.

That was the operative metaphor since talking to Blaise—and watching party guests play volleyball.

I'd been conditioned to think in terms of metaphors the whole time I was at Poverty Gulch. To the Eriksons and their friends, everything had to have some kind of cosmic meaning. For instance, the tree house symbolized being closer to the stars. The stars represented destiny, heaven, and the celestial powers that control things.

Metaphors surrounded us like the stars. Someone at the beer station wondered aloud about the *Lord of the Rings* references everywhere, objects and sites all around labeled "Hobbiton," "Gandalf's staff," and such. Emily told her this started out as a game to teach Molly how to recognize "the fantastic elements in life," but "it eventually got out of hand."

Next to the "the road," "the garden" was probably the most enduring metaphor. The natural beauty of the valley was, of course, likened to the Garden of Eden. And Galaxy, pining for the imminent Aquarian Age, evoked the wistful refrain from the song "Woodstock"...

"We got to get ourselves back to the garden."

Now the term "spike the ball" was my own concoction. This metaphor was all about grabbing the opportunity when you have the chance, sort of like Carpe Diem ("seize the day"). It came to me when I strode past the volleyball game in the field where the Welcome Center used to be. The participants gave it all they got, though it wasn't a competitive thing. They seemed to be in it only for the fun. Half of them were probably stoned out of their minds, so it didn't seem to matter if someone screwed up. Having a major buzz myself (thanks to Blaise), I imagined their agile bodies moving in slow motion, gracefully to and fro to keep the ball in the air, within set boundaries, over the net to the opponent's side. Each move mattered.

Spiking the ball, I knew, requires recognizing when you and ball are one thing. You're at the right place at the right time, and so is the ball. When the conditions are exactly right, you slam the ball into rival territory.

One of the female players invited me to play, but I politely declined. I'm not sure what was going on in my head at the time. I was probably feeling bashful or leery about embarrassing myself in front of others. I do remember that my "no thanks" triggered a thought...

Isn't that just like me? A freaking *wallflower!*

"Wallflower" conjured up memories of my awkward high school days. Yes, I was among the socially-awkward ones who'd clung to the gym wall during school dances at Bishop Borgess High. I felt like The Invisible Man: No one seemed to notice me. Having said that, I had the sinking feeling everyone was looking and laughing at me behind my back.

Refusing to play volleyball made me question everything I'd recently said or did, or more accurately, what I *didn't* say or do. I feared my being too passive cut me off from the human race. This intense self-examination could've been a healthy thing, the kick in the ass I needed to get out of my comfort zone. But cannabis does weird things to your head, especially if you have a natural tendency to blow things out of proportion like me. It makes you paranoid. It makes you want to crawl into a hole and die.

A voice in my head probed, accused, and condemned. "Ted, what have you done for yourself yesterday and today?" Answer: *zero*, zilch, absolutely nothing but observe, ask questions, and write down stuff in my notebook. Worse yet, I struck out with Rosie while I let LeBlanc score the home run.

I remembered Professor Dutton's take on existentialist philosopher Jean-Paul Sartre: "You have to participate in life's game and not be a mere spectator," he deliberated. "You're defined by your actions." This lined up with a song by folk singer Steve Forbert. The title said it all: "You Cannot Win If You Do Not Play."

You have to do something for yourself *now*.

Well, I did not return to play volleyball, but I did make a resolution to "play" or "spike the ball" in a different sense. I strengthened my resolve to pursue three things that were widely available at the Poverty Gulch bash...

Sex, drugs, and rock & roll.

I set out to accomplish two specific things I'd never done before—first, *try acid (LSD)*... and, second, *get laid*.

It was so consistent with The Grand Experiment!

Getting on the Bus

First, there was the *idea* of acid.

Blaise's influence on me would reverberate long after Poverty Gulch. Besides introducing to me to Jack Kerouac's

On the Road and other important books, he'd be the one who planted the notion of trying LSD.

He did so as he presented to me a book called *The Electric Kool-Aid Acid* Test by Tom Wolfe in the second part of our conversation. Blaise explained that it was a kind of sequel to *On the Road* (except it used real names instead of fictitious ones). It's about a bunch of folks who called themselves "The Merry Pranksters." These Pranksters, led by author Ken Kesey, traveled across America like Kerouac on a rickety old bus, wearing outlandish costumes, pulling random pranks on people and doing so while "tripping out on LSD." Kerouac's former sidekick and muse, Neal Cassady drove the bus.

The goal was to achieve the higher consciousness.

When Blaise first mentioned "experimenting with acid," I was aghast, picturing jars of powdery stuff on the shelves of my high school chemistry lab. But Blaise cleared up my confusion.

"Acid is another word for *LSD*! I'm telling you, it's the ultimate drug, man."

"Hmmm, LSD," I replied with an ambivalent tone, hand over chin, eyes narrowing to slits.

I knew about the drug and its effects. On one hand, the TV cop show *Dragnet* taught me it was extremely dangerous. It showed young people freaking out from hallucinations of monsters and jumping out of ten-story windows because they think they're Peter Pan.

On the other hand, a documentary I watched showed a distinguished scientist named Dr. Timothy Leary and The Beatles—the smartest rock band ever—raving about LSD's effects: wondrous and weird experiences like you're in some kind of *Alice in Wonderland* version of heaven.

And, only a week ago, Mary Zarret had testified that her one and only acid trip was "a religious experience," likening it to Siddhartha's luminous "ah-ha" at the river bank.

Acid. Good or bad? I weighed the pros and cons.

"In a way, the Merry Pranksters were like the American pioneers, exploring the uncharted regions of the mind," Blaise said enthusiastically. He recounted a few of their acid-inspired antics like splattering the bus with lurid colors, decorating it with American flags, and driving it through downtown Phoenix *backwards*. Their frolics also included bathing in slime pools, running around naked, painting themselves with Day-Glo, performing bizarre street theatre skits, doing every conceivable kooky thing, and filming it as a documentary.

"I don't know, Blaise. This stuff sounds pretty crazy," I replied. The word "crazy" leaving my lips could've easily been replaced with "fun" or "suicidal." My hair stood on end.

"But that's exactly the point, Ted. You're thinking too much with your rational mind. You have to allow yourself to let go and follow your inner madman."

Inner madman! That clicked with me. What Blaise said jived with what I'd just read in Rosie's favorite book in the trailer—*Ecstasy: the Forgotten Language* by Bhagwan Rajneesh. Again, the book contended that reason and common sense are the bad guys with black hats. Thinking is hazardous to your mental health. So I exhorted myself to "throw caution to the wind" and "go for the gusto" as the beer commercial admonished. Let Pink Floyd's lunatic lead!

Ironically, I used reason to arrive at this conclusion.

And it was the exact same rationale used when I had tried marijuana for the first time two years before: "You can't really know something is good or bad, unless you *experience* it."

Randal Stark had conjured up this adage when my other friend Mick Rhodes introduced us to pot on that fateful night in the park. We agreed to try it once and only once, to see what all the hubbub is all about. But, more importantly, it was to *gain wisdom*. The thinking was you must experience *everything* to be truly wise. This required being unbiased to absolutely any experience imaginable, however extreme, outlandish or forbidden by society.

Open-mindedness to all things was the key to becoming more sophisticated.

But here's the twist. Randal and I believed you should try everything at least one time, but *never let anything master you*. In other words, we valued prudence and self-restraint. We swore on the spot, practically in blood, we'd never get addicted to pot, let alone hard drugs.

It's funny what a difference two years and five-hundred miles makes!

"Where can I find some acid around here?" I asked Blaise. These decisive words sounded shaky like a mute man who suddenly discovered his voice.

"If you track me down later, I'll see what I can do."

Sighting at the River

After Blaise and I parted ways, I went back to the stream to see what was going on there. It was the same spot I was at the day before, a clearing at the end of the valley trail. Once again, the sound of the rushing water over the rocks had a calming effect. This time I beheld several groups of people sitting, looking, and chatting on the grass and on the huge boulders along the bank. Some were sun-bathing. Some were washing stuff, clothes, pots and pans. Some were jumping in and splashing around in the water.

As I watched, another metaphor dawned on me—*baptism*. Since I was a kid, I envisioned John the Baptist, waist deep in the Jordan River, dunking a continuous line of people anxious to have their sins washed away. Though I'd rejected organized religion, I fancied myself being a spiritual person. As such, I liked the idea of baptism. Baptism symbolized rebirth, when you go from a sinner to a squeaky clean soul. The problem was I didn't believe in sin.

Thoughts of "pure souls" came to an abrupt end when something abhorrent invaded my field of vision. It started out innocently enough...

It was a whale of a man coming out of the water.

First, the plump bearded head emerged, then the flabby chest. Chopping through the water like an iron-ore barge on Lake Michigan, he homed towards shore as the surface of the water rippled.

Then it happened...

His private parts surfaced out of the river fully exposed. He was naked!

In horror, I bowed my head, closed my eyes, and buried my face in my hands.

Why couldn't it have been some beautiful naked *woman*?! After all, this was "Woodstock!" Why couldn't it have been *Breezy* emerging from the water like Botticelli's Venus?!

The fact it was male grossed me out. Don't get me wrong. It's not that I was homophobic; I was just homo-repulsed. In the past, the mere glimpse of an undressed man in a locker room (combined with the stench of sweaty socks) made me want to bolt out of there like a cheetah in a brush fire.

This particular male specimen, the one coming out of the water, made me sick to my stomach. The hair covering its shiny body was smoothly matted by water from head to toe like some newly-hatched beetle larvae. It took a moment to register that the purple splotches on his arms and shoulders were tattoos. Rolls of fat, concealed by pasty white pudgy flesh, jiggled at each step, making the dude resemble the Michelin Tire Man.

"F***in' aye, man!" the life form grunted.

Then, a friendly voice on the shore gave away its identity.

"Hey *Hooter*, how's the water?"

Blissful Finch

After the Hooter sighting, the perfect opportunity to spike the ball presented itself. At least, that's how I read the situation. It had to do with my goal to get laid.

As I said before, I was a virgin. And I did not intend to stay one until my wedding night. As far as I was concerned, it was a curse. The murmurings of couples retreating into shadowy places like vans made me envious. I desperately wanted a piece of the action.

Someone who would give me a glimmer of hope was seen in the distance.

The young woman was first seen bouncing to the beat of the song "Cocaine," Northern Comfort's tribute to the great Eric Clapton. When I saw her again, she was sitting down a few feet away from the stage while the band was retooling. Her floppy wide-rim tan straw hat could be seen a mile away.

And something quite essential stood out: She was alone.

I went on a reconnaissance mission to check her out. As to not appear conspicuous, I circled around and ogled at her through groups of talking people. About ten feet away, I caught a glimpse of her profile.

She was in her early twenties, eating off a paper plate in her lap. She was classy-looking like she just stepped out of some Louvre painting with her 36-26-36 figure and 5'4" frame in a strapless cotton dress. The afternoon sun accentuated the patterns on her garment: horizontal bands of Lavender, Fuchsia, and Teal.

But the shadow cast by her hat obscured her face. So did her shoulder-length brunette hair hanging over her left eye like actress Veronica Lake. The mystery of what she looked like made her more enticing.

I managed to size up her face from a different vantage point. And it helped when she finally brushed her hair to the side. Her beauty snuck up on me like the aftertaste of diet Coke. She wasn't wearing any makeup, but she had all the right elements: smooth complexion with a few freckles, slim nose, full lips, etc.

I took a deep breath, combed my hair with my fingers, and made my move.

"Hi, is anyone sitting here?" I asked assertively, referring to the stainless-steel Methodist folding chair next to her. The alcohol in my system from beer spurred my confidence.

"No, sit right down," she replied gesturing with her right hand. I did what I was told.

"Howdy, Bud. Mah name's Jill Finch, but m' friends call me 'Blissful.'"

Her cool, poker-face expression made her hard to read at first. But her friendly nature was also like the diet-Coke aftertaste metaphor. When she said she lived "down the road," I wasn't sure if she meant that literally or metaphorically.

Her accent revealed that she originally came from the Land of Dixie. And a name like Blissful Finch hinted she was a hippy. (For some reason, the categories of "southerner" and "hippy" didn't seem to go together.)

What now? How do I jump-start a conversation?

When I'd confided with Blaise about my shyness, he advised, "Don't worry, people around here are a different breed, totally out-front and friendly." You can be yourself here. No games. All you have to do is ask people what "their thing" is, or come right out and say what you're "into." So I followed his big brotherly advice...

"What is *your thing*?" I asked Blissful. "I'm into music."

She nodded vigorously and gave me a "thumbs up" and then a wait-until-I-swallow-my-food-gesture with her forefinger. The pause felt like eternity.

"Same here!" she finally blurted out. "How do ya like Northern Comfort?"

"Yeah, I think they're pretty good."

"Mark mah word, they're *goin' places.*"

"So I hear."

"Ah've seen 'em a lot of times. Y'know, a couple of 'em are friends of mine." Her claim to know all the right people reminded me of Rosie.

"Well then, you're all set now," I replied. "Backstage pass and everything!"

A big grin broke up her expressionless face. She may have been high, but it didn't matter. Her undivided attention was like a gust of wind in my sails.

"Yeah, yeah, *here* it is: mah backstage pass," she said holding up her napkin playfully. "This makes me *bona fide.* Yup, a bona fide V.I.P." Her southern twang (especially when she said "bona FIDE"), her impish smile, and the way she tilted her head to the side when making a point, caused my heart turn over in my chest like a rotisserie chicken.

"What other groups are you into? I'm a big fan of Bob Dylan, Bruce Springsteen..."

"Bob Dylan. Oh, Ah just *looooove* Bob Dylan."

"I-I-I-I ain't gonna work on Maggie Faaaaaaarm no more!" I intoned with a yelp and snarl like a coyote. My perfectly-honed Dylan impression.

Her face lit up like the sun, followed by a gust of laughter.

"That's purty good!" she exclaimed as she nudged my shoulder. Only a slight tap, mind you, but enough to send a jolt of electricity up and down my spine. No woman, except my mother, ever nudged me like that.

Her declaring *Street-Legal*, Bob Dylan's controversial latest album, "another masterpiece" was a sign that she was a hardcore "Bobcat" (Dylan fan). We eagerly compared notes about the enigmatic folk singer/rock star, his work, his performances, his personal life. I bragged about being a mere twenty feet from Dylan at his Detroit show back in October.

She looked impressed. We also discussed the allusions to reincarnation in the songs "Oh Sister" on the *Desire* album and "Shelter from the Storm" on *Blood on the Tracks*.

Dylan's cryptic lyrics also got Blissful and me on to the subject of poetry. Recalling how Pete LeBlanc had skillfully used the topic to win over Rosie, I told Blissful I enjoyed "reading verse in my spare time." Judging by her raised eyebrows, this lie seemed to work like magic, except it put me in a vulnerable position.

"Oh, that's wonderful! So who are your favorite poets?" she inquired.

"Uh..."

I recalled the one poet I turned to for amusement. His inscrutable stanzas had titles like "Karma Repair Kit: Items 1-4," "Haiku Ambulance," and "My Nose is Growing Old." I'd even memorized a couple of his short ditties. And I could honestly say I read his book *Trout Fishing in America*.

"*Richard Brautigan*! He's my favorite poet," I declared.

"Goodness gracious! Ah looove Richard Brautigan. Y'all like him, too!"

"Oh yeah... 'Lemon lard!... with your odd snowshoes and your ability to remember dates... and that's all you'll ever want to be.'" This is the actual poem I'd once recited in my tenth grade English class in its entirety.

Blissful obviously was taken by my eloquence. As for me, I felt the buzz from a shot of much-needed success. In a small way, at least, I'd spiked the ball. But this game was more like *baseball* than volleyball. I'd only made it to First Base. To score, I obviously needed to go to Second, Third, and Home.

The prospect of me going "all the way" with Blissful was probably as far-fetched as a Mars mission. But it was not as unthinkable at Poverty Gulch as it was back home. "Free love" was the norm here. And, being an authentic hippy chick, Blissful had to be "easy."

What next? Blissful was probably anticipating my next move, I supposed. How should I take this situation further? The question was beginning to rattle me. I couldn't let this perfect opportunity slip by.

Well... here goes... I said to myself. I opened my mouth to inaugurate the next phase. It felt like I was about to go down Niagara Falls in a barrel.

I cleared my throat to make the suggestion: "Hey, how about going *down by the river?*"

"Sure thing, hon'!" Blissful responded.

CHAPTER 6

SURRENDER TO THE VOID

B LISSFUL AND I SAT ABOUT A FOOT APART on the trunk of a downed tree. We were under a shady grove at the river's edge, not far from where I'd last seen Hooter. Willow tree branches scraped the water's surface like giant claws, creating silver streaks and whirlpools. Behind the veil of leaves, you could see the wider perspective of the river's shimmering ecosystem, gulls swooping around in the air, swimming and perching on things. The relentless current coiled around or rammed its way into parts unknown, over rocks and piled up debris in its path.

My conversation with Blissful lasted about fifteen minutes at this spot until the big surprise...

Blissful let out an audible sigh. "Sooo nahce meetin' you, Ted." She said blithely. "Time to git back to my *old man*."

Then she shook my hand, got up, and left.

Hmmm.

First off, I was confused. Did I do or say something that scared her off or offended her? She didn't seem agitated in any way. On the contrary, she seemed laid-back, upbeat, and even gracious. Secondly, when she voiced the phrase "old man," I honestly thought she was talking about her dad, but then it dawned on me later she was referring to her boyfriend or husband.

A frozen feeling settled in. Blissful's abrupt exit was like the moment you noticed your computer crashed and hours of work had just vanished into thin air. It numbed me like Novocain. Needless to say, my precarious scheme to get her to Second Base, let alone Home Plate, had completely failed.

This realization eventually made me laugh.

How could I make sense of this? I consoled myself with the notion that the encounter wasn't a failure or a waste of time. The glass is half full, not half empty. For one thing, Blissful helped me to see that there were other fish in the sea besides Rosie Smith.

As I pondered the situation for a few minutes, another unexpected thing happened. A magnificent wide-winged bird—a blue heron in fact—sprung out of a thicket of cattails and flew into the azure expanse of the sky. Was this some kind of sign? It also activated my mental juke box to play The Beatles song "Norwegian Wood (This Bird Had Flown)," John Lennon's wistful recollection of a one-night stand. How sad my "bird" had taken flight prematurely, I thought.

Then, as I stood on my feet and peered into the rolling river, another Lennon/McCartney tune came on: "Tomorrow Never Knows."

> *Turn off your mind, relax*
> *And float down stream*
> *It is not dying*
> *It is not dying*

For those who never heard or remember it, "Tomorrow Never Knows" is arguably The Beatles' most "trippy" song. It anticipated my next move: the quest to abandon *all thought* ("turn off your mind, relax"), to let *consciousness* sweep me away ("and float down stream"), and to not worry about the *consequences* ("it is not dying").

What inspired The Beatles to write that song? No doubt it was LSD, the substance that supposedly helps you to...

> *Lay down all thought*
> *Surrender to the void*
> *It is shining*
> *It is shining*

Where could I find some acid, the revered—and feared— miracle drug I'd never tried before?

The question ran through my mind like a continuous tape loop. I guess I now bought into Blaise's highly romantic narrative about acid, how it opened "the doors of perception," how it was a vehicle to get to where you're going—onward like the stream, upward like the blue heron.

I was imagining a headlong, no-holds-barred flight into the Great Beyond, the much celebrated mental state called the "higher consciousness." Like the Wright Brothers' enterprise, this inner journey would be risky, but well worth it!

This would put my encounter with Blissful into perspective. Maybe, the goal of "free love" was never about love (at least in the traditional sense of the word), nor was it about releasing a pent-up sex drive. It was all about *the trip*—the term widely used for taking acid. In other words, "getting lucky" with Blissful would be like taking LSD in the sense that it would be a consciousness-expanding experience.

But it was never to be. This fact strengthened my resolve to take an *actual* acid trip.

I now turned to drugs.

The Dragonfly

By mid-afternoon, I was wandering aimlessly through the crowd trying to shut off the spigot of my rational mind. True to Rajneesh's advice, I tried to zero in on "the Now" as I began chanting to myself "I am not Mind" over and over.

Certain elements of the party seemed to egg me on. The guy in the Uncle Sam suit freaked me out like circus clowns did when I was a kid. So did those running through the woods singing mantras with flutes, tambourines, and bongo drums in an attempt to evoke "the forest spirits." There were signs posted on trees designed to mess with your head. They had Zen sayings such as "What is the Sound of One Hand Clapping?" and random nonsensical statements like "Stopple the Orifices of Tom, Dick, and Harry." The Eriksons and the gang had thought of everything.

Getting yourself into a state of "not-mind" is easier said than done. The blaring music, crowd noises, and self-talk distracted me. Then there were the dramatic mood swings. One minute, joy; the next minute, anxiety. I felt elated thinking everything was leading up to a climax: the emerging Aquarian Age from without, higher consciousness from within.

I was at the very brink, the cusp, the threshold of a major life passage!

The anxiety arose from the realization that I was playing a dangerous game like Russian Roulette. Not only regarding the planned drug experiment, but with everything in general— getting into complete strangers' cars when hitchhiking, continually putting myself in harm's way. Living on the edge, as they say. For what? The thrill of adventure, the glory, a deep knowledge of the Universe... But all the good books, songs, and movies had warned that disaster awaits those who cross over the line from "calculated risk-taking" to hubris, like Icarus plummeting to Earth after flying too close to the Sun.

But I couldn't afford to think about that now! Thought must be obliterated! Why pass up my chance to experience acid? Poverty Gulch may have been the *only* place left to find it in these end times.

As the impending twilight cast new shades of gray over everything, I hung out at the beer station near the back of the log cabin. It was like Grand Central Station, the major hub of activity in the most crowded area. Things remained calm and orderly—but only for a while. As the evening progressed, the drinking and merriment started to get a little loud and boisterous. To my embarrassment, couples were getting hot and heavy.

I found an open chair next to a Brad, a Jim, and a Holly, as well as two women named Lee and Julie whom I presumed to be lesbians. My initial shyness was countered by folks drawing me out, asking me questions like "What's your thing?" and listening intently to what I had to say. In doing so, they seemed to go beyond practicing the Golden Rule. My table companions and I discussed music, *The Farmer's Almanac* (of all things), and "games" (negative behaviors in relationships). My heart swelled with admiration, thinking these people weren't just special. They were *extraordinarily* special. And they were just like me: open-minded, freedom-loving "individuals" who liked to talk about deep things and who relished a good time. "Everybody I Love You," another song off the *Déjà vu* album, serenaded my mind.

Unfortunately, I caught a glimpse of something that made me intensely confused and troubled.

Over in the distance, I saw children dashing around, doing somersaults, and throwing balls.

What's wrong with this picture? I asked myself. On one hand, Poverty Gulch had to be *the* family place. Kids could explore and run around the woods, climb and swing on trees, and swim. The Eriksons even considered the whole place a *classroom* where children could learn and create with available art supplies, building materials, and books galore. At their "home school," youngsters could be in an unstructured setting and express themselves to their heart's desire. Jean-Jacques Rousseau would approve!

But Poverty Gulch *wasn't* a wholesome family environment! Since seeing little Molly getting exposed to adults pot smoking on the porch, I wanted to shield the vulnerable young ones from the inappropriate things going on: people getting drunk and high, uttering profanities, and practically having sex in the open.

What's *wrong* with these parents?! I thought.

High and half-drunk around sundown, I tried to broach the subject with my table companions—but not about the kids, but about my own need to acquire some LSD.

"Does anyone know where I can find some?" I asked.

"WHAT DID YOU SAY?!" replied Holly. The music was too loud.

"DO YOU KNOW WHERE I CAN FIND SOME *ACID*?"

Just then, a little boy—one of the children playing in a distant field—rushed to our table like an excited puppy. The angelic-looking young tyke, about five years old, had wavy black hair and pudgy cheeks. He was holding a glass jar carefully as if it contained something priceless. His right hand served as a lid.

The incident blew my mind, as the hippies would say. I bowed my head in shame at the idea of me asking around for hard drugs in the presence of a child.

"Look what I found, Mom and Aunt Lee!" the boy exclaimed. "A *dragonfly*!"

"Wow! That is really fantastic, Johnny! Let me see." The boy handed his mother Julie the jar. The woman with curly brown hair and a tie-dye shirt, she held it up high as she looked through the glass at the insect in the light.

"Is it alive?... Ohhh yeah, I see it moving its wing. See it! See it!"

Both mother and child examined the captured specimen closely like trained entomologists. I admired the way Julie selflessly hurled herself headlong into Johnny's inner world. She acted just as curious and amazed as the little boy was.

Blonde-haired heavy-set Lee stood up and came over to check out the bug. With her military-style buzz cut, she was definitely the "butch" of the gay couple.

"Beautiful!" she cried.

Others at the table also chimed in...

"Hey, it's trying to fly," said Brad.

"What are you going name it?" Jim asked.

"Is it a girl or a boy?" inquired Holly. (This was a funny question to ask with butch-looking Lee standing right there.)

At one point, Julie trembled with joy at the moment of discovery. Still, her face transformed into an expression of concern and sadness.

"I'm sorry, Johnny. You're going to have to *let it go*."

There was an expectant pause.

"I know." The boy replied bravely as his voice quivered. He lowered his head and swallowed hard. You could tell he was holding back his tears. Knowing eyes and smiles ricocheted among my companions and me like billiard balls.

So Julie and Lee followed Johnny hand-in-hand into the sunset to a far-away spot to release the insect.

The exchange between the boy and his "two moms" was a show stopper at my table. Everyone got choked up, including me. You could feel the love, and not to mention the happiness for the prisoner in the glass jar. The dragonfly was going to be *free again*! I have to admit, the THC in my system made a total idiot out of me. I was weeping and blathering over a stupid dragonfly!

Though impaired emotionally, I surprisingly maintained my wits regarding the issue of children being exposed to inappropriate behavior. I realized that maybe I'd been thinking about this all wrong. Perhaps kids are like that dragonfly. They need freedom. Sheltering kids from worldly things (like sex and drugs) might end up doing more harm than good.

Look at what happened to me. My parents had messed up my mind with all their silly rules, morals, and boundaries. Their 1950s-style conservatism repressed me. As a result, I had become too rigid and judgmental like those "narrow-minded" Methodists!

"Do It Fast"

"H-h-h heeeeeeey! Whaaaaat's goooooin' on?" intoned the wild-eyed long-haired guy who was politely asking to move from his seat.

He represented a number of sloshed people befuddled by the major program change being implemented: Northern Comfort's last stand. Their drug-induced stupor made it hard for them to be uprooted from their chosen spot. Tables had to be taken down, and chairs rearranged to face the stage. It was a hilarious thing to watch. Like Musical Chairs, zombie-like individuals were herded by the hosts to move to one location, but instead they fumbled around in circles and impulsively tried to sit down again in chairs that kept disappearing.

And those of us who were not yet totally smashed were following instructions of hosts *who were*! For example, Glenn Erikson, the Master of Ceremonies was bumping into trees. (One had to wonder, who was minding the store?) I didn't want to miss the band's triumphant return which was being billed to be as earth-shattering as the Second Coming.

But then I spotted *Blaise* in the distance. I said to myself what Jesus put forth to Judas Iscariot. "What you are going to do, do it fast." So I shouldered my way through the crowd to get to Blaise.

Slightly more dazed-looking and disheveled than the last time we'd met, Blaise still maintained his cool-cat appearance with his in-style black threads and snake-skin boots. He walked with a swagger and had in tow a loopy blonde who was about three inches taller than him. He certainly didn't fit the stereotype of a book worm.

"Hey, what's up, Blaise?" I said as I shook his hand.

He looked up. "The *sky*! That's what's up," he quipped with a foolish grin and a hiccup of a laugh. He looked at me with piercing red-laced brown eyes narrowed to slits.

His pretty female companion lightly tapped Blaise on the shoulder and made a gesture informing him that the cigarette he just put in his mouth was backwards (filter end out). In response, he let out the familiar quivery pot-smoker cackle, and groped to make the necessary readjustment.

After we exhausted the preliminary small talk, I reminded him of his promise to help me find acid if I'd "track him down later." His befuddled expression communicated that he forgot all about it. For all that, Blaise assured me he'd keep his word. With his hand on his chin, he nodded his head and rolled his eyes in a state of deep contemplation. It took him less than a minute to sketch out a plan.

The guy made an OK sign with his right hand, stuck the same fingers into his mouth, and let out a shrill whistle. "*FWEEEEEEEEEEEEEEEEEEEE!* Hey, Muskrat!"

Blaise effectively got the attention of a tall, lanky dude with lengthy stringy hair. The guy resembled Donald Fagan from the band Steely Dan. He was about twelve feet away behind a dense clump of humanity.

"Yeah, Blaise?"

Blaise motioned him to come over and Muskrat did.

"Where's Valerie?" the Idahoan asked.

I caught bits and pieces of the exchange between the two men. A plan being constructed involved this Valerie person and a man who was named after the world's highest mountain range: "Himalaya." The plan was as follows: Find a yellow '76 Volkswagen van in the parking lot to meet Valerie. She would tell me where the acid supplier, Himalaya, hung out.

What have I gotten myself into?! I thought.

After repeating the instructions to myself once or twice so I remembered them correctly, I thanked Blaise amply for his generous assistance.

It occurred to me as I walked away that Blaise was the serpent in the Book of Genesis. LSD was the forbidden fruit that would open my eyes to the knowledge of good and evil.

Shocking Incident at the Trailer

It was a race against time. I needed to complete this business with the underworld before the big show. Valerie, whom I met in the parking lot, was apparently the mediator between me and this Himalaya guy, a go-between to screen out undercover cops. The thirtyish petite Latino woman was cool and professional. With very little fanfare, she looked me over and told me where Himalaya was: "by *Bob the Tree*." And she provided me code words to use once I meet him: "Tyger, tyger burning bright."

"A hit of acid will cost you twenty dollars."

Valerie's words flabbergasted me though they shouldn't have. I simply didn't realize this would actually cost me *anything*. It's not that I was stupid (but then again maybe I was). I was just out of the habit of actually *paying* for things. During the entire hitchhiking trip, I practically mooched everything from others: rides, drugs, food, lodging, etc.

Getting something for nothing was the code of the road.

"Am I supposed to give you the money *right now*?" I asked earnestly while panicking that I didn't have my wallet on me.

"No, no, you pay Himalaya on delivery," Valerie replied.

Whew! Now that I had the information I needed, I thanked Valerie, and sprinted into the twilight. Before going to the beer station at Bob the Tree, I ran up to the trailer on the hill (my supposed sleeping quarters) to get my billfold from my backpack.

I made it there in about seven and half minutes flat.

Out of breath, I turned the trailer's latch, opened the door, and got halfway into the door frame. Then I got the shock of my life...

The soft glow of candlelight revealed two naked people "doing it" on the mattress!

Holy crap!

Sheer astonishment made me recoil so violently that I flew back like a paper mache doll in an industrial blast. I slammed the door shut. Under the pale evening sky, it felt like my heart jolted out of my chest. I was panting. My face must have been beet-red from blushing.

I took a deep breath, gathered my wits, and meekly knocked on the door.

Knock. Knock. Knock. Before I could say anything, the door opened and there was this long-haired, bearded fellow standing there.

He was stark naked.

"Sh*t!" I muttered. Here we go again. Another naked guy?! What's the meaning of this? The man apparently had no sense of modesty. The door was wide open and he made no attempt to cover his private area. Talk about laid-back!

"Hey man, it's cool. It's cool. It's cool. Don't worry about it!" he muttered empathetically.

"Uh, excuse me," I interrupted. "My backpack is in there. Can I get something out of it?"

"Sure, come right on in!"

I timidly entered the trailer. To the nude guy's left was a good-looking but dopey young blonde on the mattress. She wrapped herself up with a familiar sight—LeBlanc's sleeping bag! (Yes, the very one Pete had fretted about earlier because it had Hooter's cooties.)

"Hi there!" she said. "Do you have any *weed*?"

"No," I replied awkwardly as I crawled on the mattress next to her to get to my stuff. The maneuver required me to brush up against her because it was the only way to get to my backpack. With my unsteady fingers, I unzipped one of its pockets, reached in, and grabbed my wallet.

Then I darted out of there lickety split.

As I left, the woman bared an innocent Shirley Temple smile, waved, and blurted out a friendly "Byyye!"

The man, on the other hand, kept repeating "It's cool" fifty-million times.

There was a good thing and a bad thing I took away from this. The good thing was the man's incredible concern for *my feelings*. He made my emotional well-being such a priority that he forgot he was totally unclothed. Talk about *selfless*. What an extraordinary example of Christian charity!

The bad thing was I felt embarrassed. From the hippy perspective, shame is a big no-no. It's considered a "hang up." After all, Adam and Eve were "naked and unashamed" (before the Fall, that is). And, of course, Poverty Gulch was *pre-Fall* all the way. It was all about "getting back to the garden."

Last Stop: Bob the Tree

From the trailer, I frantically scurried in the near-darkness. It would take me about five minutes to get to the "Bob the Tree" beer station.

The place was shady in more ways than one. Located in the more densely wooded area, it was an eighth of a mile down the trail from where the commotion surrounding Northern Comfort was. The more wayward people hung out there.

The famous tree looked exactly the same as all the other maples around it. Its huge trunk was where the kegs and goodies were set up on a table. Said to have magical powers, the maple tree had nailed on it a 12" x 18" hand-painted sign that read "Bob the Tree." The absurd name did not originate from acidheads as one would expect, but from the children.

When I arrived, I beheld a dozen or so unshaven, tattooed individuals, standing around, most of them males. The glow of a Sears lantern revealed that half of them were bikers with leather vests and jackets featuring images of skulls and flames. Were they Hooter's friends? All these modern-day barbarians were, to some degree or other, wasted on beer and drugs. Some of them were quiet, inert souls in their own world. Others were loud-mouths spouting out all kinds of trash and nonsense with rambling, slurred speech, forgetting their thoughts in mid-sentence. They could hardly walk, fumbling around spilling their drinks.

The sheer unpredictability of these people, saying stuff like "I love you" one minute and "I'm gonna kick your ass" the next, made you think twice about being there. And I must admit the guy uttering random gibberish to a stalk of broccoli really gave me the willies!

Part of me wanted to turn back. The other part of me pushed forward.

"Is Himalaya around?" I asked gasping for breath shortly after I had so spectacularly burst onto the scene. Scratches and scraps must have covered my arms and knees from running into and tripping over things.

A glint of compassion shone on certain faces as if I was some escaped prisoner being pursued by blood hounds. Of course I wasn't being chased. I just wanted to catch the drug dealer before he leaves to attend the show.

"Are you okay, man?

"Yeah. I'm looking for Himalaya."

"Himalaya? He's not here."

"Not here? Then where is he?"

A shrug or two was the only answer I got.

I sat down on a log shaking my head in disappointment. The idea that I went through all this for nothing—the search for Valerie, the humiliating trailer episode, and scrambling through the dark woods without a flashlight—made me want to howl at a Moon that was barely seen. I was like Dorothy who'd just missed the Great Oz.

Just then, I heard the sound of a door slamming. It came from the outhouse a few yards away. A man the size of King Kong emerged from the shadows into the bug-infested light.

I knew immediately he was the one I had come for.

If appearing inconspicuous was a top requirement for successful drug dealers, this guy wouldn't qualify. Folks didn't call him "Himalaya" for nothing. He was a *big* guy, height-wise and width-wise. About 6' 7" and obese. To add to his physical distinctiveness, he had mixed blood, predominately African-American and Asian, maybe even a little Hawaiian. (Most of the people at Poverty Gulch, by the way, were white.)

He zipped up his pants as he walked over. He was wearing blue jeans and a denim vest with no shirt underneath.

"Himalaya, right?

"Yeah, that's me."

"Tyger Tyger burning bright."

The oversized man looked me over up and down like a finicky shopper. He then sighed, made a grunt, and glanced at the guy standing next to him in Davy Crockett attire. Then he combed his kinky jet-black hair back with his fingers.

"So what kind of stuff are you lookin' for?" Himalaya probed. "Let's see here, I got some pot, hash, coke, acid, even some goofballs."

"Some *acid* please."

"A hit of acid? That will be twenty bucks."

"Sure."

I reached into my pocket and pulled out my wallet. It was the moment of truth. All abstract thought was finally being translated into action. Expectations were high. As sacrilegious as it sounds, I compared taking LSD for the first time to receiving my first Holy Communion.

When I opened and looked into the billfold of my wallet, something gave me that sinking feeling. Then something profoundly stupid left my lips.

"Do you take *traveler's checks*?"

My listeners peered at each other intently. Once what I said registered, smiles congealed, followed by a blast of raucous laughter.

I was a smash hit! However, the only one not laughing was me.

I'd bombed of course—and I did so in major way. The acid-trip-that-didn't-happen was a big disappointment to say the least, just like my misfire with Blissful Finch. Here's my Freudian take: It was all my *parents' fault.* The old-fashioned morality they'd instilled in me messed me up. Using guilt, shame, and fear of a judgmental God, they caused me to unconsciously sabotage myself.

Dear old Mom and Dad were a bad influence!

But then it occurred to me: How can you blame your folks? My parents are basically good, decent people, albeit *misled*—perhaps even brainwashed. They don't exercise that much power over my life. It was *me* who committed the sin of being uptight.

I realized *I* had to take responsibility for my own actions, as Jean-Paul Sartre would have it.

There was so much to learn! The challenge ahead seemed so daunting. When would I be able to stop holding back, relax, and surrender to insanity? I normally would've beaten myself up over it. But the night was still young. I made the determination to end the day on a high note. So I proceeded to head back to the homestead to witness Northern Comfort's last stand.

CHAPTER 7

THE SHOWSTOPPERS

A LL EYES WERE ON ROBIN HOOD in the spotlight. "How are you doin' tonight, Poverty Gulch?!" he bellowed into the microphone. He was speaking on behalf of Northern Comfort.

The crowd went wild, clapping, bouncing, letting out a collective primal scream that sounded like a mish-mash of "AWESOME!" "WONDERFUL!" and "GREAT!"

"Are you ready to *rock & roll*?!" Sir Robin who was wearing shades continued.

"YYYYYYEEEEEEEEEEAAAAAAAAAAAHHHHHHHHH!" screamed the audience.

On cue, each musician triumphantly strode out onto the brightly-lit 24'x16' rented stage. They were the epitome of "cool." They swaggered over to their designated spots where their instruments awaited them. First, the two guitarists, then the keyboard player, and then the drummer. Then finally Robin picked up his shiny Fender guitar and strapped it to his beefy shoulders.

Robin Hood's real name was Randy Lance. The front man and de facto leader of the band, Randy channeled the showmanship skills and take-no-prisoners energy of a Bruce Springsteen. His passionate words fanned the flames of anticipation. The message was clear: Northern Comfort was ready to break all sonic and psychic barriers.

"Was anyone around during our all-day jam session?!" Randy earnestly asked the audience.

"YYYYYYEEEEEEEEEEAAAAAAAAAAHHHHHHHHH!!

"I just wanted to let you know that we were just *warming up*! Here we go! ONE, TWO, ONE, TWO, THREE, FOUR..."

Like a thunder clap, Randy launched into a funky, rollicking Chuck Berry-sounding guitar lick. The other musicians jumped in, including the intrepid rhythm guitarist/violinist/vocalist, Kari, decked out in her cowgirl clothes...

I went down to the mountain, I was drinking some wine
Looked up in the heavens lord I saw a mighty sign
Written fire across the heaven, plain as black and white
Get prepared, there's gonna be a party tonight
Uhuh, hey! Saturday Night

Bull's eye! Frantic, delirious dancing broke out all over the place. With the rhythm of the music, arms glided up and down, and rocked to and fro. Hands clapped, flittered, and waved. Hips wiggled, swayed, and twisted. Legs jumped, bobbed, and kicked to the Grateful Dead song.

Everyone transformed into sweating, maniacal dervishes.

Standing at a slightly obstructed place near the stage, I took pause at the sheer mystery of the phenomenon before me. It floored me. Like sacred shamans, Northern Comfort mediated their magic to one and all. Each person there was enveloped by their song and beat, moving with it and letting it surge through them. I pictured their spirits ascending like a flock of airborne swans into the heavens.

One individual stood out in the mass of people like a fire fly—Rosie Smith. In a floral embroidered teal blouse and blue jeans, Rosie swayed her body like a gentle tide, bobbing her head up and down with eyes tightly shut, extending her arms open and wide as if she was worshiping Yahweh before the Ark of the Covenant.

I saw other acquaintances boogie as well, most notably Marcus, Emily, and even Livgren.

I couldn't get into the music as much as the others since I wasn't familiar with many of the songs being played (though I still appreciated them). A good number of these were Grateful Dead covers. I'd been recently astonished at Dead fans' vehement connection to their band. Whenever Northern Comfort played a Dead song, intense expressions of beatitude—like that of Rosie—ensued. The closest thing I could compare it to was the collective rush I'd experienced when Springsteen and his band performed live one of my all-time favorite songs "Thunder Road."

Another notable thing Rosie and the others did was dance with whoever was next to them. The music united people. All social distinctions dissolved between the respectable and the wayward, the egghead and the simpleton, the family person and the druggie.

Hooter's Spotlight Moment

As performers often do (part of their shtick), Randy and Kari teased each other between songs before the audience.

"What happens when a cowgirl marries a cowboy?" he asked her one time.

"I don't know, Randy. What?" replied Kari.

"It's a Western Union!"

"Ha, ha, ha..."

With style and verve, members of Northern Comfort performed the typical rock band antics: prancing around on stage, showing off their musical abilities, and amusing the onlookers with their wisecracks. The group seemed to have what it takes to be famous someday, a decent stage presence and the skill to balance playing crowd-pleasing covers (of songs by the Allman Brothers, The Band, and, of course, The Grateful Dead) and their own material. Most of all, they were able to personally connect with their audience.

Northern Comfort's camaraderie and frivolity reminded me of how rock stars and rock music itself had enchanted my friends Randal Stark, Mick Rhodes, and me growing up. No wonder we wanted to be in a band.

And speaking of "rock star"...

Glenn, looking less smashed than before, got up on stage and interrupted Randy in the middle of a song. He mumbled something in Randy's ear as he pointed into the distance. The guitarist motioned to the other band members to stop playing. Everyone in the audience froze in their tracks and looked at each other, wondering what was going on.

Suddenly, Glenn and Northern Comfort started chanting "Hooter! Hooter! Hooter!" and then the crowd joined in.

"HOOTER! HOOTER! HOOTER! HOOTER! HOOTER!"

Then something strange happened. Out of the thick pines, emerged the scraggly, bearded Hooter into the spotlight. All eyes were fixed on the pitiful-looking soul. This time the chubby ex-Hell's Angel was actually wearing clothes: a ratty-looking red t-shirt turned inside out and tattered jeans. His quirky mannerisms reminded me of Baby Godzilla.

Hooter made his grand entrance. A cheering, laughing crowd parted like the Red Sea to make him a pathway to the stage. At first, he paced catatonically, as if suffering a hangover, and then obviously energized by the attention, he began to run, flapping and waving his arms like the lunatic he was.

When he finally planted his bare feet onto the stage, the band resumed the song they'd been playing: "A Friend of the Devil" by Grateful Dead.

By now, most of the people there coalesced into one restless mass like Elvis had just arrived. The theatrical Hooter then zoomed up to the microphone and proceeded to sing a duet with Kari, the lead singer.

> *I take my money but I take my time,*
> *a friend of the devil's is a friend of mine.*
> *If I get up before daylight,*
> *I just might get some sleep tonight.*

Then, as the crowd went level-ten seismic, Hooter—who himself was "a friend of the devil"—started doing a combination of three dance moves: the Twist, the Mashed Potato, and the Frenzy (the dance move Fred Flintstone accidentally invented when he dropped a bowling ball on his big toe).

As repulsed as I was earlier by his presence, I couldn't help but smile at how this vacant Attila-the-Hun-looking character had managed to steal the show at Poverty Gulch—just by being himself!

"You'll never meet anyone crazier than Hooter!" I heard one admirer remark glowingly and then rattle off Hooter's madcap exploits.

The adulation and praise poured on this human anomaly was incredible. It reinforced Rajneesh's adage "Joy is *mad*." And it confirmed how Poverty Gulch celebrated all things preposterous, irrational, and psychotic.

Here, the madman was king!

LeBlanc's Moment of Glory

Then came the climax of the entire evening. Northern Comfort launched into a number that got me as riled up as everyone else: "All Along the Watchtower." After that, the band blew me away with their blistering rendition of "Wipe-

Out." As an encore, they performed "The Weight" (aka "Take a Load Off, Fanny") to end the show with a mellower note. All three songs had in common the fact that they each had distinct *solo* parts. With "Watchtower," it was Randy's killer guitar solo (modeled after Jimi Hendrix). With "Wipeout," the drummer of course did his bit. "The Weight" had three vocal solos sung by Randy, Kari, and Hooter respectively. Hooter very appropriately sang the "Crazy Chester" verse.

There was one last solo act waiting in the queue, even after Northern Comfort took their last bow, packed up, and left. The light technicians were long gone when the imaginary spotlight would beam on none other than Pete LeBlanc.

It was a performance that would not be forgotten.

I'd run into LeBlanc at least once that day circulating in the crowd. Out-of-character for him, he showed his feelings...

"Ted, this place is so awesome! For the first time in my life, I feel *appreciated!*" he exclaimed.

Was this the same Pete I knew back in Detroit? There, he was the supreme loner with his mind in the stratosphere, an enigma to those around him. As I said before, few besides me, understood him. Some—most notably, my parents and Randal—made clear that they didn't like him at all.

Now, to my bewilderment, Pete fit right in at Poverty Gulch! And, remember, on top of that, he'd won the heart of Rosie Smith. For him, it must've been his wildest fantasy come true.

When Pete said "the hand of Fate had led us here," I couldn't agree with him more. It was uncanny how we'd happened to stumble on Rosie in the right place at the right time. It was as if the whole thing was orchestrated "from above." That being said, I wished that Fate (or God, the gods, or the stars) would've shown more favor on *me*.

Now Fate would look down and smile on my traveling partner one more time.

It all began when things were starting to wind down. The crowd had thinned out and those left behind sat around and capitulated to a mellow, pensive mood before the backyard bonfire. About three dozen people took part in a sing-along. It started with "Amazing Grace."

When someone handed Pete the well-worn acoustic guitar, his face lit up. He received it with adoration as if it was a new-born baby. He examined its features scrupulously at arm's length and up-close. He studied its nicked-up caramel-colored body, its saddle and bridge, its mathematical finger board and frets. He ran his hand slowly and tenderly over its well-worn varnish. He even put it up to his nose to smell it. With his nimble fingers, Pete noodled the strings a few times and adjusted the keys in order to tune it.

After all that, he was ready to go. Closing his eyes, Pete took a deep breath and began to pluck the guitar strings again. This was *his* moment now. It was *his* time to show the world what he could do. Amongst the chorus of chirping crickets, he played an alternating string pattern of E and B, the first chords of his rendition of Stephen Still's "4+20"—yet another song from the *Déjà vu* album.

> *Four and twenty years ago I come into this life*
> *The son of a woman and a man who lived in strife*
> *He was tired of bein' poor and he wasn't into sellin'*
> *   door to door*
> *And he worked like the devil to be more*

I have to admit, I felt apprehensive for my friend. His guitar playing was adequate enough, but to me, his voice sounded kind of shaky, weak, and off-key. I buried my face in my hands, anticipating Pete's performance to be an almighty cringe-producing bomb.

But, thank goodness, this didn't happen. To my surprise and relief, nobody seemed to mind Pete's tenuous singing.

In fact, something mysterious happened. And it occurred in spite of—or perhaps even *because of*—Pete making himself so open and vulnerable.

To my disbelief, the audience appeared to actually enjoy it! The atmosphere was so quiet you could hear a baby breathe. It was as if Robert Johnson's ghost had descended into our midst and took control. Like the late bluesman, Pete had managed to do the seemingly impossible: He transcended technique and polish. He satisfied his listeners with something pure, clear, and deep as water from an artesian well. All the folks around me—including Roy, the Eriksons, and Galaxy—stared reflectively into the fire as Pete performed the next numbers: "Helpless" and "Teach Your Children," also from *Déjà vu*.

You could tell Pete was really "into it." Like musicians often do, Pete cocked his head back and forth, and crinkled his closed eye lids with the music. He was like "the sleeping prophet" Edgar Cayce in a trance. He was so engrossed in the songs that he failed to notice something rather important...

His elbow was roasting in the fire like a marshmallow!

As nasty as it sounds, I just had to laugh, because it was so characteristic of Pete LeBlanc. Nothing—even his own burning flesh—could deter him from finishing a song. It was like when Teddy Roosevelt delivered an hour-long speech, even after an assassin just shot him squarely in his chest.

"YYYYYEEEEELLLLLLP, MY ARM!" Pete finally shrieked in pain. He set down the guitar—gently, I may add—to glower over the condition of his singed skin.

Emily and another friend frantically rushed Pete to the cabin for medical attention. But, ten minutes later, my friend returned triumphantly, gauze bandage and all. His audience bountifully received him back, shouting "ENCORE! ENCORE! ENCORE!" I must admit that my jealousy flared up again when I noticed Rosie chanting the loudest.

Pete bore a sheepish grin. He nodded repeatedly with gratitude as he accepted the guitar back.

"Sorry if I don't do it exactly the same way *this* time," he quipped inciting audience laughter. He would perform a few more numbers before everyone turned in for the night.

One final observation: LeBlanc's "aw shucks" manner and self-assured glint in his eye reminded me of David Carradine's portrayal of Woody Guthrie. And, the guitar in his hand, of course, made the image complete.

As my account of Poverty Gulch draws to close, I must say that Pete's rendition of *Déjà vu*'s "Teach Your Children" probably best captured what Poverty Gulch was all about.

> *"You, who are on the road, must have a code*
> *that you can live by."*

Later in the song, you're beseeched to pass on this "code" to your children... and then to your parents "before they can die... in peace."

What was this *code?*

I took it to mean the beliefs ardently held by everyone at Poverty Gulch—Rosie, the Eriksons, Galaxy, Blissful Finch, Blaise, and all the rest. Besides emphasizing "the individual" and "doing your own thing," it was all about being super-friendly, creative, and deep.

The amazing thing about this code was the fact it turned my parents' way of thinking upside-down and inside-out. My folks had instilled in me the idea that success, happiness and heaven come through practicing self-discipline. At Poverty Gulch, these positive outcomes come through the exact opposite—*self-indulgence.* There, bad is good and good is bad, at least in regard to sex and drugs.

At one point, the realization struck me: I was now a true believer. I couldn't wait to someday teach my own children... and even Mom and Dad "the truth" being fully lived out by "the pioneers" at Poverty Gulch.

PART II:

ON THE ROAD 1979

Act One

CHAPTER 8

THE GREAT KEROUAC NATION

Sunday, July 1, 1979

THE PARTY WAS OVER. The next morning, it was time for the Eriksons to clean up the mess and for Pete and me to hit the road. We were itching to move on, to continue our serendipitous adventure across the vast American continent. As Tom Petty would say, "Into the great wide open, under them skies of blue, a rebel without a clue." The very thought of leaving energized me.

We sadly bid farewell to our Poverty Gulch brethren, including the ones who'd changed my life forever—Rosie Smith, the Eriksons, and Blaise. We had not seen the last of Rosie. However, the Eriksons and Blaise would remain my constant companions only in memory.

The books they had recommended would be my keys to unlocking life's mysteries. The most important of these were *Ecstasy: the Forgotten Language* by Bhagwan Shree Rajneesh,

The Electric Kool-Aid Acid Test by Tom Wolfe, and *On the Road* by Jack Kerouac.

Believe it or not, I did not get around to reading *On the Road* until many years later. When I did, I was gob-smacked. It was like reading the script Pete LeBlanc and I had been following that fateful summer. I was Sal Paradise, and Pete was Dean Moriarty. As Blaise had explained, *On the Road* chronicles the real-life antics of the author and his pal Neal Cassady (with the fictional names Sal and Dean). With no permanent jobs, these former altar boys crisscrossed the country in the 1950s, doing whatever they felt like doing, oftentimes drunk or high. You could say the underlying theme was freeing yourself from society's rules, and, in doing so, living a fuller life.

As I saw it, Rosie Smith lived the dream detailed in *On the Road*. She had abandoned the rat race and chose to center her life on pleasure and enjoyment. And much of that was derived from traveling around with no set schedule or plan, and yielding oneself to any random experience that came along. She "went with the flow" to the extreme.

Whether she knew it or not, Rosie modeled what Kerouac did in a big way. She savored whatever she came in contact with—encounters with all kinds of people, places, sensations in her head, or *whatever*. Each experience, good or bad, had *meaning*. In fact, with Rosie Smith, there was no such thing as a "bad" experience, just a beautiful, unusual, or hilarious one.

She was a character in her "own novel."

As for me, the hitchhiking trip's steady flow of uncommon situations—often involving eccentric, cool, and even normal folks—continued to delight, surprise, and inspire.

America The Beautiful

We got a ride out of Poverty Gulch from a man with sandy brown hair and a long beard named Francisco. The quintessential nature man, he looked like the unkempt flute-player

Ian Anderson from the rock group Jethro Tull. Before we left, he showed us something he was very proud of: a deer-skin drum that he had made out of a hollow log, adorned with feathers, bells, and carvings. It was Native American art though Francisco himself was not an Indian.

Francisco drove us a few miles on the winding valley road in his run-down Jeep Wrangler to the music of Bob Marley and the Wailers. He suddenly pulled over, stopped the jeep, and gazed into the heavens utterly stupefied.

"Damn! Look at that *biiiiirrrrrd!*" he exclaimed pointing up. He'd just noticed a hawk with a jet-like wingspan sailing across the cloudless indigo sky.

Pete and I looked at each other and laughed. He was enthralled like a child seeing the bird for the first time. It was not lost on me that Francisco had the name of the Catholic saint who loved nature and animals—St. Francis of Assisi.

I associated this with Rosie and Kerouac. Francisco's fervent reaction to the bird reminded me of Rosie's "Julie Andrews" moment in the meadow. And, it occurred to me that it was like Jack Kerouac's vision of life. To repeat Blaise's words regarding the Beat author...

> *"Awe... amazement... wonder... at the world around you. Each breath you take, each person you meet. As you behold the* beauty *of it all! Yes, that's it—beauty! Inexpressible, inexhaustible beauty in its highest and purest form, the kind that makes you tremble and cry amen, man. amen!"*

Apparently, Kerouac, this wayward Catholic author, had inspired Blaise and perhaps Francisco and Rosie to see and relish the beauty in all things.

In this vein, I thought of the song "America the Beautiful" at our next stop—the conservative Ferryville, Wisconsin. Is America *beautiful*? I asked myself.

Francisco dropped us off at Ferryville at about one o'clock. It's located along the east bank of the Mississippi River. The part of it that I saw was a postcard-perfect representation of small town America. It had well-maintained houses with glorious flower beds, freshly-cut lawns, well-trimmed bushes, clean sidewalks, and white picket fences.

When we arrived, Pete and I noticed a lot of commotion going on along Main Street. Crowds were gathering. As we came up to the town square, it dawned on me what was going on—a Fourth-of-July parade (three days early). It was about to start. Swatches of wholesome-looking people—many grouped in families and still donning church clothes—lined up along Main Street.

The events unfolding put a smile on my face.

People clapped, cheered and waved American flags as they watched floats, marching bands, and fire trucks proceed down Main Street. Children scrambled to pick up Tootsie Rolls being hurled into the crowd by parade participants.

Ferryville seemed to be frozen in the '50s, just as Poverty Gulch was in the '60s. The fact that shops were closed on Sunday indicated that religion still prevailed over consumerism. Old Glory everywhere showed Ferryville was a bastion of patriotism.

Ironically, this was in 1979, the year when being proud-to-be-an-American was considered uncool, especially in my age group. Everyone was cynical. Still reeling from the after-effects of Vietnam and Watergate, Americans in general were feeling deeply disillusioned, jaded, and pessimistic about the future. People were mostly going bonkers over the energy crisis.

In two weeks, President Jimmy Carter would deliver a major speech centered primarily on the American people's ornery mood. Famously known as the "malaise speech," it turned out to be one for the history books, right up there with the Gettysburg Address and the I Have a Dream speech. It would also be considered one of the most (if not *the* most) open, honest and realistic speeches ever.

Being politically liberal like me, Pete thought it would be funny to mock the conservatives by joining the parade. So we went into the street, got behind the last float, and joined in the procession like Peter Fonda and Dennis Hopper in the movie *Easy Rider* (except we weren't riding motorcycles). The crowd probably couldn't cared less about two young punks marching with backpacks in the parade, but we thought we were cool being rebels.

The Stumble Inn

We had a hard time getting rides outside of town, most likely because it was Sunday. It was 85 degrees, humid and sunny. After many hours of hitchhiking, a middle-aged couple stopped and drove us across the Mississippi River bridge into Iowa. They took us sixteen miles up the Great River Road and dropped us off in a rustic town called New Albin. We were in front of a modest roadside bar called the Stumble Inn.

Weary of being out on the highway, we decided to go in for a glass of water.

The joint looked pure Route 66. The interior appeared old, gritty, and grungy, and it reeked from stale cigarette smoke. The multi-color glow from the neon lights, the pinball machines, and the jukebox helped to Christmas up what would otherwise be a dim and dingy cave.

It was deserted except for three elderly men in baseball caps sitting at the bar. They were watching the Brewers game on TV and drinking beer. Another old guy with a pool stick was playing a round of Three Ball by himself. His pot belly protruded over his belt, the only overweight part of him. The bartender was bald, clean-shaven, and fiftyish. Wearing a white smock, he swatted flies with his cleaning rag. Naturally, the entrance of two young backpackers turned all heads.

As we came in, Pete and I noticed a handwritten sign beside the blaring television that read "TODAY'S SPECIAL: BUD BEER—25¢ A GLASS."

"I think we've just entered The Land That Time Forgot," I said with a chuckle as I whipped out a quarter and placed it on the counter. "Around here, they still have 1957 prices!"

The bartender handed me a cold one. It went down my parched throat like water from a Sahara Desert oasis.

"Where y'fellas from?" asked the man.

"Detroit."

Eyebrows went up, the reaction we'd come to expect whenever the name our hometown was mentioned. Like it or not, we represented the Motor City. We carried our town's disconcerting image with us wherever we went. Folks often assumed we were refugees from a war zone with bullets flying and Devil's Night fires flaring up everywhere. I found it amusing how—in spite of our scrawny physiques—people thought we were tough, scrappy, and even dangerous.

Pete and I hitchhiking across the U.S. reinforced this mystique. Astonished by our very existence, the barflies asked us questions like "Where do you sleep?"... "What do you eat?" ... and, of course, the biggest query of all: "Why?"

Why was always a good question. Folks understandably bristled at the thought of hitchhiking in general, because of the potential threat of getting run over or picked up by some psycho killer. Many wondered if it was still legal, let alone safe. Some doubted our sanity for doing it.

"It's a cheap way to get around" was our boiler-plate reply. Neither of us ventured to explain the *philosophy* behind our mode of travel—the fact we did it to fully experience freedom and adventure. We figured trying to enlighten these simple-minded rubes would be a waste of time.

Needless to say, the five men treated us like celebrities. As we told them a few stories from our trip, they were spell-bound. The guy with the green John Deere cap and glasses kept shaking his head saying, "If that doesn't beat all hell." And, when I handed him a coin, the bartender said, "Nah, this one's on me."

After chatting awhile, LeBlanc and I sat at separate tables to gather our thoughts and write. LeBlanc penned a poem; I wrote in my journal. It was the first time I had the opportunity to record what had happened at Poverty Gulch.

Out to the Wood Shed

Suddenly, everyone's attention was turned to the two attractive young women and a guy who'd just walked in.

Naturally all of us males focused on the girls. The brunette had on a stretch-knit tube top that accentuated the curves of her upper torso. The blonde's short-short jeans exposed her lovely long legs. Both girls had hair like Farrah Fawcett. The shorter one (5'1) had Farrah's feathered look, but she was a brunette. The taller blonde (5'4) had frosted hair like Farrah, but hers was straight not feathered.

All the ogling brought to mind President Carter. What he said in that *Playboy* interview was honest and realistic like his malaise speech: "I've looked on a lot of women with lust. I've committed adultery in my heart many times."

Anyhow, the young man with the girls was short, dark-haired and stocky. He wore khaki shorts and a red t-shirt. You could tell he was trying to grow a beard but wasn't all that successful.

The three sat down at the table near me. After ordering a Tom Collins from the bar, the blonde made a comment about my backpack. This got the conversation rolling. We learned that the trio came from Houston, Minnesota and were out on a Sunday afternoon joyride. The two girls were Suzette (the blonde) and Pam (the brunette). The guy named Chip was Suzette's boyfriend.

Suzette took the lead in cross-examining us about our trip while Pam mostly listened. Chip appeared to be either disinterested or preoccupied with something else.

The mountain-top feeling I had felt while writing in my notebook, primed me up for an exhilarating chat. This time I wasn't feeling bashful in the least bit. Even when Pete eventually joined in, I ended up doing most of the talking—a major role reversal from two days before when we met Rosie. The two girls listened intently, periodically smiling and laughing as I told them the stories about Poverty Gulch, the anti-nuke rallies, the Milwaukee slums, and so on.

Getting noticed by two cute babes was a major revelation.

At some point, Suzette, noticing my empty mug, motioned to the bartender to refill it. Picking up on my expression of demur, Suzette said to me. "No, that's okay, I'll take care of it." She then ordered a beer for my partner as well. This was repeated three or four more times. I think Suzette got a kick out of getting us plastered.

As we talked for maybe an hour, everyone at our table had become positively giddy—except for Chip. He remained quiet and off to the side, staring into space. I had no idea he was like a volcano about to erupt.

Then he did something totally off-the-wall.

With a clenched fist, Chip slammed on the table with all his might!

THWWWACKKKKKKKKKKK!

The sound reverberated. It echoed.

THWWWAKKKKKKKK... thwwwakkkkkkk... thwwwkkkkkk

This solitary act definitely made an impression. Everyone in the room promptly stiffened up. After that, a weird silence ensued for a few seconds.

What made Chip do that? The guy was obviously irritated about something. How come? I had no clue. Suzette, a bit embarrassed, apologized profusely about her boyfriend's erratic behavior, saying he just had a little too much to drink.

After we continued talking for another ten minutes, Chip interrupted us again...

"HEY YOUUU F***HEADS! IAMSSSSSSSSICKOFYOUR-SH*T, MANNN!"

It was now quite clear: These were vile words aimed at Pete and me! Chip looked like he wanted to punch us both out, and I didn't know why. Needless to say, I felt more than a little uneasy.

Pure consternation swept over Suzette's face, like the I'll-be-damned-if-I'm-going-allow-this-to-happen look of my sixth grade teacher Mrs. Delaney. And, sure enough, Suzette uncrossed her legs and put both feet down firmly on the floor. She leaned over and practically hurled herself at Chip. At the same time, she tried to look inconspicuous to avoid creating a scene.

"Chip! Now you listen to me. *Shut the hell up!*" she whispered with a terse, blood-curdling voice.

His reaction of a vacant look got her even more worked up. She then practically picked him up out of his chair, grabbed him by the arm and dragged him outside.

The old men at the bar shook their heads over the spectacle. Pete and I did the same, except we burst out laughing.

A few minutes later, Suzette and Chip returned. Suzette had her chin up and a triumphant look. Chip, on the other hand, looked like a contrite little boy who'd just been out to the wood shed. Suzette's serious expression changed into a smile once she rejoined us at the table.

"Now, what were we talking about before?" she asked. Then we conversed more as if nothing had happened.

★ ★ ★

It wasn't long before Suzette announced that she, Pam, and Chip had to go.

"Oh, by the way, do you guys need a lift to Brownville?"

"*Heck yeah!*" was our jubilant response. We'd been planning on going in that direction.

Chip obviously didn't share our enthusiasm. Nonetheless, he went along with the plan, remaining as quiet as a mouse. He *had* to. It was crystal clear to him—and everyone else in the room—who was boss.

We then stumbled out of the Stumble Inn and piled into Suzette's black Ford Granada.

Suzette drove us up Highway 26 into Minnesota, finishing our brief flirtation with the northeastern corner of Iowa. She even took us a few extra miles past Brownville, far out of her way.

I sat in the front seat next to Suzette the driver. Pam served as a buffer between Pete and Chip in the back seat. Fortunately, the boyfriend posed no threat as we made our way north. As Joe Jackson's hit song, "Is She Really Going Out with Him?" played on the radio, I kept wondering why Chip was so enraged at the bar.

Then it struck me like a freight train: The outburst was all about *jealousy*...

Dah?... Two girls, plus two "*rock stars*" equals...

After Pete and I got out of the car, unlocked the trunk, and retrieved our backpacks, Suzette gave us each a warm farewell hug.

That's when all hell broke loose.

Chip, still in the car, completely flipped out.

He pounded on the car's interior like an angry gorilla in a cage. At the top of his lungs, he yelled out a continuous stream of verbal sewage that I don't care to repeat.

With the Stumble Inn behind us, I was left with three thoughts. One, what did Suzette see in this guy? Two, Chip was *me*, the jealous idiot two days ago. Three, I didn't have to dream of being a rock star. I was one already.

La Crosse, Wisconsin

Pete and I took great pride in traveling *three* states that day—Wisconsin, Iowa, and Minnesota. However, if you look at a map, this wasn't that grand of an achievement. We covered only tiny slivers of Iowa and Minnesota, but we ended back in Wisconsin where we started from.

Making La Crosse, Wisconsin our final destination that day seemed to make sense. In college towns like La Crosse, you could usually find parties and open-minded people who are willing to put you up for the night.

A series of short rides got us there about seven at night.

Unfortunately, La Crosse would fall short of our expectations. It wasn't the wild-and-crazy college town that Madison was. Downtown La Crosse was lively, but, to us, it was a ghost town. Only *normal* folks roamed the streets—not our kind of people. The evening crowd stopped at restaurants, gift shops, and ice cream parlors. The opening of a brand new Radisson Hotel and special Fourth-of-July events attracted locals as well as out-of-towners, in spite of the gas prices.

The main hangout was Riverside Park. It was the ideal spot to take a stroll, read, play Frisbee, feed the ducks, or do whatever. The park's greatest asset was its panoramic view of the Mississippi River. As the sun went down, Pete and I sat on one of the park benches and watched the river boats and barges go by. To our south was the magnificent Big Blue Bridge connecting Wisconsin and Minnesota. (It was actually two-bridges-in-one, joined like Siamese Twins.) To our north was a 25-foot-high sculpture of an Indian named Hiawatha. He stands proud with his arms folded toward the spot where the La Crosse and Black Rivers converge with the Mississippi.

The Mississippi was more than a river. It had been a great symbol to me all my life. It was the border of the great mythic American West. The mental picture of Lewis and Clark rowing down the waterway in their cargo-filled canoes gave me shivers. When I was a kid, my best friend, Mick Rhodes, and I saw ourselves as the buckskin clad adventurers when we probed the "uncharted" woods near my house—the place known as "the Tracks."

Mark Twain's ghost haunted the Mississippi (in a good way). I could see him in my mind's eye making wisecracks, wearing that white linen suit, and chomping his cigar. He could crack up an entire audience by just standing there saying nothing. His characters Tom Sawyer and Huckleberry Finn lived in my soul. I imagined them both rowing a raft on the river.

Like the romantic Tom Sawyer, I innocently thought real life should conform exactly to the books and movies about swashbuckling pirates, soldiers, and robbers.

To me, Mick Rhodes was Huck Finn, my "blood brother." He was quite literally my partner-in-crime. Like Huck, Mick had a genius for mischief making. He instigated well-thought-out pranks on teachers, daredevil stunts, and all the shady business at the Tracks. Living out the adventures we'd read about or watched on TV helped us to escape reality.

That night LeBlanc and I slept beside "Old Man River." As the rhythm of the water serenaded us to sleep, I thought of life imitating art—Mick and me, a modern-day Tom and Huck; Pete and me, a contemporary Cassady and Kerouac. Then there was whatever legendary duo Randal and I were supposed to be.

CHAPTER 9

F. SCOTT FITZGERALD'S GHOST

Monday, July 2, 1979

W E CONTINUED TO CONSORT with the spirits of the dead.

At least I know what it's like to be *partly* dead. When I woke up the next day, I had the funny sensation that my right arm was gone. My brain told it to move, but nothing happened. Seeing that it was still attached was no consolation because it was as cold and lifeless as a cadaver. As I sat up, it dangled from my shoulder like a sausage in a smoke house. Sleeping on my side on the hard pavement had cut off all the circulation. Fortunately, in a matter of minutes, the blood in the unblocked artery brought the dead thing back to life.

As the brisk morning air over the Mississippi revived me, I wondered what surprises may lie ahead. Pete and I packed up our stuff anticipating a long haul to our next destination: the "Twin Cities"—St. Paul and Minneapolis, Minnesota. We chose to go there because Rosie had said it was a cool place to visit.

As we went toward the highway, a heavy-set Indian guy with a black pony tail and front teeth missing, came up and asked us for some change. He said he needed the money to buy a loaf of bread for his family. Pete handed him some coins. Feeling generous, I donated a dollar believing my good deed would be repaid.

It apparently was. Call me superstitious, but the events of the day seemed to work out smoothly. After several short rides, we practically got the chauffeur treatment from a young electrical engineer named Boris on his way to work. He took us up U.S. 52 to the outskirts of St. Paul. After an hour, Tony, an Italian widower in a white AMC Gremlin, took us right into the heart of the city by mid-afternoon.

St. Paul, Minnesota

LeBlanc and I trekked down 12th Street to the Minnesota state capitol building just to check it out. Under the vibrant Michelangelo dome, the masses went in and out of the place in their business suits and tourist clothes. There was nothing exciting happening like at the Wisconsin capitol where the anti-nuke rally took place.

Maybe it was because I was tired and hungry, but I felt apathetic about viewing the ornate government building. Its grandeur did not move me. I basically went through the motions like the vacationer who observes a tourist attraction only to cross it off his to-do list. Afterwards, I thought, if you've seen one state capitol, you've seen 'em all.

My indifferent attitude in St. Paul would change, however, thanks to our chance encounter with a certain Sam Haddad, a used car salesman. Meeting friendly people like Sam on the spur-of-the-moment was what made our method of travel so interesting. He was a young Lebanese fellow in a business suit. Pete and I crossed paths with him along Jackson Street, where he was walking to his car in a bank parking lot. Just as he was getting out his car keys, he caught a glimpse of us adventurous-looking backpackers. Curiosity prompted him to pace over to us, say hello, and give us the third-degree.

As we told Sam our story, he wagged his head with amazement. Then the light of inspiration flickered on his face.

"Say guys, I just got off of work. How would you like me to give you the grand tour of St. Paul?"

Pete and I looked at each other and exclaimed "Heck yeah, sure!"

"Come on, hop in!"

Sam took a big risk picking up strangers like us. He drove a black '77 Trans Am, a car that thieves must have salivated over. After we put our packs into his trunk, we were off to see sites such as The Landmark Center, Fitzgerald Theatre, and Hill Library.

Our well-informed "tour guide" managed to fit everything in before rush hour. A lot of places he showed us related to author F. Scott Fitzgerald, who was born and raised in St. Paul. Sam said the famous writer often mentioned his hometown in his novels. In fact, Fitzgerald even used St. Paul as a metaphor in *The Great Gatsby*, just as Mark Twain did with the Mississippi River in his works.

Sam's enthusiasm was contagious. Learning that F. Scott Fitzgerald's ghost lurked there lifted me out of my doldrums. I liked ghosts. The very idea gave me butterflies like Mark Twain did the night before.

I'd never read Fitzgerald, let alone *Gatsby*, but Sam just had to say certain words and phrases like "foreboding" and "American Dream." to set my mind reeling. The term "foreboding" made me think of Edgar Allen Poe and the sense of imminent disaster you enjoy when you read his books.

The term "American Dream" evoked different things. It reminded me of that line from Bruce Springsteen's song "Born to Run"...

"In the day we sweat it out in the streets of a runaway American Dream."

Randal Stark had talked a lot about the American Dream. He made it clear, in no uncertain terms, that he wanted no part of it.

His words: "Go to school... Get a career... Get married... Have kids... Live in a house in the suburbs with a white picket fence... It's all crap that society forces on you!"

One thing you could say about Randal: He really had his priorities straight!

In *Gatsby*, the American Dream is an illusion, a fleeting one at that. Unlike George Bailey in *It's a Wonderful Life*, the main character, Nick Carraway, actually made it out of his Bedford Falls. Nevertheless, he found out soon enough that "life in the Big City" wasn't all it was cracked up to be. The people he'd hung out with just wanted to get filthy rich and have wild parties. All life was about was "Wine, Women, and Song" (the 1920s version of "Sex, Drugs, and Rock & Roll").

Fitzgerald might conclude the same thing about America in 1979. Our country had been going through "The 'Me' Decade" when narcissism reigned supreme.

The disco scene showcased a previously unheard of level of vanity. At the Studio 54, a popular night club in New York City, the world's most beautiful people came out to dance under glittering mirror balls and before their own reflections. They'd snort cocaine and have anonymous sex with perfect strangers in dark corners and even out in the open. On hearing about it, the general public was scandalized. Has our cultural elite finally descended into the deepest depths of depravity? Some people drew the parallel between these shallow hedonistic celebrities and the gluttonous aristocrats of the Roman Empire before its fall.

In the end, Fitzgerald's alter ego Nick yearned to get back to his beloved hometown—St. Paul, Minnesota—the citadel of faith, moral certitude and family values. Our driver Sam told us that the author didn't focus on the entire town of St. Paul in his writings, only his old neighborhood—the square mile that centered around one particular street—Summit Avenue. Sam knew he *must* drop us off there, the literal place that Fitzgerald had transformed into a symbolic place of great beauty and truth.

Mansions of Glory

Summit Avenue begins at an actual summit of a hill. It is the site of the historic St. Paul Cathedral. The church's magnificent copper-clad dome overlooking the downtown area made my eyes bug out. Of course, it was named after the apostle who was "blinded by the light," as Bruce Springsteen would say. Getting physically knocked down by the Lord in heaven reminded me of when Rosie and Francisco suddenly became overwhelmed by nature's resplendence. (Again, for Rosie, it was a meadow; for Francisco, it was a bird.) Pete and I had laughed both times, but, in each instance, I took their intense moments of rapture very seriously.

I coveted Rosie and Francisco's unusual ability to relish relatively ordinary things. It was as if they were mysteriously catapulted into another realm—a holy place—and became completely oblivious to everything else. Life's cares seemed to evaporate. It illustrated to me Kerouac's extraordinary sense of wonder, something I eagerly wanted to emulate. As Plato once said, God can be grasped through truth, goodness, and beauty. But beauty is the most accessible.

For two hours, beauty smiled on us through "mansions of glory"—yet another Springsteen phrase. After our granola dinner, Pete and I began to go west down the renowned four-and-a-half mile avenue of large Victorian homes, considered one of the finest in the nation. These mansions, dating back to the early 1850s, had been meticulously kept up by their owners. It was like we were in a coffee table picture book, or else back in the Gilded Age. The sheer number of Queen Anne, Beaux Arts, and Colonial Revival-style homes blew me away. Many houses had intricate French and Italian detailing, slate roofs, and stained-glass windows. Some had American flags out for the Fourth-of-July and flower gardens that probably rivaled those of ancient Babylon.

F. Scott Fitzgerald's mansion was so wondrous it was shocking. 599 Summit Avenue looked like a castle with its bold Romanesque bricks and third story towers. You could imagine the author himself writing *The Great Gatsby* at a walnut desk behind one of those magnificent bay windows.

Reflecting on what Sam said about *Gatsby*, I realized that *I* was Nick Carraway *in reverse*. Nick (Fitzgerald's alter ego) was in the "urban ash heap" of New York City pining to return to his mythical hometown in the American heartland; I was in Nick's hometown fleeing from the blighted metropolis of Detroit. With me, it was backwards!

My city of origin had earned its reputation for being a window looking into a bleak future. Back in '79, as it is now, people came to Detroit to see the end-of-the-world. It probably looks worse than Rome did after the Visigoths sacked it. Detroit's upwardly mobile population had long fled, leaving unfortunate souls to languish in crime-ridden neighborhoods.

Why does Detroit's rot and decay fascinate people? Does it rouse that sense of foreboding perhaps? Among the ruins are remnants of a glorious past. Detroit is a real-life fable like the story of the Titanic. It was America's number one industrial boom town long before the automobile. With its success and prosperity came architecture that reflected the romance of Europe. Victorian mansions lined its rich neighborhood streets like Grand Boulevard in the late 1800s. It's hard to believe that my hometown was once known as "the Paris of the Midwest."

Now look at it! Many of the opulent homes along Grand Boulevard are run-down; some have been condemned and abandoned; others have already been demolished.

What an epic tale author James A. Michener could tell about Detroit! The saga deserves a sprawling TV miniseries like *Centennial*, about the generations who had built, lived in, and destroyed our once great city. The trouble is the ending would be too depressing to watch. At least maybe we'd find out who dropped the ball which led "Paris" to become a bombed-out Beirut.

701 Summit Avenue

A lot of my classmates had read *The Great Gatsby*, but I never cared to read it because it's about rich people and I didn't give a crap about them. I'd assumed the popular view that the wealthy are cold, stuck up, and uncaring toward others. They horded their money while people starved. And, with the exception of Bruce Wayne, they were boring. All they did was sit around and get waited on, play golf, and watch opera. My favorite Three Stooges episodes had rich people get their just desserts literally in the face.

It's funny that I didn't see people living along the radiant Summit as "rich people." ("Well-to-do" maybe.) These residents must've been loaded to be able to afford to live there, but they didn't fit my image of greedy, selfish snobs. It must have been the fact I was seeing them up close. The Summit residents looked like the average hard-working people in my Detroit neighborhood—sitting on porches, taking walks, and watering lawns.

A case in point was Louise Miller O'Neil...

It was about four in the afternoon. The weather was just right—sunny in the eighties. My partner and I covered over a mile of the pristine street when a German shepherd started barking at us through a chain-link fence in the front yard of 701 Summit Avenue. Then we heard a voice calling out to us saying, "HEY, HIKERS, OVER HERE!"

The female voice came from the front porch of a large house, but she was hard to see because of the shadow cast by the porch's imposing roof. She eventually came down the steps into the sunlight.

Our retinas locked on a chestnut-haired woman in her mid-fifties.

She introduced herself as "Louise." She had on a baggy gray sweat suit. She looked frazzled, puffing on a cigarette in one hand and holding a mixed drink in the other. In spite of her idiosyncrasies, she looked dignified and businesslike. She had on a pair of bifocals attached to a chain around her neck and an expensive pen over her right ear.

"Do you guys want a glass of water?" she asked.

"Sure," one of us replied. She motioned to us to come up to the porch. The front porch was the most notable part of the gorgeous tan brick house. It looked like a separate building, spreading across the entire width of the house. The four pillars that supported the porch's roof, also created three identical symmetrical arches. The cement steps going up the porch went through the middle arch.

The immediate problem, of course, was the dog. It was jumping on, sniffing, and licking us after we entered the gate.

Thankfully, the woman managed to grab the wily canine by the collar and tow it into the house with her.

She came out of her grand late-19th century house with our water.

"Sit down!" demanded Louise pointing to the steps. Considering all the walking we did, we didn't mind being told what to do. But it felt like we just got sucked into a black hole.

When she started asking about our safety, what we ate, and even our hygiene habits, it was easy to see where this was going. It was like déjà vu. The same thing happened in Milwaukee five days earlier when two old women on a front porch roped us in, doted over us, and kept giving us food like we were their long lost sons. Louise followed the same pattern. It was as if she was part of a vast network of mothers who had gotten together and conspired to look after each other's kids.

"You both look so skinny, what did you eat today?" Louise inquired.

"Ma'am, you don't have to worry, we keep ourselves well fed," I assured her. "We eat *healthy* stuff like vegetables, fruit, and yogurt. A couple of hours ago, we had some granola and ramen noodles."

"*Oh, my God!*" she exclaimed. "You need to eat something more substantial! Now you wait right here. I'm going to get you some *real* food." Then the vivacious woman sprinted into the house again.

As we awaited her return, I noticed a bronze sign next to the door that read, "LOUISE MILLER O'NEIL, ATTORNEY AT LAW." I thought to myself: She doesn't look like a lawyer, let alone a snobbish rich person.

Five minutes later, Louise darted out with a food tray which contained two tuna salad sandwiches, a mountain of French fries, and two large slices of cantaloupe, along with napkins and spoons.

"I'm so glad you boys came along!" Louise exclaimed. "The paperwork I was doing was driving me batty. *You* are exactly the break I needed."

Louise then described her hectic existence as a family law lawyer and a mother. By day, she dealt with cases of divorce, child custody, and child support. By night, she had to contend with her "own messed-up family," she said with a smile. Since she had her office in her house, she admitted it was difficult to keep work and family activities separate.

At one point in the conversation, something Louise said took me off guard.

"What about your *parents*? Do *they* know where you are?"

This question got me speechless like she punched me in the stomach. How did I answer that? The answer was no, but I didn't want to admit it.

Fortunately, Pete unwittingly got me off the hook. When he said that his dad died of cancer three years back, Louise forgot about the original question and started gushing over the poor orphan child. This also led to her telling us about her late husband's untimely death.

"Where are you guys spending the night?" Louise asked eventually.

"Once we cross the river into Minneapolis, we'll find some park to sleep in."

"Sleeping in the *park*?! Are you guys out of your minds? It's *dangerous* over there!" she hollered. We tried to assure her that it was no big deal.

"I won't hear of it. You're staying *here* for the night!"

Though I was taken aback by her forcefulness, I must admit the idea of spending the night in a warm bed sounded very attractive.

"No, no, we don't want to *impose* on you."

"Oh, that's a bunch of bull. You fellas would be no trouble at all. I have a clean bed waiting for you. You don't have to be in Minneapolis tonight. You can get there first thing in the morning. I'll even give you the bus money."

Pete and I looked at each other. "What do you think?' one of us asked. How could we say no? So we settled the matter right then and there.

"It's a deal," I said happily. And then we carried our packs into the house.

Louise Miller O'Neil was just one of the many people who gave us free lodging on our trip.

A Tale of Two Moms

Louise assigned us clean towels and a bedroom on the first floor (one of eight in the six-thousand-square-foot house built in 1898). The room was clean, scented with candles, and decorated like something out of the Gingerbread Era. The double-sized bed had a mahogany headboard with rich ornamental carvings. Pete volunteered to sleep on the floor that night while I slept on the bed. (Sharing a bed, of course, would be considered gay.)

With only Louise, Pete, me, and a German shepherd around, the house was pretty quiet. My partner and I got a chance to get ourselves situated, take hot showers, and even read the paper. "The Day the Funk Died" was one of the head-lines that day. (This strange intergalactic event supposedly happened on the mothership of funk music's Parliament.)

In a relatively short time, however, the place turned into a three-ring circus. Folks just started showing up. Louise's special needs daughter, Mary, returned from school around 5:30 or so. Tim, her twenty-year old son with his two pals, Ray and Steve, came from their construction jobs. Then her tenant Herman showed up. After that, Louise's secretary, named "C.J." arrived after running errands.

Before we knew it, we had a full house of folks with different agendas—putting stuff away, raiding the fridge, sharing about the day's events, and so on. You'd think it would be the opposite, but the ensuing chaos seemed to reinvigorate the once drained, haggard-looking Louise. Obviously, serving people animated her. The more people she had to boss around, the better. It did her heart good to annoy everyone with the typical mom-isms like "God gave you a brain, use it," "I just want what's best for you," and "Talking to you is like talking to a brick wall."

Just like the others, Pete and I were happy to let her wait on us hand and foot. We blended right in. Strangers or not, we found ourselves engrafted into Louise's family.

The house's interior had all the fancy furnishings you'd expect from a home on Summit Avenue like bulky parlor furniture, tables with heavy lion-paw legs, wrought-iron floor lamps, chandeliers, ornate cherry-wood beams and moldings. Still, Louise's attitude was houses were made for people, not people for houses. While her obsessive-compulsive neighbors likely regarded their homes as nothing more than Victorian showplaces, with every furnishing in place, scratch-free, stain-free, and dust-free—701 Summit Avenue was different. Louise claimed it was messed up *out of principle*. Even guests were allowed to put their feet on tables, smoke cigarettes, and let newspapers pile up. Mary's primitive works of art were taped to the wall next to expensive original oil paintings. Serious gashes marred the walls, as did wine-stains on the furniture, and cigarette burns on the pool table.

No one seemed to give a crap, much less Louise who could afford to fix and tidy things up, but chose not to.

During the course of our overnight stay, I couldn't help comparing Louise to my own mother. In many ways they were similar. Both could be great housekeepers, but didn't make it a priority. Both were hell-bent on meeting other people's needs, but also had a tendency to control you and smother you. Both were extremely warm, generous, and kind, but drove you insane with their highly-opinionated ways. If you crossed them, there'd be hell to pay. When my mother said, "My way or the highway," I took her quite literally.

How were Louise and my mom different? Since my mom put safety and security first, she would never dream of letting total strangers into the house, let alone have them stay the night. Louise was more open-minded in this regard.

My mom tended to stick with her traditional viewpoints without questioning or even understanding them. Judging by her books, Louise seemed open to different religions.

What was the biggest difference between Louise and my mother? Louise knew how to *party*.

After a delicious dinner of pork chops, apple sauce, and mashed potatoes, Louise made a surprise announcement: "Today we celebrate!" According to her, a party was absolutely necessary to show the out-of-town guests (Pete and me) a good time. She also noted that it would be the perfect way to kick off the Fourth-of-July.

Not one to refuse his mother's wishes, Tim got on the phone and invited more of his friends over. With the help of Steve, he hauled up some beer, wine, and even hard liquor from the basement. Unlike the wedding at Cana, there was no shortage of booze. Tim's buddy Ray set up the music system on the front porch. He then got out an eight-track collection featuring the likes of Boston, Kiss, and The Who.

Pete and I were delighted to say the least. To us young people, a good party was life's number one greatest event. In a sense, partying was our religion. Getting drunk or high with friends and losing yourself in mindless revelry filled our hearts with joy. In retrospect, doing so on F. Scott Fitzgerald's block seems sacrilegious. Summit Ave. was the author's symbol of moral certitude and innocence. There we were having a wild party, something *The Great Gatsby* would cast in a negative light.

What was our host Louise up to? With mischief in her eyes, she was seen rummaging through her drawers for fire crackers and other explosives. She'd been transformed from being the big boss to a big kid.

She was now one of us!

I'll forego the details of that festive evening except to say we had a blast—quite literally. The most notable thing that happened had nothing to do with the shindig. To my chagrin, the question that rendered me mute earlier came up again. Louise, the ultimate "cool mom," tipsy from drink, eyes moist from laughter, cornered me in the kitchen like some rabid dog.

Pointing to the most modern-looking thing in the room— the phone—she said with the scent of alcohol on her breath...

"Look, I want you to *call your mother* right now."

"Uh, well, I..."

"It's the *responsible* thing to do!"

The word "responsible" made me shudder like a vampire at the sight of a crucifix. Intoxicated myself, I broke out into a cold sweat and got a sinking feeling in the pit of my stomach. Responsibility?! *AAARRRGGGHHHHHHH!*

Why did she have to bring this up *now*?! I had conveniently kept "forgetting" to call home. Sure, I had done the dutiful thing of dropping my parents a postcard now and then. But I dreaded the thought of having to actually *talk* to them on the phone! I couldn't bear to hear their anxiety-ridden voices on the other end of the line, begging me to come home.

That would definitely spoil my good time!

With her blood-laced eyes, Louise demanded I call my mom for a good five minutes, but, on seeing my imploding mental state, she mercifully backed down and let me go.

Minneapolis

Tuesday, July 3, 1979

Whenever I think of Minneapolis, Minnesota, I think of *The Mary Tyler Moore Show*. Mary could "turn the world on with her smile." The actress flinging her cap in the air at Nicollet Mall during the opening credits was a big deal in the seventies. It was gesture of triumph. A single woman finally making it on her own!

This brings to mind a bronze plaque I'd noticed hanging on the wall of Louise Miller O'Neil's study. It acknowledged Louise as one of the first women attorneys in St. Paul. She was a pioneer! Other plaques recognized her political involvement and strong leadership role in the community. There were also framed written pieces about Louise that contained facts that could truly make it into *Ripley's Believe or Not!* (See Appendix A for more info about this extraordinary woman.)

The next day's activities would be as varied as the potpourri petals on the bedroom dresser. It began with doing laundry and then breakfast...

"Have another steak!" Louise insisted at the kitchen table. "Don't be skimpy. My freezer is loaded with 'em."

Pete and I stared glassy-eyed at the pile of eight-ounce rib eye steaks on a pewter serving plate. Each of us had already packed away two of them, plus three eggs, a generous helping of hash browns, and two pieces of toast, not to mention two cups of coffee and a glass of orange juice to wash it all down. We couldn't eat another bite.

Louise showed no signs she had been drinking heavily the night before. She was running on all cylinders as she ran around mothering us. Before saying goodbye, she prepared Pete and me care packages that we could barely stuff into our backpacks—three tomatoes, two heads of lettuce, three hard-boiled eggs, two steaks wrapped in aluminum foil, a can of cling peaches, even salt packets for our eggs. After that, she asked C.J. to drive us to the bus stop on University Avenue.

Retooled and revived, Pete and I were now ready to take on Minneapolis!

When the last of the city buses dropped us off at Seventh and Hennepin around 11:30 a.m., dark clouds hovered over the sky. Torrents of wind whipped up as shoppers and employees on lunch breaks scurried down Seventh Street to find shelter from the impending storm.

Apparently unfazed by the weather, a scrawny old man with white hair and purple circles under his eyes, wailed on his harmonica with his back against a wall. This defiant act touched my traveling partner's heart. LeBlanc found out that his name was William and threw several coins into the guy's cigar box.

"*Thunder and lightning were no match for William's song*" was the gist of the poem Pete would write a little while later at Butler's Square.

The steady downpour drenched everything. Pete and I found temporary shelter under an overhang on the side of a nearby Shell gas station. Since we had time to kill, I decided to unload the heaviest item in my backpack—the 6 lb. 10 oz. can of peaches Louise had given me. I opened the can and sloppily devoured the fruit using my Swiss army knife. Juice and syrup streamed down my lower lip, chin, and neck.

Undaunted by the public spectacle, Pete asked the gas station attendant for directions to a better place to loiter during the storm. The attendant suggested Butler Square just around the corner. So the two of us braved the elements and made a run for it.

Looks were deceiving. The Butler building's exterior looked as plain and utilitarian as the Hoover Dam. Built in 1906, it used to be a warehouse. However, the imposing structure featured a recent renovation—a beautiful atrium with a glass roof, an indoor mall with shops on the first two floors and offices on the upper floors. The natural light streaming in from the top window brought out the rich texture the 24-inch wide Douglas Fir timbers that formed a vast network of posts and beams.

Soaking wet and shivering in the air-conditioned building, Pete and I lounged on one of the cushioned benches for an hour as we watched the people go by. To pass the time, we captured our thoughts on paper. Pete wrote about William; I was inspired to sketch an abstract drawing of the impressive atrium with my Crayola crayons.

Our time at Butler Square may seem trivial and inconsequential, but it reflected an important aspect of our journey. I don't know about Pete, but, during the trip, I grew in my ability to *perceive* things in an original way—from architecture to the wildflowers in the cracks in pavement. Through them, I saw life from a different angle, more astutely and colorfully. People like Louise Miller O'Neil invigorated me and made me laugh. I was always on the lookout for the beautiful, unusual, and hilarious—just like author Jack Kerouac.

In retrospect, there were many other things we did that resembled *On the Road*. Pete and I were joyous and reckless "outlaws on the run" like Sal and Dean. Our thirst for novelty and adventure was insatiable.

Concerning all the dangers we faced, my mother thought we were beyond stupid. But who could blame her?

"You and that Blockhead are gonna get yourselves killed!" she'd cried in exasperation.

"I'd rather die a glorious death *being free*," I retorted, sounding like the patriot Patrick Henry.

My poor mom could not sway me. I'd drawn a line in the sand. I made up my mind to escape Detroit once and for all. And now it seemed to be paying off. Living out my romantic dream invigorated me. I savored my independence like Mary Tyler Moore—without even having a job.

However, the euphoria didn't last long. Our good luck streak would soon come to an end. The Grand Experiment would seem like the stupidest thing I've ever done.

ON THE ROAD 1979

Act Two

CHAPTER 10

ON THE INTERSTATE

FROM THE ONSET OF OUR TRIP, Pete and I understood what The Grand Experiment was all about. Again, it was to achieve freedom in its purest form. Absolute independence. But, as seen, it was also about *experience*. In particular, the experience of having a good time.

U.S. Route 66 was another inspiration. Just as I hadn't read Kerouac's *On the Road*, we had never set foot on Route 66, the fabled "Mother Road."

Still, I've learned so much about the famous highway in books, movies, and song lyrics. What is it about Route 66 that stirs people's imagination? The two thousand-mile highway running from Chicago to Los Angles means different things to different people. But I'm sure most would agree that, like America itself, "America's Main Street" has become more of an *idea* (or an icon or a symbol) than an actual road.

Bobby Troupe's popular tune said it best: "Get your kicks on Route 66." The song associates Route 66 with the pleasure of going on a road trip, taking in the sights, seeing all the great towns along the way. It's a metaphor for enjoying life. It corresponds with Kerouac's vision of perpetual wonderment. It's an extension of America's love affair with the automobile, brought to you by... *Detroit!* It's all about the joy of jumping in your car, putting the gas pedal down, cranking up the stereo, drinking a Coke and... just... driving.

Route 66 also shares in common *On the Road*'s sense of nostalgia, a yearning for something precious in the past that has been long forgotten—most notably "up close and personal" encounters with natural marvels like the Painted Desert, cool small towns, and inspiring people. American pop culture largely associates Route 66 with the innocence and the fun you have with your family at neon diners, motels, and roadside tourist attractions. While I was growing up, my family's Mother Road was M-12 which ran through the Irish Hills in Brooklyn, Michigan. Our vacations there featured extraordinary and wonderfully weird attractions like Frontier City, Prehistoric Village, and Mystery Hill.

The story is told and retold. It's a popular legend. But the Mother Road has an adversary, an arch nemesis, if you will—the Interstate Highway. (The tale is best told in the Pixar movie *Cars*.) To help people get to their destinations faster, the Interstate replaced Route 66 in the sixties and seventies. Now speed, efficiency, and punctuality are preferred over fun. Route 66 is a symbol for relishing life through-and-through via the senses; the Interstate represents missing out on life. You go from Point A (birth) to Point B (death) utterly oblivious to what's happening in between. In the end, you get that sinking feeling that your existence on this earth had been nothing more than a meaningless blur.

Up to St. Paul, Pete and I had avoided the Interstate like the plague. We knew taking the backroads was the only legit way to see the country. It was like Robert Frost's "Road Not

Taken." Along the less-traveled highway, you drank up the majestic beauty of forests, mountains, and farm lands. And you took your time doing so in order to fully savor it.

It was a tough choice, but for the next three days, we did the unthinkable: Instead of taking "Route 66," we decided to take the Interstate.

Interstate 35

Back at Louise's Victorian mansion on Summit Avenue, LeBlanc and I had planned our strategy. As we poured over the road map, we decided we'd travel down U.S. Interstate 90, the only feasible way to make it to the Black Hills on time. We figured we'd be there by Friday for the big anti-nuclear rally. To get to I-90 west, we first had to go I-35 south.

At around 2:00 p.m., when the rain ceased in downtown Minneapolis, we walked south down Nicollet Mall Street where Mary Tyler Moore famously threw up her hat. We took Nicollet to Franklin Avenue. From there, we went five blocks east to get to the entrance ramp to U.S. Interstate 35.

Hitchhiking in Minneapolis, as in any big city, was not fun. You had to deal with the negative mindset city dwellers had. We knew most urbanites were stressed out from their unfulfilling jobs. After the hectic nine-to-five grind, personal and family problems awaited them at home. When moments of rest and relaxation could be carved out, city people subjected themselves to all kinds of violence, scandal, and crises on TV.

"There are a lot of kooks out there," many people said. From this perspective, one would be nuts to pick up perfect strangers like us. We were potential con artists, rapists, and/or ax-murderers. What was it like on the receiving end? I'd grown to appreciate the alienation panhandlers must feel when people ignore, pity, and lock their doors at the sight of them. You feel vulnerable, helpless, and invisible.

The average person would be trembling in fear at the perils we'd subjected ourselves to. However, like tight-rope walkers, the sense of ever-present danger invigorated us.

Pete and I knew we had to be cautious. We weren't dumb enough to assume there were *no* sociopaths or weirdos out there to give us a hard time. However, we figured the media had exaggerated and sensationalized the few cases there were. The vast majority of people, we reasoned, were decent souls who wouldn't hurt a fly. And we figured most of the thieves, perverts, and crazies lived in big metropolitan areas. That's why we tried to avoid cities as much as possible.

The Franklin Avenue ramp we picked wasn't a feast to the eyes. We stood next to a graffiti-scarred embankment wall, a rusty chain-link fence, and grass that had been overgrown and occupied with gray-haired dandelions, nettles and thistles. Everything was on a slope. To a certain extent, wind gusts helped clear up the paper litter from the open area, but they also made the litter cling to the bottom of the fence.

Beverage containers (can or plastic) outnumbered the other types of rubbish. Paper waste—like ice cream or candy wrappers, newspapers, and receipts—came in a close second. In terms of classifying, the fast food trash deserved its own category, with the subcategories of cups with matching plastic lids and straws, paper bags with logos, napkins, etc. Litter can be grouped by *brands* as well (McDonald's trash, White Castle trash, etc.) Then there was the miscellaneous junk: a pile of cigarette butts, rusty car parts, Styrofoam packaging, a foam rubber thingy, a handle bar, tire shavings that gave off a pungent rubber smell. Naturally, all these things drew ants, flies, and other vermin.

Entrance ramps were the best place to thumb in the big city. They're obviously safer than the freeway itself, especially during rush hour when motorists have a reckless, bat-out-of-hell mentality leaving work. On ramps, drivers are going below 40 mph, plenty of time for them to look you over and make the decision to pick you up. And usually ramps have wide shoulders for motorists to pull over. On the downside, drivers entering the freeways are often preoccupied with the tricky maneuver of merging into busy traffic.

During rush hour, our first driver of the day pulled off a marvelous feat. In his blue '75 Honda Civic, he barreled down the entrance ramp a good two-hundred feet past us, before fish-tail skidding on the gravel shoulder. Then in one fell swoop, he zoomed *backwards* two-hundred feet to our spot! The grace and precision of this maneuver made my heart swoon with admiration. I honestly couldn't figure out why he'd gone through all the trouble.

After we got into his car and started driving, the man, an archetypal nerd, seemed to be totally disinterested in talking to us. Pete and I never got his name because he'd mumbled it. We kept trying to draw him out in a conversation, but he sat mute the whole way. He must have been either shy or had something on his mind (murder perhaps?). Whatever the case, the geek drove us to a safer area—a good 17 miles south of Minneapolis, the suburb of Burnville.

Seeing guys in Chevy pickups and baseball caps at the Mobil gas pump made us think we were on the threshold between suburbia and the boondocks. A quick glance at the terrain confirmed this. To our right was an Oldsmobile dealership and a condo sub-division; to our left was a corn field.

Like Robert Frost, my heart ached to be in the pastoral countryside. However, on the Interstate, you really never leave the city. The two asphalt slabs are always surrounded by a continuous, homogeneous channel of pavement, cables and wires, and urban sprawl. Highway signs, lights, and utility poles are everywhere. The familiar fast food joints, hotels, gas stations, convenience stores, and strip malls with their fences and parking lots dominate the landscape. In this elongated metropolis of concrete, metal, plastic, and glass, the herd of civilization is constantly on the move, usually going from one big city to another. Most of the time, the human face is hidden behind some tinted glass window.

Needless to say, the natural scenery—say a cow pasture or prairie in the corner of your eye—is spoiled by road signs and billboards. It's as remote as a dream, as ancillary as an afterthought.

We continued to go southward down I-35 and eventually reached our end point—U.S. Interstate 90, the highway that goes east-and-west. We got there around seven o'clock, thanks to two young men who reminded me of The Dukes of Hazard. Our next target, Rapid City, was now one straight shot west, though we still had hundreds of miles to go.

With only a few hours left of daylight, our highest ambition was finding a decent place to spend the night—such as a city park, a vacant lot, or a cemetery—perhaps in Albert Lea, Minnesota, the town just south of us. Or, perhaps, we could keep on going, just for the satisfaction of crossing the South Dakota border before dark.

Two Universes

In spite of a few puddles left from the storm, the pavement of I-90's first entrance ramp west of I-35 was almost completely dry. Judging by the clouds, you couldn't tell that it ever rained at all. The humidity in the air made us as sweaty as used dish rags. The only breeze came from passing cars lashing up the muggy air.

Traffic was too light on the ramp, so we made our way down the semi-circular slope to the Interstate, past the slightly rusty white sign that read "HITCHHIKING IN ROADWAY PROHIBITED." Once we were on the shoulder of Interstate 90, we observed three lanes of traffic whizzing by.

Traffic was relatively heavy. You wouldn't know it, but just days earlier, President Jimmy Carter had vehemently admonished the American people to not drive very much during the Fourth-of-July holiday to conserve fuel. He said the United States is alarmingly low on gas! However, most people ignored Carter's urgent pleas, presuming "the energy crisis" to be one big hoax.

The Interstate itself had two separate "universes," if you will, right next to each other. One universe was going 60 to 80 mph. Its "inhabitants," the motorists, were driving along in their gas-guzzling cars and motor homes with their heads in the clouds, reading and napping. They were safe and insulated by their protective shells on wheels. And they even brought along the comforts of home—air-conditioning, contour padded seats, stereo systems, and so on. In fact, their vehicle *was* home.

The other universe, the one we "lived" in, is the outer rim of the Interstate. It's commonly called the "shoulder." It's usually ten-feet wide (four feet of cement pavement and six feet of gravel). Separated from the traffic lanes by a white line, it's designed to be a place for vehicles to stop in case of emergency. Reflector poles that guide traffic at night are positioned at the edge of the pavement and are spaced out roughly twenty yards apart. Next to the shoulder is usually a shallow ditch. Beyond the ditch is land. If we were lucky, the land had secluded spots where we could set up camp and answer nature's call in privacy.

Being outside on the freeway shoulder, you're always at the mercy of the elements, which could be pleasant or not.

It's like being in a NASA wind tunnel. Moving vehicles, especially the big trucks, whip up gusts of air up to 50 mph, constantly blowing your hair and clothes, sometimes knocking you off balance. Under these severe conditions, you have to synchronize your body like a seagull in flight. Underpasses were convenient shelters when it rained. And, since we chose not to bring tents, we occasionally had to sleep under bridges.

On the Interstate or not, hitchhiking involves a rhythmic pattern of movements and gestures. It's like a dance. It may seem obvious to most people, but there's a standard way of doing it, as well as variations. The standard way is to stand in one spot along the roadside, face the oncoming traffic, and signal passing motorists to give you a ride. The indicator is typically an extended arm with closed fist and thumb out.

The variations include sitting down instead of standing (on a folding chair, on your backpack, or on the pavement), waving your arms instead of holding out your thumb (like Rosie did), and using a sign to indicate your destination ("CALIFORNIA OR BUST" or something). On that evening of Tuesday, July 3, 1979, we practiced our favorite variation—walking and hitchhiking at the same time.

Besides being a good workout, walking as you hitchhike has one big advantage: If you don't get picked up, you'll make it to your destination *eventually*. The disadvantage is you always have to turn forward and backward—forward to see where you're going; backward to see where motorists are going. You want to face drivers to charm them (with your captivating smile) into picking you up, but you also want to notice if they're coming straight at you at 65 mph! Most of the time, you trudge forward cocking your head back and forth as you extend out your right arm. Unfortunately, you'll probably get a kink in your neck doing so. Often you'll find yourself tipping over and running into things as you pace in reverse.

One time, I tripped on some road kill, but it wasn't road kill. It was still alive! The poor critter (I think it was a prairie dog) twitched its hind leg as it writhed in agony in a pool of blood. That was until I took a rock and put the poor thing out of its misery. The whole affair traumatized me. It's weird how an act of mercy can make you feel like a cold-blooded killer.

CHAPTER 11

CROW AND THOMAS

TRAMPING ALONG I-90, WE SPOTTED two other hitchhikers ahead of us. One was tall and lean; the other was short and chunky. From an eighth of a mile away, the pair resembled Don Quixote and Sancho Panza.

Who were they? Where were they going?

As Pete and I drew closer, the duo looked even stranger than the Man of La Mancha and his sidekick. In fact, each of them appeared like he'd just stepped out of his own adventure movie.

The tall one was the best dressed half-naked man I'd ever seen. He wore only a pair of faded cut-off blue jeans and leather sandals. Jewelry decked his neck and wrists. Thirtyish, with a wiry build and long skinny legs, he was obviously outfitted to look like a Native American, but his burnt orange "red" hair and sun-burned fair complexion broadcasted his European ancestry. And his long beard came across quite un-Indian to me. Hanging half-way down his chest, it was tied into braids and decorated with rust-colored beads and white feathers. A deerskin bag dangled from his left shoulder by a strap.

His stout partner sported a long black untrimmed beard, a plaid short-sleeve shirt, and tattered jeans, He had a blue bandana wrapped around his head. His appearance reminded me of a lumberjack, a mischievous one at that, with his slanted eyebrows and black shifty eyes. On second thought, he looked like Blackbeard the Pirate.

The four of us greeted each other.

"The name's *Crow*... like the bird," said the redhead. "This here is Thomas,"

"Nice to meet you, Crow... Tom."

"No, it's *Thomas*," the pirate corrected me. This would be one of the few times he said anything. Thomas was the silent type. He typically just nodded as he let Crow do all the talking.

"We're from upstate New York," Crow continued. "We're pushing to get to the Black Hills before the rise of the morning star." Besides sort-of talking like an Indian, there was something about the way Crow spoke that gave him a commanding air like he's your boss. And, his accent sounded Cajun to me.

"I'm sure you guys are wondering about my appearance."

Pete and I nodded in unison.

"A wise man once said that clothes are a natural extension of the soul," Crow said. "What I'm wearing reflects who I am—I'm French Canadian by birth, but my *heart* is Indian."

"Whoa."

I was dying to continue our chat. But the shoulder of a busy Interstate is a terrible place for long conversations. It's too hard to hear. Besides, we all understood that sticking together reduced the odds of getting rides considerably. As our eccentric new friends went ahead of us, I hoped we'd eventually meet up with them again.

"Nice meeting you Crow and Tonto... I mean Thomas."

Then something totally unbelievable happened. Crow and Thomas tread only thirty feet from Pete and me when a blue '78 Silverado truck stopped to pick the four of us up. I thought we'd won the Lotto! And then after traveling about a mile down the Interstate, the driver gave three more hitchhikers a lift—two guys and a girl, also bound for Rapid City. However, to our chagrin, the ride only lasted for ten miles. The motorist dropped all of us off at Exit 154.

In ten minutes time, we'd become a roving band of nomads: seven hitchhikers in all. It consisted of Pete and me, Crow, Thomas, a scraggly hipster guy, a *real* Indian carrying a guitar case, and an attractive petite young blonde named Indigo. The three newbies were obviously political activists. After beholding each other with awe and wonderment in the twilight, the different parties split up near the overpass of Highway 13 above I-90 for the final push before sundown.

Trucker City

Under the bright orange and amethyst sky, the silhouettes of Crow and Thomas remained ever-present some 500 feet ahead of Pete and me. I now imagined them as The Lone Ranger and Tonto in reverse roles (the "Indian" being the leading man; the white guy being the "faithful companion").

As night drew the final curtain, Pete and I opted to call it quits and amble over to the nearby gas station. It was the Road Runner Truck Stop, a sprawling eighteen-wheeler metropolis, with service islands wide enough to accommodate at least ten semis at the same time. The parking lot looked as vast as that of a suburban mall. There, I counted roughly thirty parked semi-trailer rigs. The intense flood lights towered over the concrete expanse like those at a ball park. They attracted a plague of insects overhead that mingled with the rising exhaust smoke.

LeBlanc and I took turns going into the convenience store. As we typically did, one of us stayed outside to watch the backpacks. The 3,000-square foot facility offered the usual provisions—hot coffee, ice-cold fountain drinks, junk food to go, munchies, newspapers and magazines. There were also trucker services like an automated car wash, CAT Scales, Western Union, check cashing, public laundry, and showers.

The store bustled with commercial drivers, from the uniformed to the casually-dressed. For a brief moment in the seventies, truckers were considered cool, thanks to the popular song "Convoy" by C.W. McCall. On the other hand, pop culture typically tagged them as "rednecks" which carried with it a certain negative stereotype—scruffy working-class white men from the rural South who were racist ignoramuses like Bob Yule in *To Kill a Mockingbird*. In spite of my tendency to size up people using stereotypes, I noticed a good number of truckers did not look the part—for instance, a couple of black men, an Asian, and even a woman.

I came into the store for two things: the men's room and an ice-cold bottle of Mountain Dew. The air-conditioning ramped up to Arctic levels made me want to linger inside a while. But, as I set the soda down on the cashier counter, I glanced out of the front window and saw two human forms consorting with LeBlanc.

It was Crow and Thomas. Pete and the peculiar duo were sitting hunched over on the curb like a trio of Rodin's Thinkers studying the road map.

When I went out to join them, I came in the middle of their discussion about logistics. Using the map, Crow calculated that Rapid City, South Dakota could be reached within eight hours (without stopping). After making this determination, my comrades took a deep breath and sat there mutely as they soaked in the surroundings. Unsurprisingly, the four of us, especially Crow, got protracted stares from patrons coming and going.

Crow, unfazed by the attention, zeroed-in to what I was holding—a twelve ounce bottle of Mountain Dew.

"Sh*t!" he exclaimed shaking his head. "Are you really gonna *drink* that stuff?"

"Uh... yeah," I replied awkwardly under my breath. I wasn't sure how to take Crow. I examined his sunburned face, those piercing eyes, that outlandish braided beard. He appeared dead serious, even fierce.

"Here, give me that bottle," Crow said gesturing with his hand. What did he want with my precious Mountain Dew? In spite of my reservations, I surrendered it.

After studying the cold, sweaty thing, he pointed to the label. "*See here!* High fructose corn syrup: worse for you than regular sugar. Can give you gallstones, cardiovascular disease. And, there... see *there*, Yellow Dye no. 5... causes allergies."

"Right."

"But that's not the *scary* stuff..."

"Hmmm."

Check this out: Sodium Benzoate. Studies have found that when it's mixed with Vitamin C, it *causes cancer!* Ironically, the only healthy ingredient—orange juice—might actually *help* the carcinogen!"

Crow and Thomas looked at each other and burst out laughing. I was visibly annoyed at being the butt of their joke.

"Look, Ted, sorry for messin' with ya, buddy," he said in a warm, conciliatory tone as he handed me back my drink. "I wouldn't deprive you of your Mountain Dew. But do you want to know the truth? You've been *conned* into thinking it's perfectly okay to pour that poison down your gullet."

"Okay, thanks, I guess."

"You got to be leery of Corporate America. It cares more about profit than people. Those greedy bastards bombard you, 24 hours a day, seven days a week, with slick ads to sway you to buy this stuff. They're everywhere: billboards, magazines, TV. They manipulate you. They *brainwash* you to drink that Drano."

"Now wait a minute, Crow," I retorted respectfully. "I *chose* to buy this. Nobody *made* me do it."

The offbeat white "Indian" just shook his head and grinned. "Whatever you say, partner. Go ahead, drink up. I'm not stopping ya. Free country." He had a twinkle in his eye when he said "free country" in a sardonic way.

Crow ranted for a while longer. He said the American ideal of liberty and justice was just "one big con job" used by the wealthy colonialists to mask their power grab. To Crow, everything boiled down to *greed*. The whites stole the land from the Indians and the labor from the blacks, all for the sole purpose of making money and hording goods. And the United States continues to exploit and subjugate people around the world today.

"Do you want to know *why* I dress the way I do?"

"You said back there your heart is Indian."

"Yeah. It's because I'm fed up with white society. With every fiber of my being, I renounce the European blood that courses through my veins. I've rejected my membership to the white race. I've been reborn."

At these words, Thomas, the man-of-few-words spoke. His utterance was like the sound of rolling thunder.

"You gotta be *radical!*" the pirate exclaimed.

The Four Winds

The caffeine from the Mountain Dew got my synapses firing as I mulled over the undeniable truths that Crow had spoken. Considering his formidable passion and all-or-nothing stance, it would be tempting to cast Crow as a half-crazed Captain Ahab obsessed with harpooning the Great White Race. But this would be a gross mischaracterization. Anger management issues aside, Crow did reveal his softer side.

It happened when a trucker family came out of the store. Enthralled by Crow's unusual exterior, the little boy and girl—ages between six and eight—came up to Crow and stared at him as if to say, "What are you, mister?" Their mom and dad, a little freaked-out, tried to shoo them away from the oddball stranger. Crow, in turn, disarmed them with his charm by introducing himself and blessing the children like St. Francis. He even stooped down to their level and let the children touch his beard.

After that, the four of us discussed our next move. The plans of both parties seemed set. Crow and Thomas planned to head west into the night. Pete and I wanted to find some place to camp nearby.

As we got ready to part ways, an interesting idea came to Crow: Why not gather our foodstuff together, divvy it up, and share a communal feast?

A communal feast. What a great idea! We all agreed to it.

But first we had to find the right spot. So we surveyed the premises, walking past all the truck stop customers who'd parked there for the night. Besides sleeping and attending to other bodily needs, the truckers used their downtime to check their loads, do paperwork, and hose down their semis. They also watched *Emergency* on TV and played cards.

The Road Runner's powerful light field created the illusion that we were on the bright side the Moon. Crow noted how the place seemed utterly divorced from Mother Earth. The ground below our feet—under a foot-thick layer of cement— was probably once a vibrant, green meadow, but now it was a barren, concrete wasteland. As Joni Mitchell sang: "They paved paradise and put up a parking lot."

A number of drivers were overheard complaining—most notably about the escalating gas prices and the independent trucker strike. But, as Crow pointed out, they were part of the problem. They wasted fuel by keeping their engines idling in order to run their air conditioning. And, they polluted the atmosphere in the process.

We settled at a spot near the east section of the guard-rail surrounding the truck stop's periphery. In spite of being alienated from nature in the physical sense, I felt "at one with the cosmos" because of Crow being there. Thanks to the "Indian" in our midst, our dinner felt like the first Thanksgiving.

The food was prepared and shared with loving hands. Louise Miller O'Neil's care packages—which included a half dozen tomatoes and hard-boiled eggs, and lettuce—likely amounted to 80% of our pot luck supper. (Unfortunately, since they were likely spoiled by now, the four rib eye steaks had to be thrown out.) Crow and Thomas contributed the other 20%: a couple of apples, five tomatoes, and a half of a four-ounce box of water biscuits.

Thomas, the shifty-eyed sidekick, sliced up the fruit, eggs and lettuce with my Swiss army knife. He then divided up the food four ways.

With our dinner plates on our laps, Crow, Thomas, Pete, and I sat in a circle; with legs crossed "Indian-style."

"This is perfect," said Crow in spite of the rumble of a huge truck driving by. "The Lakota medicine men always look at everything in terms of circles and in fours."

These cryptic words puzzled me. What do medicine men have to do with *geometry*?

"Each of us is one of the four winds," Crow continued. "Pete here is the East wind, from where the new day was born. Thomas is the South wind, which sends us comforting summer breezes. Ted is the West wind, the one who ends the day and brings rest. And, me, I am the North wind, the one whose sharp air awakens people to what's ahead."

Then Crow bowed his head and kissed the pavement still warm from the day's heat. It was a very Catholic thing to do. Then he gave the blessing:

> *"We thank the Great Spirit for the resources that made this food possible; we thank the Earth Mother for producing it: and we thank all those who labored to bring it to us. May the wholesomeness of the food before us, bring out the wholeness of the Spirit within us. Amen."*

While Crow articulated this beautiful prayer, truckers stared at us from a distance like we were visitors from the planet Zog.

After we "four winds" cleaned up, our offbeat banquet came to an abrupt end. Crow and Thomas disappeared into the night like two restless ghosts.

The Fourth-of-July

Wednesday, July 4, 1979

There were three reasons why the next morning sucked. First, when I opened my eyes, the weather did not appear very promising. Second, I did not look forward to being on the Interstate all day. Third, all night, I was lying on the concrete within earshot of an endless procession of loud trucks. All that, combined with the caffeine in my system (from the Mountain Drew), were not exactly conducive to sleep. I felt lethargic, zombie-like.

This raises a fundamental question: Why didn't I bring a foam pad to sleep on? As John Wayne once said, "Life is tough, but it's tougher when you're stupid."

About a half hour before sunrise, Pete and I arose and prepared for the long haul on I-90. I packed up my sleeping bag. The ritual was the same as always: roll it up, stuff it into another bag (its carrying case) and securely fasten it with two belts to bottom part of the backpack.

By the way, backpacks came in two types: frame and frameless. Both of us had the frame kind, the best choice for loads over 30 lbs. Besides supporting your back and putting less pressure on your shoulders, framed backpacks allowed you to tie things on it like canteens, frying pans, and sleeping bags. As an added bonus, you could stand it upright and use it as a chair as you wait for rides.

After using the convenience store's facilities and splurging on a sugar-glazed donut and a twelve ounce coffee in a Styrofoam cup, I, along with LeBlanc, lumbered toward the Interstate 90 entrance ramp to start hitchhiking again.

As we did so, it dawned on me: *It's the Fourth-of-July.*

But this fact seemed irrelevant, oddly enough. That year, the Fourth wasn't a day; it was a *week*. The Fourth that year was maxed-out like a rubber band on the verge of snapping. The long holiday really began on the evening of Friday, June 29th—the day we met Rosie. Since the actual holiday fell on a Wednesday in 1979, many Americans had decided to launch their vacations after work on the 29th to take full advantage of the weekend, plus Monday the 2nd, Tuesday the 3rd, and Wednesday the 4th. (As we'd seen, the towns of Ferryville and La Crosse held official celebrations over the weekend *before* the Fourth.) But many people also considered the *days after* Independence Day as part of the holiday too—Thursday the 5th, Friday the 6th and the subsequent weekend.

When all is said and done, the Fourth-of-July that year lasted nine days.

★ ★ ★

The United States of America: what did this geopolitical entity mean to people? Many things of course, but over the past few days, I'd encountered two polar opposite views: On one hand, the town of Ferryville was unabashedly patriotic. It reflected the "beautiful" America I grew up with, the one of John Phillip Sousa, Walt Disney and John Wayne. To them, it was an *exceptional* country. They would vote for Reagan in a heartbeat.

On the other hand, Crow hated America with every DNA strand in his body. In his eyes, the United States was the evil empire in *Star Wars*, an imperial power that exploited people, most notably the Indians.

Though my opinions weren't yet fully formed, I sympathized with both positions. As we'd seen, Pete and I mocked the people of Ferryville by "marching" in their parade. Their patriotism came across naive, outdated, and corny.

Having said that, I must admit, seeing marching bands, children waving flags, and uniformed war veterans stirred up something in me. It made me almost teary-eyed. Maybe I was like Kerouac, Twain and Fitzgerald yearning for an irretrievably lost past. Maybe, deep down, I still loved America and fully embraced the American Dream.

But, reluctantly, I had to agree with Crow: the way the U.S. treated the Indians (and the blacks) was despicable. Yet, I had a hard time swallowing the notion that America is *totally* evil, past and present.

In the end, I guess I fell into both camps. I reasoned that America is *evolving*—from an imperfect nation to a perfect one. In other words, the U.S.A. had started out seriously flawed, but, its ideals of freedom and equality would gradually make it better over time.

To me, the sixties was a clear sign that this was the case. Minorities and women were starting to gain more rights. The "consciousness" of America was being transformed by the Woodstock generation. It was entering a new age when total freedom and equality would win out and prevail forever. That is, if we survive the current state of malaise.

Something that happened at Poverty Gulch made me think along these lines.

Once again, Poverty Gulch was located near a village called "Liberty Pole." As Rosie had alleged, the town was named after a flag pole just before the Civil War. The pole was in front of the house known as a stopover point for the Underground Railroad, the story goes. And "Old Glory" was the signal to runaway slaves seeking a safe haven in the North.

However, this story couldn't be true because Wisconsin was too far north to be part of the Underground Railroad!

At the big bash the previous Saturday, Blissful Finch offered a different explanation of why the town was called "Liberty Pole."

"It's because of its *liberty!*" she said with a wry smile, tongue firmly in cheek.

We laughed because we both understood what she meant by "liberty" and it had nothing to do with runaway slaves. It was the radical freedom we were seeing all around us at Poverty Gulch. It was freedom to be yourself... freedom from being told what to do... freedom to get high and make love with whomever, whenever, wherever you choose...

"Liberty" of course is the bedrock principle of the United States. Blissful made me ponder how elastic the term is. At first, it had meant freedom from the rule of Great Britain. Then it meant the black's freedom from slavery. Then it meant black, woman, and gay freedom from prejudice and discrimination.

But Blissful took the definition even further. When she equated "liberty" with "doing your own thing," she pegged it right there. That's what America was all about: doing your own thing and let the consequences be damned!

Was *this* what the Founding Fathers had in mind?

The Hitchhiker's Handbook

Call it wishful thinking, but I predicted we'd end up watching a spectacular Fourth-of-July fireworks display in some Mayberry-like small town by the day's end. It was just another romantic fantasy. I pictured the bright, sparkly, globe-shaped peonies bursting over Cinderella's Castle during the opening credits of TV's *Wonderful World of Disney*. I also thought of the idyllic images in the Springsteen song "4th of July, Asbury Park (Sandy)." Of course, this imagined outcome depended on several variables, most notably chance or luck—or, something LeBlanc kept referring to: Fate.

Whatever the case, our long streak of good fortune had me spoiled. I repeat: over the past week, we'd consistently met the right people at the right place at the right time. Our encounters with Rosie Smith and Louise Miller O'Neil were prime examples. Crossing paths with each of them had set off a chain reaction of wonderful events.

I was beginning to think, in the grand scheme of things, we were among God's Chosen Ones. Since we were enlightened idealists, we *deserved* our good fortune. The stars or the gods looked down on us and smiled. But the night before seemed to be a toss-up. Karmic retribution was split both ways. Ending up at the Road Runner Truck Stop looked like a bad omen. On the other hand, the sheer coincidence of meeting Crow and Thomas seemed to be a sign from God.

Weather-wise, July 4, 1979 didn't appear like it was going to be a glittering jewel of a day. This made me feel depressed.

A cold front had commenced, resulting in showers of mist. A canopy of dreary stratocumulus clouds hovered overhead making it hard to locate the sun. The temperature dropped a good twenty degrees. We started out welcoming the idea of a cooling trend. But standing on the entrance ramp for an hour or so in drizzly fifty-degree wind made my teeth chatter. Jogging in place and rubbing my hands together, I was ready to take out my sweater and rain poncho.

The unusually straight and long entrance ramp, with its reflectors embedded in the pavement, resembled an airport runway. Obviously, coming from the truck stop, the traffic was mostly made up of semis, but some regular vehicles were mixed in, one per every two eighteen-wheelers. Sadly, the chances of getting picked up by a big rig were practically zero. Most companies had prohibited their drivers from doing so, for insurance purposes. Some states even made it outright illegal. And the independent truckers couldn't give us a lift because they were all on strike.

Hitchhiking required real discipline. This meant following certain rules, which we typically broke, such as illegally thumbing on the Interstate. Nevertheless, we respected other people's advice, most notably from the book I brought along, *The Hitchhiker's Handbook* by Tom Grimm—and from Dave Zarret, Pete's friend and mentor.

Like Yin and Yang, Grimm and Dave complimented each other. *The Hitchhiker's Handbook* emphasized the outward appearance, while Dave the inward. Grimm's formula for getting rides was to look clean and neat, use hand-lettered signs (to show you're intelligent), and, above all, "Smile, smile, smile." "Too many hitchhikers look bored and unhappy. Instead try to look like you're enjoying yourself." Admittedly, I often didn't feel like smiling, especially on gloomy days like this, but I did it anyway. The thinking was "perception is everything," as they say in advertising. LeBlanc, however, didn't bother to smile. True to his Holden Caufield personae, he avoided acting phony.

Having thumbed all over the United States, Dave Zarret, like Tom Grimm, was a hitchhiking guru. His sagely wisdom made *The Handbook* seem superficial. To Dave, the experienced hitchhiker was like some kind of Jiu-Jitsu master. He thought, in order to be effective, you must rigorously cultivate your inner qualities. Attitude (not perception) is everything. "Strength within" gives you a positive energy that draws people to you. "Be prepared to be treated like a worthless piece of sh*t," he warned. "You have to remember to respond to insults with love and kindness, not spite or anger." This sounded a lot to me like "turning the other cheek."

Dave, our personal Obi-Wan Kenobi, was spot-on right about the abuse. Most of the time, it's the motorists' passive-aggressive looks of loathing: head-turning and grimacing like you're a leper. Sometimes you get the finger. Obscenities are thrown at you, not to mention banana peels and beer bottles. For me, this kind of behavior was more creepy than scary. "When this happens," Dave counseled, "Count to ten, take a long deep breath, and say "thank you" or "I love you" (even though the perpetrator is long gone). He said this practice benefits *you*, not them—in a spiritual way. It prevents resentment from eating at your insides, so that "your Jesus-self" shines out.

The worst offense of the passers-by was indifference. I started to get thoughts of victimhood: How could they be so calloused and cruel? Can't they see I'm *suffering* out here? How could you pass up God's Chosen! The drivers' apathy, combined with the Chinese-water-torture-effect of the iffy weather conditions, caused me to I blow my stack.

"*AAAAAAAAHHHHHHHHH*! I can't take this anymore!" I exclaimed.

Since there were no inanimate objects around to let out my aggression on (besides my backpack), I angrily kicked the ground. Mud, rocks, and loose gravel were sent flying every which way onto the pavement. Pete didn't even flinch as I stormed away down the ramp toward the Interstate itself.

Just then, a black 1976 Chrysler Cordoba veered over to the shoulder of the freeway ramp.

CHAPTER 12

SOUTH DAKOTA

I T'S HARD TO DESCRIBE THE HAPPINESS you feel when someone stops to give you a ride, especially after a long wait. The burden is lifted; no more worries, frustration, and depression! You feel like a game show contestant winning the grand prize. Your heart leaps.

However, when it happens, you must learn to curb your enthusiasm. You must keep your desperation in check, lest you wind up in some serial killer's car. It's a tricky business. Your intense desire to leave the hell-hole you're in can mess up your better judgment. It skews your perception, making even Charles Manson look like Jesus Christ.

In a friendly way, you have to empirically size up the driver like a hard-nose police interrogator. You need to be able to tactfully decline the ride if need be. The screening process involves observing visual and verbal cues. Does the driver look you in the eye as you speak? Does he answer questions without hesitating? Does he look like he's up to something?

The young driver in the Chrysler not only passed our test, but he evoked a smile. "Wally" from Paraguay appeared like he just came from a New York discothèque with his hair sprayed like John Travolta's, handle bar mustache, and avatar sun glasses. His lime-colored polyester long-sleeve shirt with pointed fold collar was left unbuttoned on the top to reveal a gold medallion.

Once we got moving, Wally explained he was heading to a Fourth-of-July dance party in Sioux Falls.

All and all, we liked the guy. We could handle his pungent aftershave and heavy accent, but we couldn't stand his music.

It was disco, the musical genre that became emblematic of the 1970s.

All the way from Albert Lea, Minnesota to Sioux Falls, South Dakota, Wally subjected us to the syncopating rhythms of groups like Sheik, Donna Summer and Village People. To make matters worse, Wally kept bopping his head and singing off-key with every song. I must admit, there were moments when I thought we should've screened Wally out.

Passing the "WELCOME TO SOUTH DAKOTA" sign was like turning the page to a new chapter. Louise's secretary, C.J., had warned us about riding through "the Rushmore State." She told us to be prepared for "the most boring ride of your lives."

"Once you reach the South Dakota border, you'll see miles and miles of *nothing*. You'll leap for joy when you see a single tree."

According to C.J., a prehistoric glacier had acted like a mammoth bulldozer, flattening out all the scenic hills and valleys—with the notable exceptions of the Badlands and the Black Hills. Miles and miles of prairie grass covered "the lowlands," as they're called.

In my mind, I cataloged all the pop culture references to South Dakota. It's mentioned in The Beatles song "Rocky Raccoon." Laura Ingalls Wilder from the *Little House on the Prairie* grew up there. It's the land of Red Cloud, Crazy Horse and Sitting Bull. I also remembered Bob Dylan's "Ballad of Hollis Brown"—about some guy who murdered his family—on a "South Dakota farm."

Besides Mount Rushmore, the state's most famous tourist spot is Wall Drug, immortalized by its unabashed hype. An endless procession of billboards, over a hundred or so of them, celebrated Wall Drug's gift and souvenir shops, a fake dinosaur, and generous deals like "five-cent coffee" and "free ice water." I'd read somewhere that Wall Drug billboards can be found all over the world, even Antarctica.

There were other notable attractions in South Dakota like The Corn Palace, The Flintstone's Bedrock City, and Reptile Gardens.

The Geologist

We eventually switched drivers. Wally had dropped us off north of Sioux Falls, where Cedric Voss, a geologist, picked us up in his '79 Ford LTD Wagon. He had us lay our backpacks over a half-dozen five-gallon buckets of rock specimens in the back. Cedric was in his late forties, smartly dressed in a navy blue short-sleeve polo shirt and khaki denim slacks. The shape of Cedric's balding head, his wire-rimmed glasses, and his toothy grin reminded me of Franklin D. Roosevelt.

Our intelligent conversation with Cedric helped break up the monotony. He was extremely well-informed about things. I learned a lot from him about politics and dinosaur bones. He explained that the U.S. government had commissioned him to survey shale deposits in the region. These minerals were being considered as a possible fuel source, a synthetic alternative to the gas and oil imported from the Middle East. If the technology ever got off the ground (or, more accurately, *under* the ground), he said the energy crisis could be solved. Nonetheless, it faced two major obstacles: it was too expensive and the environmentalists strongly opposed it.

Our talk hit on issues making headlines. First of all, we discussed the skyrocketing oil prices that got most people worked up that summer. Since the early part of the decade, Americans suffered from inflation due to the OPEC oil embargo. However, in the year 1979, things got far worse. The Islamic revolution in Iran—led by the religious leader, Ayatollah Khomeini—choked off much of the world's oil supply. Everything got so expensive that families had to forego eating out, which put many restaurants out-of-business. Due to shortages, frustrated motorists had to wait hours in gas lines that wrapped around city blocks. Fights broke out. All kinds of violence, including murder, flared up because of the truckers' strike.

The energy crisis may explain why certain drivers hated our guts: We were literally "getting a free ride" while they were paying through the nose for gas.

Another touchy issue was the environment. Republicans and Democrats couldn't agree over whether or not nuclear power is a safe alternative to fossil fuel. On March 28, 1979, the accident at the Three Mile Island power plant in Pennsylvania provided the liberal Democrats the ultimate I-told-you-so moment. A massive movement to shut down *all* nuclear plants boomed practically overnight.

At one point, we found out that Cedric thought we were anti-nuke demonstrators. We had to laugh because nothing could be further from the truth. The only reason we were heading to the Black Hills protest rally was for the experience.

While on the subject of politics, Cedric pointed out a couple of interesting facts about the State of South Dakota. If you look at the map, the massive Missouri River is like an aorta, going through the middle of the state, splitting it into two halves. Cedric said there are palpable political differences between each of the hemispheres. The east side's politics are "pastel colors" (meaning they're more moderate); the west side's are "bold colors" (meaning they're staunch liberal or conservative). Another thing was presidential candidate George McGovern—the hardcore liberal Democrat who ran against Richard Nixon in '72—had come from South Dakota. (Unfortunately for the political left, McGovern had lost in every State, except Massachusetts and D.C..)

Our political discussion came to an abrupt end when we had to stop at a rest area at Mile Marker 302. After using the drinking fountain, I turned around and couldn't believe my eyes. Standing twenty feet away, next to the information kiosk, were Crow and Thomas!

I rushed over to say hello. There they were in the same clothes as before, which made them shockingly out-of-place amongst the tourists. The sheer coincidence of meeting them at that particular place and time delighted me to no end. It was one more sign that Fate orchestrated earthly events.

The pair seemed pleased to see us, but now Crow, like his partner, didn't have much to say. Both men appeared dazed, haggard, and haunted. Perhaps the cops had been giving them a hard time. Maybe the Interstate wore them down. I knew from experience that both possibilities were plausible. Whatever the case, the duo just gave us friendly nods and Indian handshakes, and went on their way.

As we returned to Cedric's station wagon, I remembered what Crow had said about himself back at the truck stop...

"I am the North wind, the one whose sharp air awakens people to what's ahead."

It suddenly occurred to me that these were words of a prophet of doom.

Tell Tale Signs

Crow and Thomas' haunted looks seemed to capture the country's mood. The general weariness and apathy that had set in across the land had a name—*malaise*. This out-of-sorts feeling, from the French word for "sickness," had been building up for years. It was the result of Vietnam, Watergate, and the Kennedy and King assassinations. And now in 1979, the hyper-inflation, exasperated by the events in Iran, raised the malaise up to the highest level imaginable. The public, of course, blamed President Carter.

People were beside themselves with angst like the crazed Peter Finch in the movie *Network* screaming at the top of his lungs, "I'M AS MAD AS HELL AND I'M NOT GOING TO TAKE IT ANYMORE!"

The combination of everything listed above gave me the weird feeling that history was at a tipping point. The end of the age was upon us! In '79, things were about to go haywire—socially, politically, and spiritually. Things were strained, spinning out of control, falling apart. Pretty soon, I would wake up one morning, look around, and barely recognize everything, like Rip Van Winkle.

To say I had F. Scott Fitzgerald's deep sense of foreboding would be an understatement.

Besides the energy crisis, there were three other signs that the end was near. First, from out of the blue, traditional religion was making a comeback. For better or for worse, it was toppling entire regimes, most notably the ones in Iran and in Poland.

Secondly, the "Disco Sucks" movement, which began in Detroit, was making Wally's music a thing of the past. Again, disco defined the seventies. Its extinction would mean the era of *Saturday Night Fever* was over. (This development was the one bright spot of the end times.)

Thirdly, film actor John Wayne died three weeks ago. "The Duke" had been the king of the Hollywood Westerns, the most popular movies when I was a kid. His passing marked the end of the age of innocence that was probably long gone already.

References to "The Wild West" on billboards along I-90 made me think of the Duke a lot. I imagined the legendary cowboy wearing his ten-gallon hat, twirling a rope, and riding his horse across the Great Plains. The Duke defined what it meant to be a man—putting in an honest day's work, herding cattle, defending people with his Colt .45. He always knew the right thing to do and did it. Morally speaking, everything was black-and-white to John Wayne. He was *the* Great American Alpha Male.

Now the male role models in the seventies were Alan Alda and... (ugh!) *Woody Allen!*

Driving with Cedric all afternoon, I could confidently say we saw some hogs, cattle, and, yes, even trees. The terrain even started to roll a little. Then, near a town called Chamberlain, came the eye-opener. There it was—the Missouri River, the Mississippi's drop-dead gorgeous sister with its lush green bluffs looking down on her. Her scale is breathtaking: over five football fields wide. The steel girder bridge didn't seem to pay proper respect to this vast blue water marvel. Half of the river's flow was obstructed with a man-made peninsula to accommodate the foundation of the bridge. And the I-90

Bridge itself had no decorative features, obviously built on the cheap. Like the Interstate as a whole, utility trumped beauty.

After the Missouri River interlude, it was like we woke up from a marvelously lucid dream. The oblivion continued. We had just crossed over into the hardcore political half of the Rushmore State.

"The Great Sioux Nation" (the Lakota and other tribes) once staked their claim on this territory, which extended from here (west of the Missouri) to the Big Horn Mountains in Montana. Crow had said it was the last region the Indians had called their own—until the U.S. government took it over after Custer's Last Stand. Talk about the end of an era!

Dudley Do-Right and the Indians

Cedric let us off near the minuscule town of Reliance, just south of the Lower Brulé Indian Reservation. While waiting for our next ride, I stepped into some tall grass to take a leak.

Just as I was zipping up my fly, a rusty black '71 Chevy pickup swerved ahead of us in a zig-zag pattern onto the shoulder until it came to a complete stop. The vehicle was part way on the gravel shoulder and part way on the grass. The height discrepancy between the two made the truck tip practically forty-five degrees.

We walked a good two hundred feet to get to it. After the dust settled, we observed four males in the truck, two in the cab and two in the bed. The three-minute jaunt to the vehicle gave us ample time to check out its young occupants. Even from a distance, you could tell from their black hair and skin color that they were Indians. And from their loud chatter and obnoxious kidding around, you could tell they were drinking. However, as we got closer, they became quiet and serious.

The young shirtless one worried me. He looked wild with his long unkempt hair, partially obscuring his face. His well-sculpted shoulders and chest showed he must be a disciplined body builder. The way he bobbled his head around revealed a certain nervous energy. He appeared as volatile, unpredictable, and threatening as a twister.

"*H-H-H-HEEEEEEEEEYYY!*" he slurred with a puerile smirk and finger pointing at us. "Wheeeeere d'ya think *yeeeeer* goin'?"

Taken aback, Pete and I turned to each other and frowned. Was this a provocation or what? My fight-or-flight instinct started to kick in. My heart started to pound like a bass drum.

The driver's door opened. Under the door, you could see cowboy boots hit the dusty gravel forming a small cloud. A big man—6-foot-3 feet tall and 250 lbs.—donning a well-worn straw cowboy hat emerged out of the cab and strode over to us. He appeared a little older than his companions. Also a Native American, he had short black hair and a copperish complexion with a reddish tinge. Beard stubble on his face culminated to a tuft of hair on his chin. The man's blue-black-white pattern plaid shirt was open, revealing a plain white t-shirt underneath. His wide leather belt had a large buckle with a Red Man Tobacco logo.

"Hey guys... oh, don't mind him," he assured us referring to his intimidating companion in the back. "We're just going a few miles down to the next exit. *Hop in!*"

I breathed a sigh of relief when I saw his gentle, friendly face. To assist us, he lifted our backpacks like Styrofoam and hoisted them into the truck bed next to his plastered chums. There was other stuff back there under a 10 x 10 blue plastic tarp. I couldn't tell what it was.

"My name is Jack Buffalo," the man said with a firm handshake. "I always make it a point to pick up hitchhikers. That's because I hitchhiked a lot myself when I used to ride the rodeo." When he said that, I felt we'd met a kindred spirit.

After we got in the cab and starting moving, Jack related that he and his three buddies were on a mission to "go into town, get wasted, and raise hell." The fellow in the cab next to Jack was "Mark Holy." The two in the back were "The Running Deer Brothers."

Jack shared a couple of stories. Then he explained, "What I like best about hitchhiking is the freedom of being on the road. And it's a great way to see the country and meet all kinds of interesting... people..."

Suddenly distracted, Jack's face got even redder as he abruptly interrupted himself.

"OHHH SH*T! IT'S *DO-RIGHT* AGAIN!" Jack exclaimed pounding on the steering wheel. The reason for the outburst was what he saw in his rear mirror—a highway police car with its flashing lights signaling to him to pull over.

"That guy is *always* hassling us!" Jack said shaking his head in disgust. He groaned as he made a gradual stop. Meanwhile, Mark was laughing as he hummed the familiar theme song of Dudley Do-Right, the dim-witted Canadian Mountie from *The Rocky and Bullwinkle Show*.

The officer barked into the hand receiver of his radio and stepped out of the car. He fit the stereotype of the tough highway patrol cop—all uniform, from the top of his wide-rim hat to his shiny black regulation shoes. He wore dark wire-rimmed glasses and a smug expression on his face.

He came over to the truck.

"OK, boys, Get out!" the trooper muttered calmly and firmly once he got there.

The six of us followed his order and proceeded to line up in single file along the passenger's side of the pickup. The volatile Running Deer brother could hardly stand.

After the lawman checked our ID's and frisked us, he searched the pickup, most notably the stuff under the tarp.

"Ummm, lookie here! Three rifles...and hooooly sh*t! They're *loaded*."

Oddly enough, the cop's blasé affect doesn't seem to match this highly dramatic utterance. In fact, he sounded bored.

"What do you fellas have to say about *this*?"

"Well, officer, *sir*," Jack said with mock respectfulness. "We were just doing some target practice." Jack lied. He told us later the real reason they carried the loaded guns was to defend themselves against "crazy Indians shooting at them on the reservation."

The cop rubbed the back of his neck and sighed. "Christ, Buffalo. When will you ever learn?" He articulated this in such low-key manner that you could barely hear him. I got the sense he and Jack knew each other a long time.

Do-Right whipped out his pad and pen, and started to scribble out one ticket after another.

"Let's see, carrying loaded firearms... Open alcohol in a vehicle... Contributing to the delinquency of a minor (one of the Running Deers was underage)... And...uh... picking up hitchhikers."

Jack looked stunned as he examined each ticket handed to him.

"Thank you, officer!" he said sarcastically. Do-Right didn't seem to notice or care about Jack's thinly-veiled disrespect.

As soon as the patrolman drove off, the other Indians exploded with laughter. It took a minute or two for Jack to finally crack a smile.

"Do-Right's been pretty *easy* on us today!" joked Mark Holy patting Jack on the shoulder.

When he stopped flipping through the stack of tickets, Jack pulled out the truck keys. As he did, he let out an audible sigh. Then his face suddenly brightened once his pent-up anger fully dissipated. Like an enthused Captain Kirk, he proceeded to declare the next mission:

"Well, guys... it's time to get us some SQUAW!"

"YYYYYYEEEEEEEAAAAAHHHHH!" the four exuberant Indians belted out as we all filed back into the pickup.

The Yuri Geller Method

Things got gloomy again once we parted ways with Jack and the boys at the crossroads. My high hopes of reaching the fireworks by nightfall were starting to dwindle. We found ourselves in a worse position than before, surrounded by a panoramic field of wild-rye and pronghorn without a single object to focus on except a faded billboard a half a mile away. It read, "FREE ICE WATER WALL DRUG."

An hour turned to two hours, then three. It infuriated me to realize that many of the passers-by were also heading for the anti-nuke rally. How could all those enlightened, sophisticated, liberal types refuse to give us a ride?

"BUNCH OF PHONIES!" I blurted out shaking my fist, sounding like LeBlanc who sounded like Holden Caufield.

Around six, Pete complained of hunger pangs, so we decided to have a bite. The spot we chose to dine made the Road Runner parking lot look like a Howard Johnson's. It was a shallow gully twelve yards from the white line. Even from that distance, the freeway noises still made it difficult for us to hear each other talk.

Small plants covered the ground, but they barely carpeted over the gravel-mixed dirt. Was there any poison ivy? Other life forms made their presence known. I noticed a couple of Monarch butterflies fluttering among the taller weeds. Swarms of grasshoppers sprang into the air. South Dakota had been suffering a biblical-scale plague of them that summer.

Each of us reached into our backpack zipper pouches and pulled out a can of Chef Boy-Ar-Dee. Pete had a 15-oz can of spaghetti. I had Beefaroni. Typically, we'd open the can, pour the contents in a sauce pan, and cook it over a 7-oz can of Sterno—a cooking fuel that looks like Jello.

Anyhow, the un-specialness of the occasion prompted us to forgo the usual civilized routine. We spooned and gobbled up our Chef Boy-Ar-Dee cold out of the can, all the while trying to shield ourselves from the Attack of the Airborne Grasshoppers. Unfortunately, one managed to land in my Beefaroni. Disgusted, I picked the thing out by its hind legs and threw it down.

After we washed our utensils and dried them off with our bandanas, we rested awhile on the ground. Once we regained our stamina, we got back to the job at hand (or, should I say, thumb).

As we did so, I couldn't help thinking that our bad luck streak had to do with the incoming historical era. In the late seventies, hitchhiking had gone out of fashion. It was definitely not as hip, cool, and romantic as it used to be. People used to believe it was perfectly safe, but times had changed. Too many hitchhiking horror stories had circulated and swayed public opinion in the negative direction. Resentment of free-loaders increased, especially in tough economic times.

Unless you were able to pay drivers for rides, hitchhiking is freeloading by definition. It's all about getting something free at other people's expense. In some folk's eyes, it was on par with living off the government dole.

When you're stuck in one place, you try everything to get rides—well, almost everything. We ruled out *The Hitchhiker's Handbook*'s recommendation to dress up like girls (to get drivers' attention). LeBlanc shot down many of Tom Grimm's suggestions because he considered them dumb or uncool. My former hitchhiking partner Randal Stark was more open to creative stuff like using signs that make people laugh like "HOPELESSLY LOST" or "ANYWHERE BUT HERE." One time, Randal and I had found a large piece of cardboard, cut it out into the shape of a hitchhiker's hand and extended thumb, and wrote our destination on it.

The weirdest technique I used to get rides is what I call the Yuri Geller Method. *The Handbook* didn't give me the idea, but it got the ball rolling. It said you need to look directly at the passing motorist. "Eye-to-eye contact makes him feel uneasy about driving past you," it states. I took this further by trying to *control the thoughts* of drivers by staring at them and mentally commanding them to stop. It was based on the idea that I—like everyone else—have untapped superhuman powers at my disposal, such as psychokinesis (ability to move physical objects using only your mind) and telepathy (ability to communicate to others through extrasensory means).

The Zarrets had alluded to this idea. But I first picked it up while watching "The Phil Donahue Show." Phil's guest, Yuri Geller, demonstrated on live TV how he could bend spoons with his mind.

Heading toward evening, we faced another conundrum—the weather. A cold front had set in across the Great Plains producing continuous cloud cover, shifting winds, and drizzle. In spite of struggling with it all morning outside the truck stop, we eventually got used to it. However, the weather report on Cedric's radio had raised concerns. It predicted that severe thunderstorms were heading our way.

On the roadside around 8 p.m., we sensed it coming about fifteen minutes before it hit. Night came crashing down quickly. Winds whipped up, vapors in the air got thicker, the whole atmosphere grumbled. We braced ourselves for the worst.

Then came the downpour.

It was as if the clouds finally collapsed under the weight of something enormous and pent-up. Lighting flashed overhead. The accompanying thunder even undermined the hundred-decibel growl of a passing eighteen-wheeler, which is saying something. Of course, we were drenched, but, fortunately, we had shielded ourselves with our hooded rain ponchos. Still, cars and trucks zooming by, pummeled us with water, getting our hats, athletic shoes and socks thoroughly soaked.

You'd think drivers would pick us up out of sympathy. We probably looked pitiful standing out there on the highway in the storm. But I think the rain made matters worse. You have to figure people don't like getting their upholstery wet. And, besides, we must've looked scary like two Grim Reapers in our ponchos.

The Niagara Falls over my glasses distorted what I spotted next—the blue and red flashing lights of a highway patrol car. The vehicle stopped along the shoulder ahead of us. When we walked up to it, the driver's side window opened and we were confronted by a certain "Officer Kowalski."

"Boys, do you mind getting off the road?" the cop said almost politely. "We've been getting complaints about you. It's for your own safety. You're liable to get yourselves killed."

"But, officer," I answered perplexed. "We're stuck here."

There was a pause. Kowalski let out a sigh. The nature of our predicament seemed to dawn on him. It took him a few seconds to process what to do as he rubbed the tired eyes under his glasses.

"OK," he verbalized reluctantly. "Get in the back seat and I'll give you boys a lift."

When the officer said that, I thought I was going to kiss him. At last, there was hope. *Maybe we could see the fireworks after all!*

Soaked backpacks and all, Pete and I gladly entered the back seat of the patrol car and rode off.

The hard plastic back seats smelled like bodily fluids. The seat cushion was as hard as a rock, no doubt designed to make criminals squirm. And I felt like I was in a cage. Wire mesh reinforced the side and back windows. There was bulletproof glass between the front and back seats. Needless to say, the rear door could not be unlocked from the inside.

By and by, Kowalski dashed my last hope of fulfilling my Fourth-of-July fireworks fantasy when he announced he was only taking us to the nearest rest area.

The Out-Post

Once we arrived, there was some good news and some bad news. The good news was the rain let up. The bad news was what Kowalski had called a "rest area" was more like a wayside stop. It had only three decrepit picnic tables, a water fountain, and two outhouses. This rinky-dink operation was more suitable for a county road than the Interstate.

We dubbed the place "The Out-post," a combination of the words "*out*house" and "com*post*." And because it was like the last *outpost* of civilization. The name stuck.

The Out-post privies were basically rectangular boxes on platforms, four feet wide, four feet deep, and seven feet high. They were painted flat brown and had four-inch tin pipes protruding from their roofs. Like most porta-johns, each gave off a pungent stench of the usual suspects: urine and feces.

Pete and I took full advantage of the precious little the place had to offer. We replenished our canteens and brushed our teeth using the fountain, and made use of the john. Flashlights helped us get around in pitch-black darkness.

Sadly, we couldn't find any dry place to lay our heads for the night. The downpour had turned the ground into a virtual swamp. The only reasonable place to set up camp was on a sloped section of sidewalk. At least, there were no puddles there. Though the surface was still pretty wet, I thought my "water resistant" sleeping bag could handle the moisture. I was mistaken.

After I slipped into my bed roll, I immediately felt a soggy sensation at my feet, and, a little while later, I felt it directly under me. As a result, a groan escaped my larynx, but I was way too exhausted to give a crap at that point.

Just as my mind began to drift off, an unwelcome sound invaded my ears.

"ZZZZZZZZOOOOOOOMMMMMM! HUM! HUM! HUM!"

It was of an eighteen-wheeler truck pulling into the rest stop.

The cab door slammed. Lights perched on two utility poles revealed a silhouette of a male trucker coming out of his vehicle and plodding over to the outhouse. He did his business, zipped up his pants, and went back to his rig.

"Oh good, he's leaving," Pete said with a sigh.

This shared sentiment was short-lived, however. The booming vibration of the idling truck engine lingered on for another five minutes, then ten minutes... then fifteen ...until finally the realization came...

"*Oh crap! He's not going away!*"

Apparently, the driver had decided to take a snooze in his truck with the motor running (to keep the air-conditioning going, I suppose). This was a problem of course. Number one: he was wasting gas during the energy crisis. Number two: he was polluting the air. Number three: How can one get any shut-eye with the semi's incessant rumble?

I told myself maybe our situation's not that bad. At least, the rolling din was a *consistent* sound like the "white noise" of a refrigerator. And something Dave Zarret had related occurred to me: "Master your circumstance, and don't let it master you."

So, to get to sleep, I made the decision to ignore the blare and think about something else. Instead of counting sheep, I imagined John Wayne on his horse... galloping in slow motion... through the wind-driven field of wild rye... across the vast plains... and... zzzzzZZZZZ.

It was a light sleep but at least it was something. After three hours went by. I detected rain drops on my face with the accompanying pitter-patter on my sleeping bag.

This combined with a night breeze woke me up.

Then what started out as a shower intensified into *another downpour*! The rain came in sheets, then buckets.

The deluge put us in a dilemma. Where do we go now?

The only dry place was *inside the outhouses*.

Pete and I hastily gathered our stuff. Since each privy could only accommodate a single occupant, Pete scrambled to the men's outhouse and I bolted to the women's.

An outhouse is never a place you want to remain very long. I turned on my flashlight to a house of horrors. There were dead flies in a spider web and, lo and behold, a live Daddy Long Legs. There were the typical things that make you recoil with revulsion in a porta-john, especially that disgusting black hole. Of course, the smell was abhorrent. The fact the women's john was messier than the men's surprised me. I'd previously thought it would be otherwise. And there was also some notable graffiti: a haiku about poop and "STACY LOVES MICHAEL FOREVERRR."

The rain showed no signs of letting up. As time lapsed, it was a daunting challenge just to remain in standing position. The relentless walking all day had practically reduced my legs to jelly. How long could I bear it? The revolting sight of bodily excretions on and around the toilet seat prevented me from sitting down. I could always *squat* down, but that would bring my eyes and nose closer to the filth.

Just as I thought my legs were going to give out, I had the bright idea of using my standing backpack as a chair.

Problem solved, but then the next issue came to mind: How do I manage to get some sleep?

The outhouses being just three feet apart allowed me to communicate with my partner.

"Pete."

"Yeah."

"I... can't take being in here any longer."

"Neither can I."

"So..."

"So what?"

"So what do we do?" A pregnant silence ensued. A rare kind of dilemma confounded us: Do we spend the night with spiders and sh*t—or get walloped by rain?

But there was a third option we hadn't considered. When the sound of the idling eighteen-wheel truck was realized, the idea struck me like an apple falling from a tree.

"Pete, what if we *wake up* the driver?"

"The driver in the truck? What good will *that* do?"

"Don't you see? He's got room, lots of *dry* room... in his truck. Maybe he can let us in."

A desperate Pete LeBlanc agreed to my plan. So, at the count of three, we peeled out of our respective outhouses like race horses out of the gate. With flashlights in hand, we braved through the rain, over to the front of the semi truck.

If I wasn't thoroughly soaked before, I was now.

The machine looked like some giant prehistoric beast, reverberating continually in its parking place. Smoke stacks attached to the cab looked like giant bull horns. Another mental image for truck was a dragon. I pictured myself as St. George the Knight jousting the colossal thing if it ever woke up.

The headlights had been kept on, so we positioned ourselves right smack in the middle of their intense beams. It was like we were swimming in the glare of a lighted *stage*.

And the "show" was about to begin!

The windshield towering above us was like a theater's balcony. Behind those two black rectangles, was our mystery man presumably sleeping. He was our audience!

"WAKE UP, WAKE UP, WAKE UP, RISE AND SHINE! HELP US PLEASE!" we shouted at the top of our lungs as we tramped in the puddles and flapped our arms in the rain.

No response.

We did this again two and three more times, but again we received no reply. Only crickets.

Just as we were starting to become despondent, a funny thing happened: We began to laugh. It wasn't a contrived chuckle. It came from deep within, in waves—a full-fledged belly laugh at the utter ridiculousness of our situation. We recognized we were in some comedy movie, albeit a dark one.

We started singing and dancing to refrains "Singing in the Rain" like Gene Kelly. We performed the Robot as we did Devo songs and pretended to be Led Zeppelin. Then came the bright idea of fetching some props from our backpacks (of course, still in the outhouses), pots and pans to bang together, miscellaneous items to perform a juggling act. We had to take this vaudeville thing to the hilt!

If the driver was awake, I can't begin to fathom what must've been running through his mind!

My partner and I laughed until our sides ached. The joy of this unexpected frivolity at The Out-post floored me.

We'd missed the fireworks. We were stuck in the driving rain in the dead of night in the middle of the Great Plains. No place to go for shelter but a sh*t house. And yet... I was blissfully happy.

How could this be? Things couldn't possibly get any worse—or could they? Then I remembered what Blaise said at Poverty Gulch:

"Ted, you know, Kerouac came up with this word 'beat'... It's the state when you're so beat down, you're looking up into heaven..."

ON THE ROAD 1979

Act Three

CHAPTER 13

THE ROUTE 66 TOURISTS

A S DAVE ZARRET HAD SAID, hitchhiking has its ups and downs. The Out-post experience could well be the best depiction of hell since Dante's *Inferno*. But the surprising thing was "heaven" was close at hand. The joy and laughter that ensued felt *heavenly*.

But surely, the Out-post was purgatory, not hell. The two realms in the afterlife often get confused. Purgatory and hell are not the same thing. What we experienced—the deprivation, the revulsion, the anguish—seemed like hell but it wasn't. In hell, you're totally and permanently cast away from God's presence. On the contrary, in purgatory, God is right there. In fact, he's the active agent, purifying your soul through the fire of suffering until it's clean enough to enter heaven. It's like iron ore going through the blast furnace at the Rouge plant to remove impurities. The final product is pure and refined metal.

Speaking of metaphors, we need to revisit the Interstate highway. As I said before, the Interstate is all about rushing through life until it's utterly meaningless. In contrast, Route 66 represents slowing down to delight in one's surroundings and loved ones. To put it another way, it signifies being aware, engaged in, and appreciative of where you're at *right now.*

Enter Lou and Doris Czeizinger, a middle-aged couple from Westfield, NY.

They would be the ones destined to take us all the way to Rapid City. But they did another thing I'm grateful for: They rescued us from the oblivion of the Interstate and they gave us the chance to see the sights. You might say, the Czeizingers were the ambassadors of Route 66.

Travel Information Center

Thursday, July 5, 1979

The extraordinary day began back at The Out-post. Pete and I had failed to get the truck driver to let us into his rig, but, fortunately, the rain let up. So we managed to get some much-needed rest on the pavement. When we woke up, the eighteen-wheeler was long gone.

At the crack of dawn, we repacked our stuff, strode over to the Interstate, and held our thumbs out. Then, after a while, we started walking.

Though hitchhiking was our primary means of travel, Pete and I had done our fair share of traveling by foot. If the average person can hike 36 miles a day, I wouldn't be surprised if we had paced over two hundred miles that summer.

Pete could win an Olympic gold medal for his endurance. I really had to push myself to keep up with him. His drive to keep moving often infuriated me because I often lagged behind. There were times I had to practically beg him to stop for a break. Even getting him to turn around was a major task. Pete wasn't necessarily ignoring me. He was just spirited away to another realm—La-la Land to be exact. He stayed in cruise control, totally unaware of his surroundings, as when he kept on playing his guitar as the bonfire grilled his elbow at Poverty Gulch.

Hours dragged on as we trotted along Interstate 90 until a guy named Bob Bailey picked us up. Bob was a middle-aged African-American man from Minnesota on his way to Pierre. A devout Jehovah's Witness, he initiated a favorite topic of ours—the end-of-the-world. Also, at one point, Bob made the claim that the buffalo on the plains were once so plentiful that they managed to stamp out all the trees. I found that hard to believe, but I didn't say anything out of politeness.

Bob drove us a half hour before he dropped us off at the Travel Information Center near the Highway 83 interchange. This glorified rest area was crawling with tourists. Staff and different displays informed travelers about road conditions, the weather, and, of course, all the neat vacation spots.

Countless racks of glossy color brochures were devoted to western South Dakota's main attractions. Mount Rushmore, Wall Drug and the Badlands definitely fit the "must-see" category. The Information Center also promoted a number of "maybe" tourist traps such as The Corn Palace, Flintstone's Bedrock City, and Reptile Gardens. The sight of more ads made my eyes roll. We'd already been exposed to an endless parade of billboards hyping up these places.

Another annoying thing about this tourist headquarters was the *tourists*.

Young and old, they came from everywhere, in all shapes and sizes. To us, they were like a herd of cattle. Many wore the stereotypical shorts, fishing hats, sunglasses, Hawaiian shirts, and suntan lotion—others did not. Their numbers included mothers yelling at their brats, sporty-looking dudes who looked like they were ready to play tennis, and slow-moving grannies with varicose veins. Whoever they were, we held them in contempt. We could see right through them!

Besides being loud, rude, and clueless, tourists had one thing in common—superficiality. They were as shallow as a puddle on your driveway. Their idea of "experiencing a place" was nothing more than gawking at a few designated points-of-interest, taking pictures, and moving on. As far as we were concerned, they were just going through the motions like the walking dead.

Desperate to get rides, Pete and I implemented another idea from *The Hitchhiker's Handbook*: Why not just approach people at the Travel Center and simply ask them for a lift? It seemed easy enough. It would be as straight forward as asking your next-door neighbor for a cup of sugar.

But two things made me leery about this method. The first was the fear of rejection. I felt too shy and awkward to walk up to strangers randomly. (This was ironic of course, because a hitchhiker afraid of rejection is a like a doctor afraid of blood.) Secondly, I thought, since the odds of success were so slim, why waste our time? Tourists never gave us rides before. Living in the comfort zone of their car or camper, they ignored cool folks like us. Shallow people and deep people don't mix. It's like Apartheid.

To address my objections, I conjured up antidotes. The first objection was countered with FDR's words: "The only thing to fear is fear itself." On the second objection: What do we have to lose? We were already "wasting time" doing things the normal way. These, along with Pete LeBlanc's unshakable confidence, persuaded me to carry out *The Handbook*'s tip.

Looking our Personal Best

We knew appearance mattered in getting rides just like on a date or job interview. So the first thing we did was hightail it to the restrooms so we could make ourselves presentable. (Another great purgatory metaphor: You have to get "cleaned up" before you enter heaven.)

Compared with The Out-post, the Travel Center's lav was the Taj Mahal, with its grand corridor of stalls, sparking tiles, and Pine-Sol aroma. After we utilized the urinals, we proceeded to wash up and change.

Personal hygiene was the first order of business. As we did throughout the trip (mostly at gas stations), we brushed our teeth, shaved (with disposable razors), and combed our hair using items from our zipper toiletry pouches.

When there was no one else in the restroom but Pete and me, I decided to wash my greasy hair, so I stuck my head in the sink and let the tap run. I started to lather my head with the liquid soap in the dispenser. Just then, a couple of tourist guys walked in and looked at me weird. In spite of them, I proceeded to finish the job.

Then I took a paper towel bath and changed my clothes, replacing my filthy threads with those we'd laundered at Louise's house.

What did I wear on our trip? What practically everybody else my age wore in the seventies: t-shirts and blue jeans (cut-offs or bell-bottoms). I sported Adidas sneakers and a red baseball cap. For special occasions, I dressed in my taupe and black Western shirt. For chilly days, I wore an olive-drab army jacket, which I got from Harry's Army Surplus. (These coats were very popular at my high school, especially amongst the "stoner" males who wore them with ripped blue jeans or jeans that dragged on the ground.)

Once I got myself all spiffied up, I left the restroom and began asking random tourists for rides. Pete LeBlanc would be joining me shortly.

"Excuse me, sir, ma'am... uh, we're on our way to Rapid City," I sputtered nervously with a gooey grin. "We were wondering if we could, uh, possibly get a lift."

In spite of my newly freshened up appearance, a vacationing couple looked at me like I had leprosy and bolted away. How degrading!

I checked over the crowded Tourist Center for my next prospects. As I did, I heard a gruff-sounding man's voice that seemed to come out of nowhere:

"Hey, man, *get a haircut!*"

"Huh? What?" I wondered where the words were coming from. Who were they addressed to?

"Yeah, *you!* The young man in the U of M shirt with the backpack. GET A HAIRCUT."

Once again, I recoiled, despondent over the fact that I'd spent an hour trying to look my personal best, only to have someone zero-in on my hair.

Standing before me was a middle-aged tourist couple. The man was smiling ear to ear, with a twinkle in his eye. The woman (presumably his wife), on the other hand, looked mortified.

"Hello, young man, my name is Lou. This is my wife Doris. Would you mind doing us a favor?"

Meet the Czeizingers

A few minutes later, I was looking at "the Czeizingers" through the lens of their Kodak Brownie camera. I snapped the picture. As it turned out, Lou Czeizinger, a balding man in his late-fifties, was only joking about my hair. He said that to get my attention so he could get me to take the photo. And besides, he was the type who liked teasing young people.

Just as the portrait was taken, my partner came out of the men's rest room to join us. I introduced Pete to my new acquaintances.

"As I was telling your friend here," Lou relayed to LeBlanc. "We have enough room in our car to take you guys to where you're going. But there's only one catch."

"What's that?" Pete asked.

"Doris and I plan to do some sight-seeing before we head over to the Black Hills. I'd be glad to take you guys there, *if* you don't mind being around us old fogies awhile."

Pete and I looked at each other like we'd just hit pay dirt.

"No problem with that!" LeBlanc exclaimed. We now had the chance to see the Badlands and Wall Drug—*and* make it to Rapid City by nightfall!

Lou Czeizinger didn't dress in flashy clothes like other tourists. He wore a pale blue button-down shirt, the blandest kind imaginable. Barrel-chested, he was only a couple inches taller than his wife. A pair of brown-rimmed aviator-style glasses rested on his nose. His round head and double chin reminded me of my middle-aged male Polish relatives. His bright smile was a wide line that nuzzled up to his nose. Crinkles deeply etched in along his lower jaw insinuated the smile.

His gregarious, happy-go-lucky personality could even put Edgar Allen Poe in a good mood.

Doris looked much younger than Lou. Like her husband, she had a warm, tender *neighborly* look. Her full head of sable brown hair was permed like Margaret Thatcher's. She wore a frilly white blouse. Personality-wise, she was a little uptight and reserved at first, but she loosened up later. You could tell she'd been having a good time, although she looked dubious about Lou asking two strange young men from Detroit into their car.

The Czeizingers led us to their olive-green Dodge station wagon in the parking lot. It had a colorful decal collection on the rear driver side window. Each decal represented one of the half-dozen States they had visited. This was a sure sign they were dedicated tourists.

We loaded our packs and drove off.

As we traveled down I-90, Lou, a machinist by trade, entertained us with his stories and jokes. For example, he told us how a beard once "saved his life." While in the U.S. Navy during the Second World War, he served as the ship barber. (He got the job based on his experience shaving the rear ends of cows at a dairy farm.) Once while on furlough, Lou decided to grow a full beard. He chanced upon a former shipmate in a seaside bar. The guy told Lou he'd long held a grudge against the barber who once made him "look like a freak." Little did the guy know, he was talking to the incompetent hair stylist that he once "wanted to kill."

The reading material in the car revealed that the couple was religious, although Doris seemed to be a little more fervent in the faith than Lou. When asked about it, Doris said they had attended the First Baptist Church of Westfield back home. When she uttered "Baptist," I thought of evangelist Billy Graham whom my parents liked to watch on TV.

"Do your *parents* know where you are?" Doris asked.

Here we go again! I thought to myself. The last time that question came up was when Louise Miller O'Neil practically nailed me to her kitchen wall. In contrast to Louise, however, Doris came off low-key and winsome.

"Well... sort of..." I responded.

"Boys, you really should keep in touch with your mom and dad. It's the *considerate* thing to do."

Then Lou piped up (and he said this with total sincerity, without a hint of irony). "Dear, that reminds me of something in the Bible that always made me wonder—you know, that part when Jesus was twelve. Why didn't *he* tell his parents where he was going?"

On noticing the pained expression on his wife's face, I think Lou realized that he should've kept his mouth shut.

A Blast from the Past

Though Lou used the Interstate most of the way, we occasionally got off at exits to see and do things. I enjoyed the quirky stuff. In the town of Kadoka, we chanced upon a cool sculpture of an elk made out of car scrap metal at the Sinclair gas station. There was also The Fountain Motel which had a gaudy turquoise-painted fountain that resembled a giant three-layer wedding cake. In Murdo, we noticed the town had a consistent pattern along Main Street—plain rectangular buildings with signs too small to read and generic names like "Drive-In," "Restaurant," and "The Diner."

One time along U.S. Interstate 90, we passed a figure of a skeleton man with his ax in hand walking a skeleton dinosaur on a leash. It was intended to draw attention to the "Original 1880 Town" just ahead. Doris couldn't photograph it properly from the moving vehicle, so she talked Lou into getting off at the next exit so she could get a decent shot.

However, we got more than we bargained for. As we got closer to the tourist spot, curiosity drew us in like steel to a magnet.

We'd give the "ghost town" mixed reviews. It consisted of real and fake stuff, as well as that which is cool and kitschy. I think it would've been better if real historians ran the place instead of a "mom and pop." For instance, some items— such as antique toys, weapons, and clothes—didn't match the historical period. Buildings were in disrepair. Signs even warned to "ENTER AT YOUR OWN RISK." Lou shared with us a large bag of popcorn he bought at the "museum" as we surveyed the old train and station house (which I admit were pretty cool). Before we left, Doris finally got her picture of the skeleton sculpture, plus a shot of some longhorn cattle and even a camel.

After the ghost town, the Czeizingers decided to stop in the nearby town of Murdo. To our delight, our guides treated us to lunch at a greasy-spoon restaurant that was called "The Diner." There, the four of us sat down in a booth. I ordered a grilled cheese, French fries, and a Coke.

Even if it didn't have all the features of a Route 66 restaurant, it didn't matter. Route 66 was the going fantasy. The Diner had a service counter with floor-mounted stools, a food prep area against the back wall, and small booths. The aroma of coffee, bacon and toast filled the air. There was a cook behind the counter wearing a white smock and holding a soup ladle. There was a uniformed waitress with her order pad in her apron and pencil behind her ear. The customers included a guy at the counter reading a newspaper and a typical family of five talking as they sipped on sodas in a booth.

WHOOOSH! Shivers went up and down my spine. I was utterly *enchanted*.

Why?

It was all about the fantasy, like we were in a movie that took place in the 1950s. The scene before our eyes was, as they say, *iconic*. TV shows, Hollywood films, and painters like Norman Rockwell and Edward Hopper gave diners a certain mystique. The neon lights, American flag decal, burgers, Coke, a juke box, and whatever else fit the "Route 66" motif— and it also fit like a hand in a glove into the even broader "Americana" theme.

Another thing that contributed to this "whoosh" feeling was nostalgia.

The sight of neon lights, for instance, brought me back to the days when my dad wheeled me around in a stroller. He'd take me to the local bowling alley where the multicolored glow of neon sent my mind reeling with wonderment. I even liked the sound of the falling bowling pins and the smell of the stale cigarette smoke. Over and over, the lounge jukebox played Motown hits by the Supremes, the Temptations, and the Four Tops. The atmosphere felt exultant and hopeful, which went along with that time period—the first half of the sixties. Back then, Detroit beamed with pride over being the home of Motown Records and the world's leading auto maker. It was like "Yeah, rah, rah, Detroit is number one," "We built that," etc.

Indeed. the *whole road trip thing* began in the Motor City! Who could argue otherwise?

Why did I obsess over ancient history? It had to do with something more than curiosity. It was something deeply personal. Memories of the era of prosperity and optimism in Detroit—and the whole country—had instilled in me a vision of hope. So my reverie was not so much about the past but the future—the future of mankind.

During those glory days, "the little guy" felt empowered. Henry Ford had made it possible for ordinary working class guys like my dad to afford to take his family on fantastic, whimsical road trips along M-12, southern Michigan's very own "Route 66."

Being with Lou and Doris Czeizinger was like going back to those days. I felt like a kid again. In my imagination, the Czeizingers were Mom and Dad taking my brothers and me on cool vacations. I was reliving those magical moments through them.

The Badlands

Near Cactus Flat, we took a major turn in more ways than one. Lou Czeizinger got off Interstate 90 at exit 131 to make our way to Badlands National Park. We went down U.S. Highway 240, which is also known as the Badlands Loop. It runs 22 miles through arguably the most bizarre terrain on the planet. Whenever I heard the word "Badlands," Springsteen came to mind. He opened his most recent album, *Darkness on the Edge of Town*, with a song bearing that name. The first listen of "Badlands" was one of those rare events when I remember where I was at and what I was doing at the time. (I was in my basement playing pool with Randal before our high school graduation ceremony.) The song's epic drum beat and exuberant rhythm section hit me like a heat-seeking missile. *WHOOOSH!* I got that burning in my bosom! The lyrics went straight to my soul:

> *Lights out tonight,*
> *Trouble in the heartland,*
> *Got a head on collision,*
> *Smashin' in my guts, man,*
> *I'm caught in a cross fire,*
> *That I don't understand...*

It was like the voice of God speaking to me through the burning bush! "Badlands" the song felt so epic and grand like a John Ford movie. I desired something in it, yet *beyond* it.

The more I played the tune and the rest of the album, the more I appreciated the contrast between *Darkness* and its predecessor *Born to Run*. The two Springsteen albums were polar opposites, yet complimentary. *Born to Run* dealt with the hopeful fantasies of youth, *Darkness* had to do with the sobering realities of adulthood. Taken together, the albums were like William Blake's "Innocence and Experience."

Now I found myself in the geographical Badlands. The Lakota gave it its name, *mako sica*, which literally means "land bad." John Steinbeck once said the landscape was "like the work of an evil child. Such a place the fallen angels might have built as a spite to heaven." Theodore Roosevelt said, "They look like Poe sounds." They made me feel like I was surrounded by the ruins of New York City after a nuclear holocaust. Wind, water, and natural processes—both cataclysmic and undetectably slow—had sculpted an environment so strange you feel like you're in a Salvador Dali painting.

It's a bleak desert now, but you could imagine the ruthlessness of an ancient sea carving out a terrain chock-full of random, contorted rock formations, such as twisted towers, gnarled cliffs, and contorted canyons. Weird shapes besiege the landscape, most notably giant pillars that are wide on the top and narrow on the bottom like wine glasses. Others look like tea pots, salt shakers, and hourglasses. Patterns of roundness and sharpness bewilder the eye. At the same time, you're dazzled by the contrasting color of the sedimentary layers, combinations of purple and yellow, tan and gray, orange and red. They even create the illusion of movement like they're actually alive and changing before your very eyes.

The Badlands is a juxtaposition of stunning beauty and shocking desolation.

Stories of the Badlands evoke *dread*. They conjure a more extreme kind of foreboding than F. Scott Fitzgerald. They have to do with nature and survival-of-the-fittest. Rhinos, saber-toothed tigers and, the most epic beasts imaginable— the dinosaurs—once roamed here, but they are now extinct. Why? Things changed. They couldn't adapt because of the shift in climate, predators moving in, or perhaps because of their own complacency and hubris. The fact that nature is so indifferent, so *merciless*, doesn't seem fair. You and fellow members of your species stumble into a tar pit and that's it. You're done! There are no second chances. You just have to suck up to your fate and die.

Another grim story is that of the Ghost Dance. Crow had told us that some Indian prophet instructed his people to dance in "ghost shirts" in the Badlands to generate magical powers. Performing this dance was supposed to shield them from bullets, make the white man extinct, and restore the ancestral hunting grounds. But it didn't work out that way. The ghost dance ceremony—carried out during the gloom of encroaching winter—spooked the local U.S. Army brigade into massacring 300 native people at nearby Wounded Knee. Call it evil or stupid or whatever, the whole business was just plain wretched!

To be sure, the meandering two-lane highway snaking through such surreal terrain was a welcome departure from the dull, straight-and-wide Interstate. Lou tried to have us cover the major points-of-interest—especially the lookouts and spots where you could see wildlife like bison, mule deer, and prairie dogs. When he came to a good place to turn off, we parked and took our sweet time walking around and viewing stuff with keen interest through Lou's binoculars.

The Czeizingers, Pete, and I talked along the Door Trail, a short hike on a series of boardwalks along the rolling mud hills. Our jabber somehow swerved into the cheery subjects of human strife, misery, and "the dark night of the soul" that St. John of the Cross referred to. I equated this state of mind—the worst mental suffering imaginable—to the deep despair addressed in the song "Badlands."

"Lou, did you see any action when you were in World War II?" I asked.

"No, son, thank God, no. We were 'all at sea'—literally." Then Lou suddenly got serious and pensive. "I did come away with a bad case of what they call 'survivor's guilt.' So many good men ended up at the bottom of the Pacific, but me? I walked away without a scratch. Was it sheer coincidence? Was it dumb luck? Was it God's plan? It's really hard to wrap your mind around that."

"Fate smiled and destiny laughed..."

"But it's not that simple, Pete. Bad things happen to good people. As the Bible says, the Lord sends the rain on the just and unjust."

"Unfortunately, if it isn't one hardship it's another," Doris added with a sigh. "Like the time our spouses died."

"What!? Your *spouses?*"

"Yes, we were both married before. We're two widowed people who got married."

"Whoa!"

Detecting our interest, Lou weighed in. "Yeah, it was all very strange. We were actually friends at the church before it all happened. I was happily married to Alice, as Doris was to Don. Each couple even had their own kids. But then disaster struck. Both families were in total shock and disbelief when our spouses were diagnosed with cancer!"

"*Holy crap!* How did you deal with that?"

"Lord knows, it wasn't easy. The grief of losing your loved one is devastating to say the least," remarked Doris. "Different people deal with it differently, of course. As for me, I felt like Jonah inside of the whale, cut off from everything, in utter darkness, lost."

As Lou recounted his experience, the anguish on his face was palpable. "I couldn't sleep. My family and friends kept trying to get me to eat something. I must have lost twenty pounds after losing Alice. I had to steer clear of certain rooms that reminded me of her. It was horrible. I even imagined her visiting me in a dream."

"But, having said all this," Doris added. "The Lord works in mysterious ways."

The rest of the story, as told by Doris, was Lou and she started dating about two months after Lou's wife's died. While doing so, neither of them stopped grieving. In fact, the mourning process brought them closer together. Eventually, they got married and formed a large blended family with seven children "like The Brady Bunch," Doris added in jest. (Lou and Doris did not have children together.)

Doris added one more thing. "Remarriage doesn't mean forgetting about the past. Instead you honor and treasure it."

"It's very strange." Lou said. "I love Doris with all my heart. And yet, I still think of Alice a lot. It makes me feel like Trent, an old shipmate of mine whom we used to tease for having two girlfriends at the same time. We used to call him 'Trent the Two-Timer.'"

Wall Drug

Still reeling from the gut-wrenching conversation on the Door trail, we made our way to the world famous tourist attraction—Wall Drug. It's located in the heart of Wall, a small town just outside the northwest rim of the Badlands.

A framed photograph on display piqued my interest. It dated back to 1932, shortly after the place first opened. Taken during the Great Depression, the sepia-toned picture shows a young man and woman with bright smiles.

They were holding coffee cups upside-down.

The caption under it identifies the beaming couple as Bill and Dorothy Hustead, the founders of Wall Drug. It says the Husteads were having fun with the fact that their restaurant tables had to be set with cups upturned—to prevent customers from getting a *mouth full of dirt*!

Like practically everywhere else in the country, South Dakota at the time was going through the Dust Bowl, the worst ecological disaster in U.S. history.

How appropriate! The Dust Bowl is also the setting of John Steinbeck's epic novel *The Grapes of Wrath*. However, in this literary masterpiece, the Joad family had nothing to smile about. Talk about human suffering! The infamous dust storms had killed off all their livestock and reduced their farm to a virtual Sahara Desert. The Joads had to flee to survive. The only way out was west down, none other than, the "Mother Road," Route 66.

Then it hit me. Route 66 is like a coin: It has two sides. One side is the best of times; the other is the worst of times. To me, the Diner in Murdo—representing "the best of times"—is an icon of heaven as it were. Conversely, the Badlands signifies "the worst of times"—or hell.

On second thought, the Badlands must be *purgatory*. This is obvious because, in the Springsteen song, "the Badlands start *treating us good*." They do so once a certain "price"— presumably human suffering—is paid, much like purgatory in Catholic theology. However, purgatory in *this* life (as opposed to the afterlife kind) involves *the will*. Determination makes you a better person. In hard times, you develop resilience. You persevere through all of life's crap to get to the glory.

Back to the subject of the old photo: How could anyone— let alone the Husteads—be so happy and content during America's darkest hour?

And why *start a business*?!

Here's how we made it to Wall Drug: Once we finished touring the Badlands, Lou followed the Badlands Loop until it changed into Glenn Avenue in Wall at I-90. We immediately turned right down "Loup 90" to see the 80-foot brontosaurus. After that, we turned around and drove past several Route 66-looking motels with neon signs advertising air-conditioning, color TV, and heated pools. Then, we turned right down Main Street, went two blocks and there it was—the focus of all the advertising build-up—WALL DRUG!!!

It spanned at least two city blocks. Like a river emptying into a lake, the traffic on Main Street flowed into a parking lot with three rows of cars parked diagonally. License plates probably represented every State in the continental U.S.. Tourists surged en masse down the sidewalks.

The storefronts of Wall Drug and its associated shops shared common elements—a Western-style type font along with the branding colors of golden yellow and pine green. Under wood-shingled overhangs on both sides of the street, stood a complex of stores like the Badlands Trading Post, Gold Diggers Gold Shop, and Legacy Old Time Photo. Window shoppers could check out bull horns and buffalo skulls, Native American trinkets, and portraits of modern people dressed late-1800s style. There was even a Traveler's Chapel to accommodate those of different faiths. One could easily identify the nucleus of the sprawling operation under a huge sign that read WALL DRUG STORE SINCE 1931.

The faces of Lou and Doris lit up as we set foot in this empire of refreshment, shopping, and entertainment. The place was colossal. In addition to being a shopping mall with all kinds of souvenir, clothes, and jewelry shops, it had a main restaurant where you could help yourself to Wall Drug's world-renowned five-cent coffee and free ice water. The establishment offered various props you can use to take photos with, such as stick-your-face-into-the-hole images of cowboys, Indians or pioneers; a scaled-down version of Mount Rushmore; and a saddled "jackalope" you could climb onto for an imaginary ride.

I had mixed feelings about Wall Drug. That's putting it mildly—I was being pulled in two directions like a game of tug-a-war. It was a contest between opposite views.

On one hand, I slipped back into my resentment of tourists and tourism in general. I cringed at how they wasted money on things like stuffed prairie dogs, t-shirts with tired old slogans, and ridiculous knick-knacks like "pet rocks." At that point, I was strongly influenced by Crow and Thomas' opinions. Crow would consider the owners of Wall Drug as nothing more than greedy capitalists, profiting from merchandise likely manufactured in low-wage sweat shops in Malaysia. Crow's object lesson with my Mountain Dew made me more aware of the exploitive nature of the unholy trinity—capitalism, consumerism, and commercialism.

On the other hand, I continued to revel in the Route 66 fantasy, appreciating Wall Drug's quirky, fun, and friendly atmosphere. The place was wholesome, decent, and down-home, just like our new friends the Czeizingers. It had a homegrown feel. Sure it was tacky, but it was original and folksy, unlike the overly-slick generic chain stores you find everywhere else. Its corniness made my eyes roll, yet that very thing gave it its distinctive charm.

For better or for worse, Wall Drug capitalized on tourists' romanticism of "the Old West." Virtually everything—from menu items to clothes to arcade games—seemed to revolve around the theme of "cowboys and Indians." Another one was "pioneers." I must admit, I loved the swashbuckling tales about these heroes. I needed to keep reminding myself that they were only fantasies largely concocted by Hollywood and slick marketers going back to Buffalo Bill Cody.

At least part of my enchantment with Wall Drug had to do with the Czeizingers themselves—their sunny, earnest, and innocent demeanor. It was heart-warming to see Doris in her element shopping around for gifts for her children and grandchildren. She checked out the porcelain "Precious Moments" figurines, ornaments, and plaques with sayings like "GOD BLESS THIS KITCHEN" and "YOU CALL IT CHAOS, WE CALL IT FAMILY." Doris' sentimentality over kitschy stuff made me shudder like my reaction to Southern-style "sweet" tea—but there was also something deeply compelling about the way she cherished all the things related to family and home. She reminded me of the Blessed Virgin Mary, who "treasured these things in her heart."

True, Lou had shown his serious side in the Badlands, but I believe, he was a really big kid deep down. I pictured him as a much younger man on his battleship in the Pacific making his terrified shipmates laugh with his erratic antics and wisecracks. We had a blast taking turns with him firing at the "bad guys" in the Wall Drug shooting gallery. One time, he goaded me to play Frisbee with him down one of the aisles. Another time, he had Pete and me in stitches when he went into the men's fitting room and yelled out "Hey, we're out of toilet paper in here!"

After all that could be said about July 5, 1979, the day definitely belonged to the Czeizingers. It was their movie, but one I thoroughly enjoyed being in.

The fact I thought Lou and Doris were so refreshing is very odd, considering they were so *normal*. In another context, they'd be dismissed as boring. They were all about the family-oriented Route 66 rather than the decadent Kerouac. They were as *un-Poverty Gulch* as you could possibly imagine. In fact, they shared many of the conservative values of the much-maligned Liberty Pole Methodists and my parents.

When we finally parted ways with Lou and Doris in Rapid City that evening, I was astonished by how heartbroken I was. I felt like bawling like a kindergärtner separating from his mother on the first day of school.

I'll always remember the Czeizingers' positive attitude. In spite of their past troubles, they were obviously enjoying life. I imagined them being the Husteads in that old photo, holding their coffee cups upside-down smiling defiantly at the Dust Bowl.

And spitting in the face of the Badlands.

PART III:

THE BLACK HILLS

CHAPTER 14

NO NUKES!

A S LONG AS I CAN REMEMBER, I had two life objectives: "do your own thing" and "change the world." These two things seem to be what all young people want. And, coincidentally, they also seem to capture what the sixties were about in one fell swoop.

From the onset, the hitchhiking trip had only one goal: "do your own thing"—total autonomy, absolute independence, complete self-rule. When Pete and I arrived in the Black Hills, "change the world" was the furthest thing from our minds. We laughed when we had found out that Cedric Voss thought we were political activists. Again, we were only going to the anti-nuke rally for the experience and no other reason.

"Do your own thing" was the point of everything. It was all about being selfish and the absolute center of the universe. I'd focus on me and Pete would focus on himself. Each of us would not be expected to be responsible for the other—

unless, of course, Pete or I *chose* to. Being forced to take responsibility for anyone other than yourself would betray our philosophy of "the individual."

The Grand Experiment was to live this notion out fully. No holding back.

By and by, we had met our match—Rosie Smith—by far, the most free-wheeling, self-reliant, and American person we'd ever met. Rosie was the perfect embodiment of the ideal. And, so was the special place she had introduced us to—Poverty Gulch.

I repeat: changing the world was not on my radar. Or so it seemed. Maybe it was just dormant in me like a seed planted in the soil. Perhaps John Lennon's spirit never went away.

Lennon—of course the most outspoken member of The Beatles—championed the notions of "making a difference," "making the world a better place," and "world peace" which had burned in my bosom since first grade. His signature song "Imagine" expressed the hope that fellow dreamers would join forces so "the world will be as one." The song also implied that I was accountable to humanity as a whole. I had a responsibility to help save the planet.

Marvin the Rancher

Friday, July 6, 1979

The Black Hills are located immediately west and south of Rapid City, where Lou and Doris Czeizinger ended up spending the night. Lou graciously went out of his way to drop us off at the foothills of this relatively small, isolated mountain range. "Black Hills" is a translation of the Lakota *Pahá Sápa,* named after their dark appearance from a distance. But, to be honest, they didn't look black to me at all. Interestingly, the region is said to be at the exact center of North America, in terms of latitude and longitude. That means it's quite literally

America's heartland. Indeed, the Lakota Sioux elders refer to it as "The Heart of the Earth." They say its oval dome shape resembles a physical human heart.

Like the Badlands, the Black Hills comes as a surprise. The range pops out of nowhere from the Great Plains like an island in the middle of a vast sea. (In fact, millions of years ago, it was a literal island in a literal sea.) Moreover, it has nothing to do with any of the other mountain ranges in the western United States. Unlike the Badlands, it looks like it belongs to the Earth. Its one-and-a-half million acres of granite highlands are covered with pine trees. The elliptical shape of its inner core reaches almost four thousand feet. The entire range is encircled by limestone deposits, evidence of an ancient shore. Of course, the most famous feature of the Black Hills is the national monument dedicated to four U.S. Presidents—Mt. Rushmore.

Our overnight stay in the Black Hills was as pleasant as The Out-post was unpleasant. And the place didn't even have a restroom. It was in a section called the Red Valley because of the color of the oxidized iron particles in the soil. A dense grove of ponderosa pines—trees with thick trunks and scaled, rusty-orange bark—fully concealed our campsite. The grassy undergrowth was sparse, but the fallen evergreen needles could be bunched together to make a bed as soft as a haystack. The aroma from the bark, which resembled vanilla or butterscotch, accentuated that of the pine. The nocturnal sounds of the locusts, coyotes and owls made you feel like you were right there in nature. We even saw a pair of white-tailed deer galloping around early the next day.

In the morning, around seven, we climbed down the slope about seven-hundred feet and started to hitchhike down Highway 44 toward downtown Rapid City. Our destination, Heritage Park, was only about twenty minutes away. Just a mile down the road, beyond the curve and a trailer park, you were back on the prairie, an altogether different ecosystem.

A red Chevy pick-up stopped. The truck's flat bed—where our packs went—contained a half-dozen coiled up ropes and smelled like manure. The fortyish motorist—who identified himself as Marvin—was a rancher. Tall and lean, he definitely looked the part with his straw cowboy hat, ruddy complexion, and tightly muscled shoulders and arms. He wore a scarlet bandana around his neck.

Marvin the Rancher gave us a brief low-down of the area.

"Here's what you need to understand, boys," Marvin said earnestly. "The Indians consider the Black Hills the holiest place on Earth. It's like what Jerusalem is to Jews and Christians. Are either or both of you guys religious?"

"No. At least not in the traditional sense," answered Pete.

"I'm spiritual, not religious," I replied.

"Well," Marvin continued, "Imagine, if you will, you're a devout Christian or Jew. And foreigners start invading your most sacred grounds in pursuit of silver and gold. You'd be a little pissed off, wouldn't you?"

"Of course."

"Well, that's how the Indians see it. And I'd venture to say that the animosity over this tract of land is just as intense as what's going on in the Middle East."

"You mean between the Israelis and the Palestinians?"

"Yeah, this place is a powder keg like Palestine. The Indians see the Black Hills as a spiritual place. Their national pride and identity is wrapped up in it. The whites, on the other hand, have always wanted the Black Hills for its natural resources. By a cruel twist of fate, the Hills happen to contain the largest and most valuable mineral deposits in the world. It's got gold, silver, you name it—or used to anyway."

"And *uranium*."

I informed Marvin that the mining of uranium—the raw material for nuclear energy—had prompted the political face-off downtown. That and Three Mile Island.

However, Marvin expressed that he knew this. In fact, he was one of the activist organizers!

"They're tearing the guts out of Jerusalem," he continued grimly. "The sad thing is there can't ever be any compromise. The stakes are high. Either the corporations win or they lose. If they win, we *all* lose."

"Doesn't it seem like the greedy power-grabbers always have the winning hand?" I lamented. "Like Bruce Springsteen says *'Poor man wanna be rich, rich man wanna be king, and a king ain't satisfied 'til he rules everything.'*"

Marvin went on, "We've all been taught in school that the U.S. government is based on 'the rule of law,' right? Well, what about the Treaty of Laramie of 1868? It declared that the Black Hills is off-limits to white settlers—*forever*. If you read it, it's plain as day. Both parties signed it into law."

Little did I know, just one year later, the U.S. Supreme Court agreed that the Laramie Treaty had been broken. It's now official. The United States had finally admitted it stole the land from the Indians! However, the Indians were only awarded a measly sum of money which the Sioux ended up turning down. They wanted *all* of their land back.

(Learn more about Marvin in Appendix B.)

The Big Protest Rally

By this point in time, LeBlanc and I had already been to two anti-nuke demonstrations—one in Zion, Illinois, site of a nuclear plant, and the other at the Wisconsin State capitol in Madison. The growing numbers at both events, plus the third in Rapid City, South Dakota, seemed to show that the movement was picking up steam. We seemed to be right smack in the middle of something big.

The carnival atmosphere was beginning to build when we arrived. Activists set up booths and tables along the main walkway in Memorial Park. You could feel the excitement mount. People from all over were itching for a nonviolent fight. Officially, things would begin at high noon with a "teach-in," as they called it. That's where you're invited to walk from booth to booth and gather information about given topics. Each booth, representing some organization, displayed posters and literature, and usually had live staff available to educate you, answer questions, or have you sign some mailing list.

As previously said, protests all over the United States began as a reaction to an accident at the Three Mile Island nuclear power plant. Located near Harrisburg, Pennsylvania, the facility nearly melted down and radioactive material seeped into the atmosphere. No injuries were reported, but public concern, even hysteria, spread like wildfire. "What about the long-term health risks?" Americans were asking. "Are other nuclear plants safe?" "What if one of them explodes big time?"

Attempts to calm people's fears apparently backfired. Leaders withholding information gave the impression of a cover-up. (Americans were in no mood for cover-ups after Watergate.) And, by coincidence, the recent movie *The China Syndrome*—starring Jane Fonda, Michael Douglas, and Jack Lemmon—dramatized the nightmare scenario. The setting? A nuke plant that eerily resembled Three Mile Island.

A newly-formed activist organization called the Black Hills Alliance (BHA) was sponsoring this three-day series of events called "A National Gathering of the People." BHA was a coalition of Indians and whites like Marvin opposed to the careless mining of uranium and other minerals. Positively stated, it served to "protect the land and its people."

Pete and I were glad to make it for the opening. Day One's agenda would consist of the aforementioned teach-in—held throughout most of the day—and the big evening event. The latter was scheduled to begin at 8 p.m. in the Rushmore Plaza Civic Center. It would consist of political dignitaries making speeches and then—the *rock concert!*

Of course, the concert was the main thing that interested us. It would feature the famous rock stars Jackson Browne, Bonnie Raitt, and Jesse Colin Young. And the price was the best part—free!

Once we got tickets at the box office (seating was on a first-come-first-serve basis), we spent the morning wandering around until things got seriously underway. Memorial Park, Rushmore Plaza, and the shops along Rushmore Road and Main Street were practically brand new. They'd been built or rebuilt during the years following the Great Flood of 1972 which had all but destroyed Rapid City. Civic planners had constructed Memorial Park (where the teach-in took place) as a tribute to the two-hundred or so flood victims. Its thirty acres consisted of picnic areas, a rose garden, a fountain, tennis courts, and a pond. The four-block Rushmore Plaza and Civic Center complex was just north of Memorial Park.

Hordes of people arrived by bus or by other means of transportation. It seemed most of them came from the big college towns like Madison, Boulder, and Ann Arbor. A good majority of these "concerned citizens" were white students on summer break. Their appearance ranged from derelict to clean-cut. Some of the older adults—presumably professors, community organizers and such—erred more to the derelict side with their long hair, grown out faces, and earthy clothes. They fit right in with the dealers, beggars, and crazies who also showed up.

Overall, the mood was festive, which is weird when you consider everybody talked about death, impending doom, and world annihilation. People toted coolers, sat on blankets, and tossed around Frisbees like they were having a beach party. Pot-smoking was common though organizers discouraged all alcohol and drug use. Vendors came around selling stuff—such as raw coconut bars, trail mix, and banana-carrot juice—like peddlers at a baseball game. A few Indians in body paint and traditional garb did ceremonial dances, as well as Hare Krishas in their peach-colored robes. Eccentrics came out of the woodwork, such as a gentle fellow with a W.C. Fields hat and cane going around trying to play Skip-to-My-Lou with random people.

It may have been a party, but folks were "taking action." Taking action meant getting out "the message," even if it involved making a spectacle of yourself. Guitarists performed protest songs along the sidewalk. Leaders with bullhorns led chants like "TWO, FOUR, SIX, EIGHT, WE DON'T WANT TO RADIATE!"

Holding up signs was another form of taking action. Banners, poster boards, and t-shirts featured slogans with bold lettering and provocative images. Slogans went from statements of the obvious ("NUKES KILL LIVING THINGS") to the poetic ("BETTER ACTIVE THAN RADIOACTIVE" and "HELL NO WE WON'T GLOW"). The most often used graphics were crossed-out radiation symbols and skulls.

Theatrics seemed to be the order of the day. With masks, costumes and face paint, several individuals pretended to be the Grim Reaper or fallout victims. Others strolled around in gas masks and head-to-toe radioactive gear. With a tape recording of an explosion blasting from a "boom box" (no pun intended), a group of thespians acted out what would happen in the event of a real nuclear detonation.

As far as Pete and I were concerned, we got what we were looking for—an experience. It was fantastic. To expand one's consciousness, the experience had to have an element of novelty, in other words, *out-there-ness*. And this scene was definitely "out there." In fact, in some ways, it was probably more so than Poverty Gulch (which is saying something!)

To get the most out of a particular "out there" experience, one last thing is required: You have to move from being a spectator to participant. You have to be part of the action like you're the leading actor in a movie—your *own* movie. As I'd come to realize at Poverty Gulch, you've got to *play the game*. And, once you're in a situation, you have to give it your best shot. You've got to spike the ball!

What exactly is "spiking the ball" at a protest rally? Unlike Poverty Gulch, it isn't about sex, drugs, and rock & roll (although more than a few in Rapid City that day were inclined to think so). The answer is obvious: A protest rally is all about *protest*.

This realization took me off-guard. As previously said, my impulse to "change the world" was nonexistent or at least dormant. But I suppose a certain principle came into play: "When in Rome, do what the Romans do." In other words, your actions are determined by *where* you're at. While in Italy, you eat pizza; in Mexico, tacos, etc.

Again, what do you do at a protest rally? You protest. You join the crowd and sing with gusto "We Shall Overcome," you grab a placard and shout "NO NUKES!" at the top of your lungs. You pass out literature.

And that's just what I did—when Pete wasn't looking.

The Gullible Cynic

From dawn to dusk, the political ferment went on. The booth for an activist group called Students Against Nuclear

Energy (SANE) served as our base of operation. The activist group graciously allowed us to keep our backpacks in their storage bin so we could move around more freely. Their canopy and water dispenser made the booth a kind of oasis, the ideal place to hang out. The three students who ran it had driven all night from Lawrence, Kansas. Throughout the day, they took turns crashing on the lawn to make up for the lost sleep time. The awake ones informed booth visitors on the perils of nuclear power using colorful diagrams, charts, and graphs.

A talkative young woman named Jessica led the team.

From the start, Pete had designs on Jessica. As for me, I wasn't in the least bit interested in her. She was a twenty-year old blonde, tall and thin. As far as looks go, Springsteen might say, "you ain't a beauty but, hey, you're alright". This spirited young activist evoked the "hippy chic" archetype with her wire-rimmed "granny" glasses, straight hair falling halfway down the back, and cut-off denim shorts. That look was on its last legs.

I liked her t-shirt. It read "GULLIBLE CYNIC." "Gullible" implied a certain innocence or naiveté that comes with starry-eyed idealism. "Cynic" suggested a person who is experienced and jaded. If the t-shirt was intended to be an ice-breaker, it worked. I asked Jessica about it and she confirmed it captured who she was. She said she was "cynical" about the well-laid plans of "the establishment" and she had to do something about it.

"When I see something's not right, I speak my mind!" Jessica said with a self-satisfied grin. And "speak her mind" she did!

Jessica strumming an acoustic guitar clinched it for Pete. He venerated the Joni Mitchell type. As I watched him make his move, I just rolled my eyes. Granted, I admired Jessica's enthusiasm, but she didn't hold a candle to Rosie Smith in terms of being radical. In fact, she came across as a closet normal person. She reminded me of a class valedictorian, the kind whom the teachers adore but the other kids sneer at. She seemed too smart for her own good. I expected graduation speech drivel like "reach for the stars" and "follow your dreams" to leave her lips at any second. (Now I was playing the cynic!)

At one point, Pete managed to borrow another guitar so he could play a duet with Jessica. How appropriate! They performed Dylan's "The Times They Are A-Changin'" They also did "If I Had a Hammer," "We Shall Not Be Moved," and other classics from the Kumbaya Days. Eventually, however, Pete saw the light about Jessica.

Looking agitated, he pulled me aside and whispered, "I can't believe it. She's a nun."

"She a what?" I replied perplexed.

"A *nun.*"

I was imagining Jessica as a *literal* nun with habit and all. Though far-fetched, it seemed plausible. After Vatican II, the sisters didn't wear habits.

"C'mon, I don't mean *literally*," Pete said visibly annoyed. "She's a nun *for 'the cause.'* I mean, the only thing she talks about is nuclear power."

This cleared it up for me.

Pete's credulity really gave me a smug satisfaction. First, I enjoyed seeing him stumble with women after his mind-boggling success with Rosie. Second, it demonstrated my superior ability to size up the female species. I had determined Jessica wasn't worth the trouble two hours ago. But, to me, she was more like an evangelist than a nun.

That said, you couldn't knock Jessica for her effectiveness at activism. She was truly righteous and she knew all the hard facts about nukes. By the time she was done with us, we were well-informed on how high-level wastes are disposed, how radiation messes up your chromosomes, and how nuke plants are susceptible to meltdown. After a while, the steady barrage of information, statistics, and terms like "plutonium," "mill-tailings," and "strontium-90" reduced us to nodding bobble heads.

We remained on good terms with the Gullible Cynic mainly because of the storage space. But it was time to branch out and do other things. Pete felt inspired to sit on a park bench to compose a poem. I went around checking out the various other booths erected by political organizations like Greenpeace, the Sierra Club, and ones that probably had little or nothing to do with the environment, such as the National Organization for Women (NOW).

A pamphlet I picked up at the NOW booth helped me grasp Jessica more. It read "Transforming Conversations that Matter into Actions that Make a Difference." With these political activists, it's all about *urgency*. There's no time for small talk. You need to act *now* to alleviate strife, end oppression and save mankind. (The feminists at NOW corrected me: It's *"humankind"* not "mankind."). The clear-and-present global threat was not the Soviet Union, OPEC or the Ayatollah Khomeini. It was big corporations.

Planetization

The next stop was the American Teilhard Association (ATA) booth. It had a poster featuring a picture of Earth with stick figures holding hands around our planet's circumference. Above it was the inscription "THE WORLD IS ROUND SO THAT FRIENDSHIP MAY ENCIRCLE IT."

After listening to Jessica's incessant talk about nuclear catastrophe, it was refreshing to meet people who put more emphasis on dreams than nightmares. The representatives of ATA highlighted what they're *for* rather than what they're against. The married couple manning the booth put me at ease with their cheerful disposition. They allowed me to browse through their literature rack without saying anything, for a while at least. The crosses around their necks revealed they were Catholics. I felt right at home.

Their names "Kazuka and Kari" sounded poetic to me. Kazuka was a handsome, physically fit Asian guy in a white polo shirt. He was originally from Japan (so he must have been quite familiar with Hiroshima and Nagasaki). Kari was one-quarter this and that, but her auburn hair and blouse made her look "Celtic." They were both around thirty.

"Do you have any questions?" Kari asked.

"Yeah, who is Pierre Tee...?"

"Oh, Pierre Teilhard de Chardin. I'm glad you asked. He was a French Jesuit priest who lived in the first half of this century. He was a great visionary. His writings inspired (among other great people) leaders of the United Nations. The late Fr. Chardin started out as a paleontologist. His observations on how evolution works convinced him that humankind is moving toward world peace."

World peace. That's a loaded term! The very thought of it made me shudder.

"Is it even possible?" I muttered under my breath. I was beginning to wonder, given all the frightening news reports. Muslim radicals were taking over. President Carter was in over his head. Nukes were destroying the planet. What else could go wrong? Surely we were on the eve of destruction.

"Look, Ted, if you think about it, world peace is not only possible. It's *inevitable*," Kazuka replied with a combination of wistfulness and steely resolve. "We're beginning to see it happening. The present crises are only the birth pangs of something wonderful—*planetization*."

"What's 'planetization?'"

"Planetization," Kari replied, "is the cosmic phenomenon where all humans will achieve total *interdependence*. Through the process of evolution, the human race is finally coming together—politically, ecologically and spiritually—into one unified framework."

Kazuka continued. "It's all part of the emerging global consciousness. More people are realizing that unconditional love is the answer to the world's problems. It's dawning on us that human solidarity is the only way we can save ourselves from ourselves."

"It's about time! Mankind... uh, I mean, *human*kind has to get its act together," I injected. "We've been so thick-headed for so long."

I'll never forget the way Kazuka and Kari spoke. It had a breathless quality that indicated an emotional level *beyond* enthusiasm. They were alluding to humanity's highest dream— *utopia*, the perfect world that's spiritual and everlasting. Great philosophers, poets, and such have fantasized about it since the dawn of time, most notably John Lennon, who challenged us to "imagine" a time and place when religion, countries, and possessions no longer divide people. Everybody would work together to eliminate war, poverty, and pollution—once and for all!

The result would be a paradise, literally heaven on earth!

Meeting Kazuka and Kari was a breakthrough of sorts. Thanks to them, I wanted to read Pierre Teilhard de Chardin. From the little I'd just learned, his visionary insights clicked with me. I felt, on a gut level, the truth of his ideas.

Kari handed me something for my intellectual appetite: a pamphlet. It was called *Toward the Omega Point: Understanding Pierre Teilhard de Chardin.*

The funny thing was, in 1979, "working for world peace" seemed quite out-of-date, a throwback to the touchy-feely Kumbaya days. It came across silly, over-sentimental, and naive. "Peace and love" was out; cynicism was in. Even the cynical Elvis Costello lamented over this fact in a song called "What's So Funny 'Bout Peace, Love, and Understanding?"

Kazuka and Kari said they didn't like this disturbing new trend. They were nostalgic about the sixties when young folks selflessly flocked to civil rights marches and joined the Peace Corps. The couple yearned to go back to those heady days. At least during that weekend, they could enjoy reliving the past. Or maybe—just maybe—the recent anti-nuke protests would reignite the sixties.

Nothing to Crow About

Again, there'd been anti-nuke rallies going on all over the country that summer. What made this event unique was its location—the Black Hills. It introduced the Indian angle. Native Americans and the environment seemed to go together like bread and butter. Since, they're so "close to nature," Indians were the perfect spokespersons for the cause.

Ironically, the only "Indian" I talked to that day wasn't an Indian. *It was Crow!*

Over the past couple of days, I'd thought a lot about Crow and Thomas. Rapid City was supposed to be their final destination. Where were they? Crow's Mountain Dew speech at the Road Runner Truck Stop remained fresh in my mind. Again, he had railed against America's greed and injustice. He condemned capitalism for exploiting workers and defiling the environment. He even denounced his own white skin to show his solidarity with the oppressed people of the world.

Though he was the silent type, Thomas made almost as much impact as Crow. His passionate words "You gotta be radical!" ricocheted in my soul. They were so appropriate for the Black Hills!

Lo and behold, I saw their forms in the distance—Crow and Thomas in the flesh!

Like two Buddhas, they were sitting under a tree near the fountain. I rushed over to see them, anxious to compare notes. The men were in much better spirits than before. When I shook Crow's leathery hand, I forgot to do it the Indian way. Crow was still shirtless, wearing only aboriginal jewelry around his neck and wrists, and his "loincloth" (that is, his cutoff shorts). His long, burnt-orange braided beard looked bristly and stiff, almost dead, no doubt from constant exposure to the sun. Thomas. his sidekick, remained at Crow's right hand.

"How did you guys make out the rest of the way?" I asked.

Crow just smiled and shook his head. Thomas the Pirate rolled his eyes.

"It was a *wonderful* experience! Right, Thomas?" Crow was of course being sarcastic. He told me about their hassles with the cops and I recounted our run-ins with Officers Do-Right and Kowalski.

"Those pigs have an attitude problem," he continued with his French-Canadian accent. "I think the uniform gets to their head. It's like they're God Almighty and you're a piece of sh*t. You know, they're just like *Custer*..."

Once again, Crow went on a tirade about General Custer. He had a personal vendetta against a man who'd been dead for a hundred years. To him, Custer was the symbol of everything that was wrong in the world. Custer was evil incarnate, responsible for America stealing the Indians' last bastion of freedom. The fact that so many things in the area were named after Custer drove him nuts.

"General George Armstrong Custer!" Crow said with disgust. "What a fool to think he could take on 20,000 Lakota, Cheyenne, and Arapaho warriors with his 300 men. I'm glad they flattened his ass!"

Crow spoke wistfully about the pristine Garden of Eden the Indians had enjoyed before the white man came, and how the natives saw the land as a continuous, unbroken space that belonged to everyone. They called the Earth their "mother." Then Crow explained how whites had dissected the vast virgin wilderness into plots of real estate and how they plundered the sacred Black Hills with shovels, picks, and drills. Finally, he fumed about the Indians being banished to reservations.

"Have things changed for the better since the white Europeans came here?" Crow asked rhetorically with a puff of smoke of his homemade tobacco cigarette. He then recited a litany of every societal ill he could think of and attributed them to the white man.

All the while, I wondered what was the straw that broke the camel's back? What event in this man's life caused him to reinvent himself as an Indian? Every super-hero has an origin story. I was afraid to ask Crow what his was. For better or for worse, Crow told me it anyway.

It began when I mentioned the upcoming presidential race. When I did, Crow got real emotional.

"All politicians are a**holes!" he said with lye in his voice. "They don't know what in hell they're doing in Washington. They just sit on their asses all day shoving their g*d**n laws down our throats. Not to mention getting us in senseless wars. I used to be pretty patriotic, but that was before those swine sent me off to Vietnam!"

"You were in *Vietnam*?" I was shocked and amazed. I couldn't picture Crow ever donning a military uniform, much less obeying orders. Giving orders? Maybe.

"Yeah, I was over there for five hundred and ninety days. The longest year and a half of my life," he continued. "You want to hear stories? Sh*t. Nothing could've prepared me for what I've seen over there. I was just a kid like you."

I dared to ask him more about his Vietnam experience.

"I came there thinking I was John Wayne, right? In basic training, they fed you a bunch of propaganda about fighting for democracy and all that. They brainwash you into thinking the Vietnamese were just a bunch of 'gooks' and 'slopes.' It wasn't long after I got off the plane that I started to get the full picture. Wow! When I caught a whiff of those stinking corpses in the infirmary and saw the hell on the faces of those people living there, I thought to myself, "F**k, this is absurd! What in the hell am I doing here? I've just stepped into a g*d***n nightmare."

Crow went on about the paranoia he experienced while walking around sniper-infested Saigon. He spoke about the dread of being ambushed while wading through rice paddies. Most notably, Crow impressed on us how much he felt betrayed and lied to by the U.S. government.

"I left there without a scratch," he said, "but, man, they really f***ed up my mind."

It's not necessary to recount Crow's entire speech. Only to say, it made a lasting impact on me, to say the least. First, the fact that Crow was so uncompromising blew me away. In this regard, he was like Rosie. Crow was the exact opposite of the spineless, wish-washy "cafeteria" Catholics in my life—who routinely compromised their core beliefs just to "fit in" and "be nice." He spoke the truth (his version of it of it anyway) and didn't care if he offended people.

Second, after I heard Crow had served in the military, my respect for him skyrocketed. That kind of courage inspired a sense of awe. This put him in the same special class as Lou Czeizinger who, again, had served heroically in World War II.

Third, Crow's account of the indignities he'd suffered when he came home almost moved me to tears. At least Lou returned to a hero's welcome; Crow and his army buddies did not. America shunned the Vietnam veterans because they'd "lost" the war, an unpopular one at that. In spite of the huge sacrifices made, they were treated with indifference, disrespect, and contempt.

Everything Crow said got me worked up and angry. My teeth began to grind, my fists clenched, and my temperature rose. Righteous indignation was the net effect of not only hearing Crow's words, but also those of Marvin, Jessica, and the other activists.

I had to do *something* about all this injustice!

The absurd thing was my mixed motives. I must admit, my desire to join in the protest was partly genuine and partly not. The fake part didn't necessarily stem from deceit or hypocrisy. I wanted to join the bandwagon. At the same time, I wanted to have fun *portraying* the "political activist" and/or the "revolutionary"—just for the sake of the experience.

This would be my next movie! I would now be the brave, romantic freedom-fighter Marius from *Les Misérables*—or, better yet, Woody Guthrie!

The Woody Guthrie fantasy was actually two rolled up into one. Besides being a hobo, Woody was a political activist. After he hopped trains and hitchhiked to California, Woody used his musical talent to fight for the rights of the Okies, the poor, exploited farmers from Oklahoma.

Since they literally lost everything due to the Dust Bowl, the Okies migrated to California for fruit-picking jobs. But they ended up being mistreated and underpaid by their new employers, the orchard owners. They badly needed a champion. So, with guitar in hand, Woody gladly volunteered to be their voice. In the process, he became a legend.

Optimists Versus Pessimists

I figured it was a glass-half-full-half-empty sort of thing. A matter of perception.

Kazuka and Kari thought the sixties were making a comeback in the Black Hills, but there were others there who weren't so sure. As I helped Greenpeace pass out fliers near the intersection of 5th and Omaha, one organizer admitted he was disappointed with the rally's low turnout. Crow attributed it to "today's young people" who no longer took things as seriously as "those in the sixties." Even *I* noticed that the activists' energy level wasn't quite up to par.

Siding with the optimists, I still fancied us grabbing the top headlines or even making the national TV news. That would *really* help spread awareness for the cause. Perhaps our massive fifteen-mile protest march through the Black Hills the next day would capture the media's attention. Maybe the evening's concert—with noted rock stars—would get us widespread publicity. One couldn't underestimate the power of the press to influence the masses.

I had to admit though, it was an uphill battle. Our bold rhetoric about shutting down mines and plants didn't seem very popular around here. In fact, it seemed to backfire: It made folks afraid and angry at *us* instead of the corporations. In their minds, we threatened people's jobs. This bugged me, considering how we liberal Democrats took pride in looking out for the working class.

And, due to the malaise, average Americans simply didn't give a crap about politics.

I'm sure it was much worse in Rapid City. Being a major tourist town, it was a place where folks came to escape their troubles and lose themselves in the vacation fantasy. And there we were—bombarding them with inflammatory signs, bullhorn chants, and literature—all reminding them that the country's going to hell. Politically, these tourists seemed to be the opposite of us. Many of them were conservative patriots who came to see Mt. Rushmore for the Fourth-of-July, not to be confronted by strident anti-American malcontents like Crow, Marvin, and Jessica.

The tourists generally ignored us, but some found us amusing. I noticed them across the street taking our pictures and peering at us through binoculars like we were animals on a safari.

We agitators followed the organizers' instructions: Be courteous and friendly when engaging with the public. "A smile goes a long way" brought to mind similar advice in *The Hitchhiker's Handbook*. In spite of our best efforts, the pedestrians treated us like turds. Folks typically took my Greenpeace fliers out of politeness, but ended up throwing them in the trash or on the ground. Some just said "no thank you" and kept walking. Some simply steered clear of us. On rare occasions, we got comments like "If you don't like it here, go move to Russia!" "Get a job for chrissake!" or "Take a bath, you communist scumbag!" To make matters worse, we were accused of littering.

The visceral rage aimed at us was hard to understand. Some passers-by looked like they wanted to beat the crap out of us. Fortunately, well-placed police officers—who we called "pigs"—helped keep us safe from our foes.

One fellow activist from Chicago took it upon herself to give her glum comrades a pep talk. She was a heavy-set African-American woman named Roshonda. She had an annoying habit of "reminding" you of things you didn't need to be reminded of.

"Let me *remind you* who we're dealin' with here—losers. Conservatives are basically losers because they oppose all change. We liberals forgot we've been the winners for a long time," she asserted.

"Well... I don't know..." responded the pessimistic, forty-year old white Political Science teacher from Ann Arbor, the home of the University of Michigan.

"Look, it's time for a few reminders," Roshonda said cutting in. "Conservatives have a terrible track record. They were wrong about slavery. They were wrong about the sun goin' around the earth. They've been wrong on jus' about everything: the environment, democracy, the woman's right to vote, equality, social justice. The list goes on and on. On every conceivable issue, the liberals have won and the conservatives lost."

"But, you have to admit," replied the teacher. "*They're* the ones winning the propaganda war. People like Reagan can make lies sound just like truth. They're convincing people that government is the enemy of freedom, that feminism destroys families, that the fetus is actually a person, and so on. They've even turned the term 'liberal' into a dirty word. That's some accomplishment.'"

"*Ronald Reagan!* That guy drives me crazy," muttered a male picketer just joining the conversation. "The idea of that man becoming president terrifies me."

"You're not kidding." added a woman standing there shaking her head. "Reagan keeps me up at night. He'd set the civil rights and the women's movement back a hundred years!"

"Ha, worse than that. He'd get us into World War III." There was a moment of silence. I saw a couple of people swallow hard: This ominous prediction needed to be digested.

"Relax, comrades!" said Roshonda the optimist. "There's no way that man Reagan will ever be elected president. He's way to too conservative. Trust me, the American people aren't that stupid."

"Famous last words," the teacher retorted, "That's what they said about *Margaret Thatcher*." Roshonda and I drew a blank. We knew zilch about Great Britain's recently-elected prime minister. The teacher claimed she was "Reagan's ideological twin," in other words, a dangerous right-wing fanatic. He worried aloud that a similar calamity may soon befall the United States.

At that, I left the scene to go check on my partner Pete LeBlanc. (Remember him?) The last time I saw him, he was on a park bench composing a poem. Pete was still there in a state of deep thought. I found it weird that he had produced only eight lines of poetry in two hours' time. After annoying him with my interruption, I left him alone to continue his craft.

While I was there, I noticed a commotion going on at the NOW booth. There were people crowding around watching one professionally-dressed woman interviewing another, holding a microphone. Photographers were around taking pictures. It dawned on me that the media had arrived!

Now things will get interesting. The *whole country* will learn about us!

The interviewee was an important person: Sara Nelson, the Labor Committee Chair of NOW, one of the speakers at that night's event. The newspaper doing the reporting was the *Rapid City Journal*.

I was elated over the fact that we were actually making news. That meant our message was getting out! Perhaps what we were doing in Rapid City's Memorial Park would impact society after all. Or, dare I say, *make history*. It felt good to be part of something so significant!

Well, sometime the next day, my hopes would be dashed at a newsstand. We didn't make front-page headlines. The *Journal* buried the story on Page 5A, and we got zero coverage everywhere else.

What was splashed over the headlines of all the nationally syndicated newspapers?

President Carter has *disappeared*! In bold print, the New York Post said it best: "WHAT IN THE HECK ARE YOU UP TO, MR. PRESIDENT?"

Talk about being upstaged!

"Where in the World Is Jimmy Carter?!"

All afternoon, I continued passing out fliers, singing, chanting, and holding up picket signs. I got myself on many mailing lists (which I regretted later because my mom wouldn't be too pleased about the deluge of junk mail). Pete hung out with the troubadours after his poem was done. It was about Jessica the Gullible Cynic.

After grabbing a bite to eat, we made sure we got to the Civic Center early to get a decent seat for the concert. We ended up standing in line for hours outside the main door of the theatre. It was there that we found out about the high drama going on in Washington D.C..

"Did you hear that Jimmy Carter has gone *stark raving mad*?" asked an overweight fellow with beard stubble, a double chin, and a baseball hat (a young Michael Moore?).

Pete and I looked at each other and laughed. We were both thinking the same thing. This guy one-upped one of the most bizarre Bob Dylan songs, "Clothes Line Saga," where one neighbor informs another that "the *vice*-president has gone mad."

We waited for the punchline but none was forthcoming. The baseball hat guy was dead serious. He went on to say that President Carter had planned to deliver a much-advertised TV speech about the energy crisis but, for some reason, he cancelled it at the last minute. The president then dropped out from the public eye without any explanation. The press had a field day. Nobody knew what to make of it. The mystery surrounding this unprecedented move sent the rumor mills into overdrive. The American people expected the worst. Besides the wry claim that the White House had to put up "rubber wallpaper," some speculated about physical health issues. Others claimed Carter had fled the country and even got abducted by aliens.

As it turned out, the top brass knew about the president's whereabouts. Carter took a helicopter to Camp David to meet with advisors.

Others in line weighed in. "I feel *so* sorry for President Carter," expressed a woman who looked like Cher. "He means well, but the job is just too big."

"Personally," replied a guy with a "PLUTONIUM = SLOW DEATH" t-shirt. "I can't stand that purse mouth preacher man and his ghastly family, that beer-sodden brother Billy, that grisly mother Miz Lillian. Ugh! I mean, they make me want to throw up."

"We need to draft Ted Kennedy before it's too late!" said another man.

In the early part of July 1979, President Jimmy Carter's presidency was on the skids. Practically everyone considered it a dismal failure. Carter's approval rating was almost as bad as Nixon's during the worst of Watergate. Needless to say, it did not look good for his reelection.

Who was this man Carter anyway?

James Earl Carter, Jr., our 39th president, was a former naval officer, nuclear engineer, and peanut farmer from the boondocks of Georgia. He had sandy brown hair, which for some strange reason, went from being parted on the right side of his head to the left while he was president. (I'm sure some political commentator saw the metaphorical significance.) His most distinctive physical feature was his wide toothy grin. Coming from the Deep South, President Carter talked in a soft drawl and used words like "y'all." As far as style, he preferred everything casual. He liked wearing jeans and cardigan sweaters, and holding flexible, informal meetings.

Mr. Carter was a man of peace. His empathetic nature, his unswerving concern for human rights, and his appreciation of soul-searching weekend retreats were probably his most endearing traits, at least to the Kumbaya set. He used his strong mediator skills and Camp David, the presidential retreat house, to pull off nothing short of a miracle—to get the historic adversaries, the Jews and Arabs, to not only agree on something, but to *hug each other!*

Even his enemies had to concede that Jimmy Carter was a sincere, well-intentioned man. He was impeccably honest. In this regard, he was an answer to prayer after the dark days of "Tricky Dick" Nixon. However, Carter may have been *too* honest, proving that you must be careful what you pray for. An example of honesty's detrimental effects was that disastrous *Playboy* interview.

Carter was a centrist Democrat. This created problems for him from the start. As they say, "What happens to people who stand in the middle of the road? They get run over." The Right couldn't stand him because he was too liberal. The Left didn't like him because he was too conservative.

Jimmy Carter's biggest adversary in '79 was not Ronald Reagan. It was the hardcore liberal Democrat, Senator Ted Kennedy, JFK's chubby kid brother. Many people thought of Ted as the heir-apparent to the "Camelot" throne. In public life, he was no cuddly Teddy Bear. He was a blow-hard with the disposition of a great white shark. If he detected even the slightest trace of Carter's blood in the water, he was there.

As author Kevin Mattson says, Jimmy Carter's previous roles as a nuclear engineer and a Sunday school teacher shed light on the two sides of his personality. The nuclear engineer side required him to have everything scientifically-verified, technically-precise, and meticulously-documented. In short, he was a hardcore data head. He had to have everything mapped out perfectly with diagrams, charts and graphs. For better or for worse, Carter's abilities in engineering translated into *social* engineering in the White House. His tendency to manipulate and micro-manage everything to the minute detail drove his staff crazy, not to mention Congress.

Carter's Sunday-school-teacher personae viewed everything through a moral lens. As a devout born-again Christian (a Southern Baptist), he believed there's such a thing as right and wrong (in contrast to our much better-informed cultural elite). He firmly believed everyone is a sinner and admitted that he was one too. As president, Carter honored the church-state distinction. At the same time, he presumed the American people shared a common morality. Carter took it on himself to challenge Americans to be their better selves. Nonetheless, his preachy side could rub people the wrong way. It came across to some as condescending, sanctimonious, and holier-than-thou.

These two sides of President Jimmy Carter's personality would crystallize just nine days later—in the form of the "malaise speech." The famous address not only captured who Carter was, but it also served as a snapshot of the American people's messed-up psyche.

CHAPTER 15

ACTIVISTS! LIVE ON STAGE!

THE NEW RUSHMORE PLAZA CIVIC CENTER had a 10,000-seat arena that hosted pow wows, rodeos, Broadway shows, sporting events, and, large-scale rock concerts. The No Nukes event was held in a smaller space: the 1,700 seat theater. This was fine with us. Its high-quality acoustic design would assure the best possible sound quality for the show. Besides, the cushy seats and air conditioning would feel heavenly.

The doors opened at 7:30 p.m.. It paid off to wait in line early. With the choice of sitting anywhere, we picked the middle seats, only six rows from the stage. As we made ourselves comfortable, the tech people were still moving stuff around, finishing the sets, and doing sound checks.

It didn't take long before the auditorium filled up. The incoming crowd consisted mainly of activists of course. But there was another element: The people like Pete and me who came only for the rock & roll.

In the seat to my right was Pete. To my left was a cute girl with chestnut hair wearing a purple and white striped blouse and blue-jeans.

As house lights were dimmed, I took a deep breath to mentally prepare myself for what promised to be a memorable evening. Having glanced at the program, I knew this "free" rock concert had a price: You had to endure a number of speeches before the music began.

My reaction to the speeches was mixed. Some turned out to be interesting, but others made me yawn. Comedian Dick Gregory was pretty funny though.

From Elvis to Bonnie Raitt

After a string of somewhat-interesting-and-somewhat-boring political talks, came the moment that we were waiting for—the concert!

Rock & roll was my new religion; the rock concert was the new Mass. The transformation had occurred gradually during high school. Rock music—and the philosophy behind it—had replaced my former belief system. That said, I kept my faith in the Christian principles of charity, social justice, and changing the world—minus God of course.

Wasn't this John Lennon's outlook, at least when he did the song "Imagine?"

The first ever concert at the Rushmore Plaza Civic Center was performed by none other than Elvis Presley, the King of Rock & Roll. Sadly, it was like two ships passing in the night. It was one of Elvis' last shows. He died only seven weeks later. It is fitting that the King himself would inaugurate this place at the foot of the Black Hills. Since its inception, rock music has always been about rebellion and revolution. From the scandalous hip gyrations of Elvis to the communist provocations of The Clash, rock has always been an agent of social change.

"Before Elvis, there was nothing," John Lennon had once said. But Lennon himself was no slouch. In fact, you could say he was a true blue saint (a secular one that is). He and his bandmates The Beatles—almost singlehandedly—changed the face of music forever, transforming what was basically teenybopper music into a high art form. Lennon knew he could use rock to change society. In this regard, "Imagine" is rock & roll through-and-through, though it may sound kind of syrupy.

To fully appreciate "Imagine," you have to keep in mind *who* John Lennon was deep down: that scrappy kid from Liverpool, teenage prankster, troublemaker and the street fighter who once beat the crap out of a sailor.

"Imagine there's no heaven" are truly the words of a smart ass trying to piss you off.

But I wasn't pissed off though, I was open-minded to what he had to say. The man was practically a god himself!

How was rock doing in 1979? With the scores of rock-format radio stations switching to disco, one had to wonder: Was rock & roll going extinct like the dinosaurs? What was the world coming to? Even Rod Stewart, Paul McCartney, The Eagles, ELO, The Rolling Stones, Kiss, and The Grateful Dead were doing *disco* songs!

Uggghhh! Western civilization was in deep doo-doo!

Thankfully, after witnessing class acts like Bonnie Raitt, I felt reassured. The future of rock music looked bright.

Bonnie hit the Rushmore stage around 9:30 p.m..

I must admit, prior to the concert, I wasn't familiar with her at all. (I kept getting her mixed up with Bonnie Bramlett and Bonnie Tyler.) At the time, mainstream popularity had eluded her, in spite of being consistently praised by the critics for a number of years. In hindsight, she was up-and-coming.

But it would take her ten long years (and conquering alcoholism) before she hit it big with her Grammy-winning album "Nick of Time."

Believe me, Bonnie did not disappoint. It was like she was paying you back for listening to all the boring speeches.

Like any concert, the first few minutes were the best part. Anticipation mounts as the house lights go out and every member of the band shuffles to their position. The spotlight beats down on this matchless-looking woman wielding a large electric guitar.

She's a fox. No, better yet, she's a freaking *femme-fatale* with her snug-fitting black slacks, bronzey satin blouse, and magnificent red hair shimmering.

After Bonnie was introduced, she and the band came on stage triumphantly and launched into her bluesy version of "Runaway"—her 1977 hit—a reinterpretation of the 1961 classic Del Shannon song. It was electrifying. The three guitars generated a rollicking, bouncy rhythm section. The song, of course, had nothing to do with social issues. It was time for those fighting for social justice and the earth's survival to lighten up.

> *As I walk along, I wonder*
> *A-what went wrong with our love*
> *A love that was so strong*

Bonnie's stage presence almost knocked me out of my chair. My heart pounded in my chest. Here was the Wild West legend Annie Oakley reincarnated—strong, earnest, and dignified. Sexy without trying to be, she played that slide guitar as adeptly as Annie shot her gun. Her vocals were the sonic equivalent to a hot toddy, sweet and smooth as honey, rich and poignant as a shot of Jim Beam. The way she moved around the stage drove me insane. She coolly swayed to the beat, skillfully sliding her fingers across the frets, and making those intense facial expressions, most notably smiles that brought out her dimples. Besides the dimples, her most prominent characteristic was her *hair*, a red river, so long, wavy and thick you could drown in it. Her forward and backward S-shaped locks framed her round face, one covering her eye on the left side. Even at thirty, she had a mark of maturity, a white streak that branched out where her glorious mane was parted.

The stage lights gave the whole set a golden cast. All members of Bonnie's five-piece band (and two backup singers) had long blow-dried hair. They wore t-shirts, jeans, and sneakers. Their appearance was pure late-seventies—the I-don't-give-a-crap-about-fashion look. Each band member was in a state of euphoria.

A tight, well-rehearsed band such as this could relax in its perfect synergy. They were all individuals with different roles, and yet, together, they comprised one thing. Bonnie and the others got into goofy interactions, pointing, laughing, and literally getting into each other's faces as they played. You could tell they were having a blast. They were bonding.

The audience also participated in "Runaway" by singing, clamping and dancing. You might say all present—Bonnie, her band, and the audience—embodied the single most cherished ideal espoused that day in Rapid City...

One-ness!

The total oneness or wholeness or unity resulted in something truly extraordinary, something greater and *beyond* it.

Again, just like the Mass.

This "religious" element also reminded me of the Bruce Springsteen concert I went to in Detroit, as well as Northern Comfort's stellar performance six days before.

Before The Deluge

As the musicians rallied to wind down "Runaway," Bonnie's final leap on one leg was the exclamation point to the song's theatrical finish. After that, the illustrious red head and the band finished their set with two more songs, "Angel from Montgomery" and "Under a Falling Sky."

The benefit concert that night was put on by Musicians United for Safe Energy, or MUSE, an activist group co-founded by Jackson Browne, Bonnie Raitt, and others. It was part of a series of concerts that fanned the flames of the anti-nuke movement after Three Mile Island. The concert series was gaining momentum. Although the MUSE roster in Rapid City had only Jackson, Bonnie, and Jesse Colin Young, the size and scope of the No Nukes concerts would increase throughout the summer, along with the number of performers taking part. Everything would come to a climax in September at New York's Madison Square Garden. The entourage that did five shows featured Jackson, Bonnie, Jesse, Cosby Stills and Nash, James Taylor, Carly Simon, The Doobie Brothers, Tom Petty and the Heartbreakers, and many others.

The most notable star added to the line-up was Bruce Springsteen. This marked the beginning of Bruce's lifelong involvement in politics. The most notable *non*-participant was John Lennon who lived only two miles from Madison Square Garden. Perhaps he showed up in the audience. Maybe he preferred to stay home and "watch the wheels go round."

The *No Nukes* triple live album and movie, released in 1980, documented those legendary New York performances.

On that night, July 6, 1979 Jackson, Bonnie, and Jesse just arrived from St. Paul. In my mind, each member of the trio represented rock & roll's past, present, and future. Jesse Colin Young was the past, Jackson Browne was the present, and Bonnie Raitt was the future.

We had 1969, 1979, and 1989 together in one room.

Close to forty, Jesse Colin Young was the group's senior citizen. He was the Spirit of Rock & Roll Past. He had intense eyes, long brown hair, and a droopy mustache which made him look like Sgt. Pepper. His career reached its zenith in 1969, the year of Woodstock. The song "Get Together" performed by him and his group, the Youngbloods, peaked at #5 on the Billboard chart. This quintessential peace and love song truly captured the essence of the sixties.

> *Love is but a song we sing*
> *fears' the way we die*
> *You can make the mountains ring*
> *or make the angels cry*
> *Though the dove is on the wing*
> *and you may not know why*
>
> *Come on people now*
> *smile on your brother*
> *everybody get together*
> *and try to love one another right now*

When he sang the refrain the second time, Jesse replaced the word "brother" with "*sister.*" ("Smile on your sister, etc.") Since everyone knew the lyrics by heart, Jesse invited us to sing along. Naturally, we the audience did so with gusto. It expressed our highest ideals and evoked fond memories of the glory days of the sixties.

When he told us to sing the song to the person next us, I cringed. There was no way I was going to turn to Pete LeBlanc and sing "Smile on your brother." (And I'm sure the feeling was mutual.) However, when it came to "Smile on your sister," I readily turned leftward. There she was: the cute girl next to me. I not only serenaded this perfect stranger face-to-face, but I gave her a big hug.

That leftward move felt so right!

Jesse Colin Young did two other songs and turned the microphone over to Jackson Browne.

Jackson Browne was the Spirit of Rock & Roll Present because he was so popular at the time. Granted, he didn't have a new album out that year, but the deejays kept playing his stuff over-and-over on the radio. Their playlists included Jackson's earlier hits like "Doctor My Eyes," "Take It Easy," and "The Pretender," as well as the ones from his breakthrough 1977 album, *Running on Empty*. No wonder we in the audience leapt to our feet to give him a standing ovation the moment he hit the stage.

I loved Jackson Browne. He was a great songwriter and a happy political warrior. A handsome fellow with thick eyebrows and a thick lower lip, he came across as unpretentious and earnest. His hair was perfect—straight, brown, and parted down the middle. The considerate way he treated his band and audience demonstrated his high level of class. The most striking thing about Jackson was the fact he looked so young. Around thirty, he looked a lot like a high school senior in the Drama Club. I could just picture him dressed up like Romeo in the school play.

Belonging to the early-seventies school of singer-songwriters (along with the likes of James Taylor, Carole King, and Gordon Lightfoot.), Jackson Browne specialized in songs with deep, introspective lyrics. The songs helped listeners gain a perspective on their complicated lives, particularly in the area of relationships—in a clear, straight-forward and truthful way. Pete and Dave Zarret, musicians themselves, were really deep into the whole singer-songwriter thing.

Jackson performed five songs in the following order: "For Everyman," "Rosie," "The Pretender," "Running on Empty," and "Before the Deluge." Like "Rosie," he did "Before the Deluge" on his acoustic guitar with only his fiddle player accompanying him. That particular song was, for me, the highlight of the evening. It truly captured the moment.

Some of them were angry
At the way the earth was abused
By the men who learned how to forge her beauty into power
And they struggled to protect her from them
Only to be confused
By the magnitude of her fury in the final hour
And when the sand was gone and the time arrived
In the naked dawn only a few survived
And in attempts to understand a thing so simple and so huge
Believed that they were meant to live after the deluge

By the time Jackson finished the song, there was not a dry eye in the house (except maybe the stoic Pete LeBlanc). First off, the idea of "the deluge" had special meaning to audience members from the Rapid City area. As mentioned, they'd suffered through one of the worst floods in U.S. history. There were probably those present who had lost loved ones in it.

Second, "Before the Deluge" sounded like it was about the bitter disillusionment that the staunch sixties idealists experienced as they got older. It refers to "dreamers" and "fools" who try to "journey back to nature" only to find "their feathers, once so fine, grew torn and tattered."

Naturally, the Poverty Gulch gang came to mind and it deeply saddened me.

Is "Before the Deluge" a song of hope or despair? The image of sand running out in an hourglass seemed to suggest the latter. It hinted at the imminent apocalypse.

Thirdly, in retrospect, there were ominous signs that a different kind of deluge was coming. In fact, it was at our door! When the Black Hills activists fervently sang "The Times They Are A-Changin'" in Heritage Park that day, they didn't realize how right they were.

But it was *not* the kind of change they were expecting. In fact, it was their worst nightmare! Sixteen months later, they would be like children building sand castles on the beach staring wide-eyed at the colossal tidal wave heading their way.

It was called the Reagan Revolution.

CHAPTER 16

THE TIPPING POINT?

Saturday, July 7, 1979

A FTER THE CONCERT, WE DECIDED to spend the night on the grounds of Dinosaur Park, the famous tourist attraction since 1936. It's located on top of a sandstone ridge overlooking Rapid City. Though it's only a mile and a half west of the Rushmore Plaza Civic Center, the steep assent up Quincy Street and then Skyline Drive got us as exhausted as mules on a long, arduous journey. But it was well worth it. The view of the starry night sky and the city lights was spectacular.

In the morning around seven, we awoke to the sight of life-size sculptures of a Brontosaurus, Tyrannosaurus Rex, and five other prehistoric beasts. Since the park was free, Pete and I got a chance to check out the giant green reptiles. We paid homage to each extinct creature as if we were visiting graves in a cemetery.

After that, we gazed at the panoramic view once more, but this time in broad daylight.

From our vantage point, we could see a hundred miles in all directions. Looking eastward, you could observe Rapid City right there below, and beyond that, the Great Plains to the cusp of the horizon. A hundred miles to the southeast, the Badlands stood proud and formidable like some mythic fortress.

West of us was the Black Hills. It had a special significance to Pete and me in terms of our friendship.

It symbolized adventures of the Old West. It was a shared fantasy, mine and Pete's—based on TV and movie Westerns. Story after story about the West had basically the same formula with a different spin. You start with a stark, rugged backdrop like the Blacks Hills. You dream up some wild, disorderly mining town like nearby Lead or Deadwood. Then you populate it with heroes and villains, cowboys and Indians, and, of course, whores, drinkers, hucksters, and so on. Throw in the usual props—guns, horses, tumble weeds, etc.—and presto! You have yourself a Western!

Again, it was a *shared* fantasy. On our travels, Pete and I fancied ourselves being Western-style outlaws like Butch Cassidy and the Sundance Kid.

The Black Hills was also about being *spiritual*. It was the place to go to contemplate and meditate. Young Lakota men went there for vision quests. A vision quest is a rite of passage in which you take time to discover your true self, and find meaning and purpose. Pete and I had what you might call a spiritual partnership. You could say, our entire hitchhiking trip was a vision quest. Since we'd first met, Pete helped me spiritually by directing me to the right books, music, and movies. I'm sure I assisted him that way as well.

The concept of the "tipping point" had played out in the Black Hills in a big way. What is a tipping point? The idea was popularized by author Malcolm Gladwell in the early 2000s. For our purposes, it's the moment of truth when one historic event changes everything. It's usually some small, seemingly insignificant thing that triggers something big. In fact it starts something cataclysmic like a snowflake causing an avalanche. It's the straw that broke the camel's back.

The Black Hills' tipping point likely occurred on July 28, 1874 when Horatio Ross discovered gold at French Creek. It sparked Custer's Last Stand, which led to the final white takeover of Pahá Sápa and hence the rest of the Indian-possessed territories in the United States. A whole way of life was replaced by another, just because of what one person did. It was like Eve eating the fruit.

A more personal kind of tipping point almost occurred right there in the Black Hills: Pete LeBlanc and I came very close to parting ways!

The tension between us had been building up for some time, even before the Rosie Smith affair. But meeting Rosie for the first time was definitely the start of something earth-shattering. Maybe it was the beginning of the end.

Perhaps it was the tipping point in our relationship.

Before Rosie came along, Pete and I had a certain equilibrium. Pete's superiority over me balanced out my superiority over him. Pete had the leg up in regard to spiritual knowledge and being radical. I was "better" than Pete because I was older, less socially awkward, and going to college. And, like Dave Zarret, I was a seasoned veteran of hitchhiking from of my previous trip to New York with Randal Stark in 1977.

However, Rosie had unwittingly thrown the scale off kilter. When we first met Rosie, Pete and I had simultaneously thought the same thing—"I struck gold!"

As we've seen, the whole thing tipped in Pete's favor on that fateful day along Highway 14 outside of Madison. The threshold was reached. The stage was set for everything to suddenly and completely collapse to one side—Pete's!

While my relationship with Pete would improve somewhat after saying goodbye to Rosie at Poverty Gulch, there was still some unfinished business...

Pete had Rosie's phone number burning in his pocket!

This suggested that there was something more between Rosie and Pete than a one-time fling. My imagination went wild. I entertained the notion it was already a done deal: They'd discovered each other as soul mates. And it was only a matter of time before they actually got married.

That scenario would be totally unacceptable, because I wanted Rosie all to myself.

Even the possibility of Pete marrying Rosie was reason enough to sever all ties with Pete. It was sad to think this way. We'd been good friends since the Dylan concert.

But here's the ironic twist in all this. While it's true that Rosie was tearing us apart (even when she wasn't around), she, in a weird way, actually brought Pete and I *closer together.*

This stronger bond resulted from the fact that Rosie had introduced us to Poverty Gulch. In our minds, our experience there was beyond belief. It was as if we were abducted by aliens, taken to some far-off galaxy, and returned back to Earth. Our lives would never be the same again. If we dared to tell other earthlings about it, who would believe us? People would think we were daft. And who could blame them?

At least, Pete and I had each other to confirm it was all true. The idea that Poverty Gulch was a real-life paradise was something we shared. As we traveled along the Interstate, it was all we talked about.

By the time we reached the Black Hills, Poverty Gulch was idealized, romanticized, and glorified to the level of the Lost City of Atlantis. I can't speak for Pete, but I'd already determined I would eventually go back there.

It Came from the Refrigerator

There was another universe thriving virtually unnoticed at the Black Hills, one that's only seen under a microscope—the world of bacteria, yeast, and fungi.

It was hot, sunny and muggy. Gravity helped pull us down Quincy Street back into town. When we got to the bottom of the hill, we found ourselves in a neighborhood of older homes built around the turn of the century. At 12th Street, we came upon some commotion going on down the block, generated by a throng of boisterous people. Curious, we turned and walked down 12th until we noticed everything coming from a somewhat run-down Victorian house.

The scene reminded me of a frat house party in Ann Arbor. Clusters of mostly college folks stood and milled around on the front lawn, chatting, laughing, eating pancakes on paper plates and drinking coffee. There were probably two dozen tents set up in the backyard. A good number of cars and vans were parked out front. A constant flow of people filed in and out of a house filled almost to capacity. You could tell it was some kind of activist headquarters.

Pete and I entered the crowd. With our backpacks and scruffy exteriors, we blended right in.

Things were transitioning. Besides having breakfast, folks were putting on hats, sunglasses, and sun screen. Tents were being taken down. The protesters moved stuff out, putting things into pockets and backpacks, and onto wagons. They secured things with rope and straps, most notably water containers and hiking boots.

Provocatively-worded banners and placards were the definitive clue of what was about to commence—the much-talked-about fifteen mile protest march.

A thrill ran up my leg like Chris Matthews' reaction to Obama. Associating it with Martin Luther King's freedom march, I wanted a piece of the action. I yearned to be part of a higher cause—a *movement*. The maps showed that the activist walk would start right there in downtown Rapid City and proceed up Highway 71 north to the town of Piedmont.

Oddly, Pete and I hadn't determined yet to participate in the march. We'd never even discussed it. Personally, I was all in, but we had to decide together whether or not we'd go. Out of principle, we didn't plan anything. We tended to "go with the flow." And besides, such decisions were better made on a full stomach.

Practicing the fine art of mooching food, we stealthily slipped through the back door directly into the kitchen. We timed it perfectly. The kitchen was practically deserted. The remaining house guests had either gone outside or dispersed into other rooms to get items ready for the long hike.

To our delight, the cook left quite a few pancakes and sausages unattended on serving plates on the stove. They were cold, burnt, and attracting flies, but who was complaining? Helping ourselves, we scavengers doused them in leftover maple syrup, scarfed them, and washed them down with half a jug of orange juice. We outdid the socialists by foregoing the bourgeois trappings of paper plates, plastic utensils and napkins, wiping our sticky fingers and mouths with our shirts.

When Pete left the room to use the bathroom, a slightly overweight but pretty young woman, took his place. Her pale blue eyes contrasted sharply with her jet black shoulder-length hair tied back with a red bandana. Dressed in cut-offs and a white shirt that read "CHANGE OR DIE," she brought in a pile of rags, sponges, gloves, garbage bags, a box of baking soda, bottle of ammonia, and a spray-bottle of Formula 409, all contained in a white three-gallon bucket.

Her presence made me feel awkward. Since it was only her and me in the room, introducing ourselves was inevitable.

"Hi, I'm Becky. I'm supposed to clean out the refrigerator," she said with a twisted grin.

It seemed odd for someone to be doing this now of all times. Seeming to read my mind, she shrugged and said it needed to be done right away because the lease was up on their "collective household" (a term that brought to mind "the Guardians" in Plato's *Republic*).

The moment she opened the fridge door, Becky's contorted facial expressions made it clear that she'd rather be in the thick of the Brazilian jungle than here.

I couldn't blame her. We were both bowled over by the stench and the sight of food (or ex-food) piled on the shelves—in jars, bottles, cartons, and on plates sealed with Saran wrap. The refrigerator looked like it hadn't been cleaned for months! In my estimation, it was an ideal breeding ground for e. coli and salmonella. Rotten tomatoes caught my eye, as well as mildew growing along the rubber seal.

Holding her breath and gritting her teeth, Becky put on rubber gloves, hurriedly picked out food at random, and threw it in a garbage can. Perhaps out of a morbid curiosity and/or masochistic tendencies, items that no longer qualified as food were closely examined. The chemical process of decomposition rendered them as indigestible as cardboard, lethal as venom, and as disgusting as rat phlegm.

I must say, Becky did an admirable job of doing this without throwing up. At one point though, she was so repulsed by a particular substance, her face turned literally white and her entire body froze. You'd think she'd just encountered a severed head.

"Uh, Ted, if you don't mind, would you please...?" she said looking at me with her pleading big blue eyes. She was imploring me to do "the man's job."

The significance of this didn't hit me until later: Here's this young activist woman, a feminist no doubt, entreating me to do the *chivalrous* thing. In those days, the women's libbers frowned on this sort of thing. They told men they should *not* assist a woman by opening doors, pulling out chairs, or walking on the street side of a sidewalk, lest he treat her as a "non-equal."

Without questioning, I did my duty. I plugged my nose, lowered my head before the open fridge, and peered at what was lurking in the back.

From the side, the rank thing in a glass bowl looked like it was a chicken casserole leftover from the days of black-and-white TV. But, as I viewed it from the top, I winced in horror at the sight of a mound of fuzzy mold. It resembled the planet Neptune seen through a blurry lens, in terms of its intense aqua color and its other-worldliness. In another context, it might have been admired for its beauty—except for the smell. The sharp odor of fermentation streaming from the shiny mucus-like froth (below the fuzz) assaulted my nose.

"AAARRRGH!" I muttered.

The movie *Apocalypse Now* didn't come out until next month, but I felt like Marlon Brando spewing his immortal words "The horror!"

I gingerly picked up the disgusting thing and threw it in the trash. Going the extra mile, I pulled the plastic garbage bag liner out of the basket, twisted the top, and carried the bag out to the back of the house where the other rubbish was. Feeling like a triumphant exorcist wiping the evil off his hands, I went back into house.

As if waiting for me, Pete LeBlanc stood there wagging his head.

"What are they going to have you do next?" he said. *"Clean out the toilet?"*

"Meet the New Boss..."

What happened in the kitchen was a perfect example of a tipping point. It was a small thing that triggered a big thing, a chain reaction. The "big thing" was the issue of splitting up with Pete and going separate ways.

Believe it or not, Pete and I had planned for this moment before the trip. Dave Zarret, our trusted hitchhiking advisor, told us to expect one or both partners to have the desire to break up at some point in time.

Did he think it was inevitable? Not necessarily. But Dave, speaking from experience, said, if or when someone decides to split with the other—*welcome it*! In other words, give each other permission to play their Get-Out-of-Jail-Free card when the time is right. "It's the loving thing to do," Dave asserted, "to let your partner (and yourself) go free."

It may be a stretch but the Get-Out-of-Jail-Free card is a good metaphor. Being with another person could be as restrictive as being behind bars. It forces you to deal with the other person's hang-ups. It compels you to make compromises you don't want to make. You have to constantly compete over what to do or what not to do. Just ask any married couple.

Taking Dave's advice seriously underscored how radical we were. Traveling alone must have been fifty times more dangerous than traveling with a partner. But Pete and I were each willing to take that risk, just so we could "do our own thing" unimpeded.

Fully living out freedom superseded everything.

Dave went on to say that, after the split is made, your hitchhiking experience will enter an extraordinary new phase. Sure, going solo can be lonely and even downright scary, but the experience is well worth it! There's nothing more exhilarating than being completely on your own, without another soul influencing you.

In a state of complete solitude, you can achieve the lofty goal of self-actualization!

★ ★ ★

The "chain reaction" started when Pete watched me eject that disgusting former casserole into the yard. Once again, Pete said, "What are *they* going to have you do next? Clean out the toilet?"

The operative word on my partner's lips was "they." Pete apparently saw something sinister in me helping out Becky.

"What are you implying, Pete?

"Well..."

"I know. You think I'm *following orders*, right?"

"It did cross my mind. Maybe just for a fleeting second."

"Oh, come on, Pete! What if I *wanted* to 'clean out the toilet' to help someone out? What's it to you?"

"Don't worry about it, Ted. Far be it for me to stop you. *Go for it!*" (At this point, Pete was channeling Crow during the Mountain Dew episode.)

I knew exactly what he was up to. He was, in a subtle way, insinuating that I was slavishly obeying "orders from above." Nothing could be farther from the truth.

I was just giving Becky a hand, for chrissake!

I'm sure he understood that, but he was just trying to get my goat. This was classic LeBlanc. He liked to play games. This, combined with his condescending tone, made my blood boil. To remain calm, I took a deep breath or two.

"Hey, lighten up, Ted," said Pete glibly. "I'm only kidding around."

I was probably being over-sensitive because of what happened the day before. Pete made me feel like an idiot. He didn't say it directly, but I could tell by his looks, gestures and subtle comments that he thought I'd gotten a little too involved with the protest.

Pete LeBlanc had always been cynical about the John Lennon "change the world" thing.

One time back home, when we left the theatre after seeing the movie version of *Hair*, a musical about the sixties, he remarked, "I'm sick and tired of the sixties. The sixties were phony. They're just an illusion dreamed up by the media. Who's behind it? A bunch of elitists out to control people. They're the *very thing* they claim to be fighting against—overlords, slave drivers, tyrants—all of them!

"They won't tell you this, but they want to keep the same old hierarchy—except with *themselves* in charge. It's just like song by The Who: 'Meet the new boss same as the old boss.'"

A bunch of elitists. That's what LeBlanc meant by "they."

Here's what's fascinating: Pete seemed to only associate the political activities at the Black Hills with "the sixties." But remember, he himself rejoiced in the idea that *Poverty Gulch* was "another Woodstock," I think he disliked the "change the world" part of the sixties, not the "do your own thing" part. He illustrates how the two parts of the sixties don't necessarily go together—just like oil and vinegar.

Italian salad dressing is the perfect metaphor for the sixties!

"So are we going on the march or not?" I finally asked Pete, aware that if we didn't leave now we'd miss the boat. The house was starting to get empty.

"Ah, okay, whatever...well, actually *no*."

"No? Why not? It looks like it's going to be a blast."

"Not to me. I'm not into volunteering."

"Volunteering?"

"Come on, Ted. Going on that fifteen-mile hike to 'change the world' isn't my idea of fun. It's volunteering. And volunteering is the exact same thing as *work*."

To my traveling companion, "work" was a dirty word. He was the most idle person I'd ever met (beating the slothful Randal hands down). The funny thing was Pete had no problem with the hundred or so miles we had walked so far. Not once, did he complain or call it "work."

I came up with another angle to persuade Pete: "Look, maybe it would be a great way to get our voices heard."

"What?! To get *our voices* heard?" Pete said with contempt. "Wow, they really got to you, man! Now *you're* spouting that activist bullsh*t. You're not turning into *one of them*, are you?"

"Aw, come on, man, give me break!" I replied astonished and embarrassed. He was insinuating I'd become some kind of conformist, a robot in sync with someone else's agenda. *That* would be a grave sin against The Grand Experiment.

Did Pete have a point?

Once again, Pete played the role of Holden Caufield: "Look, Ted, these people are a *bunch of phonies*. And, if you ask me, their brains are devoid of any original thoughts. What's a 'march' for anyways? To follow marching orders!"

"Hmmm."

"Well, *you* can march if you want to. Not me. I'm sick of being around these people."

Why was I surprised by Pete's vehement reaction? I knew all along where he stood. All day yesterday, he seemed more detached than usual. No doubt Rosie was on his mind. All the political chatter day and night obviously bored him. And then there were people like Jessica the Gullible Cynic imploring Pete—the proud nonconformist Pete—to think like them. To him, it was like Bob Dylan's "Maggie's Farm."

Sure, the novelty of the whole scene had amused LeBlanc, but it wore off after a while. Now, having attended the free concert, he thought he'd accomplished his mission and now wanted to move on.

But *I* wanted to stay.

It was clear that the moment of truth had arrived. We were at a crossroads. Was it time for Pete and me to call it quits?

The situation put a lump in my throat. A break-up would be just as epic as when Abraham said to Lot, "Let's part company. If you go to the left, I'll go to the right." It would be like Lennon asking McCartney for a "divorce."

There were three solid reasons to allow this happen. Number one: There was the whole Rosie thing. Would I be able to bear seeing Rosie and Pete together one more time? Number two: I wanted to go on the protest march and Pete didn't. But wasn't doing "my thing" the whole point of the trip? If I went on the march, I'd be true to myself. If I went along with Pete, I would *not* be, the reasoning went.

Number three: Pete's personality quirks were driving me crazy—his gamey-ness, his trances, even his voice and the way he talked. I had to ask myself: Which is worse? The trials and tribulations of hitchhiking (which, as we've seen, were many)—or dealing with the person you're with. Maybe the second thing is worse.

As Jean-Paul Sartre once declared, "Hell is other people." Especially if the person's name is Pete LeBlanc!

I was ready to do "the loving thing" (as Dave put it): Go my own way and let Pete go his. However, there was one thing holding me back—my pride. Was I going to leave Pete with the mistaken notion that I'm some kind of sellout? Was I going to let him to perceive me as a complete *conformist*?

No way!

So I made my decision.

"Look, Pete," I said after I swallowed. "I think we should, uh, *stick together*."

"Whatever you say."

After the choice was made, we set our sights on our next destination: Greeley, Colorado... *to see Rosie!*

Mount Rushmore

Before saying good bye to the Black Hills, we first had to see Mount Rushmore, the most revered national monument next to the Statue of Liberty. Our ride took us southwestward through the heavily forested mountains on Highway 16 to Highway 244. My ears popped as we approached the Black Hills' highest point, Harney Peak.

Along the way, we passed by the villages of Rockerville and Keystone which were once thriving gold rush towns. Since the 1870s, the Black Hills region had over six-hundred such towns with names like Tinton, Cyanide, Mystic, Preston, and Nemo. They're all gone now. A jaunt down one of the many trails may lead you to a ghost town with its ruins of a post office, a livery, or a bank still intact. At another location, you'll find only a cemetery. Somewhere else, you'd be lucky to run across even a rusty nail.

As we've seen, people value the Black Hills for different reasons. To me, its main treasure is its *stories*. And I'm not alone. Two other former mining communities—Deadwood and Lead—are now profitable resort towns. They capitalize on tourists who wish to immerse themselves in tales about colorful, violent, and lawless characters like Wild Bill Hickok and Calamity Jane. Scenes, generated by the Hollywood dream machine—like high-noon showdowns, drunken brawls in saloons, and public hangings—are all fondly remembered!

Pete and I continued traveling together as if nothing had gone down between us. The shared fantasy of the Old West overshadowed the *un*shared fantasy of changing the world.

The West had always captured the grit and passion of the individual, one who just wants to be left alone and do his own thing. We loved the fables, stories of prospectors who braved severe weather conditions to strike it rich. But these were cautionary tales. Like Howard (Walter Huston) said in the movie *The Treasure of Sierra Madre*, "I know what gold does to men's souls." Decent guys like Dobbs (Humphrey Bogart) get corrupted, go mad, and kill their partners out of paranoia or greed!

At around 2:30 p.m., we arrived at Mount Rushmore. It is, of course, the site of the four sculptured heads of U.S. presidents carved on a granite mountain side. As expected, the national memorial, about 25 miles from Rapid City, was bustling with tourists. Millions come here each year. The visitor center offers exhibits and a theatre where you can watch a documentary film. There's also a gift shop and a café. Rangers in their clean, crisp uniforms make themselves available to answer questions and guide people on the trails. One trail takes you to the presidents up close.

From the visitor center picture window, Pete and I gave Washington, Jefferson, Lincoln and Roosevelt long, protracted reflective stares. Of course, I've seen a gazillion photos of the monument, but, when you're actually there, you get a sense of its vast scale: Each head is really as tall as a six-story building.

At one point, Pete said thoughtfully, "I've always loved Lincoln; I can feel his spirit inside of me."

"Teddy Roosevelt is my favorite." I replied. "He's the Rough Rider. The human equivalent to dynamite."

I have to admit I felt patriotic. But at the same time, I harbored the uneasy awareness that many Indians loath Mt. Rushmore. To them, I'm sure, it would be just as bad as a giant sculpture of an extended middle finger aimed squarely at them. Maybe I was being delusional, but I comforted myself with the notion that America is *evolving* into something better than it had been. Someday, its *real* manifest destiny will be reached. Its citizens will receive all those who had been oppressed with open arms. And, among other things, it will honor its past treaties.

Being a history buff, I could go on and on about what I'd learned about the thirty-nine presidents. In my early days, the chief executives of the United States were practically gods—until Richard M. Nixon came along. Nixon's successor, Gerald R. Ford—Michigan's only president—was best known for clumsily tripping over things.

The president who most came to mind was our current one, Jimmy Carter.

As we had learned, Carter was in a state of crisis. At the park newsstand, I gained a fuller appreciation of how the President's alleged disappearance captivated the country. It would take months before I found out all the details. Like Rosie Smith (and us), Carter apparently "chucked it all" after deciding he's fed up with the rat race. Something inside of him "just snapped." On July Fourth, he threw away his scheduled speech and skipped town.

"There is more to it than energy!" the president exclaimed (referring to the energy crisis). "I just don't want to bulls**t the American people!"

It was a jaw-dropping moment. Jimmy Carter's inner circle registered shock, dismay, and even panic, not because this squeaky-clean religious man uttered a swear word. But it was because they thought he was committing political suicide. After his tirade, Carter did a very Catholic thing (though he was a Baptist): He went on retreat. He took a copter to Camp David to isolate himself from the world like a monk. Taking his trusted confidantes with him, he was determined to get to the bottom of things.

Eight days later, something extraordinary would happen. The President reemerged! He was like Moses coming down from Mt. Sinai with the Ten Commandments. But instead of the Commandments, it was the malaise speech.

It was as if Jimmy Carter was ready to answer Lennon's anguished cry on the album *Imagine*...

> *All I want is the truth*
> *Just gimme some truth*

PART IV:

THE RAILROAD TRACKS

CHAPTER 17

THE MYSTERY TRAIN

Sunday, July 8, 1979

WITH HITCHHIKING, YOU LEARN to expect the unexpected, but nothing surprised me more than what happened next. We got picked up by a *train*! The chain of events started outside of Bridgeport, Nebraska.

The second half of the previous day had gone smoothly. We went south from Mount Rushmore down U.S. Highway 385 which runs through the Nebraska Panhandle. It was along the legendary Gold Rush Byway which was once the superhighway to the Black Hills mining towns. In the late 1800s, it imported supplies in and exported gold out.

Once we reached Bridgeport, our plan took an unexpected turn. Local teenagers named Jake and Pixie invited us to party with them at the nearby state park.

The park was adjacent to the North Platte River and several sand pit lakes. During World War II, the Army Corps of Engineers had pumped sand and gravel from there to a local paratrooper base. When the job was complete, the military planted cottonwood, pine, and even fruit trees which over time grew into a lush forest. The place was pretty rustic. Picnic tables were badly weather-beaten, still water bred mosquitoes, and rotting fruit attracted all kinds of bugs. But these things didn't dissuade a sizable crowd from coming out for Saturday afternoon picnics. Speed-boaters and jet-skiers tirelessly circled around the donut-shaped lake until nightfall. We set up camp a good distance from the mayhem only to contend with traffic whipping up road dirt.

Pete and I carefully studied the map in the campfire light that evening. The area between the North Platte and South Platte Rivers resembled the border of a grotesquely gerry-mandered congressional district. The two branches came together at the city of North Platte, 140 miles southeast of where we were at.

You'd never know it, but the Platte River is a tributary of the great Missouri River, which is a tributary of the great Mississippi River. Author James A. Michener once called the Platte "the sorriest river in America." It winds around like intestines and becomes alternately wide and narrow to the extreme at different spots. The wide parts are spotted with islands. The narrow parts are said to be virtually impassable by boat. Canoes or kayaks can squeeze through bottlenecks, but they still have to deal with the river's shallow bottom. Its water is too muddy to drink. And, the Platte thickens. The French called the river *Nebraskier*, which is from the Indian word for "flat water." This is where the name "Nebraska" comes from.

The Platte's history reads like a Zen parable, a downright contradiction. In the 1800s, when the waterways were by far the most efficient means of travel, this utterly useless river had become a major route. In fact, it was *the* main conduit to the West, practically the horizontal version of the Mississippi! That's because its valley provided an easily passable wagon corridor.

Earlier that day, a historical marker along Highway 385 had given us a sense of the Platte Valley's significance. The sign read "THE MORMON TRAIL." Below these bold letters, smaller type detailed how "latter-day saints" from Illinois followed the river banks west to get to their Promised Land (the Utah territory). We were standing on hallowed ground! I could imagine the Mormon pioneers in their horse-drawn covered wagons riding the dusty trail like in the movies. They inspired me with their grit and determination, braving countless perils—such as treacherous terrain, deadly diseases, and hostile Indians—all the while anticipating living in a paradise on earth.

Then the thought bowled me over: a strange crossroads indeed! Imagine ghosts streaming north up the Gold Rush Byway to the Black Hills to seek earthly treasure. At the same time, restless spirits flood west to pursue *heavenly* treasure. Both parties share in common the fact they risked everything for a dream. When they were alive, their contemporaries must've thought they were mad—just like how people saw Pete and I.

When I brought this stuff up with Jake and Pixie, they just shrugged their shoulders, expressing they were clueless and couldn't care less. This indifferent attitude irritated me. Teenagers like them often alleged that older folks are boring, but I found the opposite to be true. Older people like Cedric Voss, Marvin the Rancher, and Crow had fascinated me, especially with their stories.

More importantly, they valued *history*. In my mind, history is not boring because it helps you understand the present.

My passion for learning history was insatiable (and still is). It was probably inherited from my mother, but I'm sure the place I grew up in helped a great deal. Who can deny Detroit has the greatest success story on the planet? And, it also has the most spectacular *failure* story. Its range is mind-boggling: Detroit simultaneously represents humankind's highest dreams (being the world's automobile capitol)—and its worst nightmare (being the murder capitol). Growing up in a time of optimism, I took pride in the notion that the Motor City had made the world a better place in a tangible way. It not only improved the human condition with the car, but it also helped build the fabled "Arsenal of Democracy" that annihilated Hitler.

I was raised only a few miles from Dearborn, Michigan, the home of Henry Ford. My friends and I used to ride bikes on the grounds of Ford's Fair Lane Estate. Though the auto magnate is famous for saying, "History is bunk," he had built one of the nation's finest history museums right in our own backyard. The institution, now called "The Henry Ford," is a world-class tourist attraction. Mr. Ford had commissioned the moving of the actual homes of the Wright Brothers, Noah Webster, and other notables to one spot, Greenfield Village— the outdoor part of the museum. He also acquired the actual rocking chair that Abe Lincoln was shot in, George Washington's camp bed, and even Thomas Edison's last breath sealed in a tube.

Amongst the most venerated relics is one of the largest train locomotives ever built—"the Allegheny" (one of two last remaining of its kind). It is 125-feet long, 11 ft. wide, 16 feet tall. It's a marvel to behold. I'm awestruck every time I see it.

It was the very last day of the stretched-out Fourth-of-July holiday. After an uneventful overnight stay at the Platte River State Park, we found ourselves once again with our thumbs out along a road surrounded by a rolling ocean of sun-bleached prairie grass. Rocky hills towered along the horizon. The landscape's sheer vastness was matched only by that of the sky with its humongous cumulus clouds gracefully floating along like hot air balloons. The scene humbled me. It made me acutely aware of my inability to fully comprehend the height, depth, and breadth of the panoramic mythical West before my very eyes. It stirred in me a sense of limitless possibilities, a sentiment I'm sure was shared by the pioneer ghosts.

Before me was a parched wasteland. But it might well have been the "fresh green breast of the new world" envisioned by F. Scott Fitzgerald's Dutch sailors as they beheld the sprawling American continent for the first time, an event "commensurate to (one's) capacity for wonder."

These words could have easily been penned by Kerouac. But the scene also brought to mind Steinbeck, especially its bleak, scruffy topography, a lonely road with its utility poles and lines converging into the point of infinity in each direction—and railroad tracks running roughly parallel with U.S. 385.

The tracks, to the right of us, veered away from the road as far as a quarter mile and came as close as twenty-five feet. They were the closest where we were at. And, behind the tracks was about fifty acres of tractors and combine parts, most of it, no doubt, worthless junk. A prominent sign on the corroded chain-link fence read "The Bridgeport Tractor Parts and Salvage Yard." Other signage said the place had every piece of farm equipment imaginable—new, rebuilt and used. The luminous red-orange color of the rusty metal parts over-whelmed the otherwise muted landscape.

Then there was the *train*.

Its string of freight cars appeared endless from our vantage point. It consisted of the typical boxcars, hoppers, and gondolas, each having its color subdued by a film of dust. The engine car, the dynamo propelling this massive caterpillar, just happened to be next to where we were standing, just a stone throw away. It was blue with white trim, the shape and size of the standard modern diesel locomotive. Its idling engine droned. Judging by the multiple adjacent rails a quarter of a mile back, I figured that the train must have just switched tracks.

The aforementioned surprise occurred at mid-morning. We heard a male voice coming from the locomotive: "HEY, YOU GUYS OVER THERE!"

We turned and saw a white-haired man on the front platform of the train. It had to be the engineer. Pete and I stared at each other perplexed. Looking over to him, we gestured the question, "Are you talking to *us*?" The answer came with a nod meaning "yes."

"DO YOU FELLAS *WANNA RIDE*?!"

When I realized the implications, my heart beat faster with a jubilant feeling beyond description. We excitedly picked up our packs and rushed over to the locomotive. It was like something from a dream.

It would be the only time this hitchhiker ever got picked up by a train.

The Train Fantasy

If rock & roll is a religion, its "prophets" would surely be the rock stars and its "sacred scriptures" their songs.

If you take this comparison a step further, who would be the divinely-sanctioned interpreters of rock & roll scripture, its "magisterium," if you will? It would definitely be the editors of *Rolling Stone* magazine.

Who else?

Consider the Elvis Presley song "Mystery Train" and what one-time *Rolling Stone* editor Greil Marcus wrote about it:

"The mystery train"—it was a phrase that, once Elvis made it a metaphor for fate and desire, became a signpost, a doorway to a better world, a key to the truth, a philosopher's stone."

Whoa! Greil is onto something here. Perhaps *that's* what makes trains so special. They're sacred icons! Could they be shadowy derivatives of the universal Train in heaven as in Plato's theory of forms? (I'd learned a lot about Plato in Philosophy 101.) Perhaps the original *eidos* ("form") of Train and the Mystery Train are the exact same thing!

Whatever the case, the mere sight, sound and smell of trains made me tremble. They stirred up a torrent of deep-seated emotions—that whoosh feeling, bliss, a sense of being in the presence of something mystical, even supernatural. The closest thing I can relate it to is my rapturous reaction to fully-decked Christmas trees, or the diner we ate at with the Czeizingers in Murdo, SD. While trains can elicit pleasant thoughts and memories, they can also evoke melancholy, dread, and foreboding, particularly with the sound of their whistles. Like the modern age version of the coyote, the howl of the train engine gives me shivers as I lie half-awake in bed in the middle of the night.

To fully understand my obsession with trains, I must recount my personal history. As I shared with Roy at Poverty Gulch, one particular train had changed my life forever.

It happened when I was still in high school two years back. Once again, my best friend Randal Stark and I were walking along the railroad tracks in my neighborhood when a passing train gave us the notion to hop a train to New York like hobos.

I don't know about Randal, but the original fantasy was inspired by the movie *Bound for Glory*. In the film, legendary folk singer/activist Woody Guthrie traveled by stowing away in boxcars during the 1930s. Earlier in his life, he did so out of necessity, but later on, for the adventure. As I'd told Roy, Randal and I opted to hitchhike instead of hop trains because we thought hitchhiking was safer.

However, my interest in trains, railroads and hobos goes back much further than that. I fondly remember the bedtime stories my mom used to tell about Casey Jones and John Henry. The first song I'd learned in kindergarten was "I've Been Working on the Railroad." I often hummed to myself train songs like "The Midnight Special" (CCR), "Folsom Prison Blues" (Johnny Cash) and "City of New Orleans" (Arlo Guthrie) which had received a fair amount of radio play.

Trains are a key element in rock & roll's "sacred tradition" which formed me in my teenage years. According to *Rolling Stone*, rock music is, more or less, a hybrid of blues and country. The "father of the blues," W.C. Handy, discovered the blues in 1903 while sitting at a *train station* where he observed "a lean loose-jointed Negro plucking a guitar." Similarly, the "father of country," Jimmie Rodgers, worked on the railroad since age thirteen, where he'd learned to play stringed instruments and yodel from his co-workers and hobos.

So apparently, rock & roll's "parents'—blues and country—were *both* born in a train yard!

My hometown Detroit has long been associated with trains. Though Chicago wins the title of *the* main railway hub of the United States, our town couldn't be far behind, along with other big cities in the industrial Midwest like Pittsburgh. The rail system, of course, is an integral part of the auto industry. Around the clock, trains bring in tons of the raw materials to feed the fiery furnaces in the Ford Rouge plant. At the same time, they transport countless finished parts and products to cities across North America. One of Detroit's most revered landmarks is the spectacular Michigan Central Station located near the Ambassador Bridge. This passenger depot, an architectural wonder in its day, is now our city's most famous ruin.

The symbolism of trains is strong with Detroit's African-American community. It's prominent in black art, literature, and music. Their ancestors, the Southern slaves, had seen trains as a means of escape and starting a new life on free soil (hence the name "Underground *Railroad*"). After abolition, trains signified liberation from poor working conditions, poverty and oppression in the South. A mass exodus of blacks migrated on trains to Detroit (and other northern cities) to find decent jobs in the factories. Some black men worked for the railroads as porters, brakeman, and switchman, which were considered high-status positions.

My best boyhood buddy, Mick Rhodes and I shared a passion for trains. Mick, who lived next door, was aptly named because he looked like a pint-sized version of Mick Jagger. When Mick's parents got him a Lionel train set for Christmas one year, we were in train heaven. We spent countless hours in his basement playing with it. Back in a time when model trains were just as popular as today's video games, Mick had just about every Lionel accessory you could imagine, most notably a dockside switcher engine that was styled from the Old West-style steam locomotive. It even gave off real stream! His set also included an operating dump car, gondola, and caboose as well as a transformer. We tried out every track and car configuration conceivable. Once in a while, Mr. Rhodes would take time out of his busy schedule and join us.

There was another thing besides owning a Lionel train set that made me envious of Mick: His dad was an engineer!

While my father was an ordinary factory worker, Mr. Rhodes was a modern-day "Casey Jones." I pictured him as the archetypal hero—on par with the brave fireman, soldier, and astronaut. No wonder Mick idolized his dad. Engineers, of course, were known for their courage, patience—and, most of all, their punctuality. Through night and storm, they always brought their train through safely *on time*.

Having said all this, my perception of Mr. Rhodes would dramatically change. At one point, I discovered something strange about him. When I saw him come home from work, I noticed he didn't exactly dress like an engineer. He didn't wear the striped hat and bib overalls with suspenders, red bandana scarf tied around his neck, and leather gloves. He wasn't covered with black soot. Instead, he sported a clean, neatly-pressed business suit. He carried a briefcase.

Come to find out, Mick's dad was a *mechanical* engineer at the Ford Motor Company, not a train engineer!

The Reality of Trains

Pete and I were now in a different sort of train heaven. Our forty-mile train odyssey from Bridgeport to Sidney, Nebraska lasted about an hour. The locomotive we rode was an EMD SD40, considered one of the most efficient models in the seventies, though its appearance didn't correspond to the Mystery Train in my mind's eye. (The Mystery Train was black and steam-powered like the ones on TV's *Gunsmoke*, *Wild Wild West*, and *Petticoat Junction*.) The engineer's name was Nathan Biddle. Most of the time, he sat before the controls positioned on the right-hand side of the cab. Pete and I stood behind and to the left of him.

While gazing out of the cab windows, we conversed with Nathan, who was a dead-ringer for William Frawley, the actor who played Fred Mertz in *I Love Lucy*. Looking back on the whole train ride, it was a rare treat. Nathan picking up hitch-hikers must have been considered a big no-no according to the Burlington Northern Railroad Rule Book. I figured, since he was retiring in a few months, he simply didn't give a crap.

Nathan didn't dress like a train engineer, but unlike Mr. Rhodes, he was the real deal. Instead of the typical engineer's cap (the kind with the folds, rim, flat top, blue-and-white stripes), he wore a solid teal one that looked more like a base-ball hat. Concerning the rest of his clothes, Nathan—rough-ly age sixty, white hair, average build—sported a blue denim shirt with the sleeves rolled up, and work uniform pants (also denim yet in a darker shade of blue). Truth be told, he looked like an average factory worker, perhaps a middle-manage-ment union steward. But his neatly-trimmed white mustache and wire-rimmed glasses made him look distinguished like a college professor.

More than anything, Nathan's body language communi-cated what he did for a living. Every fiber of his being exuded confidence, a hyper-awareness of his physical surroundings inside and outside the cab. The way he moved around to all the controls gave you the illusion he had eyes around his head and multiple pairs of limbs like a Hindu god. He probably knew every gauge, switch, and indicator light like the back of his hand. He must've referred to his Rolex wristwatch every five seconds. Once the train got rolling, his gaze became firm-ly fixed on the two-mile stretch of track ahead of us, as well as the signals we passed along the way. Moreover, Nathan seemed superhuman in his ability to coordinate crew mem-bers with gibberish he blurted into a hand-held radio receiver.

Nathan presented the perfect foil to my train fantasy—*train reality*. In real life, "working on the railroad" is noth-ing like the carefree existence depicted in the song. Instead of sitting around all day playing your banjo and singing "fee, fie, fiddly-i-o," you're always racing against the clock, rain or shine. The to-do list is enormous. There are a gazillion procedures that need to be meticulously carried out. Missing a beat on any given task could lead to disaster. The slightest screw up could adversely affect the bottom line, cause a crash, and even end someone's life. And there are additional headaches brought on by company, union, and government red tape, particularly a mountain of forms that need to be filled out. Talk about a stressful job!

"Look, I'll tell you straight. Railroading isn't for everyone. It's a tough life."

"Do you like your job?" I asked flat out.

"Well... Like every job, it's a mixed bag. The salary is good, not to mention the benefits package and the pension. My wife has had three surgeries in the last twenty months and we've paid almost nothing for them. And I could afford to send all five of my kids to college."

Nathan glanced at us briefly a few times, but his eyes mostly stayed glued on the tracks ahead. His right hand steadily shifted the clutch lever to different gears. His left hand periodically controlled the switch labeled "Air Brake."

He continued to speak: "I've learned to appreciate the little things. For me, it's the rush you get while starting the engines of the largest moving land vehicle on the planet. I love the way my crew is like a family—we've shared a lot of tears and laughter. And all the gorgeous scenery you see never gets old."

"What's the *worst* thing you had to deal with?"

"Hmmm. It's definitely scheduling. In railroading, your time is not your own. I mean that quite literally. You're always on-call, at unexpected times and on short notice. If you want to kick back with your friends and have a couple of beers, forget it. When they call you in, they expect you to drop everything and come right away, no questions asked."

Pete and I looked at each other pensively. I knew my partner was thinking the same thing: How could people live like that? Responsibility trumps your personal freedom 24/7!

"Like I said, fellas, railroading is hard. You must follow the rules and do your duty. The trains must be kept running 365 days a year, 24 hours a day, 7 days a week. They must take precedence over your life. I can't tell you how many birthdays, Thanksgivings, and Christmases I've missed. Imagine having to inspect the cars in the freezing rain on your wedding anniversary, or else sitting in an unheated cab when it's ten below on Christmas Eve."

One thing jumped out: Nathan seemed relatively content, in spite of it all.

"There's one other thing," Nathan said with a face as gloomy as a tomb. "It's not a matter of *if* but *when*. It's going to happen. You're going to hit someone on the tracks. It will happen when you least expect it. There's nothing you can do about it. Unless you're able to compartmentalize things like cops do, it will profoundly affect you for the rest of your life."

"Would you mind telling us about your experience?"

"Sure. I'm one of the lucky ones. As an engineer for 27 years, I've only had three incidents of hitting a person or a vehicle on the tracks. The first one happened around 10 p.m. one hot summer night when we were just coming around a curve under an overpass. I'm going maybe 40 mph and right there in front of me, basking in my headlight, is a man likely in his mid-forties, standing in the middle of the track, arms out stretched, looking square at me!"

"Oh my God! Suicide?"

"I don't know. The blood samples showed he was intoxicated. I'll never forget that face staring at me and then that deafening thud, a ghastly sound like that of a meat grinder. In that situation, the entire crew is devastated, especially the conductor who has to go out there and investigate."

"*Oh sick!* The conductor has to see the bloody body?"

"Oh, worse than that, he often has to collect body parts. It's a gruesome affair. But, look, someone's got to do it."

"Is there any way to stop the train in time?"

"Are you kidding? At normal speeds, it takes at least a mile and a half to come to a complete stop. Under certain weather conditions, it could take three miles. The fact that you're so helpless will drive you nuts. It will make you sad, angry, and even guilty though you know it's not your fault. You often lay awake at night analyzing everything."

"Have you ever hit a motor vehicle?"

"Oh yes. At a crossing near Alliance, my train struck a van with four passengers in it. Fortunately, no one got seriously injured. It infuriates me to no end to see drivers pull out and around closed gates in a mad dash to beat the train. Can't those idiots just wait 30 seconds? Why risk your life for that?"

One of us asked about the third incident Nathan had alluded to earlier.

There was a significant pause and then the engineer let out a sigh. "When it happened, I thought I'd seen everything. It was a case of dismemberment. A young man from Scottsbluff lost a leg while his girlfriend, fortunately, got away unharmed. The two were, uh, you know... naked."

"Aw, man, they were actually...?" I gasped.

"Yeah, I think you get my meaning."

"A *train fetish*?"

"I swear to God, boys, I'm not making this up," Nathan put forth grimly.

Son of the Engineer

Before Pete LeBlanc and Randal Stark, there was Mick Rhodes. Since his family moved next door in '65, Mick and I were the best of friends. We started out playing with the Lionel train set, but ended up messing around with *real* trains.

We were different in so many ways. The age gap between Mick and me was practically the Grand Canyon—almost two years. I was easy-going and amenable; Mick was loud and boisterous. His family seemed to be in a higher social class than mine: My dad worked as a clerk in a paint factory; Mick's father, in my mom's words, was a "big shot at Fords." Again, Mr. Rhodes was a mechanical engineer.

But Mick and I shared in common one important trait—an overactive imagination. Our fertile fantasy factory churned out all kinds of projects. Like the Wright Brothers, we were always bouncing off each other. It was like we were in the late-1800s, the Age of Invention.

One time, not content with the conventional Kool-Aid stand, Mick and I made a "vending machine," a large wooden rectangular box where the drink is poured through a funnel on the top and goes down a system of plastic straws before flowing into a Dixie cup below. Another time, we made a giant "spider web" out of twine on Mick's swing glider. After we coated it with Elmer's Glue, we tried to lure Mick's arch-rival Noel Cogley into it. Yet another time, we aspired to build a skyscraper in Mick's backyard, but our seemingly endless supply of lumber ran out before we could finish the first floor.

We constantly played make-believe and acted out stories. Like the other kids, Mick and I used action figures, toy trucks, and other props. We ran around the neighborhood playing the usual cops and robbers, cowboys and Indians, and war. What made our playtime so extraordinary was Mick's above-average creativity, intelligence, and wit. For instance, when we played "Secret Agent Man," we'd abruptly stop the show for a commercial and have Mick pretend he's "Bud Nicks," the actor who plays Secret Agent Man, endorsing some soft drink, toothpaste or laundry detergent. Mick was hilarious. He had a perfect TV announcer voice and the ability to voice-act characters he created on the fly like Robin Williams had done.

Our favorite characters developed intriguing personalities over time. In a weird way, they seemed real. Mick had me in stitches with his "Mr. XY Factor," the prototypical nerd who talks incessantly about mathematic equations with a thick Viennese accent. The character thinks everyone he meets—at parties, in the grocery store line, and on elevators—is just as excited about the subject as he is. He's so socially inept that he presumes everyone understands what he's talking about. It was all in good fun, of course. But I had long suspected that Mr. XY Factor was a caricature of Mick's dad.

Mr. Rhodes didn't have a Viennese accent, but he did like to talk about equations. He was sort of a nerd but a cool one. My parents used to comment about the way he carried himself, so confident, self-assured, and sophisticated—and the fact he earned a Master's degree at the prestigious University of Detroit.

He was refined in his cultural tastes. In his spare time, he drank dry martinis with an olive, painted abstract art, and listened to Esquivel and Stan Getz. He always smelled like aftershave and cigarettes. There was also something *military* about this man with his buzz-cut and commanding presence. Mr. Rhodes could be warm and friendly but also peevish when you disagreed with him. I think he still thought of himself as "the lieutenant" (he had served in the Navy), as well as the smartest guy in the room. At home, he was definitely "the man of the house," the final decision-maker, the disciplinarian.

By and by, the hero became the villain in his son's eyes.

How this happened is anyone's guess. In many ways, Mr. Rhodes seemed to be a good dad, playing with Mick stuff like model trains, chess, and Frisbee. Psychology 101 class gave me some clues: For one thing, Mr. Rhodes fit the profile of an "authoritarian parent." Authoritarian-types expect too much of their kids and enforce rules that are too strict. They tend to demand unconditional obedience and inflict harsh punishment. Even my retired sixth grade teacher, Mrs. Delaney, made this comment: "Oh yeah, I remember him. He was *the dictator*." (Which is saying something: She was one of the strictest teachers in our school!)

Mick, on the other hand, was what pop psychologists call a "strong-willed child," the sort who is naturally wired with an indomitable spirit. He could drive *any* parent mad. Highly demanding, controlling, and rude, Mick tended to be bossy and get into fights. Always on the look-out for new challenges and chances to move around and explore, he had a knack for getting into trouble. At home and school, he constantly pushed his luck to the limit and laughed aloud at the chaos and confusion he created. Sure, he could be a pain, but from my standpoint, he was as entertaining as the movie character Cool Hand Luke.

It's easy to see why the pair clashed. Mick and his dad were like the two chemicals that explode when combined. But this particular combustible mixture took a long time to simmer.

Putting that aside for now, how did *trains* factor in?

There was a region in our old neighborhood known as "the Tracks." The capital "T" indicates that it was the actual railroad tracks plus the area surrounding them. This swathe of land is called a railroad "right-of-way." It's about 400 feet wide (but got wider north of Plymouth Road) and seems to follow the rails to the ends of the earth in either direction.

Privately owned by the Chesapeake and Ohio (C&O) Railroad, the Tracks are overgrown with junk trees and other wild plants. Buildings surround them, mostly warehouses and job shops located along and between Fitzpatrick Drive and

Weaver Drive. Their chain-linked fences with barbed-wire seal off and hide the Tracks from the rest the world.

Access to the Tracks region is not difficult via the crossings at main roads and an opening designated for pedestrian traffic only. Other entry points are off-limits, including one two blocks away from my house. This entrance to the Tracks was located between two adjacent buildings along Fitzpatrick—the Nabisco warehouse and the Aspen Tool and Die shop. Directly across the street from the opening was a city park with a baseball diamond.

For a time, the posted "No Trespassing" signs deterred us kids from going through that specific opening to the Tracks. However, when one of us accidentally hit a baseball through there, temptation got the best of us.

Mick, I, and two other friends found ourselves intrigued by this mysterious area—particularly the actual railroad tracks. To get there, you had to hike 100 feet down a narrow trail through waist-high grass and weeds, and up a steep slope leading to the plateau where the rails were.

Like the typical railroad tracks, they rest on a bed of rocks called a ballast. When you observe tracks up close, you notice they're basically two I-beam-shaped steel rails, arranged roughly 4½ feet apart, laid over and fastened to crossties made out of wood. Once in a while, you'll see patches of sand on the ties and ballast rocks. I often wondered where the sand came from. As Nathan Biddle would explain, the locomotive sprays sand on the wheels to increase traction when braking.

"ZOOOSH ZOOOSH ZOOOOOOOOSH DING DING DING!" The train sound from a distance prompted us to follow our instincts and move out of the way fast. But the mischievous Mick Rhodes had something else in mind before he too bolted off. He picked up five or six stones from the ballast and lined them up on one of the rails.

"COME ON, MICK. ARE YOU CRAZY? LET'S GO!" I yelled frantically.

But these words fell on deaf ears. As the train got closer and closer, Mick reached into his shorts pocket and pulled out a shiny penny and carefully laid it on the track before he finally darted off to the side.

On the grassy slope below the ballast, we covered our ears from the blast of sound. A wind stirred up by a train moving 50 mph or so, felt like a tropical storm.

We had enough of a view to watch with amazement as the heavy train wheels pulverized the objects placed on the tracks. Sparks flew. Rocks turned into powder; fragments shot every which way like bullets from a gun.

After the train finally passed and the coast was clear, we examined what was left. The most interesting thing was the coin (or, should I say, ex-coin). Both sides were so smooth that you could hardly tell heads from tails. It was almost as thin as paper.

What we'd just witnessed blew us away, physically and emotionally. It was destruction of the highest order. The adrenaline rush we received must have lasted a half hour or so. We'd never encountered such power before in our lives.

We were like cavemen who just discovered fire.

The Lincoln Highway

"Now my life is complete!" I said to Pete after our train ride with Nathan Biddle. Little did I know, the experience would soon be overshadowed.

If you saw it marked on a map, you'd notice our day's journey took the shape of a backwards "L." We went south via train along the Gold Rush Byway, parted ways with Nathan at Sidney, and proceeded to go west by thumb.

While in Sidney, we found out more cool facts:

— We'd just passed the fabled California Trail and Pony Express Trail. And the Oregon Trail was just ahead. It roughly followed U.S. Interstate 80, the highway we were planning to take to Wyoming.

— Just north of us was America's second or third most famous highway. (Number one, of course, is Route 66.) It's the very first coast-to-coast highway—U.S Route 30—better known as the Lincoln Highway.

— Running along U.S. 30 were the train tracks of the very first transcontinental railroad.

Nathan had called this "railroad country" for good reason. Here, everyone and their brother, worked on the train lines in some capacity. We were practically at the exact midpoint between two major railroad nerve-centers—North Platte, Nebraska (120 miles east) and Cheyenne, Wyoming (100 miles west). North Platte has Bailey Yard which is recognized in *The Guinness Book of Records* as the largest railroad yard in the world. Cheyenne is the home of the palace-like Union Pacific Depot, which was once the crown jewel of all the railroads in the West.

Both North Platte and Cheyenne started out as two of the storied "hell on wheels" towns, wild make-shift settlements where the original UP Railroad crew squandered their hard-earned money on gambling, drinking, and whoring. After it grew in size and respectability, North Platte became the home base of Buffalo Bill Cody's Wild West Show.

By mid-afternoon, LeBlanc and I found ourselves treading along Interstate 80, ten miles west of Sidney. A highway patrolman named Clouse had to pull over a second time.

"You guys don't listen too well, do you?" yelled the red-faced cop. "What did I tell you? GET OFF THE INTERSTATE NOW!"

"But where else can we go?" I protested.

"I don't know and I don't care!"

"My, my, *God* himself has spoken," LeBlanc muttered beneath his breath. That was the last straw for Officer Clouse who had good ears.

"Look here, smartass! I'm losing my patience. I told you guys a half hour ago to get your asses out of here. NOW MOVE!"

Before Clouse did something more drastic (he'd already written each of us a ticket), we began to make our way through the half-mile tract of land between Interstate 80 and U.S. 30. Legions of grasshoppers shot up at the slightest provocation. What looked like an abandoned wheat field was the ultimate obstacle course. Once we pushed through the menagerie of wild plants, we had to chop our way through briers and thistles in a dried-up irrigation ditch and weave our bodies, backpacks and all, under a barbed-wire fence, before making it to the clearing on the other side.

Whew! Tranquility greeted us there. Endorphins released in my brain, the result of the workout, gave me a natural high. With the faint rhythmic hiss of locusts in our ears, we beheld a lonesome highway.

It was no ordinary one. It was the fabled Lincoln Highway, the first road to connect the Atlantic and the Pacific Oceans, the older sibling of Route 66.

U.S. 30's power lines ran to where the vantage point meets the afternoon sky in each direction. Like the Mother Road, it must have been bursting with life before the Interstate came and diverted all the traffic.

Obviously, the Lincoln Highway had seen better days. Its pavement was cracked and crumbling along the edges. The road surface markings were badly faded. An abandoned Esso gas station stood along the side of the road with boarded-up windows, weather-beaten cinder block walls, and a rusted-out oval sign and appendages where the pumps used to be. I half-expected to see a tumble weed blow by like in the movies. Mother Nature claimed the remnants of two other buildings in the distance, now hollowed-out shells subjugated by wild plants.

Pete and I started to walk. The Lincoln Highway was a nice place to wax nostalgic about the Dust Bowl days with my overactive imagination, but it was impractical. There were almost no cars. Over a period of an hour, only about five non-ghost cars whizzed by. Our dim prospects put us in a deep funk. Knowing we were going nowhere fast, I was the first to break the long and weary existential silence.

"Well, so much for the Road Less Traveled," I said with a blasé smirk.

Then something in my head came to the rescue like the arrival of a long-awaited Texas Ranger posse: Laughter. I burst out uncontrollably over our miserable situation. I pictured us in our own slapstick comedy. LeBlanc cracked up too. It was just like what happened at the Out-post.

So far, I'd neglected to mention one important detail: The ghost road had a companion. Over yonder about fifty yards or so—running parallel to Highway 30—were railroad tracks.

I didn't put two-and-two together at the time, but it was actually the first transcontinental train line, as mentioned earlier. It looked like any other set of tracks, resting on higher ground and a bed of ballast rocks. The tracks gave off numerous smells—that of diesel fuel smoke and a mishmash of oil, grease, and dirt.

The most pungent scent, however, came from creosote, the black goo the railroad ties are treated with. These strong chemical fumes might cause anyone to wince, or even pass out, but not me, It was like perfume to my nostrils because they reminded me of the Tracks back home and, hence, the most important moments in my childhood.

Holy Mother of God!

A rumble and then a thunderous toot pierced the stillness, the sound of a train coming!

Pete and I gazed to the east and recognized the headlight in the distance heading our way. Pete snapped out of his reverie. You could see a sudden spark of life in his eyes. Neither of us had to say anything. We sprinted into the overgrown foliage toward the tracks.

As it got closer, you could see all the distinguishable features of the locomotive. It looked like Nathan's, except it was yellow with gray trim, the branding colors of the Union Pacific Railroad. It rumbled along the tracks like some mighty mongrel beast with its procession of cars in tow, passing us at a relatively slow pace.

"Should we? Should we do it?" Pete was the first to say outloud what we were both contemplating—hopping the train, of course!

My mind oscillated whether to do so or not. The train seemed to be going the right speed.

There was not a moment to spare.

We had to act *now*.

"Yeah, let's do it!" I screamed.

Everything happened so fast. We ran up the ballast and alongside the passing boxcars and flat cars, ripping off our 30 lb. backpacks. Pete flung his pack on an empty flat car and I followed suit. We intended, of course, to grab a ladder or something and hoist ourselves on a car a second later.

All the same, neither of us could run fast enough to gain a hold on the moving train! It was going too fast!

We watched with apprehension as one car passed then two, then three and before we knew it, the caboose rattled by, leaving us breathless, perplexed and finally stunned over the fact all our belongings had just disappeared into oblivion!

My eyes bugged out of their sockets. My lower jaw dropped.

"Sh*t! Sh*t! Sh*t! What are we gonna do now?!" I bewailed breathlessly with clenched fists. "We're *screwed!*"

I'll never forget LeBlanc's reaction. If he was shocked, alarmed, or worried like me, he didn't show it. He appeared cool, calm, and detached like Mr. Spock on *Star Trek*.

"Don't worry, Ted, everything is going be alright," he replied in a low-key tone.

This irritated me. Pete's remarkable ability to "go with the flow" and remain calm in all situations could be inspiring. On the other hand, it could come off as condescending, holier than thou—like now.

"Well, *thanks a lot!*" I said sarcastically. "So you think I'm some kind of dork for being a little upset?"

"Hmmm... well..."

"Don't I have a freakin' *right* to freak out?! Those backpacks have *everything we got*, our clothes, sleeping bags, food, money, everything!"

"Just cool it, man. No need to get uptight. Look, everything's gonna work out... trust me... it's *Fate*."

"Fate?!" I darted back, incredulous like Dr. McCoy to LeBlanc's Spock.

Pete had gotten all mystical on me again. This ticked me off even more because he seemed to imply that he was in synch with the sublime rhythm of the universe, and I wasn't.

As we'd already seen in Poverty Gulch, he expressed his strong belief that everything happens for a reason, according to a plan ordained by some mysterious force or God. "It's written down somewhere," he liked to say. And he had an unshakable sureness that destiny would bring about a positive result.

I, on the other hand, had a sinking feeling that the stars had something else in mind.

CHAPTER 18

THE TRACKS

T HE COWBOYS DIDN'T TAME the Wild West, the history books tell us. It was the *railroads*.

Those involved with the rail lines made the once "boundless and undefined space" of the frontier accessible to all, notably surveyors who mapped it out, the government which occupied it, and the pioneers who bought it at bargain basement prices. The land boom was so immense that there would soon be no wilderness left. The pioneers and their descendants cultivated everything into neat rows. Or, so it seemed. Ironically, the parcels of land owned by the railroads, such as the Tracks area by my house, still had some wilderness left in them. You might say, the Tracks kept "the wild" hemmed in like the contents of a sausage.

The Tracks weren't exactly the Jack London kind of wild, but compared to our neat and clean neighborhood, it was. It had wild plants, wild animals, and wild people. Vegetation commonly labeled and discarded as "weeds" flourished at the Tracks. The species that stood out included the milkweed plant that attracted the monarch butterfly. There were ferns in the shade that looked sinister with their finger-like leaves. There were the annoying gnarly plants with thistles and thorns. The peskiest one was Ragweed. Clusters of its marble-sized burrs attached themselves to your clothes, socks, and shoe laces like Velcro.

The untamed critters that lurked at the Tracks were usually small furry ones like opossums, rabbits, skunks, mice, and rats. Stray cats and dogs also made their appearance from time-to-time. Pheasants nesting in the thickets would sometimes dart up unexpectedly and startle the crap out of us. If you looked hard enough, you could find garter snakes, crayfish, and frogs. Even deer made their abode in the wider wooded area north of Plymouth Road.

The Tracks were a "dangerous" place to hang out, but that wasn't the only reason they were off-limits to the public. The other reason was, since they were private property, we were trespassing. But we didn't see it that way. Like the Indians, we believed the wilderness—including the wilderness at the Tracks—belonged to everybody, so it was perfectly okay for us to hang out there.

The Cogley Twins

Tom and Huck had Cardiff Hill; Mick Rhodes and I had the Tracks. After school and during summer vacations, we kept returning to our "frontier" long after that first close encounter with the train. When my parents found out about it through my brother, they were not happy. They vehemently implored us to stay away from the Tracks, but it was too late. We caught the bug. There was something uncanny about the place that attracted us to it.

There were three things that made the Tracks so irresistible. First was the lure of nature—"the call of the wild." We enjoyed the aesthetics and the novelty of the aforementioned plants and animals, the whole environment.

Second, the Tracks were the place to go for retreat. In other words, they were a sanctuary where you could hide from the rest of the world like Camp David. It was difficult being a pre-teen with pressures coming at you from all sides. You needed a special place like the Tracks to get away from it all and chill out.

Third, the Tracks were where you'd go for adventure. If you ventured north of Plymouth Road, past the viaduct, the area widened significantly. Open field eventually turned into woods. This patch of wilderness could render thrill-seeking twelve-year-old males speechless like the Dutch sailors. You wanted to check out every square inch of it like Captain Cooke on some uncharted desert island.

The comparison of Mick Rhodes and me with Mark Twain's Tom Sawyer and Huckleberry Finn seems to fit in a lot of ways. Like Tom, I came from a stable home. Like Huck, Mick came from a messed up one. Like Tom and Huck, Mick and I were so close that we, at one point, declared ourselves blood brothers, officiating the occasion "like real Indians" by cutting our fingers and mixing our blood. Like Tom and Huck, we were hardcore fantasizers who saw the world through rose-colored glasses.

Like Tom and Huck, we pretended to be imaginary characters from TV shows, movies, and books. At the Tracks, we'd play war on the foot trails with toy guns. We'd pretend to be pirates seeking treasure. We'd portray explorers of the same caliber as Daniel Boone, Lewis and Clark, and Sir Edmund Hillary.

Another important archetype in our fantasy world was the Daredevil. My friends and I would challenge each other to perform spectacular stunts at the Tracks like Evel Knievel, the world's most famous daredevil. Various feats come to mind like barreling down a hill at top speed on our string-ray bikes and flying into the air using a wooden ramp below. We'd crawl through a dark drainage pipe to see where it led to. We'd scuttle atop of the full length of a half-mile long brick wall that we dubbed "the Great Wall," in spite of daunting obstacles such as tree limbs and thorn bushes growing over it.

Half the fun was bragging about doing it afterwards—telling the story. Years later, this would be an important aspect of The Grand Experiment.

★ ★ ★

If there was a tournament for performing daring feats, the Cogley twins would surely win first prize. Neal and Noel Cogley—the fraternal twins about my age who lived down the street—always seemed to be one step ahead of us. We watched with awe as they both climbed to the top of the railroad observation tower with the greatest of ease.

The observation tower is actually a rectangular arch with two foundations, one in each side of the railroad tracks and its ballast. It houses four traffic signals, two facing each side. To get to the main platform, you had to climb a hundred-foot ladder welded to the south end.

After the Cogleys climbed the tower, Mick and I knew we had to follow suit. It took a day or two for me and other friends to work up the courage. However, it took Mick a week to overcome his fear of heights.

Even back then, Mick and I had determined we just couldn't match the Cogleys' exploits. Some of their stunts bordered on insanity. We couldn't be that crazy. Common sense and reason got in the way.

Once, I felt my heart race and hair follicles tingle as I watched Neal Cogley shimmy his prone body through a tunnel under the viaduct, from one end to the other. The tunnel was dark, a foot high and wide. It was infested with spiders, mosquitoes, and probably bats. Passing vehicles under the bridge filled it with exhaust fumes and loud echoing noise. Worst of all, it was along a ledge. One false move and you'd end up falling fourteen feet onto the pavement below!

Another way the Cogleys followed their "inner madman" was hop trains.

One time, I witnessed Noel Cogley run next to a moving gondola car, grab the ladder, and hang on for about a minute and half before flinging himself off. He did it in such a nonchalant manner, as graceful as a ballet dancer. This got Mick and me staring at each other with dropped jaws, as if to say, "Who would even *attempt* that?"

What Now?

"Imagine no possessions," John Lennon had said. After the train took away our backpacks, we didn't have to imagine it. It was reality. We now faced our biggest challenge yet. Again, our packs contained all the essentials: sleeping bags, tents, clothes, cooking supplies, canteens, Swiss army knives, toiletries, rain poncho, maps, books, rope, traveler's checks, etc.. The thought of losing my writing journal upset me the most. At least we still had the clothes we had on, not to mention the stuff in our pockets. I still had my wallet with 26 dollars in it, some change, my disposable butane lighter, ball point pen, and my ticket for hitchhiking from Officer Clouse. The most valuable thing Pete kept on him was, of course, Rosie's phone number.

After the mad dash to hop the train, we had collapsed from sheer exhaustion in the grassy meadow next to the ballast. My incessant panting made my sides ache like someone just punched me.

As I was in the process of catching my breath, my mind went into instant replay mode. I asked myself over and over:

What in the hell had just happened? How could we have been so stupid? But, most of all, *what now*? I wasn't exactly in a state of panic, but I had a terrible sense of loss like my house just went up in smoke. Pete, on the other hand, remained unruffled and kept insisting we were going to somehow get our packs back.

This situation accentuated the major difference between Pete and me (at least at that moment)—my partner had *faith* and I didn't.

Call it admirable, misguided, or whatever, but Pete's trust in "God" (however defined) was genuine, as far as I could tell. It didn't come across forced and contrived like that of certain faith healers or "positive thinking" people who try to whip up phony enthusiasm. Remember, Pete LeBlanc was Holden Caufield incarnate, the consummate "non-phony" person.

Like the Eriksons, Pete was *laid-back*. He seemed totally confident everything was going to work out.

As previously seen, I exploded with anger when Pete kept saying stuff like "Take it easy" and "Don't worry." He sounded so patronizing. Maybe I overreacted, but Pete's encouraging words came across like he thought he was Jesus Christ or something, like when Christ told a terrified Peter, "O ye of little faith!" as their boat was being swallowed up by waves in a raging storm.

Well, I had news for him: He wasn't Jesus by a long shot.

Perhaps deep down, I envied Pete. He seemed to have it so together. Part of me wanted to share his optimism. The other part of me was resigned to the idea that our backpacks were lost forever.

Going back to the original question: What now? If we didn't find our packs soon, what would happen? Would we have to cancel the entire trip? It certainly looked that way! It was hard to imagine traveling without our stuff. But that would mean having to *go back home*.

Go home? Never!

The very idea was anathema. I'd left Detroit taking the moral high road. (Remember "Give me liberty or give me death!"?) I renounced my old life of being oppressed by my parents, the industrial-military complex, and the Catholic Church. I'd virtually cut myself off from *everybody* just so I could be free.

How could I go back?!

Returning home now would be the ultimate humiliation. My family and friends would see me and my Grand Experiment as a colossal failure. I could just hear them say, "See I told you so!"

Other alternatives?

— Option One: call my parents and ask them to wire me the money needed to replace my stuff. Out of the question! They'd send me money alright—for a one-way bus ride home.

— Option Two: steal stuff. This wasn't ruled out outright. Believe or not, we intellectually justified stealing for a "higher cause" (sort of like "the ends justifies the means"). Since this subject opens up a whole new can of worms, I will have to postpone it until the next book.

— Option Three: mooch our way through the rest of the trip. (In other words, keep on doing what we're doing.)

Why was Option Three so inconceivable? After all, free-loading had worked like a charm for us so far. We'd enjoyed much success not paying our way. Over 1,100 miles from home, we paid zero, zilch, nada for gasoline. And that is saying something, considering our trip took place during the worst of the energy crisis!

Everywhere we went, we found free transportation, free lodging, and free food—free everything! (Well, *almost* everything, we *did* use a little of our own dough.) Why would things be any different after losing our backpacks? Eventually, someone would step up and *give* us all new stuff.

Once I convinced myself of the solid reasons for Option Three, I felt fine.

Since my New York trip with Randal, I thought a lot about this phenomenon (of complete strangers giving us stuff) in terms of religion and spirituality. It's like the mysterious "law of attraction" outlined in the book *The Secret* by Rhonda Byrne. Following the immutable law of the universe referred to as "like attracts like," we could expect good things to happen because we're special and chosen.

If you're a good person (which I thought I was), karma dictates that people will be good to you back. For example, noble deeds like picking up hitchhikers will be repaid in like fashion: someone will inevitably pick you up.

Relevant to this discussion, the Bible says Jesus gave his disciples these instructions: "Take nothing for the journey except a staff—no bread, no bag, no money in your belts." I took this to mean that Christ gave his followers the go-ahead to mooch. (It didn't occur to me then that doing God's work deserves a little compensation.)

After resting up for a while, we reluctantly went back to our previous plan to walk and hitchhike along the seldom-traveled Lincoln Highway. The thought we could sponge our way through anything made me whistle a happy tune.

The railroad tracks to our right seldom left our field of vision. Like on the Gold Rush Byway, the road and the tracks seemed to have a symbiotic relationship: They went along next to each other like the paths of two mating dolphins.

I took note at how the tracks appeared weed-choked, dirty and worn out. This made me think of what Nathan

Biddle had said earlier about how bad the seventies were for the railroads. Government regulations prevented them from being competitive with other transportation providers, so the railroad companies had to cut corners on basic maintenance. But that was the least of it: Many fabled companies went out-of-business, leading to talk about trains becoming obsolete like the horse and buggy.

Interestingly enough, *Democrat* President Jimmy Carter did something very "Reagan-esque." He most likely rescued the railroads from extinction by signing into law a bill that deregulated the industry in 1980. As a result, the rail industry would stop losing money, turn over a profit, and be competitive again. This highlighted Mr. Carter's integrity and courage to dodge the party line and do what he thought was right. And, in so doing, he literally saved the railroads.

And speaking of salvation, we heard a familiar sound of a horn in the distance. We looked down the tracks and saw a beautiful sight: It was another train coming our way!

The Tower Incident

It happened quickly like what occurred after Adam and Eve ate the forbidden fruit.

During my early teen years, guilt and shame entered the picture. It was the "end of the innocence," as rockstar Don Henley would say. The Tracks—our place to commune with nature—became an unnatural place. Our retreat spot turned into a robber's den where we rode roughshod over the law. Our private adventure-land morphed into something like a dark alley where clever schemes are conceived. The fact it was shadowy, polluted and perverse made the Tracks all the more attractive.

It started with our fascination with raw physical power—when the train pulverized the rocks—and ended with us feel-ing em*power*ed by "getting away with murder."

The Tracks made us feel free and independent. Without pesky adults around, you could do whatever you wanted: smoke and swear to your heart's content, experiment with drinking and getting high, or even be a criminal for a while.

By the time I was fifteen year old, the entryway to the Tracks was like the portal to Hades, the shadowy underworld. If your goody-two-shoes brother wasn't playing across the street at the baseball diamond, you could slip in unnoticed through the lot between the two buildings along Fitzpatrick Drive.

The building on the left was the Nabisco warehouse. The "bad kids" hung out behind Nabisco, a place where there was a set of abandoned railroad tracks, a pyramid-shaped buffer stop, and a ballast of rocks littered with broken glass, rusted beer cans, wine and liquor bottles, cigarette butts, and pieces of burnt wood. In the adjacent thickets, one might come across a weather-beaten *Playboy*, syringes, and a used condom. The graffiti scrawled on the back wall of Nabisco included the f-word repeated many times, the anarchy symbol, and "666." If the wall could talk, I'm sure you'd hear many things that would raise eyebrows.

The Cogley twins were among the so-called bad kids. In addition to their aforementioned daredevil exploits, they picked fights, vandalized buildings, and cussed like prison inmates. And, since they were into heavy metal music, there were rumors that they worshiped Satan too.

Mick and I, being good Catholic kids (and altar boys to boot), had once viewed the Cogleys as belonging to a lower species, heathens, Protestants. But over time, the moral difference between us and them diminished.

The rambunctious Mick Rhodes led us into a bold new direction. This coincided with Mick's new phase of out-and-out rebellion against authority at home and school, which surely centered on his hostility toward his dad.

Whether it was because they were too different or too much alike, the father and son just didn't get along. It was a catastrophic situation. The more Mr. Rhodes disciplined Mick for his misdeeds, the more Mick retaliated. It was a vicious cycle: Mick would do something wrong, get punished for it, and then punish the punisher (his dad) by doing something else wrong. The cycle would repeat over and over, each time getting progressively worse.

It was like living next door to a war zone. With my own ears, I witnessed firsthand what became the talk of the neighborhood: roaring, vicious arguments; blood-curdling screams, shrieks and the moans you'd expect from a house of horrors, not to mention the thuds, crashes, and shattering of flying objects.

From my perspective, Mick's story had the same elements of that of rock legend Jim Morrison of the Doors: the domineering military father, the intense power struggle, and the rebellion and self-destructive behavior. It was like a real-life Greek tragedy unfolding.

Or, more accurately, a tragic-*comedy*—for Mick, at the time, seemed to get funnier as time rolled on.

Like I said, I was two grades above Mick, but the stories about his shenanigans at school spread. Even to this day, former classmates still talk about the outrageous things he had done. There was the time Mick "crazy-glued" all the locks of the school. Another time, he managed to tie the teacher's shoe laces together when she dosed off during reading time. Yet another time, he and another student snuck into the library and dubbed over the instructional audio tapes with the "Bozo's Radio Hour" –featuring Mick as deejay and the "world's most famous clown."

When I tell people at class reunions that Mick and I were best buddies, they shake their heads in wonderment like I used to be the sidekick of outlaw Jesse James.

★ ★ ★

I'll never forget the tower incident. It occurred at the railway observation tower I'd described earlier, the one we'd routinely climbed after seeing the Cogleys do it once.

I'd hung out with the Cogleys and their gang only a couple of times, but, I, for the most part, kept my distance. Mick, on the other hand, started to mingle with them more. While doing so, they introduced Mick to the fine art of shoplifting (among other things). After that, it didn't take long before Mick got me—and a new friend Randal Stark—into it.

We'd often go into department stores like K-Mart and stealthily fill our pockets with merchandise like candy and other snack items, cigarettes, and butane lighters. I think the thrill of stealing motivated us more than anything else. It was definitely an extension of our daredevil phase: the adrenalin rush derived from getting away with something, coupled with the exhilaration of one-upping your friends with increasingly risky frolics.

Shoplifting was child's play compared to what came next: dropping objects on motorists driving under the viaduct for fun, making sport of getting chased by railroad men and irate drivers, and, eventually, breaking into buildings.

★ ★ ★

It was a balmy Sunday afternoon in the spring of 1975, a time when most businesses are closed. Mick, Randal, and I made our usual rounds at the Tracks, with no agenda in mind, except to goof around. Still, like a shopper always looking for bargains, Mick kept a sharp eye out for the next opportunity to take something that didn't belong to him.

As we strode by the site of ABC Construction Company, Mick closely examined the premises through the chain-link fence on the side adjacent to the Tracks.

"Man, that place looks easy!" he exclaimed.

Mick, the impulsive personality he was, blithely leapt over the fence, swaggered over to the building, and peered in the windows without consulting us.

"Yup, just as I thought, they left the window wide open!" he yelled over to us.

Randal and I peered at each other speechless, but at the same time, we were amused by Mick's audacity. He made the most outrageous acts look so effortless. Like the Cogley twins, Mick had become immune to the fear of imminent danger and getting caught. But what set Mick apart from the twins was his distinctive charm and acumen—marks of a true sociopath (though I don't believe he was).

Mick once again worked his dark magic on us. Early on, Randal seemed to be on board with Mick's spur-of-the-moment stratagem to loot the building. I, on the other hand, hesitated—and for good reason. Months before, the police caught me helping my other friends Jeff Tarantino and Vlad Grabb, burglarize the White Pine warehouse just across the tracks. After getting arrested, I was taken to the police station, fingerprinted, subjected to the good cop/bad cop routine, and all the rest. The worst part was when my parents came to pick me up. Their disappointment in me impacted me far more than any punishment they could mete out. Naturally, I swore to never repeat the sordid episode as long as I lived and I meant it. Nevertheless, at ABC Construction, my ironclad resolution quickly succumbed to the strong peer pressure from my two closest friends.

Once in the main building of ABC, the three of us grabbed what we wanted. Whether it was his astute observation skills, keen instinct, or just lucky guesswork, Mick pegged it exactly right: the security of the place sucked. We effortlessly came in through the back window and immediately found in plain sight the master key to all the padlocks on the premises. Duh?

All and all, I made off with a dozen or so locks, a denim jacket, and a girly magazine. Among other things, Mick and Randal pillaged two fire extinguishers.

However, Mick—accidentally or on purpose—activated one of the fire extinguishers in the main office! Its foamy contents hurled into the air with the velocity of a gushing fire hydrant. Losing control of it, Mick dropped the cylinder-shaped canister on to the floor, lunged out of its way, and took cover. Randal and I followed suit. The extinguisher convulsed vigorously in different directions like a demoniac badly needing an exorcism. We breathlessly watched its snake-like hose spew white foam all over everything in sight, including desks, file cabinets, chairs, the floor, the ceiling and even us.

Energized by the spectacle, Mick created more chaos by throwing all kinds of stuff around—paper, binders, books, files, staplers, waste paper baskets, etc. He threw a mirror across the room and shattered it into a million pieces. While doing all these things, he laughed maniacally as if he was having the time of his life. He got so carried away we practically had to drag him out of there like some disorderly drunk.

The joy of thievery and vandalism eventually gave way to the deep-seated fear of getting caught. At some point, it triggered our frantic flight from the crime scene.

Before we left the Tracks entirely, Mick, to our incredulity, broke ranks with Randal and me, as if pursuing some last-minute inspiration like putting the cherry on top of the desert. He turned around and proceeded to climb up the tower!

"What in the hell is he is doing?!" Randal exclaimed.

Carrying the second fire extinguisher, Mick scrambled up to the highest platform and, with a half-crazed smile and cackle, he released the valve of the extinguisher.

"FFFFFFFFFFFFFFFFFFFFFSSSSSSSSSSSSSSSSSSSSSST!"

A continuous stream of water vapor or carbon dioxide—in the form of a dense white cloud—shot up into the blue sky!

Randal and I watched the phenomenon utterly petrified, thinking Mick's impudent "final touch" may had finally done us in.

On the other hand, you had to laugh. And we laughed our heads off hysterically. There it was: Old Faithful, the great geyser of Yellowstone Park, before our very eyes—atop the observation tower no less. I'm sure it could be spotted for miles around by everyone on that clear day, including the cops.

For better or for worse, we never got caught.

CHAPTER 19

THE HOBO ARCHETYPE

ANOTHER VALUABLE THING I had learned in Psych 101 is the theory of archetypes. According to psychologist Carl Jung, universal, mythic characters—archetypes—reside in the human psyche. Each archetype has a pattern, theme or agenda that motivates it. By far the most popular archetype is the Hero. Every culture, past and present, has heroes: Ancient Greece had Odysseus; Medieval England had King Arthur; America had John Wayne.

When we were younger, Mick and I tried to emulate our heroes like Batman, Secret Agent Man, cowboys, explorers, and pioneers. Then, at adolescence, we bit the apple. After that, our heroes were *anti*-heroes—rock stars, rebels, outlaws, daredevils, and even crooks. Our role models went from selfless, duty-bound champions, to self-indulgent, lawless rascals (with a few exceptions of course).

Writer Joseph Campbell had famously said the Hero has "a thousand faces"—the Warrior, the Rescuer, the Superhero, the Soldier, the Dragon Slayer, the Winner, etc. I'd picked a strange one to be sure—the Hobo.

Am I the only person who ever wanted to be a hobo? Not at all. Many famous people were hobos at least one time in their lives: John Steinbeck, Jack London, Louis L'Amour, George Orwell, Clark Gable, Robert Mitchum, and President Lyndon Johnson.

For me, the hobo thing started when I read in *Rolling Stone* that my idol Bob Dylan idolized Woody Guthrie. And, then when I saw actor David Carradine portray Guthrie as a happy-go-lucky hobo in the movie, I wanted to sign on.

★ ★ ★

What exactly is a hobo? Most people think it's the same thing as a "bum" but it's not.

Hobos may be homeless, but they're not destitute. They possess a certain dignity because they choose their simple way of life. They value their independence and freedom. Being a hobo is definitely a step up from being a bum. According to the Hobo Convention website,

> *"A hobo wanders and works, a tramp wanders and dreams, and a bum neither wanders nor works."*

A hobo is another name for a "migrant worker," one who travels around, yet manages to get jobs. (By this definition, Rosie was a hobo.) He'll pick only temporary jobs so he can roam to his heart's content. He voluntarily lives on-the-cheap because he understands that "(true) wealth is the ability to fully experience life," as Henry David Thoreau said.

A bum, on the other hand, doesn't go anywhere or do anything out of laziness, alcoholism, or other reasons. They lack the sense of dignity that comes with autonomy and self-reliance. They're basically trapped, reduced to begging. The common panhandler is an example of a bum.

Then there's also a category between a bum and hobo called a "tramp." Tramps like to travel, but they don't like to work. Pete LeBlanc fit this description. (And, with all the free-loading I did, I probably flirted with tramp-hood myself, to be honest.)

Hobos achieved their legendary status during the Great Depression when jobs were scarce. Like the Joad family in *The Grapes of Wrath*, some people literally lost everything in the Dust Bowl. To make matters worse, transportation was a problem.

Instead of sitting around feeling sorry for themselves, certain individuals decided to do what's necessary to get to where the jobs are—walk, hitchhike, and even hop freight trains.

Their strength, courage and determination made them, in a way, real-life superheroes.

During their travels, these brave souls forged their own unique identity—the Hobo (perhaps short for "HOme-BOund"). Along with this new personae, they created their own distinct subculture, complete with special customs and codes. (Yes, there is such a thing as a "Hobo Code.") They spoke with their own jargon. They formed communities in wooded railroad right-of-ways called "hobo jungles."

The Hobo has a certain mystique: the free-spirit who's hard to peg or pin down. He's mysterious. He typically works in one place and moves on. Why are people suspicious of him? Is he running from the law? Is he a predator? Is he a deranged misfit? Cartoons, novels, and films portray the Hobo as a ragged happy-go-lucky clown who steals pies out of people's windows. But stealing, of course, violates the Hobo Code.

The Hobo is a *romantic* figure—a rustic poet or minstrel who plays guitar, harmonica, and sings. He always has some mangy pet like a stray cat or dog. He tells stories, albeit earthy ones, before a campfire while roasting a wiener on a stick. He goes around performing random acts of kindness like Woody Guthrie did.

That's the other thing that distinguishes bums and hobos: Hobos go around and help people.

Trains-Formation

Hobos are perhaps most famous for illegally boarding trains. (I'm not saying that this is a good thing.) This involves either sneaking on a train while it's still, or getting on one while it's moving. Both options involve trespassing of course (which is not okay).

The second option—what my friends and I referred to as "hopping" a train—is obviously dangerous. You could easily slip and fall under the wheels, get dismembered or even killed. Another danger is getting hit by loose chains, straps and other equipment when you get too close to a moving train. As with hitchhiking, we teenagers pooh-poohed talk about potential risks, thinking we're invincible.

About twenty minutes after the train took away our backpacks, another train in the distance came chugging along the tracks in the same direction. It was going about 10 mph. The locomotive passed, followed by its gondolas (cars with open tops), reefers (refrigerated boxcars), stock cars (ventilated boxcars for livestock), and flats (cars carrying large bulky items).

We never caught a glimpse of the caboose. Pete managed to board one of the boxcars by grabbing a step ladder. I followed suit seconds later, except I boarded the next boxcar.

After getting a firm two-handed grip on a middle rung of a ladder, I hoisted my lean 130 lb. frame with all my strength and secured my dangling feet onto the bottom step. Once in a stable position, I contemplated my next move. Peeking around the corner of the boxcar, I noticed another ladder next to me on the side facing the coupling. Next to that was a three-foot long, one-foot wide, metal grate platform suspended just above the coupling between boxcars.

I carefully maneuvered myself over to the platform via the second ladder. It was a nerve-wracking process, to say the least. All the while, wind blew in my face. The train shook like an earth tremor as it picked up speed. In addition to the vibration caused by the wheels on the track, the boxcar jerked back and forth slightly because of what railroaders call "slack."

I let out a sigh of relief once I safely made it to the platform where I'd remain for the next two hours. Unfortunately, I could never get comfortable. The platform secured my body weight, but it was only designed for standing, so I had to crouch down periodically when my legs got tired. My senses constantly stayed on high alert, hyper-aware that my life depended on how securely I held the vertical bar next to me.

The experience of riding a train between two boxcars was a striking contrast to riding in Nathan Biddle's cozy locomotive cab earlier that day. I had a good view of the "moving" ground under the train. It produced a sort of light show that dazzled the eyes, but the rapid succession of railroad ties flashing by gave me a headache after a while. The dirty, grimy space I occupied was a high-decibel echo chamber involving three elements—the constant rumbling of the wheels on the tracks, the persistent pounding caused by the "play" between the two knuckles of the coupling, and the loud hissing of the air brake. The so-called janney-style coupler below me was very prominent in my field of vision. It looked like two giant clasped hands. Next to that was a thick black rubber hose that ran between the two cars. I found out later that the snake-like hose was part of the train's air brake system.

As physically taxing as it was, this train ride was ten times more thrilling than Nathan's! I could go on and on describing the beautiful landscapes I passed by, but I'll forego that in order to elaborate on my inward thoughts.

First of all, the ride made me reminisce about the Tracks back home. Sure, my friends and I did a lot of stupid stuff there, but it was also the place where I had my best times. I'll always associate the Tracks with fun, adventure, and bonding with my friends. For better or for worse, it was the testing ground for taking bold risks and pushing the limits.

The Tracks was where it all began, the launch pad for The Grand Experiment!

Secondly, I realized hopping an actual train was a major milestone, as important as graduating, getting my first job, and even getting married! It was a kind of initiation rite—like when a boy becomes a man on a hunting trip—or, when a young person becomes a full member of the Church through the sacrament of confirmation.

Now, at this moment in time, I *crossed over*—from being an ordinary cross-country hitchhiker to a *real hobo*!

If only Mick Rhodes and Randal Stark could see me now!

Third, it dawned on me just how profoundly my heroes influenced me. Singing train songs made me think of this, most notably the ones by Woody Guthrie's two sons: Arlo Guthrie ("City of New Orleans") and Bob Dylan ("It Takes a Lot to Laugh, It Takes a Train to Cry"). Arlo is Woody's biological son; Bob is (or was) Woody's spiritual "son."

I read in *Rolling Stone* that when Bob Dylan first started out, twenty-year old Bob (aka Robert Zimmerman) admired and identified with Woody so much that he *became* Woody Guthrie. The transformation shocked the people who knew Bob. He went from a dreamy, introverted, and restless Jewish kid from Hibbing, Minnesota to an outgoing, wise-cracking minstrel from rural Oklahoma. It was like his later religious conversion. With his newly-acquired vagabond threads, Okie twang, and acoustic guitar, Bob looked like he just got off a boxcar from the Dust Bowl days. Some said he was being phony, but Dylan would later assert that his "conversion" to Woody was the real deal. He took on the new identity because he wasn't pleased with his former "bland, directionless self."

I, like the young Dylan, went beyond being an avid fan of those I'd admired (Dylan, Springsteen, Lennon, etc.). I consciously and unconsciously directed my thoughts, intentions, attitudes, speech, and actions to be just like them—or even, in a sense, *be* them! The act of hopping the train demonstrated this spectacularly, as well as in more subtle ways.

Sure, I liked "being me" and I had a strong sense of my own identity. But, in no small part, my identity was informed by and patterned after my heroes. Their words in song lyrics and in *Rolling Stone* interviews, and their public actions guided me like the stars help navigate ships. I observed this phenomenon going on in Pete LeBlanc as well: Talking to Pete was like talking to Dylan himself, Holden Caufield, or his friend and mentor Dave Zarret. It was weird.

I'd seen other people do this as well. Glenn and Emily Erikson identified with pioneers so much that they'd built a log cabin in the woods, lived off the land, and actually wore 19th century pioneer clothes. They literally morphed into Ma and Pa Ingalls! Similarly, Crow reinvented himself as an Indian. And Rosie Smith underwent in a similar personal transformation—from a teacher to kind of a female version of Jack Kerouac or else a hobo herself.

Mick Rhodes. What can I say about him in this regard? He was on a downward spiral to be sure, going from the boy who wanted to follow in his father's footsteps, to a spiteful teenager who wanted to stick it to his dad anyway he could. In the process, he exchanged one archetype—the Hero (his father, superhero, explorer, etc.)—for another: the Anti-hero (the James Dean-style rebel, the heavy metal rock star, the daredevil, etc.). He imitated anti-heroes and *became* one himself.

In spite of this, you had to admire Mick. Like the Eriksons, Crow, and Rosie, he took his new identity to the hilt. With Mick, it was all-or-nothing, no half measures. Burgling and vandalizing ABC Construction wasn't enough for him, he had to go for the cherry—Old Faithful on the top of the tower!

This made a lasting impression on me. I'm sure Mick's uncompromising attitude contributed to me wanting to "go all the way" with becoming a hobo.

Enter Randal Stark

> *"The only people for me are the mad ones, the ones who are mad to live, mad to talk, mad to be saved, desirous of everything at the same time, the ones who never yawn or say a commonplace thing, but burn, burn, burn like fabulous yellow roman candles exploding like spiders across the stars and in the middle you see the blue centerlight pop and everybody goes 'Awww!'."*

– Jack Kerouac, *On the Road*

The above quote may help solve the biggest riddle of my youth (or it may not): Why did Randal and I allow Mick Rhodes to corrupt us?

As seen, Mick led us by the nose like a couple of lackeys into his orgy of mayhem at ABC Construction Company. In addition, he single-handedly introduced us to stealing (beginning with shoplifting) and drugs (beginning with marijuana).

It's embarrassing to think that we sophisticated tenth graders succumbed to the come-ons of this short, scrawny eighth grader with a twenty-year-old voice. Mick was certifiably insane. Ah, but herein lies the problem: His *madness* was the very thing that attracted us to him. (This naturally brings to mind the teachings of Bhagwan Rajneesh—and Hooter, their embodiment. Does it not?)

In the months ahead, we lost touch with Mick. I heard through the grapevine that he'd gotten expelled from school twice and "escaped" from boarding school. I even heard a rumor that he got killed in a drug deal gone wrong. With Mick out of my life, second- and third-hand information didn't count for much.

The spotlight would then turn to my other friend— Randal Stark.

Mick and I of course had a long history. Randal, on the other hand, came on the scene much later, when he and I were in seventh grade. When I introduced Randal to Mick, the two of them seemed to hit it off immediately. This occurred in spite of their night-and-day differences. Unlike Mick, Randal never had an ax to grind with authority. My teachers considered Randal as a positive role model; my peers recognized him as a leader. Vice-president of the altar boys, he had a strong moral compass. He certainly didn't have anger issues like Mick.

Still, Randal did have one major character flaw: *He got bored easily.*

Regarding this area of weakness, I was more than happy to help him out by pointing out to Randal my miracle cure for boredom—Mick Rhodes.

However, "the cure" was much worse than the disease!

Like what Kerouac said in the above quote (referring to Neal Cassady), Mick was the human equivalent to fireworks. Mick had an uncanny way of turning you from an enthralled spectator to an enthused participant in his reckless antics.

For a while, Randal and I were on the same page about Mick. But things got complicated after the police busted me for the White Pine break-in. I found myself between a rock and hard place. If I returned to my old stealing ways, I risked getting arrested for the second time when the cops would surely throw the book at me. If I quit stealing, my friends would view me as a "goody two-shoes" and probably never speak to me again. As far as I was concerned, there was no contest. "Being cool" in the eyes of my friends was all that mattered, so I reluctantly played patsy to them.

Randal didn't always act as Mick's flunky. For instance, he's the one who initiated the business of climbing on top of the buildings by the Tracks. When Mick abruptly left our lives for good, Randal readily assumed the role of chief instigator, inspired by our bold but messy caper at ABC Construction. He conceived and mulled over schemes far more ambitious and extravagant.

His personality made him arguably more dangerous to me than Mick (which is saying something). His levelheaded, cautious, and detail-oriented nature made him a much more efficient crook than the impulsive Mick. He was unflappable.

Randal's morally upright character made him the ideal criminal mastermind.

Randal dreamed of pulling off the perfect crime and I admittedly helped him draw up the blueprint. Fortunately, Randal saw the light before we carried out our plan. For brevity's sake, I'll forgo the details, but let's just say he had his own White Pine experience. He got the shock of his life when he got caught doing something stupid. As Fate would have it, I wasn't there when it happened, and it prompted Randal to turn over a new leaf.

I think deep down Randal didn't like what we'd become. You might say he got bored of behaving badly.

Though he'd never take part in The Grand Experiment, Mick Rhodes arguably got the ball rolling.

Mick was our founding father.

His overactive imagination, zest for adventure, and foolhardiness inspired us to do other remarkably stupid things besides committing crime. For example, Mick took part in our epic bike trips to uncharted regions across the Detroit metropolitan area. Those excursions would serve as a grid for what was to come.

After Mick left our lives, Randal Stark and I would take everything to the next level. We would raise the bar with the first hitchhiking trip to New York in 1977. The New York trip would spawn my next trip to California with Pete in 1979, as well as another California trip with Randal in the summer of 1980. Randal's wanderlust would eventually prompt him to travel all over Europe alone starting in 1982.

It's funny to think it all started with an acute case of the blahs one hot afternoon in June of '77.

To elaborate on the account I gave Roy at Poverty Gulch, Randal and I were walking along the railroad tracks between our junior and senior year in high school. I kicked along a rusty can; Randal threw rocks at things. We were so bored we could rob a bank, but we'd long given up crime. I felt as lethargic and listless as a sailboat on the dead calm sea. Randal's doldrums made him look haggard and vacant.

Part of the reason for our sluggishness was the high humidity in the air and the hot sun. The other reason was Randal being himself and rubbing off on me. He was lazy and, like I said before, Randal was highly prone to boredom. He'd be highly motivated to start something, but quickly lose interest in it after a while. The unfinished projects clogging up his basement and garage testified to this. That said, he and I had always managed to find something fun to do together—except on that muggy day.

I kept rattling off the familiar list of choices—play pool or ping-ping in my basement, shoot hoops at my garage, listen to music, compete in board games, ride bikes, etc.—but Randal shot them all down one-by-one. Even going to the Tracks had become uninteresting to him.

There was another contributing factor to Randal's deep funk: *He was in love.*

All day, he'd been talking about a girl named Constance. I kept hearing about Constance this and Constance that. After a while, it got tiresome. Randal claimed he met her one enchanted morning in Daytona Beach, Florida while he and she were vacationing with their families during Easter break. They apparently hit it off when they spent a good hour chit-chatting in the hotel lobby arcade. To Randal's delight, he managed to get her phone number.

Ever since they parted ways, he fantasized about her day and night. However, there was one small problem—distance. Sixteen year old Constance lived 650 miles away. A drive from Detroit to Commack, NY, her hometown on Long Island, would take at least twelve hours. Without a car, money, and likely his parents' permission, the prospects of maintaining a love relationship from that far away appeared bleak.

But this did not discourage Randal, the incurable romantic. To him, true love transcended everything, including logistics. He was determined to get to Constance somehow!

Fortunately for me, a thunderous drone drowned out Randal's incessant talk about Constance.

It was the sound of an approaching train.

We got out of the way fast. We proceeded down the ballast and hid in the nearby thickets to prevent being seen by the dreaded "yellow fuzz," our name for the C&O Railroad cops. They could make your life miserable. As Bob Dylan once said in a song, "the railroad men drink up your blood like wine."

As the caboose disappeared into infinity and the blare subsided, we reemerged out of the tall grass and ascended back up the ballast. Randal's face beamed; I felt jubilant. It was like we both had the same idea at the same time. Then, the immortal words proceeded from one of our mouths...

"Are you thinking what I'm thinking?"

It was like the moment when history slipped from B.C. to A.D..

The word "brainstorm" falls way short in describing what Randal and I had conceived as that train went by. No, it was more like a brain-tsunami. Of course, I am talking about the idea of illegally boarding trains to New York to visit Constance.

It took time and considerable mental voltage between us to concoct a scheme. In brief, we ruled out the notion of hopping *moving* trains almost immediately ("too dangerous"). We settled for a more calculated plan—to stealthily slip into *motionless* trains in the middle of the night. Nevertheless, under close scrutiny, that plot quickly fell apart. Our biggest problem with it was lack of information. We couldn't find any detailed railroad maps to help us strategize and navigate. We had no way of knowing what exact direction trains were going. We had no means of predicting when trains stop and go. Where would we hide from the bloodthirsty railroad men? What would we do to pass the time while we're waiting for trains to move forward? How would we eat, sleep, and go to the bathroom when we're hiding in the cargo of some boxcar for countless hours? Etc. Etc.

After wracking our brains in Randal's basement, we realized the whole notion of sneaking onto non-moving trains—let alone moving ones—was ludicrous.

Was there another way to get to New York? Other options included taking a Greyhound bus, an Amtrack passenger train, or a plane—all of which didn't appeal to us at all. First, they all cost money. Second, they were all *boring*.

In spite of its many drawbacks, train-hopping (whatever method) had one thing going for it: the thrill of adventure.

Everyone knows that authentic adventures involve some element of risk. Still, *too much* risk could be bad (in fact, *very* bad—disastrous and even fatal). Was there an alternative mode of transportation that was adventurous—yet safer?

Then the idea came: "Hey, why not *hitchhike?*"

The Agent

"HHHHHHHHHHHHHIIIIIIIIIIISSSSSSSSSSSSSSSSSSS!" the air brakes murmured. The increase of sulfur-like odor in the air, graffiti on the walls, and overall grunginess of the environment had indicated that Pete and I were entering the big city—Cheyenne, Wyoming.

The rail yard was epic scale. It consisted of rows upon rows of trains and open tracks running mostly parallel and adjacent, but also merging and converging. As our train eased into a state of inertia, the cars next to me on both sides completely obstructed my view, save for several empty flat cars like the one our backpacks were on.

The number of the trains boggled my mind. I began to worry that the odds of locating our packs in this labyrinth was a million to one. And there was no guarantee they were even in Cheyenne at all. For all we knew, they could be on their way to Denver, Boise, or God-knows-where-else.

Pete was the first to leap off the train. I did so seconds later, landing in a bed of sooty ballast rocks next to a cardboard box of flares. Seeing my partner alive-and-well made me breathe a sigh of relief. All along, I'd trusted that he was on the boxcar ahead of me, but couldn't be totally sure. You might say, I had *faith* he was still there.

We compared notes about our train ride, but, realizing time was of the essence, we quickly shifted into search mode. Our plan to find our backpacks was simple: We'd fan out, each of us pacing along our own designated row between trains.

But before we even got started, a heavy-set guy with a blond beard and black cap stepped out in front of us from between two cars about thirty feet away.

"HOLD IT RIGHT THERE!" he hollered as he came rushing towards us.

Our initial impulse, of course, was to turn around and flee in the other direction. But, before we could, another man bolted out and blocked our path from that side. He had the look of a Marine sergeant with his lean, tightly-muscled body and buzz-cut.

We were hemmed in! The two men, presumably railroad cops, closed in on us.

"WHAT IN THE F*** ARE YOU GUYS DOING?!" yelled the lean guy.

Each man pounced on us. The fat dude hoisted Pete by the shirt collar and slammed him into the side of a boxcar. The lean guy roughed me up the same way.

"Wipe that f***in' smirk off of your face, you little dumb f***!" roared the skinny guy with gritted teeth, seeing me suppress my urge to crack up. His crude characterization of me was not off the mark. It's quite stupid to show the slightest hint of disrespect toward someone who's ready to pop your skull like a ripe zit.

Nathan Biddle had confirmed earlier what I'd already known: Railroaders resent trespassers to the bone. Punks like us are a constant thorn in their sides. We cause them countless headaches due to train delays, tedious paperwork, and legal hassles. And that's the least of it. We also unwittingly turn their lives into a real-life horror movie (the un-fun kind) when we get injured.

Given our circumstances, I couldn't have sounded more pathetic: "Come on, guys, all we want is our backpacks back. Have you seen them?"

"SHUT THE HELL UP, YOU F***ING MORON! COME ON, YOU'RE GOING WITH US!"

The weird thing was I didn't feel afraid or intimidated at all. I actually felt hopeful that this episode might turn out to be a blessing in disguise. If we're lucky, I thought, the railroad men might help us find our packs.

The train cops escorted us through the smoky rail yard until we arrived at a ramshackle modular structure where the big boss' office was.

When we got there, they sat us down next to a paper-cluttered desk in a room with a small square window and huge train yard maps on the walls. The entire atmosphere was shabby and utilitarian. Nothing in there had anything of aesthetic value, except for a few family portraits, a Rock City souvenir paper weight, and a yellowed Varga girly calendar from the year 1971. The joint reeked with sweat and stale cigarette smoke. There was a lone fly buzzing around.

We waited about a half hour before a tall, bald guy with horn-rimmed glasses and a mustache came in. He sat down at his desk, took off his glasses, and sternly looked us each squarely in the eye.

"What in the hell are you guys aimin' to do, huh? Get yerselves killed?!"

We nodded our heads respectfully, pretending to be contrite. Truth be told, I was a punk with an attitude problem, ready to start laughing at any second, but I managed to maintain my composure. Pete, too, kept a poker face, probably because he learned his lesson from smarting off to Officer Clouse back in Nebraska.

"Have you ever seen a train derailment before?!" the man continued.

"No," both Pete and I answered shaking our heads.

"Well, listen to me good, boys," he said as he pounded on the desk with his clenched fist. "We've found young people like you in wreckages... in bloody CHUNKS! Do you understand what I'm saying?!"

We nodded occasionally as the railroad boss proceeded to embellish the gory details about disembodied arms, legs, and even heads strewn on ballast rocks cast in the Rembrandt light of dusk, in order to scare and horrify the crap out of us. If his goal was to make us squirm, he was certainly successful—but it was more from boredom than intimidation.

After balling us out for twenty minutes, the boss told one of his assistants to run a background check on each of us (which would come up clean).

Then, with a sigh, the railroad boss told another assistant, "Alright, go ahead... call the Agent."

Hmmm, *the Agent.*

The assistant guy dialed some special hot line analogous to the Bat Phone in the other room. You could hear, "So... when can you get here?... Yes... yes... uh huh... see you then. Thanks. Bye."

Agent? Oh my gosh! The Agent. Who is the Agent? The very word evoked the mystery, fun, and coolness of all the fictional secret agents from my childhood, like The Avengers, the Man from U.N.C.L.E., and of course James Bond 007. Talk about an archetype!

Most of all, I thought of Mick Rhodes playing our all-time favorite make-believe character, Secret Agent Man. I could barely suppress my impulse to explode with wild laugher right then and there.

What a story to tell my friends back home!

But on further reflection, my wonderment gave way to bewilderment. And bewilderment turned into panic. Another connotation of the word "agent" evoked a deep-seated dread, even terror. It made me think of "Agency"—the "A" in the acronym C.I.A.—The Central Intelligence *Agency*. Thoughts of the CIA, FBI, and NSA agents blowing cigarette smoke in my face, administering cold showers, and locking me up in a ten-foot cell made me break out in a cold sweat.

"Holy Crap!" I whispered over to Pete after the big boss left the room. "They've called *the Feds* on us!" My partner just stared blankly into space.

Time seemed to move in slow motion as we awaited the Agent to arrive. Sitting up straight instead of slouching as before, I tried to control what seemed to be a tremor in my right leg. The chair I was sitting in seemed to get more and more uncomfortable by the minute.

Forty minutes or so later, probably about five in the afternoon, a fifty year old man, presumably the one we were waiting for, came through the door. He had thin brown hair with a bald spot, high-cheek bones, and a six feet tall frame. Sporting a neatly pressed suit, a bolo tie, and cowboy boots, he fit right in with the milieu of the city of Cheyenne, but not so much with the grungy atmosphere of the railroad office. The Agent's most notable possession was an off-white Stetson Cattleman-style cowboy hat in his left hand.

"*Let's go, gentlemen*," the Agent said in a flat voice as he smoothly put on his hat.

We jumped to our feet, stepped out of the prefab office structure with our escort, and entered a running vehicle—a yellow 1978 Jeep CJ7. The man started driving, not saying a word suggesting he may be harboring dark thoughts regarding what he was going to do with us next.

I swallowed hard as the tension began to mount. My head, arms, and legs grew numb as the vehicle went along a weedy dirt path along a train.

Then it happened.

The Agent parked right next to a flat car—the very one our backpacks were on! They were laying right there next to each other, a bit sooty but just as we'd left them.

"Okay, guys, you're free to go."

Huh?

To this day, I ask myself the question: Why didn't the railroad company press charges? It seems so unbelievable. My best guess is they wanted to spare themselves the paperwork. But I like to think that the final decision-maker sympathized with The Grand Experiment.

Naturally, our hearts swooned with a combination of joy, awe, and relief. Pete and I blithely got out of the jeep, merrily picked up our belongings, and cheerfully went on our way as the motor vehicle took off.

As far-fetched as it seems, Pete's faith was rewarded! The ending of this episode seemed almost too perfect like a *deus ex machina*, a contrived tacked-on ending, where some divine entity suddenly swoops down and saves the day.

Yet that's what really happened. God is my witness.

Was it a bona fide *miracle*? As we ponder this question, I think Union Pacific Railroad deserves some degree of credit for helping us recover our backpacks. Its efficiency is amazing! As Nathan Biddle said, nothing in railroading can be taken for granted: The stakes are high and the potential for disaster is imminent. This would make necessary constant surveillance, meticulous inspections at each check point, and the timely reporting of mysterious objects like our backpacks.

True, most of life's mysteries have a rational explanation. But there's another aspect about the day's experience that's not as easy to explain: the impeccable *timing* of the second train, the one we were able to hop on so easily.

Was it sheer coincidence that it came just at the right place at the right time? Was it sheer luck? Or was it divine intervention? As for me, I must confess that my faith in the supernatural went up a few notches because of what happened.

Union Pacific Depot

As the evening drew near, motorists coagulated on I-90 and I-25. The traffic jams were probably attributed to those returning home after the nine day Fourth-of-July holiday. The vacation was over; it was time to get back to work the next day.

Pete and I restocked on provisions while checking out downtown Cheyenne, Wyoming.

Besides the state capitol, the city's foremost landmark is the Union Pacific Depot. The lavish train station was once the headquarters of the Union Pacific Railroad. Since it was a major stop along America's first transcontinental railroad, the company spared no expense in making it a monument to the railroad's triumph over the Wild West.

The Depot embodies the West. Spanning a city block or two, it appears tough, audacious, and "full-of-beans" like the Cowboy archetype. Its architecture is both traditional and flamboyant. There are all kinds of surprising intricacies, such as anomalous sculptured shapes, dormers topped with triangles, and zig-zag masonry work. This eclecticism conveys something lively, playful, and individualistic like rodeos, the city's favorite pastime.

Completed in 1887, the three-stories-high complex is crowned with a very distinctive clock tower. It can be seen for miles around. The clock itself, with its wrought iron numbers and wooden hands, is a statement of how the railroad had influenced our conception of time—by *standardizing* it. The railroad single-handedly came up with the system (Eastern

Standard Time, Pacific Time, Mountain Time, etc.) that everyone follows and takes for granted.

O, the wonders of modern life!

Having to keep pace with everything—up to the millisecond—is precisely what's driving everyone crazy.

We've come full circle! That's precisely why Pete refused to carry a watch. as he told Rosie at the beginning of this story.

And, speaking of time...

★　★　★

In my opinion, Henry Ford's words "History is bunk" are bunk. I thought a lot about history on the trip, especially important figures in my own personal history.

Mick Rhodes and I would see much less of each other after the tower incident. The most memorable last encounter is the time when Mick invited me over to his house to party. Just like old times, we joked around, laughed, and goofed around as we got high on marijuana while listening to loud heavy metal music.

Nothing in particular stands out except for the realization that we were in the same basement where we once played with Lionel trains.

By our teen years, Mick himself ended up a total train wreck (pun intended). His father no longer lived at the house, making his son the de facto master of his home—instead of his mother. He did whatever he felt like doing, which included virtually trashing the place. I heard his poor mom upstairs plead with him to do something productive, but Mick only gave her lip service.

One time my mother dared to yell at him over something and we got a brick through a window. I confronted Mick about this malicious act of vandalism, but he strongly denied doing it.

Sadly, I didn't believe a word he said. After we argued, our relationship came to an abrupt end.

★ ★ ★

I last saw the Cogley twins at a funeral home. Noel was there mourning. Who was in the casket? Neal! The daredevil he was, sixteen-year old Neal had decided to go swimming in Fair Lane Lake at the Henry Ford Estate, ignoring the "DO NOT SWIM" signs. He wound up getting tangled up in the weeds on the bottom and drowning.

Randal Stark. Much more needs to be said about him. He was always the guy you could stake your total confidence in. He knew how to get things done *exactly right*—even when he was exactly wrong. (Yes, he could be disastrously wrong, especially when he got involved with the likes of Mick Rhodes and me!) Randal demonstrated how boredom can motivate you. True, he could lose interest in things he started on, but he certainly didn't lack ambition. He could "spike the ball" when he wanted to.

The best example is when he delivered his unforgettable "Apron Strings" speech to my mother the night before we left for New York. It was one for the history books (at least my own history book), as forthright, gut-wrenching, and inspiring as Jimmy Carter's malaise speech would be, if I could be so bold. To talk my iron-willed mother into letting us go was nothing short of a miracle! How did he do it?

The other ambitious thing Randal did was help me start a new world religion, once we got back from New York.

– END OF BOOK ONE –

BONUS SECTION

Excerpt from Book 2 of *THE LAST HOBO* series:

THE LAST HOBO'S QUEST: A Dearborn student
searches America for life's meaning
the summer disco died

STRANGE REBELS

It was the best of times, it was the worst of times, it was the age of wisdom, it was the age of foolishness.

– Charles Dickens, *A Tale of Two Cities*

TALK ABOUT A TIPPING POINT! In his 2014 book, *Strange Rebels*, journalist author Christian Caryl makes an astonishing claim: The 21st Century began in 1979, the year Pete LeBlanc and I hit the road. Even back then, I sensed we were entering a new age. I submit that this hinge of history could be further narrowed down to the summer we went on our trip—the summer of '79.

Historians must have been dumbfounded because what happened in 1979 was so unexpected.

Suddenly, all their predictions of the future had to be thrown out the window. Two religious figures had a hand in these shocking developments—Ayatollah Khomeini and Pope John Paul II. Khomeini started the Islamic Revolution in Iran that's still underway today; John Paul II sparked the spiritual awakening in Poland that would eventually spread across Europe and take down America's number one enemy, the Soviet Union.

In July of 1979, a different kind of spiritual leader came to the scene. His name was Steve Dahl, the rock & roll deejay. He would lead his followers to destroy *disco*—the music we loved to hate—in a crowded Chicago baseball stadium. The war was over and the good guys won. Who knew that Dahl's Disco Sucks movement began in my hometown, Detroit?

Religious fervor spread far and wide that year. Highly unorthodox sects had gathered momentum in the Western world since the early seventies, such as Hare Krishna, Scientology, and the one started by Bhagwan Shree Rajneesh— the guru Rosie Smith turned me on to at Poverty Gulch.

What a time to be alive! What a remarkable moment in history to embark on my spiritual quest—while hitchhiking across the United States! Fortunate for me, I had people like Rosie, Pete LeBlanc and Blaise to guide me in my hot pursuit for the truth.

The St. Francis Connection

Monday, July 9, 1979

We awoke to a blustery morning on the outskirts of Cheyenne, Wyoming. I realized what it was: my traveling partner Pete LeBlanc and I were going to see Rosie again at last! She was staying with a friend in Greeley, Colorado who lived only an hour away south down U.S. 85.

Beyond the hotels, gas stations, and restaurants near the Interstate 80 - Highway 85 intersection, miles and miles of sagebrush surrounded us, save for a few farms, ranches and mining areas. The ethereal presence of the Rocky Mountains in the distance gave me a sense of reverence. We had opted to camp close to civilization because of possible rattlesnakes, scorpions, and antelope poop.

Pete and I situated ourselves along 85 in front of a farm animal feed store where it would take over three hours to get a ride. As typical during long waits, my mind would ruminate about practically everything. While I was in my mental tree house, one particular insight floored me:

Maybe I wasn't going home after all!

Up to that point, I had always assumed I'd return to the Detroit area to continue my studies at the U of M Dearborn, but now I wasn't so sure. If I'm having the time of my life traveling, why stop? Rosie was right: The road is the best school. After checking out the United States, why not go on and see exotic places like Sweden, Istanbul, or even India. Besides, why waste my time getting a formal education when the world is about to end?

But then it dawned on me: What will my parents think? I doubt that they'll approve of my career choice of being a hobo.

I grew up in a Catholic home. Being deeply devout, Mom and Dad naturally prayed my brothers and I would follow the example of the saints. But there was at least one instance, my mother may had regretted doing this.

It happened when she and I were watching a movie about St. Francis of Assisi on TV called *Brother Sun Sister Moon*. Set in 13th century Italy, it tells the story of young Francesco (Francis) who goes from a worldly son of a wealthy textile merchant, to a wandering Catholic ascetic who practically invented the vow of poverty. In the film, his dramatic religious conversion takes place in the public square. He's kneeling on the ground in his fine clothes before the town bishop.

"My soul is in your hands," cries Francesco with his head lowered. The bishop is stunned because he had heard disturbing things about this firebrand. The young man was in some kind of trouble, running from the law or something.

Francesco's father, who arrives at the scene a short time later, confirms his suspicions. The middle-aged man is totally incredulous. He claims his son threw all his material possessions out of the window!

The bishop asks the youth what he has to say for himself.

"I want to be... to be *happy*." Francesco responds. "I want to live like the birds in the sky. I want to experience the freedom and the purity that they experience... I want to feel the firm grasp of the earth beneath my feet without shoes, without possessions... I want to be a *beggar*. Yes. Yes, a beggar. Christ was a beggar, and his holy apostles were beggars. I want to be as free as they are."

Then Francesco starts taking off his clothes— right there in plain sight of the crowd! He does so until he's completely naked.

As my mother and I watched this on TV, Mom looked over at me anxiously and said, "Now I don't want *you* going out and doing that!" Knowing how batty I was, she worried about me being negatively influenced by St. Francis of Assisi!

In 1979, *Brother Sun Sister Moon*, released in 1972, was said to be out-of-date because of the movie's sixties "flower power" message. But I thought it was true to life. First, it justified me making a clean break from my parents. Second, as Thomas the Pirate had said: "You gotta be radical!" and, in the movie, St. Francis is definitely radical. Like Francesco, Thomas' partner Crow used his clothes—or, more accurately, his lack of clothes—as a symbol of his refusal to compromise his principles.

Third, the film underscores an important aspect of The Grand Experiment—spirituality. As we've seen in my first book *The Last Hobo,* The Grand Experiment could be summed up by the phrase: "Do your own thing." But *Brother Sun* introduces another element—God.

Francesco indeed "does his own thing"—but he follows the Supreme Being in doing so.

However, Francesco (in the movie at least) does not hold the common conception (or misconception) of God—a deity who is the celestial "tyrant" in the sky who always "tells people what to do." In *Brother Sun,* Francesco follows the God of nature. He's the One who sets you free and rescues you from the things that entrap your soul—like materialism, corrupt society, and the establishment.

In a way, Rosie Smith was a female version of St. Francis. Like him, she was a radical revolutionary who "chucked" everything from her former life in order to be authentic and experience nature. She quit her day job as a teacher so she would not succumb to the "loveless toil" that filled her days. She was looking for "something more" in life and fervently went after it. She pursued life itself! Without material possessions and personal responsibilities distracting her, she could focus on what's really important and "be happy."

Nevertheless, in other areas, Rosie didn't exactly emulate St. Francis. She—along with the rest of the Poverty Gulch gang—engaged in wild partying, "free love" and other activities that I'm sure my mom would not have approved of.

"Lucky"

The next car that pulled over gave me pause. It was a '71 Ford Pinto, not exactly Detroit's pride and joy. Over the years, the model has earned the dubious distinction as "one of the worst cars ever made." The Pinto's laughing stock status had been tempered by the serious fact it was dangerous to ride. Even a minor rear-end collision could turn the car into a flaming deathtrap. The Pinto raised concerns even before it went on sale on September 11, 1970. Pre-production crash tests had already confirmed that it had a faulty fuel tank, but Ford Motor decided to release it anyway so it wouldn't adversely affect its bottom line. This proved to be a disastrous mistake. At first, the small compact car sold well. But after that first highway accident, then another, then another, consumers began to sour toward the car.

Things got so embarrassing for the company that it had to drop a line from one of its radio ads: "Pinto leaves you with that warm feeling."

After we put our backpacks into his trunk, the driver, a middle-aged Hispanic man, looked Pete and me over up and down. Deciding we must be harmless, he let us into his gold-colored Pinto. Before we drove away, he made sure we buckled our safety belts.

"Man, I'm really glad I picked you guys up!" he exclaimed. "It's not safe around here. The rednecks and cowboys are lunatics. They'd beat the crap out of you and leave you to die just for fun. You're lucky to be alive!"

"*You're lucky to be alive.*" These were the exact words coming from a Pinto driver. And his nickname just happened to be "Lucky."

"What's wrong with you guys? Don't you know hitchhiking is dangerous?"

"Yeah, we know." Pete's reply sounded blasé. He tried to be respectful, but he'd heard this question so many times.

"Oh, you *do*, huh?" Lucky went on to say that murder, rape, and other crimes happened there on a regular basis. Was he exaggerating? This was *Cheyenne* he was talking about, not Detroit. It sounded like the only difference between here and back home was the part about "cattle getting gored in the middle of the night for no apparent reason."

Lucky proceeded to recount crime stories from other parts of the country.

"Have you heard about that John Wayne guy?

"The movie actor, of course."

"No, the one who lured all those young men, killed them, and buried their bodies under the floor of his house?"

"Oh, you mean *Gacy*. John Wayne Gacy," I corrected Lucky. How could I forget the name of a serial killer? My mother kept bringing him up when she tried to talk me out of going on my trip. The "Killer Clown" was arrested only six months before I left on my trip.

"With respect, Lucky," Pete finally said to the driver. "We don't worry about stuff like that. If we based our lives on the newspaper headlines, we wouldn't be able do anything. We'd spend our life away locked up in our houses."

"Yeah, practically everything you do in life is dangerous," I added. "Heck, you could get struck by lightning by just walking down the street."

"Oh, come on. You can't compare..."

"Look, the only time you're perfectly safe is when *you're dead*." I'd picked up this line from Rosie who said this on the day we first met her. Then I followed it up by paraphrasing something I'd read in Rosie's Bhagwan Rajneesh book: "Maybe life is *meant* to be lived dangerously. Danger is how you *find God*."

This deep philosophical statement left Lucky speechless. It was based on the following passage that I had scribbled down in my notebook at Poverty Gulch:

"Life exists in danger, pulsates in danger. Life exists in the ocean of death. It has to be dangerous; it cannot be safe and secure... One should live with the danger, with death hand in hand. Then tremendous dimensions open before you. Then God is revealed..."

I had found these words to be very comforting, much like Rajneesh's wise admonition to stop using reason.

The idea that "danger reveals God" seemed weird at first, but I eventually came to grasp its profundity. It was gloriously validated in our dealings with the trains the day before. Sure, what we did was extremely dangerous, but it had the positive effect of testing my confidence in the higher power. Now I had the faith that I could move mountains (well, almost). The uncanny chain of events involving the Union Pacific Railroad and the Agent *had* to be divinely orchestrated. It must've been all part of the master plan!

Impressed by these and other manifest wonders, I was beginning to think nothing seriously bad could ever happen to us. This notion made me feel safe and secure. It's like we were protected by some impenetrable force field. I attributed this to my conviction that Pete and I were special and chosen. Fate, I reasoned, always favored good guys like us. Calamity only befell fools with bad karma.

At this point in time, I thought I owed Pete LeBlanc an apology, but pride prevented me from saying, "Pete, I'm sorry I ever doubted you." As seen, his unshakable faith had annoyed me, but he was vindicated when we got our backpacks back. From the start, I'd been often skeptical of his eccentric views, but, at this point, I thought I finally saw the light.

"You guys are crazy, man!" Lucky said as he dropped us off. Then the Pinto driver shook his head and added rather ominously, "All I can say is I'll *pray* for you." Lucky was a devout Catholic. We had found that out from a religious picture attached by a magnet on his dashboard—Our Lady of Guadeloupe.

APPENDIX A

This Lawyer Spoke Loudly—
and Carried a Big Stick

By Tad Vezner, *Pioneer Press*
September 7, 2007

WHEN SPEAKING OF THE LATE Louise Miller O'Neil, many St. Paul judges and attorneys begged to talk in euphemisms about the defense attorney who married a convict, carried a shillelagh "for protection" and had her lingerie debated in the courtroom during St. Paul's most-crowded 1950s trial.

Miller O'Neil, who died Sunday at United Hospital of a heart condition at the age of 83, was the first female St. Paul courtroom lawyer many can remember. As late as last year, Miller O'Neil was still cutting a swath in the Ramsey County Courthouse in her wheelchair.

"I think I'd almost hate to have Louise on my back than some judge, frankly. She was upfront, didn't mince words. She would tell prosecutors (in chambers about her clients), 'Hey, he's guilty as sin—now what are we going to do about it?'" said Ramsey County District Judge Margaret Marrinan.

Miller O'Neil always had firm control over even the most hardened clients.

"I've watched grown men about 6-foot-6 come to tears after she got done scolding them," said son Patrick O'Neil. "I watched a guy getting lippy during a court session, she turned around and backhanded him and told him to shut it."

Former St. Paul Mayor Larry Cohen remembered one exchange between Miller O'Neil and her client while he was a Ramsey County judge. Cohen asked the client whether he'd been threatened by anyone to take a plea.

"Yeah, kinda," the client replied.

"Who?" Cohen asked.

The client pointed to Miller O'Neil—at which point she yelled, "You go ahead and tell 'em why! I told him he better damn well tell the truth and 'fess up on this case!"

Collecting fees from clients was a problem Miller O'Neil solved by going to the local watering hole on payday.

"Her clients—a lot of blue-collar guys—would go down to the bar, and she'd be waiting for them," her son said.

Miller O'Neil graduated from the University of Minnesota's law school in 1951 and that year was sworn into the bar, the lone woman alongside 42 men.

As she sought work at a law firm, the first question she faced was how fast she could type.

"All the law offices said they wanted her to be an educated secretary," said lawyer Terrance "Terry" O'Toole, who asked Miller O'Neil to join him in 1951.

O'Toole hardly regretted the decision: "She's as tough as they come," he remembered one judge telling him.

In 1956, she married Eugene Kenneth Joncas.

Four days after the wedding, St. Paul police were staking out her apartment.

Her husband—a burglar she had met while representing him—had violated his parole on a forgery charge by marrying her without the permission of his parole board.

That, and the fact he was subsequently convicted of a Rochester robbery.

"She left a note on the door of the parole board, saying, 'Kenny and I are getting married.' The parole board was very ticked off," remembered attorney Thomas Burke.

Joncas took the last name O'Neil because his wife liked the Irish sound of it, friends remembered.

The Miller O'Neil stories are nearly endless: One Duluth attorney quit the day after he lost a drug case to her. Attorney

Earl Gray remembers Miller O'Neil and her husband once drove into the side of a moving train. They sued the railroad and won.

Later, she went into solo practice, working out of her Summit Avenue home. Perhaps her most famous case, however, was filed against her when she was 30, after she had been appointed a commissioner of the St. Paul Housing Authority—a post that required she be a resident of the city. She claimed to live in a St. Paul apartment, but others said she lived in West St. Paul or South St. Paul.

Attorneys debated the size and style of underwear hanging in the St. Paul apartment, purportedly belonging to Miller O'Neil. While going to hearings, Miller O'Neil carried a shillelagh—a club—"for protection."

"The Louise M. Miller case has been drawing the largest crowds into Ramsey county district court since the Arthur Dezeler murder trial of 1946," a 1954 Pioneer Press article said.

In the end, the judge ruled against her.

Miller O'Neil attended South St. Paul High School and entered the University of Minnesota at age 16. She was a second lieutenant in the Air Force and a national officer of the Young Republicans before she became an avid DFLer in her later years.

Besides her son, she is survived by daughter Mary O'Neil, sister Henrietta Kessler, brother Gus Miller, three grandchildren and countless surrogate children.

"I couldn't even tell you how many people my mom adopted over the years that have lived in this (Summit Avenue) house. She'd take in just about anybody," Patrick O'Neil said.

A public gathering of family and friends will be held after 4 p.m. today at the North End Legion Hall, 72 W. Ivy Street in St. Paul.

APPENDIX B

Bucking the Trends: Black Hills Crusader Marvin Kammerer

By Charles Ray, *High Country News*
September 27, 2004

RAPID CITY, SOUTH DAKOTA—An old pickup rattles to the top of a grassy ridge. The Black Hills stretch across the western horizon, and in the valley below, the family ranch of Marvin Kammerer is only a dot in the fields of grass. Kammerer stops the truck, gets out and looks down on his land. Behind him, a massive runway cuts across the prairie, a pair of B-1 bombers roars overhead.

Kammerer grew up here, in the shadow of Ellsworth Air Force Base. His ranch abuts the end of the runway, and over the years he's seen several plane crashes—the cause of 36 deaths—on or near his property. "Every time one of those B-1 bombers fly over, it's a violation of my environment, not a protector of good," he says. "It's just a symbol of what we can do to destroy."

Kammerer, 67, has spent his life close to the land; he has mud caked on his boots, rough hands, and a face weathered by sun and wind. He often wears a worn-out hat, a vest over a thin plaid shirt, and a bandanna around his neck. He's also spent much of his life working for social and environmental justice in the Black Hills of South Dakota.

"I realized early that if you didn't fight for what you believed, nobody else was going to do it for you," he says. "I found out that what I thought of myself was more important than what the neighbors thought of me."

Kammerer says his beliefs stem from several influences, including his grandfather, who made himself unpopular back in late 19th century Germany by speaking out against his homeland's pro-war policies. As a child, he watched his relatives and friends go off to World War II, and he witnessed the early victories of progressive programs like the rural electric cooperatives and the Soil Conservation Service.

"I've raised seven kids, several horses, and some hell," he says. "I hope I've instilled a sense of responsibility in my children, so that if someday I have a grandkid on my lap and somehow the environment is all screwed up, I can at least say that I tried my best to not let it happen."

In the late 1970s, Kammerer helped form the Black Hills Alliance, a core group of concerned whites and Native Americans who joined forces to stop uranium mining and in the area.

Through direct action, public-awareness campaigns, national coalition building, and mass protests, the group made uranium mining in the Black Hills a national issue. As mining companies pushed into the hills, activists exposed the negative impacts uranium mining could have on the people, environment and economy of the state. In 1984, the Alliance helped to pass a statewide initiative to block low-level radioactive waste dumping in the Black Hills.

"It's only through the efforts of grassroots people that the rules and regulations were brought about to keep the corporate empires in check," Kammerer says. In 1980, Kammerer helped organize the largest mass protest in South Dakota's history. The Black Hills International Survival Gathering brought 12,000 people to camp on his property. The group built large rock symbols—a peace sign, a medicine wheel and an international symbol for the environment— that can still be seen from the air by the Air Force pilots as they take off and land. The Survival Gathering also called for an end to uranium exploration and the restoration of treaty claims of the Great Sioux Nation.

The land of western South Dakota was promised to the Sioux Nation in the Fort Laramie treaty of 1868, a treaty later broken when the Lakota, Dakota and Nakota Sioux were confined to reservations. Kammerer's grandfather—who migrated to America from Germany as early as 1881—homesteaded his ranch on Sioux land in 1886, the year he brought over his family from Europe. "We squatted on this land, and as far as I'm concerned we're still squatting," says Kammerer.

Kammerer's stance on treaty rights and environmental justice has won him many friends in the Native American community, and helped overcome some of the long-standing racial divisions in the state. "He's been kind of like a Lone Ranger," says JoAnn Tall, who was involved in the Black Hills Alliance in the late 1970s. "In South Dakota, we're in a real prejudicial and racist state, and for Marv to come out back in the day, (in support of treaty rights), many non-natives were kind of taken aback. But now, some people have come around to his way of thinking."

In the early 1990s, then-Gov. George Mickelson, a Republican, brought together natives and non-natives to talk through race issues, a process those on both sides say resulted in greater cross-cultural communication and understanding. But deep-rooted problems remain; in early 2000, a U.S. Civil Rights Commission study showed that Native Americans in South Dakota strongly believe there are racial disparities within the state justice system.

For Kammerer, the treaty rights of the Sioux people are connected to modern efforts to preserve the environment—and, ironically, to the struggle to keep "squatters" like him on the land. "The cowboys are now suffering the same fate as the Indians," he says. "We're being pushed off the land, and our way of life is dying."

Kammerer and his wife have taken second jobs over the years to keep the family ranch, which he hopes to one day pass on to his children. As the sun sets over the Black Hills, Kammerer climbs back into his truck and drives toward his ranch house. The pickup bounces across the prairie, and a B-1 bomber touches down. "This is a lifelong struggle," he says. "You don't make big waves. If you have any successes, they will be small ones. It's like taking a stone and throwing it in the water."

ACKNOWLEDGMENTS

I would like to thank the following people for making this project possible.

— Joan Kettel, my dedicated chief editor. When I compensated her with a Panera Bread gift card, she thought I was being too generous.
— Ray Kettel, Joan's husband, my former professor at U of M Dearborn, assisted in editing. Ray's biggest contribution, however, was his inspiring young adult literature class.
— Tim Grajek, my brother, for his outstanding cover art, designs, and illustrations.
— Those who proof-read and provided constructive criticism—Judy Alan, Joe Polgar, Lori Grajek, Justin Grajek, Andy Grajek, Janet Wunderlich, and Joe Cheff.
— Donna Trotter, who gave a phone interview regarding her deceased parents Lou and Doris Czeizinger.
— Marvin Kammerer, the real "Marvin the Rancher," who helped me fact-check information about himself and the Black Hills Alliance.
— Author Kevin Mattson. His popularly-written nonfiction book, *What the Heck Are You Up To, Mr. President?* (Bloomsbury USA, 2010)—about Jimmy Carter and the summer of 1979—was an invaluable resource.
— Writers Tad Vezner and Charles Ray for granting me permission to reprint their articles about Louise Miller O'Neil and Marvin respectively.
— Louis Markos who influenced the book philosophically.
— Lori, my wife, and her parents Rolf and Janet Wunderlich, who had encouraged me every step of the way.

COMING SOON...

Book 2 of THE LAST HOBO trilogy

THE LAST HOBO'S QUEST:
*A Dearborn student searches America for
life's meaning the summer disco died*

Based on a true story, *The Last Hobo's Quest* picks up where *The Last Hobo* left off. President Jimmy Carter at last delivers his historic "malaise" speech. Ted and Pete reunite with Rosie in Greeley, Colorado. Rosie has a deep dark secret and so does the town: It's haunted by the ghosts of author James A. Michener—and the mysterious wallflower who inspired none other than *Osama Bin Laden*!

As Ted makes his way west to San Francisco—through Boulder, Colorado; Salt Lake City, Utah; and Reno, Nevada—he continues to ponder Bhagwan Rajneesh's gospel of insanity, the coming New Age, and the event in Chicago that finally put disco music out of its misery.

The Last Hobo's Quest is an emotional roller coaster ride! Will Ted find the true spiritual path? What perils await him once he separates from his partner Pete? Will America heed the President's dire warning?

The story often refers to the unique city where Ted had spent most of his time—Dearborn, Michigan—the home of Henry Ford, America's largest Muslim population, and the ancestors of the ancient Phoenicians, the world's first swashbuckling adventurers.

...FROM ROUND BARN MEDIA

Book 3 of THE LAST HOBO trilogy

THE LAST HOBO FINDS PARADISE:
*A Motor City hitchhiker stumbles on the perfect world,
but is it too good to be true?*

THE LAST HOBO trilogy dramatically concludes when Ted continues to pursue his ambition to "change the world." He ends up in "Boonville," an isolated farm in California. It's some kind of training camp where "doing your own thing" is not okay. Every move you make is watched. Ted attends lectures all day and writes rambling letters to Randal Stark, claiming he's found The Promised Land.

Most of Boonville's inhabitants are nerdy. They subscribe to a faith that uncannily resembles "Karma," the religion Ted and Randal had concocted half-seriously during their New York hitchhiking trip!

Did Ted discover utopia—or the outpost of some bizarre religious cult? Will Ted sacrifice his freedom to join a movement that advances human solidarity and world peace.

Or, will he escape from being indoctrinated and stripped of all his individuality.

The Last Hobo Finds Paradise is a cautionary tale that's very relevant to today's headlines. It's "California Dreamin'" meets George Orwell's *1984*!

RoundBarnMedia.com

ABOUT THE AUTHOR

Dan Grajek grew up on Detroit's northwest side. By age twenty, he had hitchhiked to New York once and California twice. Once he settled down, he earned a Bachelors degree in Psychology at the University of Michigan Dearborn (UM-D). For over 20 years, he worked as a graphic designer and a marketing coordinator at two corporations and a non-profit organization. Later in life, he returned to UM-D to earn his Masters degree in Teaching. He had taught high school English at a residential detention facility for young women in Dearborn Heights. His all-time favorite accomplishment was marrying into a violin-making family. He is married to Lori, has three sons—Andy, Justin and Ben—and lives in Dearborn, Michigan.

ABOUT THE ILLUSTRATOR

Tim Grajek, Dan's older brother, has been an art professional for over thirty years. His illustrations have appeared in many major publications including *The New York Times, The Wall Street Journal*, and *US News and World Report*. He is the illustrator of *Hoyle's Rules of Games*, one of the most widely distributed books in the world. His picture book *The First Dog* is a collaboration with writer Benjamin Cheever. Tim has received awards from *Print* Magazine, Art Directors Club, and American Illustration. He earned his Bachelor of Fine Art degree at Eastern Michigan University.

DEAR READER...

Thanks for reading *The Last Hobo*! Now that you're done, do us a favor...

- Give us your **feedback** on TheLastHobo.com.
- **Friend us** on Facebook. Find us there at "The Last Hobo by Dan Grajek."
- **Spread the word**! Tell your family and friends about *The Last Hobo*.

Do *yourself* a favor...

- Go to TheLastHobo.com and **subscribe** to get access to **free bonus materials** delivered via a monthly email. Think of it like the "special features" option on a DVD. Get the inside scoop about me and the rest of the *Last Hobo* series as it's being developed.

  Sincerely,
  Dan Grajek

Books by Chester Himes
(First American editions and books published only in France)

If He Hollers Let Him Go. New York: Doubleday, 1945.
Lonely Crusade. New York: Alfred A. Knopf, 1947.
Cast the First Stone. New York: Coward-McCann, 1952.
The Third Generation. Cleveland: World Publishers, 1954.
The Primitive. New York: New American Library, Signet Book 1264, 1956.
For Love of Imabelle. Greenwich, Ct.: Fawcett World Library, Gold Medal Book 717, 1957 (republished in a revised and expanded edition as *A Rage in Harlem.* New York: Avon, Avon Book G1244, 1965).
The Real Cool Killers. New York: Avon, Avon Original T328, 1959.
The Crazy Kill. New York: Avon, Avon Original T357, 1959.
The Big Gold Dream. New York: Avon, Avon Original T384, 1960.
All Shot Up. New York: Avon, Avon Original T434, 1960.
Pinktoes. New York: G. P. Putnam's Sons/Stein & Day, 1965.
Cotton Comes to Harlem. New York: G. P. Putnam's Sons, 1965.
The Heat's On. New York: G. P. Putnam, 1966.
Run, Man, Run. New York: G. P. Putnam, 1966.
Blind Man With A Pistol. New York: William Morrow, 1969.
The Quality of Hurt. New York: Doubleday, 1972.
Black on Black: Baby Sister and Selected Writings. New York: Doubleday, 1973.
My Life of Absurdity. New York: Doubleday, 1976.
A Case of Rape. New York: Targ Editions, 1980 (republished 1994 by Carroll & Graff with a preface by James Sallis).
Le Manteau de rêve. Paris: Edition Lieu Commun, 1982 (translated by Hélèn Devaux-Minié).
Faut être nègre pour faire ça . . . Paris: Lieu Commun, 1986.
Un joli coup du lune. Paris: Lieu Commun, 1988 (translated by Hélèn Devaux-Minié).
The Collected Stories of Chester Himes. New York: Thunder's Mouth Press, 1991 (with a foreword by Calvin Hernton).
Plan B. Jackson: University Press of Mississippi, 1994 (edited with an introduction by Michel Fabre and Robert E. Skinner).

Contents

Introduction

Though much of Chester Himes's work was not widely read or appreciated during his lifetime, in the years since his death in 1984, interest in his writing has grown tremendously. Indeed, scholars increasingly rank him, along with his contemporaries Richard Wright, James Baldwin, and Ralph Ellison, as one of the more vibrant African-American writers of the post-World War II era. His early evocations of black men, hurled by racism into a self-destructive rush to oblivion, are as electric today as when they were written. Later, in his Harlem Domestic series, Himes offers a vivid portrait of a black underclass trapped in poverty and terrorized by criminals as much victims of racism as their prey.

The reappearance of nearly all of his fiction in the recent past suggests we are very close to a major reappraisal of Chester Himes, and this collection will help in that process. More than just a complement to or commentary on his creative work, these interviews are as much the story of Himes's career as his formal autobiography. To say that Chester Himes was obsessed with his own personal history is perhaps a bit of an understatement. His early novels are all highly autobiographical, and even his more popular fictions, published after he had become the darling of the French literary establishment, reflect his varied experiences as a petty criminal, convict, would-be writer, and expatriate. As these interviews make evident, perhaps the only thing he liked better than writing about his experiences was talking about them. As an interviewee, he could be charismatic, and with the right interviewer, such as his friend John A. Williams or French critic Michel Fabre, he could be quite revealing about himself and his contemporaries.

He showed a marked consistency in the subjects he discussed in his interviews. The importance of violence to American culture, the need for organized revolution in the fight for equality, the plight of the black writer exploited by a white publishing industry, as well as his sometimes acerbic judgments about his fellow writers, come up time and again.

During World War II, Himes had addressed the need for coordinated action in a fight for equality. In his essay "Negro Martyrs Are Needed" (*The Crisis,* May 1944), a publication that led the FBI to open a file on him, Himes offered the planned and organized martyr-dom of black citizens in forced confrontations with white authority as the most effective route to equality. The three-pronged approach he expresses is remarkably similar to that which Martin Luther King, Jr., would use in the 1950s.

Later, however, perhaps in response to the more violent revolution-ary feelings stirring in America, Himes altered his thesis, now advo-cating organized and violent rebellion. In an interview with Philip Oakes for the London *Times Sunday Magazine,* Himes said, "I've come to believe that the only way the American Negro will ever be able to participate in the American way of life is by a series of acts of violence . . . Martin Luther King couldn't make a dent in the American conscience until he was killed." Perhaps the most detailed expression of this philosophy came in a ground-breaking interview with John A. Williams in *Amistad 1,* in which Himes said, "for a revolution to be effective, one of the things it has to be is violent."

As Himes further developed this notion, it came to have political and economic implications for him. He told Michael Mok in a *Publish-ers Weekly* interview that the failure of such a revolution would exert such pressure on the American economy that the government "would give blacks whatever they wanted." Of course, one suspects that in trying this scenario out on interviewer after interviewer, Himes was actually perfecting the plot elements of his last two novels, *Blind Man With A Pistol* and *Plan B.*

A theme that appeared even more often in his interviews was the story of how his career was destroyed in America by a publishing industry dominated by communists and racists. A variation on this included how often he had been cheated by all of his publishers. He told John A. Williams that "the American system toward the Negro writer is to take great advantage of the fact that the black writer in America is always in a state of need." Charles Wright, in a feature in *The Village Voice* based on an evening he spent with Himes, quoted the writer as saying "you know, there is only one black writer. Just as soon as he makes it, they tear him down. We black writers have got to stop fighting each other. Whitey has always pitted one black against another.''

There is some irony in this charge, since Himes was often less than generous with the other black writers of his generation. Speaking of Richard Wright's motion picture production of *Native Son,* Himes said "I didn't discuss that film anymore with Dick because I thought it was the worst film ever made." Speaking about Ralph Ellison's *Invisible Man,* Himes said "while I think *Invisible Man* is a great book, I don't think [Ellison] introduced any new technique." He later holds up Ellison as a figure of fun when he condescends with the remark "he's very pompous, but when he relaxes he's quite congenial, quite a good chap." James Baldwin fares the worst, when in a comment about the black writers he esteems the most, Himes first gives a roll call of Ishmael Reed, Cecil Brown, and Ronald Fair, then concludes with "I hate to say this, but the only piece of James Baldwin's I've ever read was *The Fire Next Time,* which I read in *The New Yorker.*"

By the 1960s, Himes was well-known and highly-esteemed among the younger black writers. John A. Williams admires him almost unreservedly in his *Amistad 1* piece, and introduces the interview with the remark that "*The Quality of Hurt* is a fantastic, masculine work. American writers don't produce manly books. Himes's autobiography is that of a man." Williams, whose novels often reflect themes and ideological anger very close to Himes's own, makes it clear throughout the interview that he feels great sympathy for Himes's travails and indicates he has suffered some of the same misfortunes.

The British tended to unreservedly admire Himes, too. Philip Oakes, in the first of two pieces he did on Himes, refers to the writer as "a founding father of the Black Power movement," a claim that the expatriate writer, cut off from the mainstream of black American political activity, clearly relished.

Perhaps no one was more enthralled by Himes than Charles Wright of *The Village Voice.* Grandly referring to Himes as "Don Chester Himes," Wright gives a vivid picture of having been in the company of a witty and worldly man with whom he discussed everything from books to women. Himes's customary bitterness is missing from this

unusual interview, and Wright at one point rhapsodizes, "Chester
Himes might have been my father who had been away at war, away at
sea, or in prison for a decade."

The 1960s and '70s, in which these and other interviews were
published, were a golden moment in Himes's life. The hectic, peripa-
tetic early years in Europe, during which his work was largely forgotten and his career seemingly at an end, were far behind him. The
socio-political themes of his popular Harlem Domestic Series naturally stimulated interviewers to solicit Himes's opinions on racial
politics in America. At the same time, his cultured demeanor often
provoked discussions about his literary tastes and influences, and his
love of jazz.

One of the more interesting interviews is a conversation published
in France by the impressionist painter Jean Miotte. Again, Himes the
ravaged, embittered black artist is nowhere in sight. In his place is a
man of obvious sophistication and learning, commenting on everything from philosophy to music. There is a tremendous sensitivity
evident in Himes, too. After Miotte speaks admiringly of New York
City's stimulating environment, the pain of Himes's alienation from
his native land rises to the surface as he talks sadly of the rejection he
suffered there.

Much of what we know about Himes comes from these interviews,
and by putting them together with the identifiably autobiographical
portions of his novels and his two volumes of autobiography, something of a whole picture of the man emerges. Once readers get past
his frustration and anger at American racism, they discover that
Himes, although self-taught, is widely read, an expert on jazz, and a
keen observer of people, places, and things. Readers also cannot
overlook Himes's isolation in his adopted land and his intense loneli-
ness for the country he left behind.

It is worth noting, however, that the picture is sometimes confusing
because Himes occasionally contradicts himself and other times gives
out information that is incomplete or erroneous. More than once, for
example, he refers to a Communist denunciation of *Lonely Crusade*
that he says appeared in *The Daily Worker*. The review, which is
indeed unflattering, actually appeared in *New Masses*. He told a
British columnist he "was kicked out of Ohio State University for
spending too much time in the red light district." [Pendennis (column

title) "The Man Who Got Twenty Years," *The Observer* (June 29, 1969), p. 32] A columnist for *Jet* wrote that "Himes was studying medicine at Ohio State University. He was asked to leave because his health was poor, and as a result his grades were poor." [M. Cordell Thompson, "Chester Himes: Portrait of an Expatriate," *Jet* 42 (June 8, 1972), p. 29] Neither of these gives a picture that is quite consistent with the known facts.

Over the years, Himes either forgot much of his early career or made greater drama of it than was actually there. Several interviewers were told that *If He Hollers Let Him Go* made the best-seller list, when there is no evidence to support this claim. He told Philip Oakes that "*Esquire* bought one story, but there were no others," when in actuality *Esquire* bought seven stories from him between 1934 and 1942. He told yet another interviewer that *Esquire* bought his first story in 1934, for some reason forgetting the eight known stories that preceded it in black periodicals and newspapers. It bears mention that Himes's recollections of where his early work appeared have confused bibliographers and scholars for decades. Himes, on rare occasions, told interviewers things that do not appear elsewhere in his autobiographical writings. The most important example was when he told Michael Mok that "the two cops, Coffin Ed Johnson and Grave Digger Jones, are roughly based on a black lieutenant and his sergeant partner who worked the Central Avenue ghetto in L.A. back in the 1940s."

Himes uses interviews not only to tell the story of his career, but also to emphasize his successes and air his grievances. In this he was remarkably effective, because it is generally accepted by biographers and critics that his life and career are a triumph of perseverance over adversity. As in the case of his fiction, Himes is both the teller and the hero of his own tale. The interviews give us an indelible portrait of a proud, brilliant, and combative man who commands both our attention and respect. At the same time, they help forge an heroic legend around Himes that continues to endure long after his death.

As in other volumes in the Literary Conversations series, these interviews appear uncut and in the order in which they were conducted. Throughout, book titles have been italicized and typographical and factual errors have been silently corrected. Interviews being published here for the first time have been edited for publication.

Although every interview conducted with Himes in his lifetime was read and considered for this collection, some were eliminated from this volume because the editors felt they were too insubstantial to warrant inclusion. Others do not appear here due to an inability to obtain permissions from the original publishers.

Michel Fabre, Paris
Robert E. Skinner, New Orleans
April 1995

Chronology

1909	Chester Bomar Himes is born in Jefferson City, MO, on 29 July, to Professor Joseph Sandy and Estelle Bomar Himes.
1926	CH enters Ohio State University.
1927	CH is expelled from the university over a prank. He begins associating with criminals in Cleveland's Scovil Avenue district.
1928	CH is sentenced, on 27 December, to twenty years at hard labor in the Ohio State Penitentiary for armed robbery.
1930–31	CH begins writing in prison, probably at his mother's instigation.
1932	CH's first known story, "His Last Day," is published in *Abbott's Monthly,* an African-American magazine.
1934	"Crazy in the Stir" is published in *Esquire.* It is CH's first publication in a major periodical.
1936	On 1 April, CH is paroled after serving seven and a half years of his sentence.
1937	On 13 August, CH marries Jean Johnson in Cleveland.
1937–39	CH works at a variety of jobs to support his writing habit. He is known to work as a laborer, and as a writer of pamphlets and information circulars for the WPA. He is believed to have worked for the CIO as a writer of news articles and a history of the union.
1940	CH secures a job on novelist Louis Bromfield's farm. Bromfield takes him and Jean to Los Angeles where he tries to help him find movie work and to publish one of his novels. Bromfield is not successful.
1940–43	CH works in a variety of war industries, and begins writing *If He Hollers Let Him Go.*

1944   CH is granted a Rosenwald Fellowship to complete his
          novel.

1945   *If He Hollers Let Him Go* is published and receives a
          generally positive critical reception. His mother dies.

1947   *Lonely Crusade* is published. Critical reception is mixed,
          and CH draws sharp criticism from communist, Jewish, and
          African-American critics who are offended by some of his
          characterizations. He begins thinking of leaving the United
          States for Europe.

1948   CH is invited to Yaddo, a writers' colony at Saratoga
          Springs. Later, he delivers a speech entitled "The Dilemma
          of the Negro Novelist in the United States" to a group at
          the University of Chicago in which he tries to answer some
          of the criticism levelled against *Lonely Crusade*.

1948–51   CH's writing career goes into a decline, and he is forced to
          work at a number of menial jobs in order to support himself
          and Jean. Their marriage ends.

1949   *If He Hollers Let Him Go* is published in France under the
          title *S'il braille, lache-le* and is generally well received.

1952   *Cast the First Stone* is published. *Lonely Crusade* is pub-
          lished in France as *La Croisade de Lee Gordon,* with a
          preface by Richard Wright.

1953   CH leaves the United States for Europe on 3 April.

1954   *The Third Generation* is published.

1956   *The Primitive* is published simultaneously in America and
          France. It attracts little critical notice in the United States.

1957   CH meets Marcel Duhamel, the influential editor of Editions
          Gallimard's *Série noire*. Duhamel induces him to write a
          detective story, and guides him through the process. The
          story is published in America as *For Love of Imabelle* by
          Fawcett Gold Medal, and is largely ignored.

1958   Gallimard publishes the novel as *La Reine des pommes*. CH
          becomes an overnight sensation in France, and the book is
          awarded the prestigious *Grand prix de la littérature poli-
          cière*. He is the first non-French-speaking author to be so

honored. Gallimard brings out the second novel in the series, *Il pleut des coups durs*.

1959   The second novel is published in the United States as *The Real Cool Killers*. In France *Couché dans le pain*, *Daredare*, and *Tout pour plaire* are published. CH's reputation in Europe grows.

1960   Gallimard publishes *Imbroglio négro*. In the United States Avon publishes *The Crazy Kill*, *The Big Gold Dream*, and *All Shot Up*.

1961–69 CH publishes the rest of his Harlem Domestic Series, as well as the novels *Pinktoes* and *A Case of Rape*. He begins to receive some positive critical notice in the United States.

1972–76 CH publishes his two-volume autobiography, *The Quality of Hurt* and *My Life of Absurdity,* and a collection of short fiction and prose entitled *Black on Black*.

1978   CH marries Lesley Packard. His health begins to decline.

1983   Editions Lieu Commun publishes *Plan B,* an incomplete entry in the Harlem Domestic Series. It is the last of CH's fiction to be published in his lifetime.

1984   CH dies in Benissa, Spain on 13 November. His death sparks an outpouring of critical and popular interest in France and the rest of Europe.

1991   *The Collected Stories of Chester Himes* is published in America. It is the first publication in English for many of the stories in the collection.

1994   *Plan B* is published in English by the University Press of Mississippi.

Conversation with Chester Himes

Annie Brièrre / 1955

From *France-USA* (December 1955), pp. 8–10. All rights reserved. Translation copyright by Michel Fabre.

This American writer of five novels and numerous short stories, left the United States two years ago, and has lived in the Baleric Islands and London. He is now in Paris for a long stay, although he doesn't like everything here. About the nightclubs in St. Germain-des-Prés, he says, "The jitterbug looks like a grand, primitive ballet in the large dance halls of Harlem, but in these small clubs it loses everything that makes it special."

He is, he tells me in confidence, over forty years of age. Yet his looks and smile are those of a college student, a boy whose smile hides a stubborn will, an insatiable drive. A finely chisled face, bright eyes, the manners of a gentleman. He is optimistic, perhaps with good reason. He landed here with only 1,200 francs in his pocket, but a friend helped him out. "Otherwise," he says, "I would've been forced to go to the U.S. Embassy and throw myself on their mercy."

Born of a black father and of a white mother[1], his dual heritage is reflected in his works. But his characters always rise above the handicap of race. French readers have been able to enjoy *If He Hollers Let Him Go,* a first novel which got him a Rosenwald Fellowship, and of which some four hundred thousand copies have been sold; and *Lonely Crusade,* a powerful and gripping work, which deals with social, racial, political, and emotional problems. But I personally prefer *The Third Generation.* Its directness of style, structure, and human drama, place it, in my opinion, among the greatest novels of all times. If you find autobiographical elements in all of his novels, says Himes, *The Third Generation* explains more about him than any of his other books. In it are scenes from his own childhood and adolescence, spent with a father, whose character is particularly

---

[1] Estelle Bomar Himes was of mixed race according to Himes's autobiography.

1

moving, and with a mother Himes adored, but whose overpowering
ambition destroyed her husband's career and life. We talked about
this book while having lunch in a St. Germain-des-Prés restaurant.

CH: The scenes in my novels are usually based on my own experience. They remain so strongly in my memory that they help me paint
a more authentic picture. I always try to find material for my novels
within myself, and in my own experience, instead of borrowing from
other writers.

AB: Hemingway, too, attempted to avoid external influences.

CH: It isn't always easy to do this. For instance, in Hemingway's
early work, you can find the influence of Stephen Crane, who's not
well known in France, of Conrad, and others. In my opinion, though,
the influence of Ford Maddox Ford on Hemingway's work is the most
obvious. Hemingway is tremendous, particularly when he describes a
character's emotions. He's a writer of great emotional power. He
doesn't make any judgements about man, society, or life in general.
On the other hand, you find all of that in *The Grapes of Wrath* by
John Steinbeck. In French literature, I think *Nana* is a masterpiece,
thanks to the thorough development of the character of Nana, on the
one hand, and of French society on the other.

AB: Just like the characters in your own *The Third Generation*. But
tell me why you chose that title.

CH: Because my brothers and I belong to the third generation of
Negroes born after emancipation.

AB: Your family did well. Your father was a teacher and one of your
brothers became a university professor. Did the accident you describe
in your novel which caused your brother to lose his eyesight, really
happen?

CH: Yes, this is the same brother who's now a college professor at
Berkeley. He was well taken care of after his accident. Institutes for
the Blind are marvelous and, even in those days, they showed no
racial discrimination.

AB: Some American critics thought they could discern an Oedipal
complex at work in *The Third Generation*. This seems inaccurate to
me, since there's nothing ambiguous in the deep attachment between
the son and his mother.

CH: Freud's influence on modern psychiatry has people seeing

Oedipus complexes everywhere. To me, that book is closer to *Sons and Lovers* by D. H. Lawrence. Our mother was fiercely ambitious for us. In order to make successes out of us, she made us study the violin for five years, which we thought was a complete waste of time. Any perceived weakness in us worried her. She wanted us to go out and conquer the world.

AB: She seems to have done well by you. The fall down an elevator shaft that forced you to abandon your studies, all of which you describe in the novel, must have been a blow to her.

CH: Yes, but I left college mostly because I was a bad boy.

AB: If we are to believe the misbehavior attributed to Charles, who represents you in the novel, you certainly were very bad. Yet I get the impression that this bad boy might have been better if he hadn't had so much money at his disposal.

CH: Probably, but even if many of the scenes in the novel are based on real occurrences, the things causing and linking them, as well as the dramatic climax, are completely imaginary.

AB: Along with the psychological quality of your work, there is a documentary quality, too. Many Frenchmen are unaware that there is a black middle class in the United States, made up of highly-educated lawyers, doctors, and even millionaires. I have another question: Your protagonists are usually intelligent people, yet they seem enslaved to their passions, and never use the brains you give them. Why is that?

CH: I think this is typically American. We're still a young nation and we seldom think before we act.

AB: Other black writers tend to depict their race as victims of oppression. This doesn't seem to be true in your case.

CH: Well, first of all, I don't believe that all white Americans hate Negroes, but I do believe that they feel a kind of hostility to people different from themselves. In the South it's also directed at Catholics, in the West at Asiatics, elsewhere at the Irish, the Jews, and so forth.

AB: Like a lot of writers, you've worked at many kinds of jobs. Weren't you once a civil servant?

CH: Not quite, but I did work for the Works Progress Administration in the 1930s. That was an organization founded by Franklin Roosevelt to help the unemployed, including writers. Orson Welles and Richard Wright benefited from it, and I believe John Dos Passos did, too. I was working for the WPA when I worked on *The Ohio Guide*. I lived in Cleveland for quite a while when I was a kid.

AB: Didn't you also spend some time at Malabar Farm, the estate of Louis Bromfield, the famous writer?

CH: Yes, I worked there as a field hand during the holidays. Bromfield always welcomed would-be writers. He even invited me into his home during the evening. We became pretty good friends.

AB: Have you read his latest political essay, *A New Pattern for a Tired World?*

CH: Not yet. Bromfield has to do a lot of writing to be able to meet the expense of running his model farm, and an essay is a lot less work than a novel.

AB: You think so?

CH: I know from experience. It's always easy to tell other people what they should be doing.

AB: Do you believe, then, that a writer should let the world know his opinions only through the characters in his novels?

CH: It's the reader's job to discover it. It'd be too easy a gimmick for a writer to speak through his characters. The writer's thinking should always be implied through the character's actions.

AB: You often use dreams to reveal your protagonists' aspirations or inner turmoil. However, none of that tells me whether or not you believe in God.

CH: I'm a Catholic, but a pretty bad one. But I believe staunchly in God. You can't help believing in him.

Interview with Chester Himes

Michel Fabre / 1963

January 14, 1963

This previously unpublished interview is Fabre's first with Himes. It was conducted in New York City, when Fabre was doing research for a biography, *The Unfinished Quest of Richard Wright*. Copyright by Michel Fabre.

MF: What do you remember about your friendship with Richard Wright that you think might help me write about his life? When did you first get acquainted with him?

CH: I had already read *Uncle Tom's Children* and *Native Son* when I first went to New York and met Dick in 1940. That was in Washington Square. He was a member of the Communist Party then, and I remember he spoke at some length about his efforts to organize the people who worked as janitors, cleaners, etc. in his house. He had gone to see Benjamin Davis, the black Communist Party leader, told him about his efforts, and asked for some support. Davis let him down, and Dick was very much hurt. Dick had also tried to organize workers in Mexico, where he'd stayed for a while, but he got into trouble with the government down there.

When Dick and Ellen came back from their first stay in France, they owned a house in Charles Street. As a favor to a friend of Ellen's, they rented part of the place to two white college girls. They also rented the basement to two colored girls. Because some of the girls dated soldiers, *The Daily Worker* insinuated that Wright's place was being used as a bawdy house, something that upset Dick a lot. He was as moral a man as I ever knew. I suspect that the Communist Party was just trying to get back at him for leaving the Party in 1942.

MF: Did you know Ellen very well?

CH: She was a good friend, and could be very funny sometimes. I remember she once bought Dick dozens of cashmere sweaters on sale, then made sure he wore every one of them. Dick, himself,

5

bought several hundred ties one time. That way, he told me, he wouldn't have to buy any for the rest of his life!

Dick was rich but he wouldn't buy an automobile. He was on some kind of "anticapitalist" kick. I told him I thought he ought to buy a car. He replied, "I had to drive a mail truck in Chicago. I'll never drive again." Finally, he broke down and bought an Oldsmobile and learned to drive it.

MF: What struck you as his most important quality?

CH: His human decency. He was generous, intelligent, and outgoing. Once, he did an extraordinary thing for me. I was broke and asked him for a loan of $500.00. Dick had no money on him, so he telephoned his agent, Paul Reynolds, and within a half hour he had a check for $1,000.00 ready for me. That's how generous he could be. On another occasion he helped [James] Baldwin get a Saxton Fellowship. He went to see the manager of the Saxton fund and told the man he had just discovered a young boy who he thought was a genius. Baldwin was completely unknown then. On another occasion, Dick got him an advance of $500.00 to tide him over while he revised his novel.

MF: Did he help you get to France?

CH: He gave me advice when I first got there, but he also insisted that I bring him a lot of paper for his typewriter, and six author's copies of *The Outsider,* which had just come out when I left [America] in the spring of 1953. Edward Aswell, Dick's editor at Harper's, had gone to McGraw-Hill at the time, and the son of Dorothy Canfield Fisher had taken over for Aswell. That fellow was a jerk, and pretty unsympathetic to Dick.

Aswell was a Southerner, and he should have been a Negro; that's how opinionated he was. For some reason, though, Dick was the only writer he really liked out of all those he helped into print.

MF: Was Wright much influenced by other writers?

CH: He wrote exactly what he wanted to write. He wasn't even influenced by the Existentialists. *Savage Holiday,* for example, is an extraordinary book that Dick wrote simply because the idea of a psychotic hero interested him. The plot, as I understand it, was based on an actual event. Dick never wrote for anyone but himself, and he created characters out of his own emotions, uninfluenced by anyone else.

MF: What did Wright like most about you, in your opinion?

CH: I think he loved my inner toughness. I once told him, "Nothing can hurt me," and Dick liked that.

Dick changed when he got to Paris. I think he basically wanted to be part of the bourgeoisie. He wanted a pleasant life. He was already so successful that journalists asked to come up to see him, instead of his having to go to them. He was a great man. French intellectuals accepted him as an equal, they really liked him. Americans didn't treat him that way.

I think Dick wanted the kind of place in society that only an aristocrat, a man of means, can have. I don't blame him for that, like Baldwin does. There's a genuine class system in France, with a bourgeoisie, an aristocracy, and an intellectual class. Dick moved with ease through all those levels of French society, even though Frenchmen are as racist as anybody else. But I don't think that was enough for Dick. He wanted to be an aristocratic gentleman, too. I think that by the time he wrote *The Long Dream,* he realized it was impossible for him to achieve the place in French society he aspired to. "Why can't you face it?" I asked him. "Some things can never be."

Dick was obsessed with the plot to *The Long Dream.* Every time I saw him, it was all he would talk about. Ellen scolded me for causing (or so she thought) Dick to write about his earlier life in Mississippi. The truth is, he wrote *The Long Dream* out of frustration with his inability to become a European aristocrat. Left with that, he began to focus on his past in Mississippi.

Although he would sometimes cite the example of the Russian novelist, Pushkin, Dick's experience as a lower-class black man made it difficult for him to write certain types of novels. He had no experience to draw upon once he got away from the wellsprings of his past life. Writing a novel is an emotional experience, and he eventually realized that he could successfully build on what he'd done with *Black Boy.*

I think that *Black Boy* achieved more than anything James Baldwin has ever written or will ever write. There was a genius in it, true universality of emotion. That quality made it possible for Dick's stories to be understood all over the world, in any language, in any country. Like Hemingway's, Dick's was a literature for the world.

MF: What was Baldwin's relationship to Wright?

CH: Baldwin was never intimately associated with Dick. The story Baldwin tells about the night they had a such an intimate, meaningful conversation is nonsense. Dick never considered Baldwin a friend or an enemy. They had nothing in common. Dick didn't particularly like Jimmy, even if he did help him occasionally.

Dick was a great tease, and he loved needling people. Some of them didn't like it. He did that to George Lamming, whom he didn't like very much either. Baldwin tried to make people think there was a deep friendship between him and Dick, but that's nonsense. Once I was with Dick in his home when Baldwin telephoned. Dick said, "Let's go and meet Baldwin. He wants to borrow money from me." We met Jimmy at a cafe together, and Dick loaned him some money. When we tried to leave, Baldwin kept tagging along. Dick picked on him until I finally said, "Leave him alone, will you?" I don't think Dick liked that very much. Baldwin is nothing but an opportunist, with more ambition than anything else. He takes ideas from more successful writers, and uses them in his own novels.

MF: Were you always good friends with Dick?

CH: Yes, for the most part.

MF: What about Ralph Ellison?

CH: Ellison disliked Dick. I liked Ralph all right, but once at a private party, he pulled his knife on me because I teased him, saying, "You're going to be the big man now, aren't you, Ellison?" He got so mad that his wife, Fanny, got between us and they ended up fighting with each other.

When Ellison finished *Invisible Man* in 1952, *Time* or *Life* interviewed him, and devoted about five pages of the magazine to him. I think somebody there decided to help him get a big award because they wanted to hurt Dick, and Ralph knew it.

All that aside, Dick was a great man. He survived and prevailed over racial oppression to become one of the great writers of this century. He left behind a legacy of honest protest against injustice that is known all over the world.

Chester Himes Talks about
Negroes and Harlem

Pierre Ravenol / 1964

From *Paris-Presse*, July 23, 1964. All rights reserved. Translation copyright by Michel Fabre.

Even though it's a thriller, *For Love of Imabelle* is a masterpiece! And the author has written other thrillers, all realistic and pulsing with life. His name is Chester Himes. His skin is the color of burnt ochre, because Chester Himes is an American Negro. He talks about the Harlem riots, and has plenty to say.

PR: Why are American Negroes fighting now, since the world of *Uncle Tom's Cabin* no longer exists?

CH: I disagree, and I'm not talking about just the South. I can't get a taxi in New York City. My only chance is to find a black cab driver. Look, at least five percent of New York's black population tried to move to the suburbs and leave Harlem. It was impossible. Before long, their white neighbors had fled, and they found themselves living in new all-black communities. A Negro keeps out of trouble as long as he stays in his own part of town and keeps his mouth shut.

PR: What's the point of all the rioting in Harlem?

CH: Well, this is nothing compared to the old days. In 1948 in Harlem, I saw much worse rioting than this. The rioters tore up everything. Jewish stores . . .

PR: Why Jewish?

CH: Black people don't like Jews. Jews are racists. They're the ones who own all the property up there, so Negroes destroyed their property. You see, they become so frustrated that after a while they can't contain it anymore, and they just start tearing everything up. In 1948 the police just waited until everybody calmed down, because as long as the riot remained in Harlem, they knew there was nothing to worry about.

PR: Did things get worse recently?

CH: Well, this year it's real hot in Harlem. The streets stink, the air

9

is stifling. Black people don't have any money to spend on vacations. They're stuck in their tiny, miserable apartments. Finally it just gets to be too much, and they come outside and start blowing off steam.

PR: What about the shooting?

CH: That's a lie, everything the press printed is a lie. Those people weren't armed. I know the streets of Harlem as well as anyone, and I know that if they'd wanted to, those people could've mowed the police down. No, they weren't doing anything but expressing their frustration. You know, people can only take so much before it becomes unbearable.

PR: Have you ever taken part in a race riot?

CH: No, I've kept out of that. But you know, Negroes don't go out and attack white people.

PR: Do you know about the Black Muslims?

CH: Yes. I'm not a Black Muslim myself, but I understand their point of view. Black people are so gullible. The Muslims tease them, try to wise them up. They've tried to make them understand that somebody's always out to cheat them.

PR: What about the recent legislation?

CH: It hurts black people in the long run. Besides, there have been civil rights laws on the books for years, but nobody enforces them. You might as well pass a law that says "restaurants must serve dogs," but President Johnson wouldn't prosecute you if you refused the dogs service.

PR: But if integration isn't the answer, what is?

CH: The Muslims are a religious group. They're pretty self-sufficient, and integration is unimportant to them. But white Americans will never embrace integration. I think they have an inferiority complex. It's useful for them to have a group of scapegoats at their disposal. Without that, white Americans would probably devolve into something vicious and criminal.

PR: Then, you don't see any hope for the people in Harlem except for a few riots that let them blow off steam?

CH: None. Imagine a population of two million blacks in Paris. You wouldn't be able to get away from them. This is what it's like for Americans. They feel surrounded.

PR: Is it possible they're afraid?

CH: No, not yet. Negroes aren't rebels. They're just whining beggars. "Just a little integration, please!" No, things won't get better unless . . .

PR: Unless what?

CH: Unless there's a change in the way the U.S. economy works, in the way the world economy works. Until everyone realizes that Negroes are human beings.

Chester Himes: An Interview

Francois Bott / 1964

From *Adam* (November 1964), pp. 74–75. All rights reserved.
Translation copyrighted by Michel Fabre and Robert E.
Skinner.

"In no other city in the world are there more liquor stores, more
churches, more brothels, more lies than in Harlem. . . ."

This is the opening line of *Pinktoes,* an early novel by the black
American writer Chester Himes. Some twenty years later, he says,
nothing has changed.

"Harlem," he says today, "is just a huge mass of people. Negroes
are still the first to pay and the last to benefit. They've become bitter,
hungry, and violent."

A man of gentle demeanor, with a nearly square, well-proportioned
face, and a slim elegant build, Himes speaks slowly, and there is
something aesthetic about his personality. His appearance is something of a surprise, because to the French reader, Himes is the
quintessential *noir* writer, the author of *For Love of Imabelle* in which
he disguises a con artist as a nun, and the father of Coffin Ed and
Grave Digger, the two black cops whose popularity now rivals that of
Lemmy Caution, Maigret, and James Bond.

His latest books, *Back to Africa [Cotton Comes to Harlem]* and *Il
pleut des coups durs [The Real Cool Killers],* each take us to an exotic
underworld, peopled with nymphomaniacs, suckers, thieves, killers,
sociopaths, and con men. But Himes also exhibits a cool, sardonic
kind of humor that fits in with the angry desolation of Harlem.

"Unemployment, an incredible level of unemployment, was the
reason for the ghetto riots last year," he says. "Harlem is located in
Manhattan, and Manhattan symbolizes wealth. Manhattan is automobiles, television sets, fully-equipped kitchens, overfed children, clean
streets, and houses that don't stink of urine and sex like the lousy
hallways of Harlem. The trouble in Harlem is the result of that
contrast. Harlem is poverty. The black musicians who played in the
big orchestras couldn't stay there. Most of them got out. Those who

stayed got killed. Their money made them targets.'' Chester Himes
hands me *Muhammad Speaks,* the radical newspaper from Harlem.
A caption reads, ''Don't Cry when They Lynch Me,'' quoting a young
girl as she pleads with her mother. Himes smiles slightly.

''You ask about the Harlem riots, the anger in Harlem, the revolt in
Harlem? They'll go on. There's no reason why they shouldn't. No
government can rehabilitate Harlem, or provide the people there with
a decent life. Billions and billions of dollars would be needed. No
banker's going to invest in Harlem. Everybody was quick to vote for
Civil Rights for Negroes, but that didn't cost anybody a cent.''

Himes lives at Saint-Germain-des-Prés, in a top-floor studio on rue
Bourbon-le-Chateau. You have to stoop in order to get inside. Nearly
everything there is red: the carpeting, a vase of roses, and even an
angrily-daubed abstract canvas.

He says, ''Lock up a white woman and a black man in an apartment
in the United States with a bottle of whiskey, and what you'll get is a
violent, tragicomic story.''

His latest book, *Cotton Comes to Harlem,* and his first novel, *If He
Hollers Let Him Go,* a best-seller that was translated into twenty
languages and which sold millions of copies in the United States, are
built around a theme of Southern racism. The other side of this vicious
stupidity—the victim's side—Chester Himes has never stopped
feeling.

His wounds from this battle have never healed. He said, ''Writing
that novel hurt me.'' Seated in a leather armchair beside a framed
mirror, he speaks in a low voice in which you can hear fatigue and
resignation. His hair and mustache are greying, his cheeks sunken,
his voice subdued. This face mirrors his bitter experience.

According to Leonardo da Vinci, we've settled into our faces by
the age of 40. Chester Himes is now 50. He is the son of a black man
and a white woman. With white people, childhood ends at 12, 15, or
20, and they never stop trying to come to terms with the loss of that
childhood. In Himes's case, his innocence was gone when he turned
26. In 1940, he realized that he was born with the handicap of mixed
blood, and that the pale color of his skin, lighter than that of his
brothers, was a terrible burden, one that didn't help the misery
they shared.

Until 1940 his life had been an unhappy one. ''My father was a teacher in a colored college in Jefferson City, Missouri. Later we lived at Alcorn, Mississippi, then in Arkansas, then St. Louis. We always lived in the colored community, without any contact with white people. We travelled in segregated transportation, but I didn't mind.

"My parents sent me to the co-ed university in Columbus, Ohio. There was segregation in the city, but it seemed far away, and didn't really bother me.

"I got married in 1937. Industrial production was booming in the United States as we were preparing for war. In spite of the creation of so many new jobs, and in spite of my education, I couldn't find a job. This was my initial shock, the first time I realized how things really were. The only employment young Negroes could find were jobs as street sweepers or porters.

"After I worked at Louis Bromfield's estate, Malabar Farm [so called because the hills looked like those of Malabar in India], we moved to the Los Angeles area. There, racism became an inescapable fact of life for me. I'd been able to ignore segregation up until then, but now I couldn't. I felt I could 'see' racism, and it seemed to stick to me. It contaminated everything. It was like a disease I couldn't shake. My wife was black and beautiful, with the same shade of skin as Josephine Baker. We stayed together for fourteen years, but I could never provide the kind of life for her I wanted because we were Negroes. In the end, we separated."

Chester Himes worked at dozens of jobs: keeper, porter, doorman, hotel waiter, manual laborer. He worked for several months unloading trucks full of sand. In 1945 he published *If He Hollers Let Him Go,* his first novel, telling the story of a Negro who is continually threatened with unemployment and violence. I asked how he decided on this particular title.

" 'If he hollers let him go' is a line from a children's rhyme, but the title also suggests the spiritual, 'Let My People Go.' "

When Chester Himes showed his manuscript to his cousin, now an executive of the NAACP, his cousin said, "Everything you say here is true, but these aren't things that white people want to hear about. Things like this need to be kept quiet, between colored people."

Himes adds, "My novel, which Malcolm X read when he was twenty, is a violent, angry story. I meant for it to be a shock treatment, the same kind of treatment that Malcolm X wanted to inflict on the American public. *If He Hollers Let Him Go* expressed feelings that black people had always known, things that were always kept quiet, but are today exploding into the American consciousness. My novel is being reprinted, in some measure because of today's racial climate. But when it was written, even black people were shocked by what I wrote.

"All that suppressed hatred and anger makes Negroes schizophrenic. They show one side of their personality to white people, and keep the other side hidden. Let a white man come into a room where a group of black people are talking, and his presence distorts everything they do—their conversation, their jokes, their smiles. Once a white man comes in, black people change their personalities all of a sudden."

I ask Himes why he writes novels, instead of essays and pamphlets.

"I'm not trying to write about a political situation, but an emotional state. What segregation does to people."

According to Chester Himes, segregation produces a neurosis that afflicts every person of color. It makes people crazy. In Harlem, there are many "needle parks," or underground drug parlors. Chester Himes says, "There's an obvious link between drug addiction and this craziness. Drugs help people relax. Drugs are like whiskey or jazz music; they make them feel normal again."

The taboo of interracial sex is, for many black men, an obsession, Himes says. When a black man lands in Europe, the first thing he thinks of is dating a white woman. "For him, going out with a white woman is a source of revenge against the white man, and a way of affirming his manhood."

"Do you think you've changed since you've been living in Europe?" I ask.

"Yes, here a Negro can find a sense of normality. He can calm down a little. He can meet a woman and forget what color her skin is. Right now, I'm writing a love story about a Negro and a white woman in Spain and France. A story like that couldn't happen in the United States. Over here there's nothing bizarre about it."

Himes recalled the dream of thousands of Harlemites, going back to Africa, in his new novel, *Cotton Comes to Harlem*. In the story, a bale of cotton, where the "bread" is hidden, travels all around

Harlem. Reverend Deke O'Malley, a fake preacher and an ex-convict, loses the money he stole from the people of Harlem, and finds himself the target of both the police and the Mafia. Coffin Ed and Grave Digger recover the money by going underground to find the gangsters. *Cotton Comes to Harlem* has some of the elements of a classical detective story, but in it, Himes captures the reader's imagination with his colorful evocation of the ghetto locale and its citizens.

Himes's motive in writing detective stories was to reach a larger audience than he had with his earlier novels. "A black person writing the kind of novels that Hemingway or Steinbeck wrote has a pretty small readership," he says.

Himes tells me that he doesn't think of his novels as true detective stories. Most of his characters are gangsters and killers. Harlem, he says, is "the crime capital of the world." In *Cotton Comes to Harlem,* Grave Digger says, "Here in Harlem, the crime rate is the highest in the world. There's only three ways to stop it: put the criminals in jail, pay people enough to have decent lives, or let them eat each other up."

Himes calls his books "domestic novels." He describes the miserable lives of a half million Negroes, some of whom are addicts, bums, crooks, pimps, prostitutes, or suckers. They live in a drab, dirty ghetto, in miserable hovels, with cheap whiskey and drugs everywhere.

This is a city of shadow in the shade of the white metropolis, where half a million Negroes exist on the crumbs of plenty, while they dream of an escape to Africa or the South, and more often than not are cheated by the con games of vicious black criminals and white racists. These are the pictures that haunt Himes's imagination.

"Are these detective stories? Maybe," he says. "But so is *Crime and Punishment,* and so is some of the work of Faulkner, and Kafka too. The reality of crime exists in all our lives."

I asked Chester Himes where the names of his detectives come from. He replies, "Black policemen in the ghetto are pretty violent characters, and very often they adopt nicknames like 'Pistol Pete,' 'Big Six,' and 'Gravedigger.' " For these cops, life is all dull routine and hard luck. This is Harlem, where even the dead can't get any peace.

"Funerals can be tragic in more ways than one," says Chester Himes. "They cost a lot of money."

The Man Who Goes Too Fast

Philip Oakes / 1969

From *The Sunday Times Magazine* (November 9, 1969), pp. 69, 71. Reprinted with permission.

Chester Himes has always driven too fast. He still does, aged 60. Forty-one years ago on the eve of Thanksgiving Day 1928, he was speeding to Chicago in a stolen Cadillac when it left the road, smashed through a fence, and rolled to rest in a field leaving Himes to slog five miles through snow to the shop of a pawnbroker where he tried to hock a pocketful of hot jewelry. In his other pocket was a .44 calibre revolver, and 20,000 dollars taken at gun-point from a householder back in Cleveland.

Unknown to Himes, a woman staying at the Blackstone Hotel in Chicago had reported a theft of similar jewelry two days earlier. The pawnbroker alerted the police. Himes was arrested, given the third degree (his ankles cuffed together), and convicted of armed robbery. Two days after Christmas he was sentenced to 20 years in the Ohio State Penitentiary. Weeks later the woman at the Blackstone confessed that none of her jewelry had been stolen. She was trying to bilk the insurance company.

Himes caws with soft laughter when he tells the story. He savours irony, using it urbanely in conversation, seeing it as bed-rock to his violent tales of cops and robbers which have made him the world's top-selling Negro author (until recently, the only one) of detective novels, and—according to Maurice Richardson—"the greatest find in American crime fiction since Raymond Chandler."

In fact, there's no similarity. Chandler was a romantic and a moralist. Himes is a realist who deals in bloody nihilism. His heroes are two Harlem detectives named Grave Digger Jones and Coffin Ed Johnson, whose punch-ups and pistol-whippings punctuate eight novels of ghetto life in which conmen, thieves, whores, and perverts tend their trades and frequently die about their business. In Himes's novels murder is a small occasion. Throats are cut, skulls are broken without much fuss. Death is not seen only as grotesque, but grotesquely

17

funny. A hit-and-run victim, jammed against a wall, and frozen stiff on a sub-zero night, is stripped of her finery and revealed as a transvestite. Dr. Mubuta, inventor of an elixir distilled from the mating organs of baboons, rabbits, eagles and shellfish, is butchered while arguing the true cost of rejuvenation. A white homosexual, whose jugular has been severed, expires on the sidewalk, remarkable only because he's not wearing trousers.

None of his material is invented, says Himes. He's seen it all for himself. "When most people write about the American Negro he is either a functional character, or a vehicle for sociological comment. In my case the two are indivisible. My books are as authentic as the autobiography of Malcolm X. But I don't strain after authenticity when I'm writing them. I sit there laughing at the people, I believe in them so completely."

There's more to it than that. Himes is a founding father of the Black Power movement ("I was advocating Negro revolution back in the 1940s") who has become increasingly despondent over the course of events. His latest novel, *Blind Man With A Pistol,* published in hardback by Hodder and Stoughton, is a detective story in name only. Murder goes unsolved. Its true subject is violence itself. "A friend of mine told me this story about a blind man with a pistol shooting at a man who had slapped him on a subway train and killing an innocent bystander peacefully reading his newspaper and I thought, damn right, sounds just like today's news: riots in the ghettos, war in Vietnam, masochistic doings in the Middle East. And then I thought of some of our loudmouthed leaders urging our vulnerable soul brothers on to getting themselves killed, and thought further that all unorganized violence is like a blind man with a pistol." Few critics took note of Himes's reflections, and his book was reviewed— enthusiastically—among run-of-the-mill thrillers.

Perhaps what baffles the reviewers is Himes's immense facility. He is too racy, too funny, too *knowing* to be credited with a message of grave import. He is not seen to be suffering. He's black (light copper, actually), but he mouths no slogans. He drives a Jaguar—still too fast—and has a white English wife, named Lesley. At present he is building a house midway between Valencia and Alicante. The small estate is to be fenced in completely to contain his Siamese cat, Griot.

America is a place he visits once a year to check up on the Harlem geography, vital to his books. "Each year they pull something down, or put something up. Right now, they're making a movie there of one of my stories and the whole thing's become a kind of community project." The film is *Cotton Comes to Harlem,* and the enterprise, apart from United Artists money, is wholly black. Ossie Davis is the director. Raymond St. Jacques plays Grave Digger, and Godfrey Cambridge plays Coffin Ed. What they'll do about the language in the book Himes can't forecast. In print the swearing is ritualistic, but it's unlikely that much of it—even the necessary, if bowdlerised 'mother-raper'—will be used in the film.

Himes isn't perturbed. He was, after all, a well-brought-up boy and he still has good and gentle manners. Both his parents were school-teachers. His father was a skilled blacksmith and wheelwright, and lectured on Negro history at the Lincoln Institute in Jefferson, Mis-souri. When the family moved to Cleveland he bought a house in a white district, and Chester went to high school, where he graduated to Ohio State University. Between times he took a job as a bus-boy at a fashionable hotel, fell down a lift shaft and broke three verte-brae—an accident which provided him with a pension for several years, and helped pay for the education of his blind brother, now an academic sociologist.

At college, says Himes, he was a bad influence on his fellow students. His mentor was a Chicago gambler named Bunch Boy who had been kidnapped and held to ransom for 8000 dollars by Al Capone. Bunch Boy paid up and moved to Cleveland where he opened a club called the Tijuana House. Himes was given the job of running the blackjack game. "I was so young, he reckoned I had to be honest. He felt he could trust me. All sorts of people used to play, including a lot of Negro chauffeurs who sat around talking about the rich men they worked for. I got so tired of hearing about the furs they gave their wives and where they hid their money that when the Tijuana House closed down I decided I'd rob one of them. It was pretty easy. I just walked in and showed them the gun—the .44 calibre's so big you can see the bullets—and told them where the safe was, at the back of a closet behind a stack of hat-boxes. It was stuffed with money, more than I thought there'd be, and I put it in my pocket, along with the jewelry, and just walked out. It was a completely amateur job, which is why I got away with it." Until Chicago, that is, and the State Penitentiary.

This was where Himes's life became hard times. "It was a stinking place, hardly changed since the Civil War. Cells were overcrowded. Conditions were bad. On Easter Monday, 1931, some scaffolding caught fire and 321 convicts were burned to death. The National Guard was called in. There was a bloody riot." As stud poker king of the jail, Himes was otherwise engaged, but looking up from the game he saw a man scalped by a burst of sub-machine gun fire. "It's the kind of thing you remember, so that when you come to write about it you are able to describe the mechanics. You are able to do it as a documentary."

Following the riot the law was overhauled, and Himes's sentence was reduced by two-thirds. "When I could see the end of my time inside I bought myself a typewriter and taught myself touch typing. I'd been reading stories by Dashiell Hammett in *Black Mask* and I thought I could do them just as well. When my stories finally appeared, the other convicts thought exactly the same thing. There was nothing to it. All you had to do was tell it like it is."

Esquire bought one story, but there were no other sales. Released from jail in 1936, Himes found himself jobless, his accident compensation at an end, in the middle of a worsening Depression. He married a Negro woman, and found work as a labourer. He also wrote indignant letters to city officials as a result of which he was installed in the Cleveland Public Library writing vocational books for young people. As an afterthought his parole was terminated, and his citizenship restored. "I was writing for myself too. I finished a long manuscript about prison life and showed it to Langston Hughes who passed it on to Louis Bromfield who thought he could place it for me in Hollywood. He had no luck with it, and neither did I. After two years I found that it had travelled from studio to studio, and they'd used it for reference for all those prison movies they were making then."

The film colony offered no work of any kind to Himes. "MGM was making *Cabin in the Sky,* the all-Negro musical, and the consultant on the score thought I might fit in there. Not a chance. For one thing there was complete segregation. Even the stars were forbidden the use of the commissary. Lena Horne and Ethel Waters had to bring lunch and eat it on the set like day labourers. That is, until Lena met

Louis B. Mayer in the street one day, and told him about it. Things
changed after that."

America joined the war and Himes went to work in Henry J.
Kaiser's shipyard at Oakland until his novel *If He Hollers Let Him
Go* ("The most angry thing I've ever written") won him a Rosenwald
Grant, and he moved to New York, the darling of white, left-wing
intellectuals. It was a brief honeymoon. Years later, the intelligentsia
was bawdily mocked in Himes's novel *Pinktoes* (". . . a term of
indulgent affection applied to white women by Negro men, and
sometimes conversely by Negro women to white men, but never
adversely by either"). But what first set him beyond the pale was his
novel *Lonely Crusade,* which looked bleakly at the leech-like relationship between Negroes and Communists. "Negroes hated it. Jews
hated it. Communists hated it. *The Daily Worker* ran a headline:
'Himes carries the white flag!' Radio talks and lectures were cancelled. Eventually the publishers withdrew the book."

Two books later Himes decided that he and America were incompat-
ible, and sailed for Europe. In London he sought his publisher to
collect outstanding royalties and found him in jail. In Portugal he
looked for the sun and found the almond blossom blanketed in snow.
His wife divorced him, and in desperation he accepted the suggestion
of a French publisher that he might try his hand at writing detective
stories. "I didn't believe I could do it, but I was flat broke." What
evolved was the first of the Grave Digger and Coffin Ed stories,
entitled *A Rage in Harlem.* To Himes's astonishment it won the *Grand
prix de la littérature policière,* and became a best-seller.

Curiously, the book has never been published in Britain, and its
absence from the canon troubles Himes, who says it explains much
of the subsequent violence. "It has a scene in which acid is thrown in
Coffin Ed's face, which turns him into a psychopath. People should
understand about that."

The Harlem books were written quickly, and for cash, but there is
no doubt that Himes takes them very seriously indeed. Increasingly,
he feels they have become parables of the Negro's plight in the United
States. "They offer no solution. But they go some way towards
explaining the violence of the current situation. In fact, I've come to
believe that the only way the American Negro will ever be able to
participate in the American way of life is by a series of acts of

violence. It's tragic, but it's true. Martin Luther King couldn't make a dent in the American conscience until he was killed.''

Himes is turning to autobiography, and he has completed his first volume. But he is also attempting to finish the saga of Grave Digger and Coffin Ed. ''It's the final book. They get involved in trying to prevent a black revolution in the United States, and they both wind up dead. I've tried to imagine what would happen, and write it as a documentary. But I've had to stop. The violence shocks even me.''

He's worried and he is right to worry. So, perhaps, should we. For, as Himes points out: ''I have never had to strain for authenticity.''

The Hard-Bitten Old Pro Who Wrote "Cotton" Cashes In

Rudolph Chelminski / 1970

From: *Life* 69 (August 28, 1970), pp. 58–61. Reprinted with permission.

Hollywood has finally cottoned on. The amazing success of the wild detective comedy *Cotton Comes to Harlem* has proved once and for all that movies do not have to be lily-white—or even "integrated"—to be big box office. They can be jet black. Directed entirely in Harlem by black actor-playwright Ossie Davis, *Cotton* has grossed over $6 million in three months. The movie is full of black stereotypes no white director would dare include—but which delight black audiences. Even the plot revolves around a black-oriented gag—a missing bale of cotton stuffed with the ill-gotten gains of a phony "Back to Africa" preacher. *Cotton's* producer, Sam Goldwyn Jr., has acquired six other detective stories by Chester Himes, so other black comedies will be on the way—now that Hollywood has discovered that black makes beautiful box office.

Chester Himes, *Cotton's* author, is a tough, hard-bitten writer of the old school—a grizzled old pro whose first literary model was Dashiell Hammett and who is now writing some of the toughest, bloodiest detective stories in print. He spent most of his twenties behind bars, he has endured years of near destitution, and for the last 17 years has led the life of an angry expatriate in Europe.

Until he was 17 years old, no one—least of all Himes himself—had any idea that he might one day become a professional writer. The son of a schoolteacher, he seemed set for a respectable career as a doctor—until, one day, he fell down an elevator shaft. "I was just out of high school," he recalls, "working as a room-service busboy in a fancy Cleveland hotel. I was already enrolled to start my premed studies at Ohio State. When I fell down that shaft I got so banged up that the hotel gave me a cash settlement of $5,000—and that was big money in those days. Well, I stuck out college for two years, but

23

between my medical condition and too much money I soon got bored. So I just dropped out and drifted back to Cleveland and started hanging around gambling clubs."

For a time Himes ran the blackjack game in a club called the Tijuana House. But soon he got restless again. "I was fed up with the States, so I decided to leave. I wanted to go somewhere I wouldn't suffocate. Thought I'd try Mexico. But first I needed a small stake."

For a schoolteacher's son his approach to the stake was remarkably simplistic. He walked into a Cleveland Heights house, held up a wealthy couple at gunpoint and left with $20,000 and a fistful of jewelry. A few weeks later he was caught in Chicago trying to fence one of the rings. For his pains he got 20 years in the Ohio pen.

Faced with years of incarceration, Himes spent the last of the $5,000 the hotel had paid him on a typewriter. "I'd been reading stories by Dashiell Hammett in *Black Mask* and I thought I could do them just as well. When my stories finally appeared, the other convicts thought exactly the same thing. There was nothing to it. All you had to do was tell it like it is."

Still, it took him five years to sell his first short story—a tale of prison life. It appeared in *Esquire* in 1934, complete with his prisoner's number as the by-line.

Paroled in 1936 after serving eight years, Himes bounced from place to place and job to job. All the while he kept doggedly at the writing. Finally, in 1945, he produced his first novel—and hit the jackpot. *If He Hollers Let Him Go,* based on Himes's experiences in a Los Angeles shipyard, became a best seller and won Himes a literary award.

In the following decade Himes published two more novels, *Lonely Crusade* and *Cast the First Stone,* but neither of them sold. Finally, in 1953, he packed his bags and left for Europe. He lived in England for a while, then in Portugal. For two years he seemed drained of all inspiration. He was out of money and unpublishable. Then a new career unexpectedly opened up—writing in a new style and for a new audience. Marcel Duhamel, a French publisher, suggested he write a detective story.

Himes was aghast but hungry. So he decided to give it a try. The result was *La Reine des pommes* (published in the U.S. as *For Love of Imabelle*), the first of the Grave Digger and Coffin Ed stories. To

Himes's astonishment, it became a sensational best seller in France and was named best detective novel of the year.

A few years later Himes scored another hit—this time in the United States—with a sex farce called *Pinktoes,* which he wrote between detective stories for the Olympia Press in 1961. When Editor Maurice Girodias first looked over the manuscript, Himes recalls, he was not entirely satisfied. " 'If you incorporate eight sex scenes,' Girodias told me, 'I'll publish it.' 'Okay,' I said. I went to work and put in so many sex scenes that Girodias had to censor it!''

Released in the States in paperback and without fanfare, the free-wheeling adventures of Pinktoes—a sort of middle-aged black Candy—brought Hines overnight fame. But he refused to be seduced by this sudden success. Since then, he has stuck doggedly to detective stories. Though they are written quickly (few of them take more than a month), and for cash, Himes is extremely proud of them. "My books are set in the Negro ghetto," he says. "They are as authentic as the *Autobiography of Malcolm X.* But I don't strain after authenticity when I write them. I tell it like it is, and the truth comes out as a matter of course.''

Conversation with Chester Himes, the American Crime Writer

Willi Hochkeppel / 1970

Transcribed from a broadcast by the South Bavarian Radio in September 1970. Translated from the German by Michel Fabre. Printed with permission.

This interview begins with a brief introduction of Himes's literary career as a detective story writer. It includes an interview conducted with him in Moraira, which records his statements on his craft, the origin of his detectives, his political and racial views, and his thoughts on writing.

WH: Mr. Himes, your perspective on things, events, and people, whether white or black, seems to be expressed as a strange mixture of tragedy and comedy, to which you seem to be either sympathetic or aloof. Or are we to take these characteristics of your style as expressions of personal bitterness, which you've thinly shrouded in a kind of gallows humor?

CH: I see things as a writer, and I write about black crimes in a black ghetto. I'm a kind of reporter who offers solutions to the problems in a ghetto where crime just happens to play a part. The humor in my stories is the dark humor of the ghetto. I didn't invent it, because it was there already. I just use it.

I'm not attempting an indictment of black or white racism. My stories are about people, about their lives and crimes in the ghetto. Most of the people I write about are only vaguely conscious of oppression and discrimination. It's part of their existence, and they don't even think about it.

WH: Some critics haven't liked the way you blame white America for racial problems in your detective novels.

CH: As I said, I am not protesting against anything in my novels. I just write stories about crime in the ghetto, and those kinds of stories need a definite solution, just like an arithmetic problem. But more and more readers have realized that the essence of these stories lies in the fact that there really are people who live like this, and because they do, this is the way they will act when living under racist oppression. Recently, people have begun to think that these stories represent a bolder kind of racial protest than the explicit protest novels I wrote years ago.

WH: How did you happen to create the heroes of your series, Grave Digger and Coffin Ed? Were there any models in real life?

CH: Oh, yes, the prototypes were a pair of black police lieutenants in Los Angeles. They were more or less the lords of the L. A. ghetto in the late 1930s, just before the war. They were the most brutal cops I ever heard of.

WH: Have you, yourself, committed crimes and acts of violence like those you describe in your novels?

CH: Yes, even worse, you might say. I first came into contact with ghetto life in Cleveland, one of the most violent I have ever seen. When I came to Harlem, I didn't see anything I wasn't used to. It was another ghetto like any other, although it was more picturesque, and there were distinct social classes among the people there.

WH: What, in your opinion, are your best detective stories?

CH: That's a tough question. I think the first one that comes to mind is *For Love of Imabelle*. I like it because, from a literary standpoint, it's a classic story. And there are many serious writers out there who consider it to be one of the classics of modern literature. Several French writers I have known, such as Jean Giono, Jean Cocteau, and others such as Picasso, have really been impressed by this story. In America I understand that they found a copy of it in Faulker's own library after he died. I think it's comparable to novels written by Dostoyevsky, because it's more than just a thriller. I guess that's why it's my favorite.

WH: Will you work with Coffin Ed and Grave Digger in your upcoming books?

CH: No. *Blind Man With A Pistol* was meant to be the end of the series. Everything I'd tried to do in my previous stories came together in that one. I also tried to make use of the different attitudes exemplified by the characters in my other stories, at least as many of them as I could put into the same book. But I didn't offer any solution to the race problem. Given that, I think I really have come to the end of the series.

WH: Where do you fit among the many Negro movements in the United States? Do you lean more toward the use of force, or toward the one that Martin Luther King, Jr. represents?

CH: My position is hard to explain in a few words. For more than forty years, I have written the most militant prose ever printed to condemn American racism. At the same time, however, I don't consider myself an activist. I don't think that all the books and speeches of any writer can have any direct influence upon racism, or the other problems experienced by black people in the United States.

I believe it was Flaubert who said that rebellion was the most effective tool in politics. I share his opinion. I believe in rebellion, although up to now it has really been disorganized and ridiculous. Yet Negro activism in the 1960s had more success than anything since the Civil War. Since that period of activism, though, no more progress has been made.

WH: Mr. Himes, do you consider yourself a Marxist?

CH: I don't believe that Communists have ever really worked toward any solution to the Negro problem in the United States. I think the whole strategy of the Communist Party has been to use the civil rights struggle to help the cause of Communism. I think they had no interest in black political struggles unless they helped Communism. All of the important black writers who belonged to the Communist Party in the early 1940s left it long ago. I don't believe a Negro exists who believes in or accepts Marxism. It's a dead issue as far as we're concerned.

WH: What do you think about the future of integration? Can you envision a separate black America?

CH: The only possible solution to the race problem lies in integration. There's no solution unless black people have a share of the American dream. It has to be that way, and they can't get it except through integration.

I remember that during World War II, Communists declared that American blacks were a nation unto themselves, and that the Southern states ought to be given to them to form an autonomous nation. I couldn't see any sense to that, and don't see how blacks could form any nation without the support of white people. If that's the only way it can happen, it seems to me that integration makes a lot more sense than segregation.

My Man Himes: An Interview with Chester Himes

John A. Williams / 1970

From John A. Williams and Charles F. Harris, eds. *Amistad 1*. New York: Random House, 1970. Reprinted in John A. Williams. *Flashbacks: A Twenty-Year Diary of Article Writing*. New York: Doubleday, 1972. Reprinted with permission of John A. Williams.

New York was chilly that Friday, disappointing after a couple of days of hot weather. Then spring had beat a hasty retreat. London the next day was London: chilly, gray and somber at Heathrow. Then we boarded a Trident, as tight and crowded a plane as the Caravelle, and split with a full passenger list, mostly all British except us, to Spain and Chester Himes.

Lori brightened considerably when we crossed the Pyrenees. (Once we had driven through them, back and forth from the Spanish to the French borders, pausing now and again to picnic in the hot green areas between the snow-filled slopes.) Not long after, the Mediterranean flowed out beneath us as the coast of eastern Spain bent to the west, and we prepared to land in Alicante.

It was clear, bright and warm there, and going down the ramp I was conscious once more of the strange sweetness that lingers in the Spanish air, as though the entire nation had been freshly dipped in sherry or cognac. Down on the tarmac we saw Chester and Lesley waving, and I felt great relief. For Himes is sixty-one now and is not well, although he takes extremely good care of himself, mostly under Lesley's guidance. He smokes a great deal less, drinks mostly wine and adheres to a strict diet. Himes' life has been filled with so many disasters, large and small, that I lived in dread that one of these would carry him away so that I would no longer have the chance to see or talk to him.

I suppose it is known that I admire the man and his work. This began late in 1945, when I was a boy of twenty. I was then on Guam in the Mariana Islands with my outfit, the 17th Special Naval Con-

struction Battalion, waiting to be shipped home. There was not much
to do. The war was over; we were all waiting.

I was a hospital corpsman and we held two sick calls a day;
otherwise we slept, swam or read. Mostly I read and tried to write the
kind of jive poetry a twenty-year-old will write. I don't remember
how the novel came into my hands, but I never forgot it. It was *If He
Hollers Let Him Go.* The author was Chester B. Himes. Years later,
long after it was published, I read *Third Generation.* Until 1962 that
was the extent of my Himes.

That year I met Himes in Carl Van Vechten's apartment in the San
Remo on Central Park West. I had met "Carlo" when *Night Song*
was published in 1961. Van Vechten met, photographed, knew and
corresponded with every black writer who ever came down the pike;
now that I look back, perhaps he anticipated their importance in and
to American letters fifty years before anyone else.

If anything, Himes was even more handsome than his photographs.
Not terribly big, about five-nine or ten. One remembers his eyes
mostly; they sit in that incredible face upon which ravages show—but
which they have been unable to destroy—and at certain angles the
long-lashed eyes are soft, *soft,* as though clinging to some teen-aged
dream of love and goodness and justice. The eyes have remained that
way, although today, at certain other angles they clearly reveal the
pain of life as a black man and artist.

Himes is perhaps the single greatest naturalistic American writer
living today. Of course, no one in the literary establishment is going
to admit that; they haven't and they won't. Reviews of his books
generally wind up in the last half of the Sunday *New York Times Book
Review,* if they are reviewed at all. Himes will tell you that he doesn't
care; that all his career he has been shuffled under the table. Perhaps
this is, after all, the smallest of hurts he has suffered. He is a fiercely
independent man and has been known to terminate friendships and
conversations alike with two well-chosen, one syllable words. Worse
than the words is his silence. I swear I have felt him glowering at me
across the Atlantic from Paris at times.

Soon after I met Himes for the first time, Van Vechten told me:
"Chester doesn't like many people. He likes you."

Well, I liked him. We corresponded regularly after our meeting; we
exchanged books and he gave me a quote for *Sissie;* as I recall, it

wasn't used. Himes was still publishing in France in the Gallimard *Série noire*. Although he had won the Grand Prix for detective novels for *La Reine des pommes (For Love of Imabelle,* it was called here) he was still living pretty much from hand to mouth. I managed to see him once in Paris, but most often I saw him here after he arrived on the *France*. He stays at the Hotel Albert on 10th Street and University Place when he comes. In Europe I missed him often enough, for he would move frequently to avoid having his work disturbed by other expatriate Brothers. Then he would undergo periodic fits of disgust with the Parisians and go to Scandinavia or Holland. Sometimes, through Daniel Guérin ("The French expert on the Brother," Himes says), he went to La Ciotat near the Riviera to be isolated and to work. (La Ciotat, Himes says with the pride of association, is where André Schwarz-Bart wrote *The Last of the Just*.)

Chester Himes finally got a piece of what he deserves through the American publication of *Pinktoes*. He was back with an American publisher after almost a decade away from them. His detectives, Grave Digger Jones and Coffin Ed Johnson came back to America in hardcover after titillating (one of Himes' favorite words in describing the effect black people have on white people) the French for several years. The early novels of their adventures had been spirited away, more or less, by softcover publishers—often without Himes' knowing they were being published in America. He would write and ask me to confirm their presence, for word would have been brought to him by visitors to the Continent. That he was being paid little or no money for these rights only supported his contention that publishing was a brutal business and brutal businesses always take advantage of black people.

In both 1965 and 1966 we missed Himes in Europe; he had reserved a hotel for us in Paris and we were to have dinner, but he had fled France, leaving his flat to Melvin Van Peebles, the film-maker. We were to visit him in La Ciotat, but he'd packed up and taken off again. The next time we saw him was in 1967 when he and Lesley and their Siamese cat, Griot, flew to New York. That was when he started working on a film treatment of *Cotton Comes to Harlem* for Sam Goldwyn, Jr. (I read the screenplay by Ossie Davis and Arnold Perl while in Alicante and thought that if Davis as director could put on film what he has put on paper, the movie would be a very special thing.)

So, it was almost two years to the date when we saw them again in Alicante. Lesley had reserved for us around the corner from their small apartment. Lori and I unpacked, grabbed a couple hours of sleep, then went around the corner to pick them up for dinner. Chester and Lesley lived on the ninth floor of number 2 Calle Duque de Zaragoza, a step off Rambla Mendez Muñoz, four short blocks from the Promenade and the port.

With some writers you get the feeling that you are interrupting their work; that they wish you to be gone, out of their homes, out of their lives. I've never had that feeling with Himes; he has always made me feel welcome whether it was in the Albert, in the Quarter in Paris (I repaid the hospitality that time by falling asleep in front of the fire and holding up dinner) or in Alicante. Besides, Himes deserved a break away from his typewriter. He is always at it. If not books, then letters; he has always been a compulsive letter writer. (He once wrote a letter to President Roosevelt.) So I was, I think, a welcome interruption.

While Lori and Lesley shopped (Lori has a thing about Spanish eyeglasses, that never fit once we are back home) Himes and I talked endlessly in the room he uses as a study, in the living room with its balcony that overlooks the city and the port, and on walks down to and along the Promenade. There was never a time when I dared to be without the recorder, for out of Himes pours so much, at any time and at any place.

He's slower getting about than he used to be, but intellectually he is as sharp as ever and his opinions as blunt and honest as always. I am always impressed by how well he has kept up with what's going on in the United States. Most expatriate blacks I know tend not to care. Not so Chester Himes; his information is as fresh as the morning paper. Another thing: over the years he has repeated many anecdotes to me. What amazes me is that they are always the same. They are never embroidered or exaggerated. They are exactly the same. Most of us, with the passage of time, tend to embellish.

Last fall Chester and Lesley moved into their new home near Javea, still in Spain, still in the province of Alicante. We were to have seen it one day, but something came up so we were unable to make the trip.

It gave me the greatest pleasure to be able to see Himes again, to see him at a time when a kind of physical comfort was coming his way at last; to see him still producing long, articulate and sensitive works. He let me read the first volume of his autobiography, *The Quality of Hurt* (394 pages, ending in 1955). It is a fantastic, masculine work whose pages are haunted by vistas of France and Spain, of family life in the United States, of his first marriage, of Richard Wright and Robert Graves and others. American male writers don't produce manly books. Himes' autobiography is that of a man. So we talked, and the sound of bronze churchbells filled the background, and the sweet smell of Spain blocked up our nostrils and my man Himes rapped . . .

This Publishing Business

Williams: How do you feel about the double standard of payment, say, advances—this amount for black writers and that amount for white writers?

Himes: It's pitiful, you know, it's really pitiful, pitiful. You know, the double standard of advances is so pitiful. Even friends took advantage. . . . I got a thousand dollar advance for each of my last three books.

Williams: Really?

Himes: Yes. And they resold them to Dell for $15,000 reprint.

Williams: Each!

Himes: Yeah, and then in the end they didn't want *Blind Man [Blind Man with a Pistol]* and I thought—

Williams: Goddamn! Are you kidding me?

Himes: I'm telling you the truth. You know, I have never been paid anything in advance. I'm the lowest-paid writer on the face of the earth. So . . .

Williams: Now wait a minute, Chester, people have known you since the forties. They know everything that you produced and they offered you a thousand-dollar advance for each of these three books?

Himes: Oh, yes, that's what they paid, a thousand-dollar advance.

Williams: Goddamn!

Himes: You talk about double standards. I find this quite annoying. Y'know, I have been in desperate circumstances financially, which everybody has known and they've just taken advantage of this—

friends and enemies and everybody alike. I remember in *The Third Generation;* I was paid a two thousand-dollar advance and they resold the reprint rights to Victor Weybright of NAL for ten thousand dollars, and that's the money I came to Europe on. But then when I got broke in Europe and I had to spend a year's time helping—, the woman I was living with at the time, write a book of her own which never made a cent . . .

Williams: That was the book you said was much better than the Caldwell-type books—*The Silver Chalice?*

Himes: *The Silver Altar.* I have it in my autobiography. You can read it if you like.

Himes: Can I take it and read it tonight?

Himes: Sure, you can read it tonight or you can take it back to New York as far as I'm concerned. [Laughter.] I have two copies. I think if you want to do any background on me, some of the things you should know you'll find in it. But going back to the payment, you see. Now, I couldn't find a publisher for *The Primitive.* I was very broke and desperate for some money, and I finally thought that I would send it to Weybright because they had begun to publish originals. So I sent it to Weybright, and Weybright wrote me this long letter about how we'll pay you a thousand-dollar advance on this because we feel it's best for the author to have a small advance and have substantial accruals [laughter]. I'll never forget that phrase. I never got any accruals, substantial or otherwise, from that book [laughter], until five or six years later they brought out a new edition for which they paid a fifteen-hundred-dollar advance. That's why I began writing these detective stories, as a matter of fact. Marcel Duhamel, the editor of the *Série noire,* had translated *If He Hollers Let Him Go.* The *Série noire* was the best-paid series in France. So they started off paying me a thousand-dollar advance, which was the same as the Americans were paying, and they went up to fifteen hundred dollars, which was more.

Double standards are so pitiful. Well, as I said, the American system toward the Negro writer is to take great advantage of the fact that the black writer in America is always in a state of need, and they take great advantage of that need. They take advantage just willy-nilly. Then one or two will get through. Not one or two—I mean, the American system works like this: *Time* magazine and a few other

sources and the *New York Times* and all feel that they'd like to be
king-makers of a writer and they put him in a position so that he can
earn some money, like Baldwin. Now Baldwin got into a position
where he could command sizeable advances and royalties. But the
average black writer is never paid in comparison to the white writer.

Williams: What is the most you ever made on an advance of a book?

Himes: Morrow, I suppose. Morrow paid four thousand five hundred advance, which was just for *Blind Man With A Pistol* . . .
No—that's right, Putnam paid a ten thousand-dollar advance for
Pinktoes. Walter Minton was buying up Girodias' [Olympia Press]
books. He had been successful with *Lolita* and *Candy* and he was
anxious to get *Pinktoes*. Stein & Day had offered me seventy-five
hundred, so Minton upped it twenty-five hundred. And then Stein &
Day and Putnam started a lawsuit against one another, and that's why
they published it jointly. They figured it'd be more expensive to go to
court so they just decided that they would work out a system, a very
elaborate one, so elaborate that I ran into difficulties with Stein &
Day because—Putnam kept the trade book edition, they were responsible for that and for collecting my royalties—Stein & Day were
responsible for the subsidiary rights and the reprint and foreign rights
and so forth. And finally Stein & Day began rejecting various offers
from foreign countries. The last one—the one that really made me
angry—was that they had an offer from a German publisher to bring
out a German edition of *Pinktoes* and Stein & Day rejected that, and
I went to the Author's Guild and to the lawyers to see what I could
do. And they said that that was the most complicated contract they
had ever seen. Even now, even a couple of weeks ago I wrote to
Walter Minton to find out what happened to my royalties because
Corgi Books brought out a paperback edition in England which has
seemingly been very successful. I know that they have reprinted the
jacket design so I figure they must have sold quite a number in the
first design to have brought out a different one.

Williams: Well, you know the younger black writers back home
always say that Chester Himes has given away more books than most
people have ever written.

Himes: Yeah, that's right. I must tell you the truth. You know that
the younger generation of black writers are getting paid far more than

I'm getting paid, even now. Even now I get paid so little. I just got disgusted with the whole business.

Actually, I have a good agent now. Rosalyn [Targ] for me is a very good agent because she will fight for whatever she can get, you know. And she tries everything she can.

Williams: How about some of the experiences, other than royalties, that you've had with publishers? You once wrote me something about an award you were supposed to get at Doubleday when Buck Moon was your editor.

Himes: Yes, well you know, *If He Hollers* sold I think it was eight thousand copies before publication. That was Doubleday. Well, then *If He Hollers* hit the bestseller list. Then I received a number of letters from all over the country. I'd been in Los Angeles and San Francisco—one brother was living in Cincinnati, one was down in Durham, North Carolina, teaching at the North Carolina College—and I received letters from all of these people and other people whom I'd forgotten, that they'd been in stores to buy copies of *If He Hollers* and they had been told that book stores had sold out, and had ordered copies, and the orders were not being filled.

Williams: That's something that happens to me all the time, too.

Himes: So I went to Doubleday and complained and said the same thing and showed them the letters, and at that time Doubleday was being run by five vice-presidents. I think about a month afterward Ken McCormick was promoted to editor-in-chief, and he was in control of Doubleday. He became the top vice-president, or maybe he was the president. So I talked to him. He said my complaint didn't make any sense because if they published a book they were going to sell it. I couldn't argue with this. But it got to be rather dirty. Doubleday was in the *Time* and *Life* building on 49th Street at that time and I was going up in the elevator with Hilda Simms and her husband and a joker who was doing free-lance promoting for Doubleday, and I was telling them that the book orders weren't being filled and this joker rushed in and told Ken McCormick that I was complaining about Doubleday. So I got in Ken's office and we had some bad words, you know. I said to Ken McCormick, "You know that you got this black corner here . . ." He said, "No, we haven't. It's not a black corner," and I said, "You got Bucklin Moon, he's the head of the black department in Doubleday." So then I didn't get any more information from Doubleday concerning anything. So, I think seven years later when I was living with Vandi [Haygood], Buck stopped by one day and Vandi was in the kitchen making some drinks, and Buck said that I was right about the whole thing, but he had felt it would do me more harm to tell me the truth than to let me remain in ignorance. That what had happened was Doubleday was giving an award called the George Washington Carver Memorial Award of twenty-five hundred dollars each year for the best book. And that year Doubleday had *If He Hollers*, the outstanding book on the black theme that they had published. But there was one white woman editor whose name was never told to me, who said that *If He Hollers* made her disgusted and it made her sick and nauseated, and if *If He Hollers* was selected for this memorial award that she would resign. They gave the award to a book called *Mrs. Palmer's Honey*, written by some white woman. It was about a Negro maid in St. Louis.

When Doubleday advertised *Mrs. Palmer's Honey* in the *Saturday Review*, they said this book has a nice story that will appeal to a lot of people and it was not like some other books that they had published, and they referred, but not by actual name, to *If He Hollers Let Him Go*, and called it a "series of epithets punctuated by spit." This was their own advertisement. I complained about this, too. But what had actually happened to *If He Hollers* was that this woman editor—Doubleday was printing their own books in Garden City—had telephoned to their printing department in Garden City and ordered them to stop the printing. So they just arbitrarily stopped the printing of *If He Hollers* for a couple of weeks or so during the time when it would have been a solid best-seller.

Williams: You were at Knopf too, for a while. *Lonely Crusade* was a Knopf book, wasn't it?

Himes: Yes, well, that's why I went to Knopf. I went to Knopf because of this. I was talking to Van Vechten, whom I had met, and . . .

Williams: You met Van Vechten after *If He Hollers* came out, which would be late '45 or '46.

Himes: That's right. Richard Wright had taken me over to meet him. Dick was going over to get his picture taken. And when Van Vechten was taking his picture he acted so pompous I got hysterical and I was sitting there laughing away and Van Vechten was peeping at me and . . . So he was intrigued with me and we became quite good friends because of that. But Dick was a real friend despite his eccentricities. He had reviewed *If He Hollers Let Him Go* in *PM,* a good review, and took me over to the Book-of-the-Month Club. Well, *If He Hollers* was being distributed by the Book-of-the-Month Club. So when I told Van Vechten that I was unhappy at Doubleday he said that he would talk to Blanche Knopf and she would buy my contract from Doubleday. So she bought the contract ultimately. It wasn't a very large sum because Doubleday had only given me a thousand-dollar advance for my next book, and then I went on and wrote *Lonely Crusade,* which she liked very much indeed. I'd say she liked that book as much as any book she ever published. She gave it a very good printing, very nice—you've seen copies of the book, haven't you?

Williams: Oh, sure, sure.

Himes: Very nice book, and she lined up a lot of radio appearances for me. I don't remember all of them now—Mary Margaret McBride, CBS book shows—and I was to talk to the book department at Macy's and Bloomingdale's on the day of publication. So I sent for my father to come to New York from Cleveland and I went out early that morning to go to Macy's and this joker down at Macy's—the head of the book department—was looking guilty and said, "Well, we're going to stop this procedure of having authors speak to the book sellers because they would show favoritism since we couldn't do it for all the authors." So they canceled the whole thing. So then I went over to Bloomingdale's and at Bloomingdale's there were no books, no *Lonely Crusade* on display whatsoever. So I realized that something had happened. The director of Bloomingdale's book department didn't want to talk to me at all. So then I rushed home to get my wife and go to the Mary McBride radio program but she said she'd been trying to get in touch with me because they had received a telegram from the radio that I'd been canceled off that program. And then before the day was over, they canceled me off the CBS program. Then I learned that the Communist Party had launched a real assault on the book.

It had some of the most terrible reviews, one of the most vicious reviews I ever read. *The Daily Worker* had a picture of a black man walking across the page carrying a white flag—catch the caption:

"Himes Carries a White Flag." In some of the passages they had they compared the book to the "foul words that came from the cankerous mouth of Bilbo" [Sen., D., Miss.], and so forth.

Williams: Didn't you tell me once that Jimmy Baldwin did a review too?

Himes: Jimmy Baldwin did a review for the Socialist newspaper, *New Leader* I believe, under the heading "History as a Nightmare." I don't remember the gist of the review. But all of the reviews I remember seeing were extremely critical, each for a different reason: *Atlantic Monthly, Newsweek, Commentary, New Masses*—the white press, the black press, the Jewish press, reactionary press—*all*. Willard Motley, whom I had met at a party given for the publication of *Knock on Any Door* at Carl Van Vechten's house, wrote an extremely spiteful review for the Marshall Field newspaper in Chicago.

Williams: Was that the only book that Knopf did for you?

Himes: Yes. Knopf had given me an advance for another book, but then they . . . I had trouble with Knopf too. I tried to have some kind of dialogue with Blanche to discuss some of these reactions. I said, "Now, you have all of these reviews from *Atlantic Monthly, Commentary, New Masses*, the *New York Times*, the *Herald Tribune*, and *Ebony*, the black press. All of these reviews have different complaints about this book, different ways of condemning it. Well, this doesn't make any sense, and these reviews should all be published in an advertisement showing that all of these people from the left, the right, the blacks, the whites, that if all of these people dislike the book there must be some reason. It would stimulate interest; people would want to know why." Because I never found out why everybody disliked this book.

But I know why the black people disliked the book—because they're doing the same thing now that I said at that time was necessary. I had the black protagonist, Lee Gordon, a CIO organizer, say that the black man in America needed more than just a superficial state of equality; he needed special consideration because he was so far behind. That you can't just throw him out there and say, "Give Negroes rights," because it wouldn't work that way. And so this is what most of the black writers had against it; in saying that, of course, by pleading for special privileges for the black people I was calling them inferior.

Williams: And now that's the route that everyone is going.

Himes: Yes.

Williams: Except that they're not saying it. I think a few years ago they were saying it, but now it seems to me that what the kids are saying on the campuses is . . .

Himes: Yes, that's what they're saying, that's what I'm saying. It's the same theme because it's obvious, you know, that the black man in America must have, for an interim period of time, special consideration.

Williams: What about your experiences with editors?

Himes: Well, as a rule, the whole of my experiences has been bad. Over a long period of years the editor whom I got along with best as an editor was Marcel Duhamel, the editor of *Série noire,* because he was a friend, but more than being a friend he was an honest man, which is very rare among editors. He was honest and straightforward, although he was surrounded by a bunch of dubious people at Gallimard. But he did as much as he could. A journalist from *Combat* once said, "You know, Marcel is a good man, but Marcel is a three-legged duck as far as Gallimard is concerned." I always remembered that. They never really included him until later years. *Série noire* became so successful that he became a capitalist.

Williams: You know, over the years in many conversations we've had I get the impression that, well, it's more than an impression now, you never found much difference between American and French publishers and editors.

Himes: No, no, I didn't, because the only difference—it goes like this: the French don't have the difficulty that Americans do because most black people that come to France realize that they are from the undeveloped countries and they keep their place. And very few of them feel any injustice when they're not given the same accord as the French writer. They don't feel that this is unjust.

The American black man is very different from all those black men in the history of the world because the American black has even an unconscious feeling that he wants equality. Whereas most of the blacks of the world don't particularly insist on having equality in the white community. But the American black doesn't have any other community. America, which wants to be a white community, is their community, and there is not the fact that they can go home to their own community and be the chief and sons of chiefs or what not.

Williams: That old lie again, huh?

Himes: [Laughter.] Yeah. The American black man has to make it or lose it in America; he has no choice. That's why I wrote *Cotton Comes to Harlem*. In Garvey's time the "Back to Africa" movement had an appeal and probably made some sense. But it doesn't make any sense now. It probably didn't make sense even then, but it's even *less* logical now, because the black people of America aren't Africans anymore, and the Africans don't want them.

Williams: Yes, I found this to be true.

Himes: Yes, they wouldn't have him in their world, so he has to make it in America.

Williams: You were saying that New American Library once gave you a contract with sixteen pages.

Himes: Yes. Well, I was in Paris, and like George Orwell's book I was down and out in Paris and I had submitted this book, *The Primitive,* to Gallimard. But I was in a hurry and Gallimard was taking their time, so I sent it to NAL. So NAL took it and at the same time they took all of the rights, took every right worth considering, and they sent me a sixteen-page contract to sign. So Gallimard had to buy the book from NAL. What they paid for it I never discovered. I don't remember if anyone ever paid me for that. So at that time I realized that contracts were getting much more intricate than they had been previously, much more detailed. Publishers stipulated their rights. Of course, then publishing was getting to be a big business. The artists who could command a lot of money—and who could command a lot of attention, I should say, from publishers—were also getting more rights, so they could keep their subsidiary rights, even their paper-back rights.

Williams: I think there's a move in the direction to recapture these rights for the writers once more. It's going kind of slowly. There're some writers whom I've heard about who manage to keep their subsidiary rights, or most of them, like the reprint rights. I understand Robbins is one of these guys.

Himes: Yes, that's right. The first one who I heard of who was able to keep his subsidiary rights (I heard about but probably a lot of them did before) was Wouk, when he wrote *Marjorie Morningstar.* Well, you see, that's a considerable amount of money. You take a writer like John Le Carre, I don't know what Putnam paid him for the advance for the book rights, although Putnam did very well with the book, but Putnam sold the reprint rights for I think twenty-five or thirty thousand dollars, and then Dell, on the first three months of publication of *The Spy Who Came in from the Cold* made three million dollars. So that's a considerable amount of money involved.

Williams: I recall that Lillian Ross story about Ernest Hemingway that appeared in *The New Yorker,* where he got a twenty-five-thousand-dollar advance from Scribner's. And now these guys are getting like a quarter of a million. What do you think about that? People like Roth and . . .

Himes: Yes, I read that piece. Well, the industry has gotten to the place where they make considerably more money out of, say, Roth's book [*Portnoy's Complaint*]. They'll make more money out of Roth's book probably than the American publishers have out of all of Hemingway, because the industry is so much bigger. The whole process of circulation of books. There's so much advance. You know, America is a very big book market, and I wonder if these people read these books. I suppose they do. But anyway, as long as they get something that will titillate them, they will read them.

I remember when the book industry was very much afraid of television. They thought that television would do damage to the book industry. It didn't make any difference whatsoever. As a matter of fact, the book industry is very healthy now from the point of view of profit systems.

Williams: Well, I think it's healthier now than it was ten years ago.

Himes: Yes, it's healthier now than it ever was.

Williams: Who's your favorite American publisher in terms of what it does for blacks, producing good books?

Himes: Well, I couldn't say. I don't know enough about American publishers to have an opinion. As far as publishers are concerned, in talking to other people, all publishers, Morrow has a very good reputation as a publisher with other publishers. Has a better reputation I think than Putnam. But as far as publishers are concerned, that is very difficult to say.

Williams: What was the print order for *Blind Man With A Pistol?*

Himes: I don't know. Once upon a time you could get the figures. I couldn't get these from Morrow. As a matter of fact, I haven't been in close contact with them at all.

Personal Worksheet

Williams: Well, how would you place yourself in American letters? [Himes laughs.] You're sixty-one years old now, you've been writing long before *If He Hollers* came out—You've been writing now for thirty-four years.

Himes: Yes, I've been writing since 1934. Let's see, how long is that? My first story in a national magazine was published in *Esquire* in 1934. That's thirty-five years. Well, I don't know where to place myself actually on the American scene of letters because America has a highly organized system of reputation-making which I'm afraid would place me in the bottom echelon. The American communications media are very well organized about what they intend to do and how they intend to show that this person is of great importance and that person is chickenshit. So they work this out and they make reputations. Not only do they make reputations of writers, which is insignificant, but they take people like Roosevelt and they will set out systematically to break his place in history. They'll spend millions of dollars to do so if they wish. And the same thing happens with the literary scene. That's why I never contemplate it, because I realize the Americans will sit down and they will take a white writer—he will be one that appeals to their fancy, one that has been abroad and clowned around, like Hemingway—and they will set him up and they will make him one of the most famous writers on the face of the earth. And not because of anything he has written, because his work is not that important, but because they wish to have an American up there at the top of the world literature. Anyone reading him will realize that Hemingway is a great imitator of the styles of Ford Maddox Ford, James Joyce and D. H. Lawrence. As a matter of fact, if you have read the works of these four writers, you can see the lines, you can see the exact imitation. So there's nothing creative about even Hemingway's form. This was borrowed, as Gertrude Stein says.

But the Americans set out and they made him a legend. Now, it's very difficult for me to evaluate any of the people on the American scene, because if I take my information from the American white communications media then, of course, it is slanted to whatever way they wish to slant it to. So one can't form any opinion, unfortunately.

Williams: Do you foresee the time when you'll ever quit writing?

Himes: Well, no, no I don't foresee it. I mean writing is like . . . I remember I have a line in a book—I've forgotten now what book it was—where I quote [Max] Schmeling. He said a fighter fights, and I went on to say ". . . and a writer writes." That's what I do, that's all I *do,* and I don't foresee that I will quit, as long as I'm able to write. No. I do foresee the fact that age will deteriorate my writing, as it does everyone else's writing. I don't foresee the fact that because age will deteriorate my writing, and that I will realize that I can't do what I could do when I was young (I know damn well that I can't do what I could do when I was young) that I am going to blow out my brains like Hemingway did when he discovered that.

Williams: It seemed to me when I started reading the first couple of pages of your autobiography, *The Quality of Hurt,* that you were sort of preparing yourself for the time when you wouldn't write any more. But then I also noticed that this is Volume I, the carbon that I have. How many volumes do you foresee in this autobiography?

Himes: I imagine there will just be another volume in which I will write about the change in my writing habits or change in my attitudes toward the entire American scene, and my change from pessimism to optimism. I became much less subject to the inroads of the various attitudes of people that I didn't particularly respect. I know that I will write another volume that will concern my beginning to write detective stories, and then my beginning to write the last ten or twelve books that I have written.

Williams: In one of your letters you said—and you've mentioned it since I've been here—that you were working on the bloodiest book that you have ever worked on, that you'd ever conceived, but you didn't expect (you said in this letter) to have it published in America, that it would be difficult to have it published. Do you remember that?

Himes: Well, yes, because I can see what a black revolution would be like. Now, first of all, in order for a revolution to be effective, one of the things that it has to be, is violent, it has to be massively violent; it has to be as violent as the war in Vietnam. Of course, in any form of uprising, the major objective is to kill as many people as you can, by whatever means you can kill them, because the very fact of killing them and killing them in sufficient number is supposed to help you gain your objectives. It's the only reason why you do so.

Now, when you have resorted to these means, this is the last resort. Well, then, all dialogue ceases, all forms of petitions and other goddamned things are finished. All you do then is you kill as many people as you can, the black people kill as many of the people of the white community as they can kill. That means children, women, grown men, industrialists, street sweepers or whatever they are, as long as they're white. And this is the fact that gains its objective—there's no discussion—no point in doing anything else and no reason to give it any thought.

Now a soldier, if he would have to think about the morality of going out and killing the enemy, or if he had to consider his feelings about killing people, he would be finished. To do so, he would get courtmartialed or shot on the scene. A soldier just goes out and kills; no one thinks anything about it; that's his objective. The objective for a foot soldier is to kill the enemy, and that's all. It's very simple. There's nothing else to be added to it or subtracted from it.

Well, that's what a revolution by the black people in America will be; that's their only objective. Their objective is not to stand up and talk to the white man and to stand him in front of a gun and say, "Now you did so and so to me"; the only objective is to blow out his brains without a word, you see. So I am trying to show how this follows, how the violence would be if the blacks resorted to this. Even individually, if you give one black one high-powered repeating rifle and he wanted to shoot it into a mob of twenty thousand or more white people, there are a number of people he could destroy. Now, in my book all of these blacks who shoot are destroyed. They not only are destroyed, they're blown apart; even the buildings they're shooting from are destroyed, and quite often the white community suffers fifty or more deaths itself by destroying this one black man. What I'm trying to do is depict the violence that is necessary so that the white community will also give it a little thought, because you know, they're going around playing these games. They haven't given any thought to what would happen if the black people would *seriously* uprise.

The white community gets very much upset about the riots, while the black people haven't seriously undertaken in advance to commit any great amount of violence; it's just been forced on them. What little violence they have done has actually been for protection; it's been defensive, you know. So what I would hope is to call to mind what *would* happen, what *should* happen, when the black people have an armed uprising, what white people should expect. It seems that the whites don't understand this.

Because one thing is sure—I have said this and I keep on saying it over and over again—the black man can bring America down, he can destroy America. The black man can destroy the United States. Now, there are sensible people in America who realize this, regardless of what they might think about the black man. The black man can destroy America completely, destroy it as a nation of any consequence. It can just fritter away in the world. It can be destroyed completely. Now I realize of course that the black man has no money, he has very little equipment to do this, he has very little fire power, he has lots of things against him, he hasn't been trained particularly. Even a Southern white cracker colonel . . . I remember a Southern white cracker colonel in the army in the Second World War got up and he made this famous speech about the black people, saying, "You have never been taught to use violence and you have never been taught to be courageous, but war calls for these things and you must learn them." Well, he's right. That's the most right thing he ever said.

Williams: Do you think the publishers will be . . .

Himes: I don't think . . . I don't know what the American publishers will do about this book. But one thing I do know, Johnny, they will hesitate, and it will cause them a great amount of revulsion, because the scenes that I have described will be revolting scenes. There are very few war books written that have ever described actual scenes of war, 'cause in war people are killed and blown to pieces, and all. Even when they just say "blown to pieces" that doesn't describe what they *look* like blown to pieces. When a shell hits a man in a war, bits of him fly around, half of his liver is flying through the air, and his brains are dribbling off. These are actual scenes, no one states these outright.

Williams: How do you think the majority of white readers react to your books and other books by black writers?

Himes: The white readers read into a book what they wish, and in any book concerning the black people in the world, the majority of white readers are just looking for the exotic episodes. They're looking for things that will amuse or titillate them. The rest of it they skip over and pay no attention to. That was one of the remarkable things about Richard Wright's autobiography—that the white community was willing to read his suffering and poverty as a black man. But it didn't move them, didn't move them one bit. They just read it and said, "Tsk, tsk, isn't it awful?"

Williams: Well, you know, I sometimes have the feeling that when they read books like that, they say to themselves, "Boy, ain't we a bitch! Look what we're doing to them people."

Himes: [Laughs.] Yeah, something like that. They're thinking along those lines; certainly they're not thinking in the ways you'd like for them to think. That's one of the saddest parts about the black man in America—that he is being used to titillate the emotions of the white community in various aspects. Now I couldn't say exactly how he titillates them, but in any case it's titillation in a way that's not serious. America is a masochistic society anyway, so they probably just like being given a little whipping, enough to get a feeling out of it, a sensation, but not enough for them to be moved. I want these people just to take me seriously. I don't care if they think I'm a barbarian, a savage, or what they think; just think I'm a serious savage.

Williams: There's a rash of books, I hear (I haven't read them)—detective books—in which there are black detectives, and of course one of these books was made into a movie with Poitier, *In the Heat of the Night*. Do you feel that these people are sort of swiping your ideas?

Himes: No, no. It's a wonder to me why they haven't written about black detectives many years ago. It's a form, you know, and it's a particularly American form. My French editor says, the Americans have a style of writing detective stories that no one has been able to imitate, and that's why he has made his *Série noire* successful, by using American detective story writers. There's no reason why the black American, who is also an American, like all other Americans, and brought up in this sphere of violence which is the main sphere of American detective stories, there's no reason why he shouldn't write them. It's just plain and simple violence in narrative form, you know. 'Cause no one, *no one,* writes about violence the way that Americans do.

As a matter of fact, for the simple reason that no one understands violence or experiences violence like the American civilians do. The only other people in the white community who are violent enough for it are the armed forces of all the countries. But of course they don't write about it because if the atrocities were written about the armies of the English and the French in Africa, they would make among the most grisly stories in the history of the world. But they're not going to write about them. These things are secret; they'll never state them.

American violence is public life, it's a public way of life, it became a form, a detective story form. So I would think that any number of black writers should go into the detective story form. As a matter of fact, I feel that they could be very competent. Anyway, I would like to see a lot of them do so. They would not be imitating me because when I went into it, into the detective story field, I was just imitating all the other American detective story writers, other than the fact that I introduced various new angles which were my own. But on the whole, I mean the detective story originally in the plain narrative form—straightforward violence—is an American product. So I haven't created anything whatsoever; I just made the faces black, that's all.

Williams: You know, I'm always amazed when I read your books. Here you've been out of the country for twenty years, but I'm always amazed at your memory of things and how accurate you are in details, like the guns that the cops use. In rereading the screenplay last night, there was the business of the drop slot in the car. How do you come by all this knowledge?

Himes: Well, some of it comes from memory; and then I began writing these series because I realized that I was a black American, and there's no way of escaping forty some odd years of experience, so I would put it to use in writing, which I have been doing anyway. I had always thought that the major mistake in Richard Wright's life was to become a world writer on world events. I thought that he should have stuck to the black scene in America because he wouldn't have had to live there—he had the memory, so he was still there, but it was subconsciously, which he discovered when he went back to write *The Long Dream* and the sequel (which was never published, I don't think).

Well, then, I went back—as a matter of fact, it's like a sort of pure homesickness—I went back, I was very happy, I was living there, and it's true. I began creating also all the black scenes of my memory and my actual knowledge. I was very happy writing these detective stories, especially the first one, when I began it. I wrote those stories with more pleasure than I wrote any of the other stories. And then when I got to the end and started my detective shooting at some white people, I was the happiest.

Harlem Renaissance

Williams: Chester, how about the Harlem Renaissance? You were just arriving in New York when it was . . .

Himes: It was on the wane when I got there. I knew a lot of people involved in it. There was Bud Fisher . . .

Williams: He was a doctor or a radiologist, wasn't he?

Himes: I don't know what Bud Fisher was. I only know he was a writer. And there was a young man whose name I should know, I think he wrote *The Blacker the Berry, the Sweeter the Juice*.

Williams: Was that Braithwaite?

Himes: No, Wallace Thurman, I think. He went to Hollywood and he was one of the most successful black people writing out in Hollywood. He did very well on the Hollywood scene at that time.

Williams: How would you evaluate the Harlem Renaissance?

Himes: Well, I think it was one of the greatest movements among black writers that existed up to then.

Williams: But then Hollywood wasn't interested.

Himes: No, Hollywood had no interest in the black writer, but the black writers like Claude McKay and Countee Cullen and all, produced things of substantial consequence, and so as a group, the writers of the Black Renaissance produced works that were encouraging; it encouraged all black writers.

Now, the way I look at it, the next movement of any consequence was when Richard Wright hit the scene. Nothing happened between the end of the Renaissance and the time Richard Wright came on the scene. I always had a great respect for Richard Wright because of the fact that I believe that his first works, *Uncle Tom's Children, Native Son* and *Black Boy,* opened up certain fields in the publishing industry for the black writer, more so than anything else that had happened.

The Black Renaissance was an inward movement; it encouraged people who were familiar with it, who knew about it and were in contact with it, but the legend of Richard Wright reached people all over.

Williams: Well, he hit it about the same time you did.

Himes: Yes, that's quite true, but his name was taken to the masses, and that is what is important.

Williams: I somehow had got the impression from something that you had said that they didn't think that much of him.

Himes: No, I didn't say they didn't think much of him. I said that Wright's works themselves did not make any great impression on the white community, although they read them. As a writer, he made an impression on the publishing world. Although the white community read his works and gave a performance of being moved and touched and so forth, it didn't mean a damn thing to them—they just shed it. It's unfortunate but it's quite true.

A few white people around were considerably shocked by some of it, but I remember in Cleveland—I think it was with *Uncle Tom's Children;* no, it was *Native Son,* which was published about 1939 or early 1940—I remember various white people expressing amazement at being told that black people hated them. But these people were people of no consequence. I'd like to talk a little bit about Langston. He was in Cleveland; he didn't live too far from where I was; he was living with his aunt. He was writing plays for Karamu House. As a matter of fact, it was through Langston that I met the Jellifes; through the Jellifes I met Louis Bromfield, and that's how I went to Hollywood. But most of his plays were produced first at Karamu before they were produced in New York. And Langston stayed there a great deal. He lived there, as a matter of fact, and only visited New York. It was some time before he moved to New York.

Williams: Well, he's gone now. Tell me, when did you first meet Carl Van Vechten?

Himes: The year that *If He Hollers* was published. I knew very little about him, other than the legend. He was only connected in my mind (until I met him) with *Nigger Heaven,* which I think was his most successful book. Although when he published *Nigger Heaven* he was on very good terms with most of the writers of the Black Renaissance, but after he wrote it they practically never spoke to him again. He told me, "Countee Cullen never said another word to me."

George Schuyler was also in this group. I knew him, and Philippa Schuyler [killed in a helicopter crash in Vietnam in 1967] when she was a little girl. She used to go down to Van Vechten's.

Williams: But Schuyler became terribly, terribly right wing.

Himes: Yes, well Schuyler was a man whose life was plotted like Pegler's. He is a man who wants to say strong things, individual things and all, and he makes some statements which are contradictory, which Pegler did all his life. Pegler contradicted himself so much that he wound up, I suppose in an insane asylum, or wherever he is now . . . [Editor's note: Westbrook Pegler died in June 1969.]

Hollywood

Williams: Hoyt Fuller [Editor, *Negro Digest*] mentioned your *Cotton Comes to Harlem.* How do you feel about that? With Ossie Davis directing the film and all. Are you pleased with it?

Himes: Well, I was talking with Sam Goldwyn, Jr. and he agreed with me that he wanted Ossie Davis in it whether he directed it or not. He had this Arnold Perl, a Hollywood screenwriter, write the first version of it. First he had a young man, whose name I've forgotten, who did a version. Then I wrote a version, a quickie, about a hundred and thirty pages, which he paid me practically nothing for. Sam Goldwyn, Jr. is a nice man to talk to, but he doesn't say anything about money.

Williams: You were working on it, then, the last time we saw you in New York.

Himes: Yes, that's night. Then Goldwyn couldn't use it, which I knew would be the case, because I'm not a screenwriter. But I told him that in advance. I said, "Now listen, you need to get a professional." He said he had sounded out LeRoi Jones, for whom he had great admiration as a playwright. As a matter of fact, he had extreme admiration for him as an artist, for his sharp scenes. He said that he had taken many screenwriters and producers to see LeRoi's plays when they were showing in Los Angeles, and he contacted LeRoi. LeRoi said it was a matter of money; what LeRoi wanted was for Goldwyn to pay him in advance (I don't know how much it was).

Anyway, he would undertake to write the screenplay and he would do as many revisions as were required, and then he would get a second payment. And Goldwyn said it didn't work that way—which was a damned lie.

Williams: Of course it is.

Himes: Anyway, the reason he didn't get along with LeRoi was because LeRoi wanted to be paid like the Hollywood writers—

Williams: Like the white writers.

Himes: —and Goldwyn didn't want to do that, so that was that.

Williams: Are you pleased with the present screenplay of *Cotton Comes to Harlem?*

Himes: Well, no one could be pleased with that. But I don't know enough about screenplays to know what it'll be like when it's finished.

Williams: That's true. But in terms of what you see on the paper . . .

Himes: Well, it's not as bad as it was. It's much improved. Ossie Davis improved it considerably over the Perl version . . . And he has some good things in it.

Williams: He's updated it a little, with the militants and . . .

Himes: Yes, he has a black orientation, which I like. That's what I told Sam Goldwyn, Jr. That's what I like best about Ossie Davis' treatment of it. He took the Perl treatment, which had some stuff in there that was really offensive. The treatment of the blacks in there was so offensive . . . You know, some of the Jewish writers, because of the fact that they belong to a minority too, can get more offensive than other writers do.

Williams: They mistake closeness for familiarity.

Himes: What I dislike most about the screenplay—and I told Goldwyn—it's a good story, but it's a story about Deke, and the main purpose of Goldwyn is to make a series of movies of Coffin Ed Johnson and Grave Digger Jones; he wants to keep them alive. But if this is the purpose of the first movie, they are dead because they are of no consequence in the movie. He has to bring them out stronger if he wants to keep them. What you have now is a movie of a swindler, which is a good movie. But it's about Deke; Deke is the character in this movie. As a matter of fact, in Ossie Davis' treatment he comes through very fine; he comes through as a real solid character.

Williams: I started reading it. I got about a quarter of the way through just since we left you, and it recalled the book for me, which

I guess is good. As you say, the difference between the printed page
and what they put on the film can be—

Himes: Oh, yes, I will give them credit; they have stayed closer to
the book than the usual Hollywood treatment of a book, because as a
rule Hollywood lets it go altogether. It was to Hollywood's advantage
to keep the story in this book because they couldn't improve on it. If
they're going to depart from the story altogether, then it would
deteriorate and I'm not a big enough name to carry it. Like Hollywood
buys a lot of name writers and they do what they want to because the
name of the writer is sufficient. The treatment of the book doesn't
make any difference. But Hollywood is a strange business; don't get
me talking about Hollywood.

Williams: Well, talk about it.

Himes: I went out to Hollywood because I had been working on
Louis Bromfield's farm in Malabar, and he read my first version of
my prison story. He became excited about it and said he'd like to see
it get submitted to the movies. So Bromfield was going to Hollywood
to work on a screen adaptation of Hemingway's *For Whom the Bell
Tolls*. They paid him five thousand dollars a week, but finally they just
threw his version away and they got a screenwriter to write the movie
version. But he took my book out there and he gave it to some
producers and I followed him. I was trying to get work. And then I
went to the shipyards in San Francisco.

Williams: Were you aware at this time—or did you have the feeling—that your work would probably outlast Bromfield's?

Himes: No, it never occurred to me at all. But I didn't think that
Bromfield's work was substantial enough to last. It didn't occur to me
that Bromfield had been very successful then with *The Rains Came*.
He was making quite a bit of money at that time. This was in the late
thirties or 1940, and writers like Bromfield were getting that large
money from the serialization in magazines. They were not so much
concerned with things like book clubs or reprints and so forth. But
the magazine serializations: *Cosmopolitan* was paying Bromfield seventy-five thousand dollars for the serialization of the book. Anyway,
I went out to Hollywood—Los Angeles—where I met Hall Johnson
and a number of other black people on the fringes of the movie
industry. As a matter of fact, Langston Hughes gave me a list of
names of people to see when I went out there. Most of them were

connected with the Communist Party. I saw these people and then I got involved also with the communists out there. Politically I was never intrigued by communism. Communism was very strong in the States, in Hollywood particularly. — was out there; he was the dean of the communists. Great numbers of stars and producers and directors were fellow travelers, at least. There were two young men, black men, who had been in the Abraham Lincoln Brigade in Spain. — was the one I knew. I forgot the other's name, but his brother had been wounded and he was quite a celebrity among the Communist Party there. But anyway, the Communist Party was collecting old clothes, which they sold and then sent the proceeds to a refugee camp for Spaniards from the Spanish Civil War in Mexico. I would go around with — in his truck to pick up these clothes and various stuff. And we would drive up to many, many big Hollywood estates, of producers and various people (I wish I could recall the names) and they'd come out and set us up a few drinks in the kitchen.

Williams: In the kitchen! But you were supposed to be a part of them, right?

Himes: Yes, but this was their home; it didn't mean we got out of the kitchen! [Laughter.] I swear to God, my material for writing *Lonely Crusade* came from these experiences. I met these people. And the CIO union there was beginning to print a newspaper. At the same time I had been considered for a place on the staff. But, you see, the communists were also playing a game. They wanted people like me to help break the color line. I was a tool; they wanted to send me to thousands of places that had no intention of employing blacks at that time because Los Angeles was a very prejudiced place and the only jobs black people had were in the kitchens in Hollywood and Beverly Hills.

Williams: But they liked them; that was a status job.

Himes: Yes, but the point of it was the Negro ghetto at that time was not Watts but Central Avenue from 12th to about 40th, I guess. And you know, they didn't open those night clubs and restaurants on Central Avenue until Thursday.

Williams: Maid's day off.

Himes: Yeah, they were closed. Because, you know, some of Raymond Chandler's crap out there, he writes in *Farewell, My Lovely*, he has this joker ride about in the Central Avenue section. Some of that's very authentic—it was like that. A black man in Los Angeles, he was a servant. So there was nothing I could do out there and that's why I went to work in the shipyards. And then someone told me to come back to Los Angeles because they were filming *Cabin in the Sky*.

Williams: Oh, yes, the great all-Negro epic. [Laughter.]

Himes: That's right. And Hall Johnson was the technical director, getting twenty-five thousand dollars. They used his music, anyway. I don't know what he was—musical consultant or something. Anyway, he was being paid quite well. And I went back to Los Angeles, to MGM, because I had been told (I don't remember who had told me) to go out there and see a joker named Wheelwright, who was head of the publicity department, and I could probably get an assignment doing publicity. So I went out to get a job doing publicity for the Negro press, but they had already hired a young black man named Phil Carter. Well, when you go into MGM, just to the right of the entrance was the publicity department. And then you go in a little more and you come to what they called "Old Dressing Room Row"—a long string of old dressing rooms. Well, they had this young man named Carter to do the publicity for the black press in America. They gave him, for an office, one of the old dressing rooms, at the very end, as far as they could get from the publicity office.

I got on fairly good terms with the editors of *Collier's*. I felt I could get an assignment from them to do a *Collier's* profile on Lena Horne. But then one of *Collier's'* white writers, Kyle Crichton, decided he would do the story. It was one of Lena's first big publicity breaks.

Williams: You'd said something once about the black people in the cast—no matter how high up they were—and the extras . . .

Himes: Being jim-crowed in the "commissary"—the public diner. Yes, what had happened was that I had been out to MGM several times. But first, let me tell you this: One time Marc Connelly, who wrote *Green Pastures*, had a number of screenwriters, so-called intellectuals, and various others whom he had invited to a conference to discuss a film on George Washington Carver—along with two black faces for color, me and Arna Bontemps, I think.

Williams: The story of Stepin Fetchit. [Laughter.]

Himes: Marc Connelly was sitting at the head of the table with about twenty people sitting around, and he said, "Well, now I know how we're going to start this film; I know that much about it, and then we can go on from there. Well, you see, Dr. Carver was a very humble man and he always ironed his own shirts. So when we start this film on Dr. Carver, he goes into the kitchen and irons his shirt.'' So at that point I left.

At that time, they had black people out there for décor. They almost always had some black face out there. I was reading something recently in the paper about black technicians and various people who are beginning to break through out there, making it seem like a real advance, when actually so few, if any, technicians are employed by studios. But to get back to my story, later I made my efforts to get work in Hollywood. I met the head of the reading department, I suppose they call it, you know, where they have people read the novels and write a one-page synopsis, which is all producers ever read; they don't have time to read a book. So I was tried out by the young man who was head of this department at Warner Brothers. It was a job of no consequence. They were only offering something like forty-seven dollars a week to start, whereas you could make eighty-seven a week as a laborer. Anyway, he offered me the job and I was going to take it. I wrote the synopsis for *The Magic Bow,* a well-known book about Paganini, and submitted it. He said it was a good job and that they would employ me. And then—this is what *he* said: he was walking across the lot one day and he ran into Jack Warner and told him, ''I have a new man, Mr. Warner, and I think he's going to work out very well indeed.'' Warner said, ''That's fine, boy,'' and so forth. ''Who is he?'' And he said, ''He's a young black man.'' And Warner said, ''I don't want no niggers on this lot.'' [Laughter.]

But what I was going to tell you about *Cabin in the Sky* . . . Well, in the commissary they had a sort of reserved section for people like producers and the like. Everybody ate at the commissary, and if people had a guest they would just bring them to the commissary. When they were making *Cabin in the Sky* they had this entire black personnel, and they wouldn't serve the blacks in the commissary at all. They couldn't go in there and get a piece of bread. And so, Lena Horne stopped Louis B. Mayer on the lot one day and told him that none of the cast of *Cabin in the Sky* were permitted to eat in the commissary; they had to bring their lunch. And then he made out like he was amazed. [Laughter.]

When you think about how things happen, then you get very discouraged about what the white community is doing.

Black on White

Williams: What about today's racial scene?

Himes: Nowadays, since twenty-five years have passed, my opinions have changed; because I don't believe the whites have any desire, any intention whatsoever, of accepting the Negro as an equal. I think the only way a Negro will ever get accepted as an equal is if he kills whites; to launch a violent uprising to the point where the people will become absolutely sickened, disgusted; to the place where they will realize that they have to do something. It's a calculated risk, you know, whether they would turn and try to exterminate the black man, which I don't think that they could do.

Williams: You don't think so?

Himes: I don't think the Americans have the capability, like the Germans, of exterminating six million. I don't think the American white man could. Morally, I don't think that he could do this; I don't think he has the capacity. Even to kill a hundred thousand blacks I think would disrupt America, actually ruin the country.

Williams: You're saying that *morally* the white man in America is unable to do what the Germans did?

Himes: Yes, he's unable to do it because it would destroy America. He doesn't want America to be destroyed, you see. I think that if he has to take the choice between giving the black man his rights or destroying the entire economic system in America, he'll give the black man equality. But that's the *only* reason he would do it now. Appeal to him—doesn't mean a thing. I think that he just has to be given a choice, because America is very vulnerable, you know. Armed uprisings by millions of blacks will destroy America. There's no question about it. There's not any question in the fact that the Americans can release enough power to destroy the blacks. Obviously the Americans could destroy North Vietnam and the whole people physically. It's not a question of whether they could destroy the blacks physically; it's the fact that they can't do it *morally*—and exist in the world. Because America exists in the world by a certain balance . . .

Williams: A sort of jive morality.

Himes: Yeah, a certain balance in more than just morality. It's just a certain balance in its relationship with other nations in the world, so that it cannot do this. It cannot destroy the black man. The black man in America doesn't realize this, or probably he doesn't act because he doesn't want to get killed; of course, life is precious. I can see why no one wants to get killed. But other countries realize the fact that the blacks have the power to destroy this necessary balance. When Israel first got its independence, you realized that Britain couldn't kill all the Jews that were in Israel, and the Jews were damn few in number compared to the blacks. Israel realized they couldn't kill them all, so Britain gave them independence.

Williams: Yes, but weren't those different times, though? Everyone was feeling guilty because of what had happened to the Jews in the camps?

Himes: Different times but the conditions now are the same—even more sensitive. Even America cannot afford to fall out, not only on account of the economic balance of the world, which is so sensitive; it cannot even afford to form any enmity with all the nations with whom it collaborates, even the small nations in South America. It's just an absolute fact that if the blacks in America were to mount a revolution in force, with organized violence to the saturation point, that the entire black problem would be solved. But that is the only way the black man can solve it. So the point is, that the white people are jiving the blacks in America by putting on this pretense of wanting the blacks to suggest how *they* can do this without submitting the white race to violence; whites want the blacks to find a solution where the blacks will keep themselves in a secondary state, which would satisfy the whites perfectly, because the whites themselves haven't been able to devise any way acceptable to the blacks.

Williams: It's quite a theory, and it's one I've not heard anyone discuss. I find that younger kids are all for insurrection and rebellion and rioting on an indiscriminate, unplanned, unorganized kind of thing. I discourage it.

Himes: Yes, well, I discourage that too because what that does—by means of the white communication media, the press and television and radio—is divide one group of the black race against the other group, and thus damage the progress the blacks are making.

Williams: How big a role do you think that book publishing has in all of this?

Himes: Well, the book publishers, first of all, are trying to exploit the black consciousness to sell books. As long as it titillates the whites, they will do so to sell books.

Williams: Except that there are some books that frighten them, like your book [*Lonely Crusade*] that they pulled off the stands.

Himes: Very few. And when they do, the white press kills them. White people in America, it seems to me, are titillated by the problem of the black people, more than taking it seriously. I want to see them take it seriously, good and goddamn seriously, and the only way that I think of to make them take it seriously is with violence. I don't think there's any other way. I see it on the faces of the whites around the world—the smirks, the sneaking grins and all this stuff; I realize they're not taking the blacks seriously. There are certain segments that are beginning to take them seriously, but they are so isolated and so unrelated to the entire problem. Like the uprisings in the colleges and the elementary schools. Of course, the white people realized the uprisings in the elementary schools [school decentralization] in New York created an extraordinary amount of resistance and enmity and animosity. But since that was in one small section they felt that they could contain it, put it down with force. But if the conflict had been enlarged to the place where every black man was out on the street popping down white people right and left, this might have achieved the black goals, as in the African countries. Africans killed the colonials and burned their flags. I remember the time in London when they thought of Kenyatta as being a black murderer of the most depraved kind. Well, then the Mau Mau killed enough of these Englishmen over there so that there was nothing else they could do but give Kenya independence.

Williams: That's kind of remarkable, because I think in total the Mau Mau killed maybe fifty-four or a hundred fifty-four whites and just hundreds of blacks, so that if you can kill a small number of whites, then the effect is . . .

Himes: Yes, now in black uprisings in America, blacks would have to kill considerable numbers of other blacks in order for it to move, because the whites will employ some of those blacks to speak up against uprisings. In addition to this, the white press will find enough blacks to publicize. When they do, they *know,* of course, that they are weakening the position of the black leaders. Take Stokely Carmichael, for instance. They give him enough publicity to realize that they are weakening his position so that in a period of time that will make him absolutely valueless.

Williams: In the black community.

Himes: Yes, in the black community. So they give him publicity to the saturation point, where his value in the black community is just dissipated. They devised that technique from handling Malcolm X. They figured that they would give Malcolm X the saturation of publicity so that eventually his effectiveness in the black community would be weakened. Of course, when you sit and look at it from a distance you realize exactly what they're doing, and I think part of the reason my relationship with the white community in America is so bad is the fact that they know that I know this. My relationship with the white community in America is as bad as a black man's could be. But what saves me is I'm not important.

Williams: Would you then agree that the amount of publicity that they gave Martin Luther King created the same reaction?

Himes: Yes, yes. Of course, absolutely.

Williams: Now, you knew Malcolm pretty well.

Himes: Well, I knew him, not very well. I met him in 1962, I guess. He told me he had read *If He Hollers Let Him Go*.

Williams: He used to visit you when you were on rue Bourbon; well, how do you feel about his death? Most people feel that the government killed him.

Himes: Yes, well, personally I believe—and I will always believe this—that the CIA organized it and black gunmen shot him. Because it would take an organization, the way it was so perfectly planned and executed with certain methods that blacks don't generally use. It's the first time that I ever read of black gunmen employing gangster techniques from Chicago of the 1920's. And we know the CIA has employed these techniques before. So the way that it was so perfectly organized—that with all of the bodyguards that he had they were able to rise up there in that place and shoot, gun him down—it had their trademark on it. And then the fact that the Black Muslims had already threatened him gave the CIA a perfect, ready-made alibi. They were doing this in many countries until lately. They were doing this in the

East, in Morocco and North Africa, all over. If one studied their techniques, one would realize that this very easily could have been done by the CIA. And since I'm the type of person who believes it *was* done by them, I *do* believe it was done by them. Nothing will change that. They can say what they want to; I believe it.

Williams: How do you feel about the kind of mythology that has grown up around Malcolm? Last night we were talking about the movie that they're making now.

Himes: Yes, well, I think the reason why they became frightened about Malcolm X is, as I've always said, as long as the white press and the white community keep throwing it out that the black man hates white people, he's safe. It doesn't do a damn thing to him; he can walk around wherever he wishes to. Look at LeRoi Jones, who stands up there and tells those white people whatever he wants to tell them. Stokely Carmichael, Rap Brown, anybody—they're safe. They might find something to put them away, but most of the time they don't do a damn thing to them. But then, you know, when the black man enlarges this philosophy and includes a greater scope of people in it who will understand . . .

Williams: He'd opened his own mind.

Himes: Malcolm X had developed a philosophy in which he included all the people of the world, and people were listening to him. And then he became dangerous. Now as long as he was staying in America and just hating the white man he wasn't dangerous. But then when he involved others, they figured that if he kept on—since they themselves had brought him to the attention of the world—that he could use this; that they had set up for him to bring in masses of other people, masses of whites, masses of North Africans, masses of yellow people, all that would make him dangerous. So the only thing to do with him was kill him. Because that's the way white Americans solve every problem. You know, I have never even thought for a moment that the Black Muslims organized his assassination on their own. It never even occurred to me. First of all, there are a few Black Muslims who are rehabilitated from prisons and drug addiction and various things; there are a few that are personally dangerous to each other. But when a person gets the stature of Malcolm X at the time that he was executed, I think that he is absolutely safe from the Black Muslims. It would take an organization which is used to toppling kings and heads of states and big politicians to organize his assassination. I think he was absolutely untouchable by the Black Muslims.

Anyway, you know, there is no way that one can evaluate the American scene and avoid violence, because any country that was born in violence and has lived in violence always knows about violence. Anything can be initiated, enforced, contained or destroyed on the American scene through violence. That's the only thing that's ever made any change, because they have an inheritance of violence; it comes right straight from the days of slavery, from the first colonialists who landed on the American shores, the first slaves, through the Revolutionary War, the Civil War, the Indian wars, and gunslingers killing one another over fences and sheep and one goddamned thing or another; they grew up on violence. And not only that, it's gotten to be so much a part of the country that they are at the place where they are refining the history of their violence. They don't refer to the massacres of the Chinese during the last century out on the West Coast in California.

Williams: But not until they'd helped put the railroads in.

Himes: Yeah, that's right. They got all the labor that they could out of them before they killed them. Yes, they grew up on violence, and this is the only thing that they're going to listen to, the only thing that will move them. The only people that the white community in America has tried to teach that it is Christian to turn the other cheek and to live peacefully are the black people. They're the only people they have said bounce back. They have never even suggested it to anyone else. That is why the whole legend of Martin Luther King is such a powerful legend—because his was the teaching of nonviolence.

Williams: Right. He was a godsend to the American white people.

Himes: Absolutely. There's no question about it.

Black Writers

Williams: What happens, Chester, to young black writers who go over to Europe? It seems to me they're not producing like you and Wright and Harrington and Gardner produced. You were talking about Lomax [S.P.], who started out to be a writer. William Melvin Kelley was in Paris for a while and I think he got disgusted with it and now

he's in Jamaica. What's happening to these younger guys who go
over there?

Himes: Well, I don't know. I never met Kelley. Some of them
continue to write, you know; some of them work very hard at it. But
it's just the fact that there is a great resistance among American
publishers against expatriate blacks, so that they have a much better
opportunity of getting their work published in America if they're
living there. Because if they are living abroad the American publisher,
as a rule, will just reject their works out of hand. Now this I know for
a fact because I sent a number of manuscripts, recommended them,
to American publishers myself, which have been turned down flat.
Now the American publishers feel that the blacks should live in
America and they have a sort of spiteful attitude toward blacks who
escape from getting a head-beating in America.

Williams: They don't want them to get away.

Himes: Yes, that's another thing. That's part of the scene that
makes magazines like *Time* have such a great and hard and relentless
fury against Richard Wright, because Wright got away and *Time* never
forgave him for that. And they continued to pick at him in one way or
another. They thought, "Now, we helped this black man to become
famous and so forth, and here he is escaping us." So they set out to
punish him. Well, Dick was suffering under these various things—
being the black writer who was best known in the world—he was the
one that the white communications media could pick on. He was the
only one who was vulnerable enough, being famous as he was. They
could conceivably pick on me, but there wasn't any point 'cause
nobody knew me [laughs]. When people began finding out who I was,
they did begin picking. Until then they just left me alone entirely.

Williams: So your advice would be for them to stay in the States?

Himes: My advice to the black American writer would not be to
stay in America, but just to continue to write. Not to be concerned
about the attitudes in any place they are because one thing is for sure:
there are great segments of the world who will be opposed to them,
and this opposition, if they let it hurt them, will destroy them. That
will happen anywhere they are. But there's no particular reason
why—if they are young, have great vitality and a great love of
life—why they just simply shouldn't stay in the States and write there.
There's nothing they can learn here, that's for sure. There's nothing

they can learn about their craft or anything else from going to places like Paris. The only reason for going to Paris is just to have a certain amount of freedom of movement for a limited period of time. But they won't even get any inspiration from being in France. I don't think they will.

Williams: Let me ask you kind of a cliché question. Two questions, really. What is the function of the American black writer now, and what do you think his role will be in another ten years?

Himes: Well, I think the *only* function of the black writer in America now is just to produce works of literature about whatever he wants to write about, without any form of repression or any hesitation about what he wishes to write about, without any restraint whatever. He should just produce his work as best he can, as long as it comes out, and put it on the American market to be published, and I believe now it will be (which it wouldn't have been ten years ago). All right, now, what will come out of this ten years from now? No one knows. But at least the world will be more informed about the black Americans' subconscious. And it is conceivable, since black people are creative people, that they might form on the strength of these creations an entirely new literature that will be more valuable than the output of the white community. Because we are a creative people, as everyone knows, and if we lend ourselves to the creation of literature like we did to the creation of jazz and dancing and so forth, there's no telling what the impact will be.

Williams: Can we do this? Can we make this impact without owning our own publishing companies?

Himes: I suppose so. Look, I have talked to black sharecroppers and convicts and various black people who could tell, without stopping, better stories than Faulkner could write. And they would have the same alliteration, the same wording. Some of them couldn't even read and write, but they had the same genius for telling stories that Faulkner had, and they could tell continuous stories, too. The narrative would go on and on, and they would never lose it. But then these people couldn't write, you see. So I believe that the black man certainly has a creativity that is comparable to the highest type of creativity in America because he has the same background. And probably even greater. And then the blacks of the Northern ghetto have an absolutely unlimited source to draw their material from.

Somebody else comes up—like Upton Sinclair—and draws a little from this material, and builds a great reputation. Well, look at the black man now in the slums in Chicago; look what he can do. If Richard Wright had kept writing about Chicago he could have written forever.

Williams: But isn't there a kind of censorship that goes on if you don't have your own publishing outfit?

Himes: Yes, that is very true. You say "censorship"; the American publishers have what is called a conspiracy of censorship where they don't even need to be in contact with one another to know what they are going to censor; there are certain things that they just automatically know they are going to censor, and they all will work in the same way. Yes, it's true that this automatic and unspoken conspiracy of censorship among white publishers works against the black man. He has an absolute wall against him, but in the course of time this will break down. In literature, it seems as if it's already breaking down, and it will if black writers particularly find that they need their own publishers very badly. Then white publishers, faced with competition, will have to change. That is one of the unfortunate parts of the entire American scene, that the black—well, I wouldn't say industrialists— but the black heads of firms who have sufficient money to do these things won't do them. And one doesn't know why, because it's possible for everybody else. One doesn't know why a black publisher wouldn't come up and tap this source of wealth of the black community of writers, because it seems to me it would be unlimited wealth. One wonders why one of them doesn't do so, since the white publishers realize it is rich and they are tapping it as best they can, even with their standards of censorship.

Williams: There's another young black writer on the scene. His name is James Alan McPherson. He's just published a collection of short stories called *Hue and Cry,* and most of the stories are pretty damn good. Ralph Ellison has a blurb on the back of the book in which he says that this kid is great, this is real writing. The implication is that a lot of black writers whom he considers "obscenely second-rate" use their blackness as a crutch, as an excuse for not learning their craft. What do you say?

Himes: Well, I don't know what to say about that. If Ralph means that the black writers are writing about their experiences of being black in the world—what else can they write about? Now, that reminds me of this famous conversation between James Baldwin and Richard Wright that various people have written about, this confrontation they had in Paris. Baldwin said to him, "You have written my story." He meant, of course, that when Dick wrote *Black Boy* he had written the story of all black boys. Anyway, the point I'm trying to make is what else can a black writer write about but being black? And it's very difficult to hide. It's not insurmountable, but it's difficult. And then, any beginning writer will always write about his experiences.

Well, you know, I think that Ralph is rather a little bit hipped on the business of learning his craft. I remember when he was imitating Richard Wright to the point where there was a confrontation and Wright accused him of it. Dick told me that Ralph said to him, "Who else can I imitate if I don't imitate you, Dick?" So I think he's gotten a little bit pompous in making the statements about the craftsmanship of the young black writers of the world. *Invisible Man* was a very good book, but that didn't make Ralph an authority. It didn't mean to me that Ralph was a particularly outstanding craftsman in relationship to other black writers. I think that particular remark is uncalled for; it's not a particularly beneficial type of criticism. It seems that a remark like that appeals more to the white community than the black community.

Williams: What advice do you have for all these young black writers who are growing up and getting on the scene?

Himes: Well, I was reading that book *Yellow Back Radio Broke-Down* by Ishmael Reed out there, and I agree that there's no reason why every black writer shouldn't produce a style of his own. If he has the talent. No particular purpose is served by imitation in writing, you know. You take a writer like Joyce. He had to produce his own narrative style, which any black writer can—I don't say that they can produce what Joyce produced, but they can produce a style of their own whatever it might be. Like Ishmael Reed. And I think that's what they should do. And then in the course of time this will make an impact. They will have their style. I find that hard to do myself. I can give that advice, but people are creatures of habit. I would like to produce a definite style. Of course, I won't be able to do that now, that's for sure. But I have always wanted to produce an entirely different approach to the novel form.

Williams: Than what you now use?

Himes: Yes.

Williams: What do you find lacking in the form you now use?

Himes: Well, I would like to see produced a novel that just drains a person's subconscious of all his attitudes and reactions to everything. Because, obviously, if one person has a number of thoughts concerning anything, there is a cohesion. There has to be because they belong to one man. Just let it come out as it is, let it come out as the words generate in the mind, let it come out in the phrasing of the subconscious and let it become a novel in that form. Of course this has been done, but not purely; there's always been an artificial strain. Since the black American is subject to having millions of thoughts concerning everything, millions of reactions, and his reactions and thoughts will obviously be different from that of the white community, this should create an entirely different structure of the novel. Of course, that requires youth . . . I remember when I used to be able to write creatively thirty-five or forty pages a day. When I first began writing I was doing much better in introducing a story than I was doing in later years, because I would put down anything. I would be going along in a narrative form and listening to jazz and then a trumpet solo, say, would take my mind off for a second, I would follow it and write about it, and then go back to the narrative, and that would become part of the narrative. But of course this was always rejected by the editor.

Williams: You know, we once had a conversation about *The Primitive* and I told you I'd been reading it on the subway and I missed my stop. Remember? And I told you I thought it was a brutal book, I think a great book, and I remember that you apologized for its being a brutal book. But I hadn't said that it was brutal in the sense that an apology was necessary. If you're talking about attacking the sensitivities on all levels, this is what I mean; this is what *The Primitive* did.

Himes: Yes, but that was what I was able to achieve in Mallorca because I didn't have any distractions with *The Primitive*. I wrote that out of a completely free state of mind from beginning to end; where I saw all the nuances of every word I put down, so *The Primitive* is my favorite book.

Williams: Yeah, that's a fantastic book. It's my favorite, too. But you once said *The Third Generation* was your most dishonest book. Do you remember?

Himes: Yes, yes. I had read a number of pages of a manuscript that my mother had written about her family. Her family was one of these slave families that had been interbred into the Southern white slave-owners until the time of the Civil War. My mother's grandfather (I think it was) was the half-brother of his master; they were about the same age and they looked a great deal alike. When his master went away to the war, this half-white slave of his went with him as his body servant.

Well, she had produced this novel in detail and I thought that that should have been part of the book. The reason I didn't use it was that—I needed for it to be published and I thought that would be offensive to the publishers and would make it difficult for publication at that time. That was some time ago. Nowadays, the black man has got over that thinking. They do have the freedom to write, more or less, what they want. Many books I read now by black writers would not have been published fifteen years ago under any circumstances. And there are a number of themes that won't be published now, and that's why I want to write a book and break through a certain reticence on the part of the publishers.

I read *The Godfather* [Mario Puzo] and the author has experienced a certain hesitation on the part of the publishers to publish a book that relates all the gruesomeness and the power of assassination, of ruling by this power; that relates the effect that a group of people can have by controlling—by simply shooting other people in the head. Shooting people in the head generates power. This is what I think black writers should write about. I remember Sartre made a statement which was recorded in the French press (I never had any use for Sartre since) that in writing his play *The Respectful Prostitute* he recognized the fact that a black man could not assault a white person in America. That's one of the reasons I began writing the detective stories. I wanted to introduce the idea of violence. After all, Americans live by violence, and violence achieves—regardless of what anyone says, regardless of the distaste of the white community—its own ends. *The Godfather* is not only a successful book, but it's a successful book about a successful organization that rules by violence. And not only do they rule by violence, but the American community has never been able to do anything about them.

Williams: Well, I think this is largely because people who control the American community are in cahoots either directly or indirectly with the Mafia.

Himes: Yes, that was the same thing during all the days of prohibition, when everybody realized that the gangsters and the politicians worked side by side, close together. As a matter of fact, the gangsters were only servants of the politicians, the servants of the rich. That's why the gangsters in America were almost an untouchable breed during that time.

White Writers

Williams: What about your experiences with white expatriate writers?

Himes: I don't have any experiences with white expatriate writers.

Williams: Remember once you told me a story about how James Jones used to hold this soirée every Sunday at his place, and he said he'd like to meet you and you should come over, and you said, "What the hell do I want to see James Jones for?"

Himes: Yeah, that's probably true. I never met James Jones all the time I was in Paris. I actually don't know if I'd know him if I saw him. Lesley's pointed him out once or twice, but I don't remember what he looks like. I have nothing to say to James Jones, absolutely nothing to say to him whatsoever. And from what I've heard about his career and so forth, I don't *want* to know anything about him.

The thing about white writers . . . it's very pitiful you know. Take white writers like Hemingway, for instance. Now Hemingway became one of the great writers of the world, but as far as I know Hemingway never, one time, in one book or one story, had any message or statement to make about anything other than what he called courage or bravery and so forth, which I think is simpleminded. And that is all. But then, you see, to a black writer they say, "Well, what statement is he making?" He could write a book, one of the most fabulous stories in the world, and they'll say, "That's a good book, but what is the statement? What is he saying about the conditions of the black people in America?" Well, most black writers have something to say about this because most black writers from America—what else can they say, what else can they write about, what else do they think about? So that is why it becomes an absolute part of their writing, because it's part of their thinking. But I don't think that it's all done deliberately—just to sit down and make a statement; it's subconscious. Of course, most writers of any consequence are against various forms of social injustice. Take them all—even go back to old Russian writers like Dostoyevsky, old English writers, Dickens and so forth, and the new English writers, Joyce and all. Because this is part of the human emotion, you know, to protest against various forms of social injustice. And all the rest of them who are famous throughout the world. So the black writer does so because as a writer this is part of his trade. But to sit down and deliberately do so, results in a tract which quite often gets away from the author.

Williams: Are there any white writers that you admire? Not necessarily contemporary. You mentioned Dostoyevsky . . .

Himes: Yes, I mention Dostoyevsky so much because I've always admired him to a great degree because by reading him I understand his process of writing. There was a man who wrote very rapidly and very brilliantly all the time, and the reason that he did so was that he needed money all the time. He'd need it all the time, and as soon as he'd get money he'd throw it away. Also, being epileptic he had this extraordinary perception that most epileptics have.

But then I also like Faulkner because when Faulkner was writing his stories, his imaginative stories about the South, he was inventing the situations on sound ground—but still inventive. He was inventing them so fast that if you breeze through Faulkner you can find any number of mistakes. Faulkner would forget characters. You can read certain books, especially *Light in August,* and Faulkner has forgotten the names that he attaches to certain characters, then he goes on and he gives them other names.

Williams: I've noticed this, but I always figured it was something I had misread.

Himes: No, no, he was writing so fast he forgot. I do that myself. I remember years ago when I was starting to write short stories I had a joker shot in the arm but later I forgot he was shot in the arm. [Laughter.] Yes, you know this happens quite often, especially in the movies. Not that they forget it; they just pass it over.

Williams: You know, Chester, there seem to be more white guys who are writing about black people today than ever before. There have always been some, but now they seem to be crawling out of the woodwork.

Himes: Oh, yes, everywhere, everywhere. This has been happening about the past five or six or seven years. And you know why this is? Because at the beginning of the black uprisings in America, when the blacks were seemingly going to use violence to the point where it would have some meaning, well then they had world coverage. They had the greatest coverage of any story—more than even the assassination of Kennedy or the politics in Russia. Total saturation in the world press made the white writers eager to cash in on what they figure will have the greatest appeal, so as you said before they came up with the idea. On the whole, the white writers are better trained than the black writers, because they've had more facilities for education in many of the techniques and crafts of the trade. So a white writer can sit down and he can write some of the goddamnedest, most extraordinary bullshit about the blacks, but he will successfully project his story since he's not interested in having any authenticity. All he's concerned about is reaching the largest audience and what he can do with it. Like this joker who wrote the book, *The Man*.

Williams: Oh, Irving Wallace, yeah.

Himes: He didn't give a damn about whether this story was possible or whether it had plausibility; the main thing was to write a story that would titillate the greatest number of whites and make them buy the book. It wouldn't even make them think; it would be a diversion. It is true that the white writers of the world have a much better chance of learning their craft.

Then, the white writers in America conduct writing as a major business, which it is. Harold Robbins has more writers working for him than Shakespeare had. All he has to do is just sketch out the plot and put his writers to work and knock out his books.

Williams: I didn't know he used other writers.

Himes: The way I found out, I was in New York talking to Bucklin Moon, who had become, after some hard times, the editor-in-chief of Pocket Books. And I found that in addition to working as editor-in-chief, he was also working on Harold Robbins' *The Adventurers*. Yes, he was a competent writer, so he was writing some of the passages.

Harold Robbins didn't have time to write. [Laughter.] After all, it was a million-dollar project. He could afford to pay Bucklin Moon probably better than Pocket Books was paying him as editor-in-chief.

Williams: Did you read the Styron book, *The Confessions of Nat Turner?* You know the big stink about it.

Himes: I didn't read very much of it, just off and on. I read in an English paper that Styron was employing a gimmick there. He figured that he could write about Nat Turner as long as he made him a homosexual, lusting after white women. That was the only way the story of Nat Turner could be acceptable, because Nat Turner was one of the only black slaves who had the right idea: the only thing to do with a white slave-owner was to kill him. But Styron couldn't have him just kill him outright because he wanted to be free; he had to make him a homicidal homosexual lusting after white women. Which I find very . . . [laughter] funny. It was a cute gimmick, you know, and it went down very well.

Williams: Yes, it was an immediate best-seller.

Himes: Yeah, obviously. Black homosexuals and black eunuchs have always been profitable in white literature. The profit incentive has corrupted American writing, but that's what writers write for anyway—white writers as well as black writers; they write for profit. The only thing is black writers get such very little profit. In the last ten or fifteen years it's become very big business. Now, whether this is true or not, I heard that when Martin Luther King was assassinated, no serious money-making publisher was particularly interested until they realized the world was not only incensed but extremely interested in the life of a black Christian who had been assassinated, and that it was a very big story, a tremendous story. So the publishers began bidding for the biography of Martin Luther King which was to be written by his widow. I don't know who told me this, but probably my editor, that the publishers bid for this book, unwritten of course, but it didn't make any difference whether she could write or not because they would supply any number of writers to write it. But anyway, McGraw-Hill won it on a bid of a contract to pay her $500,000 advance.

Williams: I heard it was $450,000, but who the hell is going to quibble about $50,000 when you're talking about that kind of money.

Himes: Yeah, well, there you are—half a million dollars.

Williams: That's a lot of money involved in that book.

Himes: Yes, because anything which will hold the public interest, for the next ten years anyway, will be popular. King was a much greater man in the world and a much more significant personality in the world and touched more people in the world after he was killed than before. That's when most of the people in the world even got to know who he was. But everybody knows who he is now—even the people walking down the street here, and most of the people who live in Spain.

Williams: So you say that for the next ten years he'll be a viable subject?

Himes: Yes, that's the way I feel. It might be longer than that, but I think certainly ten years.

Williams: The piece that you have in here [*Beyond the Angry Black*, 1966] I see quoted pretty frequently; "Chester Himes says . . ." And you told me that you did that piece in nineteen-forty . . .

Himes: I guess I must have done that when I was at Yaddo [a writers' colony] and that was in 1948. Horace Cayton, who was the director of the South Parkway Community Center, and the woman who was teaching creative writing out at the University of Chicago got together and decided that they would bring me to Chicago to read a paper on "The Dilemma of the Negro Writer." When I finished reading that paper nobody moved, nobody applauded, nobody ever said anything else to me. I was shocked. I stayed in Chicago a few days drinking, and then I was half-drunk all the rest of the time I was in Yaddo. That was the time I started getting blackouts, I was drinking so much. I would get up in the morning and go into town, which you weren't supposed to do, and by eleven o'clock, I was dead drunk.

Williams: Into Saratoga . . .

Himes: Yes. I lived across the hall from Patricia Highsmith who wrote *Strangers on a Train* which Hitchcock bought for practically nothing but made a classic out of. He bought the full movie rights for five thousand dollars. Hitchcock doesn't believe in paying writers either, you know.

Williams: Who else was up there in Yaddo when you were there?

Himes: Well, part of the time, there was Truman Capote. I think he had already published *Other Voices, Other Rooms*.

Williams: He's done very well.

Himes: Yeah. I don't remember any other people who were there. I think Katherine Anne Porter, who wrote *Ship of Fools,* was also there most of the time, but I didn't see her. She spent almost all her days when she was in America up at Yaddo. She had a special room up there in the big house in a tower.

Williams: What did you think of *Ship of Fools* as an example of an American book that's supposed to be long-awaited, with the great writer?

Himes: I found it innocent enough but I didn't think it was a serious book that had any particular meaning other than the fact that I could see her up there typing away. It wasn't worth waiting twenty years for it. I would think that the book that — and I wrote, called *The Silver Altar,* was certainly as good as *Ship of Fools.*

Black Anti-Semitism

Williams: What does the "B" in your name stand for?

Himes: That was my mother's family name, Bomar.

Williams: Because when I first read *If He Hollers . . .*

Himes: Yes, I was using the "B" then.

Williams: Chester, let me ask you, do you know what your name "Himes" is derived from? Is it English or . . .

Himes: It's Jewish, like "Chaim," "Jaime" . . .

Williams: Spanish Jewish?

Himes: I don't know. It came down from "Heinz." Anyway, my father's grandfather's owner was "Himes." I don't know, maybe it was his father's—my grandfather's—owner. He was a slave blacksmith, that's how my father got into that. It was a trade that came down from father to son. My father was able to go to college and learn a few other things, like wheelwrighting and various skills. But the trade of blacksmithing was a hereditary business. It came out of slavery and the owner of our family was named in a certain variety of "Heinz," but it was a Jewish name. My forebears just took the name "Himes"—that's the way it was pronounced by the slaves. It was a literal translation, whether it was "Chaim" or "Jaime" or "Heinz." I don't know. But the "Bomar" of my mother's family's slave name is Irish, of course. I should call myself Chester X.

Williams: That's interesting. That's interesting. Let me ask you one final question and we'll quit for the day. I see you sitting there getting kind of wilted. I'm getting pretty tired myself. I don't know whether you've been reading about it or not, but there appears to be growing animosity, at least in New York City, between blacks and Jews (though one can't really trust the press). Do you think this is a result of the closeness, as I said earlier, whereby familiarity breeds contempt?

Himes: No. You know, I have a very long discussion of this in *Lonely Crusade*. That whole business between the black people and the Jews in America is part of the book, and that's the part the Jews disliked so much. As a matter of fact, I have a copy of the French Jewish magazine which has a photo of me on the cover. They ran an eighteen-page interview on my discussion of the relationship of blacks and Jews in *Lonely Crusade*. It was obvious, even when I was a little boy in the South that the only stores black people could go to, like hardware and department stores, were owned by Jews. When you went to non-Jewish stores you couldn't get in the door. So, where the black man and the Jew are concerned, the Jew has always taken the black man as a customer. Because the Jew has always been in business, and he found out that in a basically anti-Semitic country like America the most available market for a poor Jew on the lower rung of business was the black man. That was his market. He could rent them houses and he could sell them food.

Well, because the blacks were ignorant and the descendants of slaves, the Jewish merchants and landlords misused them. Where blacks might have been creative in other ways, in the ways of the commercial world they were babes in the woods. They were pigeons; anyone could take advantage of them who wanted to, so the Jewish merchants did—and the Jewish landowners (the ghettos were owned by Jews). It's very seldom any other name than a Jewish one appears as a landlord or proprietor in any ghetto in any city of America. All businesses in the ghettos were owned by Jews, and then a few of the blacks were eventually able to buy some of them. Then, of course, the black majority developed an unspoken anti-Semitism, even though they were doing business every day with the Jew around the corner. The black had an ingrown suspicion and resentment of the Jew. He realized that he was being used in certain ways by all Jewish landlords and merchants. Even today a Jew will make a fortune out of the race problem, and this builds up a subconscious resentment—although

most of the white people I do business with, who help me, whom I
love and respect, are Jews. But that doesn't negate the fact that the
Jews are the ones who had contact with the blacks and took advantage
of them. Now the gentiles had enslaved the blacks and worked them
as beasts, but when they were freed, the gentiles didn't want to have
a damn thing to do with them. They left the blacks without food or
shelter. They worked them for a pittance and that was all. Whereas
the Jew realized that to house and feed the freed black man was a
business, a business that paid off. This paid off better than any other
business because where else could Jews, who were in a ghetto
themselves, open up any kind of a business and have customers, other
than in the black ghetto?

Williams: Well, then, why is there such a great reaction—as in New
York—to the fact that, particularly in the school system, the black
teachers want their thing, the black people in the community want
their thing? The Jews are saying this is anti-Semitism—which to a
large degree it is—but it's also, as you seem to imply, an awakening
to the fact that they have been used.

Himes: Yes, that's right. You see, the way it is in the city school
system in New York, a quarter of a century ago the only white
teachers who would teach in black communities were Jews.

Williams: That's where the Irish sent them.

Himes: Yes, they're the only ones who would go there. So, over a
period of time they got entrenched, and now that the black people are
rising up, they're resentful of the kind of uncommitted teachers, more
so than the fact that they're Jewish teachers. It just so happens that
most of them are Jewish teachers and that they are guilty. The blacks
claim they're guilty of giving kids bad education, ignoring them on
certain points. These teachers on the whole are Jewish, but they have
been entrenched in the school system because this is where the
gentiles sent them. It's an unfortunate situation but it's inevitable,
because as the blacks begin to have any kind of protest, it's a
spontaneous protest against the first individuals whom they have had
direct contact with—who they know are guilty. They have not looked
back far enough to realize that the Jewish schoolteachers are no more
guilty of actually misusing black students than the white gentiles who
exiled them there in the first place. No one is looking at it that way,
because no one ever does. The younger Jews, I read, seriously are

trying to get the older Jews, who are people of great habit too, to see
that there is a different side . . .

Williams: Yeah, this is something that I've noticed too.

Himes: Well, this whole problem in America, as I see it, developed
from the fact that the slaves were freed and that there was no
legislation of any sort to make it possible for them to live. So this is
what has built up to such a tremendous problem that now . . .

Williams: Right. They felt that freedom was enough by itself.

Himes: Yeah, what is it that they have in heaven—milk and honey?
That some poor nigger could go and live on nothing. Just to proclaim
emancipation was not enough. You can't eat it; it doesn't keep the
cold weather out.

Wright

Williams: What was Paris like, with you and Wright, Harrington,
William Gardner Smith and Melvin Van Peebles? It must have been a
pretty great scene.

Himes: Well, we always met at the Café Tournon. In fact Dick
Wright wasn't in it as much as Ollie Harrington, who was actually the
center; and Melvin wasn't there then. Ollie was the center of the
American community on the Left Bank in Paris, white and black, and
he was the greatest Lothario in the history of the whole Latin Quarter.
And he was a fabulous raconteur, too. He used to keep people
spellbound for hours. So they collected there because of Ollie. Then
the rest of us came. Dick was a good friend of Ollie's; as a matter of
fact, he used to telephone Ollie every morning. Dick was a compulsive
conversationalist in the early hours of the morning. When he woke up
he had to telephone somebody and have a long conversation. When
Ollie wasn't there he had to find someone else—Daniel Guérin or even
Jean-Paul Sartre. But they got tired of these conversations, so he
chose Ollie. As long as Ollie was in town Dick would telephone him
as soon as he woke up in the morning, whether Ollie was awake or
not (it didn't make any difference) and have long conversations about
the CIA and the race problem and all. You know, that kind of
conversation doesn't go down too well at seven-thirty in the morning.

Williams: What did you decide about the CIA in Paris? I know that
Wright had some pretty positive ideas about what they were doing.

Himes: I don't know really. You see, I can't make any definite statement about the CIA in Paris because I didn't have any knowledge or even any thoughts about their operation. I realized that the FBI had a dossier on me going back to my childhood anyway, so it didn't make any difference to me one way or the other. And when I got my passport from the State Department I had to go and send my certificate for the restoration of my citizenship.

Williams: What's the restoration certificate?

Himes: Well, you know, when you've been to prison they take your citizenship away. And then the governor of the state returns your citizenship after a period of time. And my citizenship had been returned to me by a governor named Burton, who later became a Supreme Court Justice. He was a Supreme Court Justice at the time I applied for my passport. So I realized that the CIA knew everything they wanted to know about me already. They weren't interested in me anyway. The CIA was only interested in Richard Wright, and only because of the fact that they thought that he might have had information concerning the communist affiliations of people in high places in government, and that he might conceivably be having a dialogue, not a conspiracy or anything, but just a dialogue with people that they considered dangerous such as Nkrumah or Frantz Fanon. The only other person I know they were seriously interested in was Malcolm X. And of course everyone knows the CIA was interested in Fanon. They went to Fanon's assistance in the last years of his life to show that they had good will. Took him over to America and put him under medical treatment. By the way, he wrote a long article on my Treatment of Violence which his wife still has, and which I've thought I might get and have published. Because he had the same feeling, of course, that I have.

Williams: How long is the piece?

Himes: I don't know. Julia Wright told me that she had read it and that his wife has it.

Williams: You know, Julia is in New York. No . . . it's Rachel.

Himes: Yes, Rachel. Well, Rachel never got along with her mother. Rachel was Papa's daughter all her life. 'Cause she was a little blond daughter, you know, and Dick was devoted to her. But Julia looks just like her father.

When Dick died Ellen was in London and then she didn't know

what to do. When she came back she wanted to have a private funeral. Ellen and I personally had a furious argument about this. I told her she couldn't do that. When Dick died Lesley and I were spending the winter in St. Tropez and our landlady asked us if we knew a man named Richard Wright. And she said he had died; it had just come over the radio. So we got into our little car and rushed up to Paris and when we got up there we found that Ellen had said that she was going to have a closed funeral, and that no one was going to be admitted, and that Dick's body was going to be cremated.

Well, we were staying with Ollie Harrington. As a matter of fact, he had just moved into this apartment, so were sleeping on a mattress on the floor. So Ollie didn't say anything—he didn't want to cross Ellen. Ollie was a great diplomat. But anyway, I telephoned Ellen and told her she couldn't possibly have a closed funeral for Dick. So she decided after Dick had been dead three or four days and the funeral was rapidly approaching that she would open it. Which meant that a great number of people were not there who would have been if they had known earlier that it was to be an open funeral. But as it was, Dick had been on the outs with great numbers of people by that time. The head of *Présence Africaine,* Alioune Diop, was one of the people who gave the funeral oration. But at that time, before Dick's death, Dick and Diop weren't speaking. It was a relatively small funeral and he was suddenly cremated. After his cremation a very strong rumor started in Paris that he had been poisoned.

Williams: I remember hearing about it at the time.

Himes: Yes. Now, Ollie was supposed to have more testimony; he had more evidence than anyone because Dick had sent Ollie a telegram, which I saw when I was in Ollie's house, which said something like "Come to see me right away." And Ollie hadn't gone because, as I said, Dick was always telephoning him early every morning and he was sort of pissed off with him, so he didn't go. Well, the next Ollie heard of Dick, he was dead. He *did* die suddenly. Everyone knows the circumstances of his death—the fact that he was being released and was in supposedly good health. And then supposedly a mysterious woman had come to see him. Whether this is true or not, I couldn't say; this is the essence of the rumor. And the rumor still persists. Personally, that is one death I do not connect with the CIA, although of course with these things one never knows because the CIA was interested in many, many things . . . And Dick realized that he was a sick man and he might have had some revelation to make and decided to make it, and people might have decided he was better off dead. This is all guesswork on my part.

Williams: Had he made a public talk in the American Church two or three weeks before this, in which he was running down the CIA activities of people connected with the arts? Connie mentions it in her book.

Himes: Yes, well, everyone was doing that too, you know. And whether that has any relation to his death or not I couldn't say. I wasn't there anyway. I had been away from Paris for some time, moving around. I wasn't close enough to the scene to have any definite information until I arrived back and talked to Ellen, mostly just about the funeral.

Ellen and I never got along, as you already know. We got along very well once upon a time, but then we fell out just around the time Richard Wright was writing *The Long Dream,* because she didn't want him to write it. She didn't want him to go back into his Mississippi childhood and write about the black oppression in America, because he had written a number of books on the world scene. And I felt just the opposite. I felt that he should go back to the roots, the sources of his information, and write about the American scene. As a matter of fact, I was doing the same thing myself at the time. And Dick had come and talked to me at great lengths before he began writing this book.

Then Ellen stopped me on the street one day and said that I shouldn't encourage Dick. And I said, "Well, you know, I can't encourage Dick to do anything." And she said, "Yes, you're encouraging him to go back and write this book, and he's a big man now and he should not do this." So that made me so angry that I said some very impolite things, and we were shouting at one another on the Boulevard St. Germain. After that Ellen and I never got along. I see her now, I kiss her and embrace her because we've known one another many years. But it's just the fact that I know without a doubt that she wants certain information about Richard Wright's life not to be revealed. If Dick hadn't had his sexual relationships, if he hadn't seen the people that he had, if he hadn't had that certain type of curiosity that he had, he wouldn't have been Richard Wright. So there's no point in trying to hide the character of a man. But Richard Wright also reached a point, after he had been in France for four or five years, where he was well entrenched, had a really splendid apartment equipped in the American fashion, was a real celebrity to the press and everybody else. As my translator said, he was such a celebrity that if he had called a press conference at the foot of the stairs leading up to the Sacré Coeur and said, "Gentlemen, I want you to run up these stairs," they would have done so. But anyway, after a time, Dick became ashamed of his own image. The French continued to think of Dick as "Black Boy," and Dick was beginning to think of himself as a world figure, which he was. But at the same time, he was still Black Boy. The French were subject to thinking of him as Black Boy exclusively and excluded the fact that he was a world personality. Also, the French liked to believe that he belonged to them.

Williams: Why did they turn on him?

Himes: Well, they turned on him primarily because just that—the fact that he began writing on the world political scene. The French are very sensitive to any world figure in France who writes on the world political scene, especially if he's a black man. They are very sensitive about it. And then what the French do, they just take him out of the press. And to take Dick out of the press, since he had been such an extraordinary celebrity . . . He was plagued by it—this sort of comedown bothered him. So eventually this sort of corroded him and he decided he was going to move from France and go and live in England. But then he discovered England wouldn't give him the— racism in England had tightened up to the point where they wouldn't even consider having Dick living there.

Williams: I remember Ollie's description about when Wright went in to see about his passport, his permanent visa. He wanted an explanation from this official, who threw his passport at his feet and said, "I don't have to explain a goddamned thing to you."

Himes: Horace [Cayton] actually knew quite a bit about Richard Wright from the time of the publication of *Native Son* until Dick left for France. He was quite close to him. He'd have Dick up to the South Side Community House in Chicago, where he was director. Dick was very naive, you know, and Horace used to get embarrassed because he was such a slick cat himself, and he'd have some of these white chicks over from the University of Chicago, and Dick would get excited and wouldn't know how to behave. Dick was a strange man anyway. He was not only a genius but an astute political tactician—but in some ways he was very naive, too.

Interview with Chester Himes

Michel Fabre / 1970

Originally published in part in *Le Monde des Livres*, November 10, 1970. Reprinted with the permission of Michel Fabre. Copyright by Michel Fabre.

MF: Well, Mr. Himes, since a very long interview by John A. Williams appeared recently in *Amistad 1*, I think I'm going to concentrate on things that weren't really covered in it, and which may interest the French public more specifically. Could we start with your relationship with your French publishers and how you came to write here?

CH: On the whole, my relationships with French editors have been sympathetic and encouraging. Albin Michel published my first novel many years ago, and as far as I know, they have done well by it. Corréa published my second novel, *La Croisade de Lee Gordon*, and it received great critical acclaim in France. The critics admired it very much.

MF: It didn't do well in the States, did it?

CH: No, it was my least successful book but, like I said, it was pretty well received in France, although, as far as I know, it wasn't a commercial success. My third novel, *La Troisième Génération*, was published by Plon in the *Collection Feux croisés*. It's a good collection. *La Croisade de Lee Gordon* was in the collection *Le Chemin de la vie*, one of the best collections. My first book, *If He Hollers Let Him Go*, was published by Albin Michel, but I don't know which of their collections it was in.

MF: It was in their standard collection, which means that here your work was considered as real literature.

CH: Yes, the first three were published in the best French collections. My next book, *La Fin d'un primitif*, was published in the Gallimard collection *Du Monde entier*.

MF: When did you start writing the detective stories? Did it start with your agreement with Marcel Duhamel, or had you written them a long time before?

CH: No, no, Marcel Duhamel had been one of the co-translators of *If He Hollers Let Him Go*, and he had just become the director of the *Série noire*. He asked me would I write a detective story for the

83

series, and I told him I didn't know how to write detective stories. I'd never even thought of doing it, although I was a great admirer of Dashiell Hammett. One of the magazines that we got in prison was called *Black Mask*, and Dashiell Hammett's novel *The Maltese Falcon* was published there as a serial. He became one of my favorite writers, so, you could say my writing in France was influenced by him.

MF: The *Série noire* had already been publishing Hammett and Raymond Chandler.

CH: Yes, right, but I hadn't attempted to write mysteries before then. I'd only read Hammett and then, later on, I read Raymond Chandler, but I didn't think Chandler was in the same class with Dashiell Hammett. For me, Dashiell Hammett was the only mystery writer who mattered up to that time. Of course, I've begun to realize that crime is a factor in many other books. When I read Dostoyevsky's *The Brothers Karamazov*, I realized that there's a perfect detective story in that book. It has the kind of solution I can appreciate, because there's no sense to the murder.

MF: And you use that in your own novels, too, as a way of stressing the absurdity of the situation.

CH: Yes.

MF: When you wrote those detective stories, did you have a French audience in mind?

CH: I didn't begin to think in terms of a French audience until after I had begun writing them. I was too busy just thinking about the story. I didn't worry about the story making any sense to anyone but myself. To tell you the truth, I was having a very difficult time financially, and I wrote the first story because I needed the money pretty desperately. I also enjoyed writing it. When I began working on it, it became a pleasurable experience just to create a story out of my own particular experience.

MF: You put a lot of your own experience in those stories?

CH: Absolutely. That's one of the reasons why I enjoy this so much. Taking fact and using it as a foundation for fiction is what makes it so pleasurable. *La Reine des pommes* begins with a confidence game that is well-known in black neighborhoods, called "the blow."

MF: Why didn't you make the con man into a kind of hero?

CH: Because black people in America are preyed upon by con men.

Con men in black neighborhoods make a good living because Negroes are such suckers.

MF: Are they admired by black people?

CH: Admired? Well, it depends on how much success they have. You can be successful in anything, even in the police, and other black people will admire you. Now white confidence men can't work in the black community because black people won't believe anything a white man tells them.

MF: I had the feeling that in all your detective stories the real heroes are Coffin Ed and Grave Digger, even though they're cops.

CH: Sure, that was my aim, to make the detectives the heroes.

MF: Doesn't it create a strange situation, since they work for establishment?

CH: They do, but they don't. Most genuine black detectives are reactionary, fascist-minded, and very unlikeable. I had to create a pair of characters the reader would like.

MF: So you don't think they betray the black community?

CH: Not the way I created them. This is what makes my creation unique. In real life, black detectives are commonplace in black neighborhoods, but they're brutal and reactionary. The interesting thing is that official law enforcement only moved into the black ghetto during this century. When black people were first free, and lived in ghettoes or in communities of their own, white policemen never went into those communities. Black people had to create their own laws to protect themselves.

MF: So you don't believe that Coffin Ed and Grave Digger are traitors to their race?

CH: Not the way I've portrayed them.

MF: So, Coffin Ed and Grave Digger could be said to represent the kind of detectives that should exist, living in the community, knowing the people, enforcing law, dealing humanely with everyone.

CH: This is what I thought. I replaced a stereotype. I've taken two people who would be anti-black in real life, and made them sympathetic.

MF: Did the fact that you were published in cheap, paperback collections in the U.S. affect your writing?

CH: No.

MF: Did you feel you were writing down to your readership?

CH: No. There are those connected with French publishing who might think I lowered my standards by writing for *Série noire* after having been published in collections like *Feux croisés*, and *Du Monde entier*, but you've got to understand that at the time, I wasn't being published at all in the United States. I was blacklisted there, so I didn't worry about what anybody here thought.

MF: Do you think your books give some of your readers, white or black, a better understanding of the race problem?

CH: I've gotten letters from people who read my books, most of them black, but it didn't seem from reading them that my books had done anything to help race relations. And I don't think they do, either. I doubt any book helps the race problem. I've never believed that literature has any effect at all on social or political issues.

MF: Wright became quite disillusioned when he realized that.

CH: Yes, this is very true, but you know . . . well, this is something I shouldn't talk about.

MF: Did you think people react differently to your more literary books, like *If He Hollers Let Him Go* and *The Primitive*, than to your detective stories?

CH: Well, in America the only honest audience reactions that showed came from *If He Hollers*, and it was a good reaction. But *The Primitive* reached a very small audience, that audience was white, and ninety percent disliked it. Times have changed now, and they might better understand my motives in that book if they read it today.

MF: I am sure. You were talking about race relations and sexual relations, too, earlier.

CH: In America, people have to be told what to think. Few people think for themselves. Many are told how to think by certain magazines, and television and radio. *Time* and *Reader's Digest* control more American minds than anything ever conceived. Those magazines tell people what to think, and how to think. I suspect that ninety-nine percent of all Americans have never heard of me, and never will.

MF: They began to hear about you when *Pinktoes* was published. America rediscovered you then.

CH: Yes, but what actually began making some Americans think about me was being published in *Série noire*, and then the news of the prize given to *La Reine des pommes* that appeared in the American press. Most of the French press ran the story.

Paris Match prepared a story about me in 1959, but for some reason didn't publish it. They came down to Saint-Paul de Vence where we were staying, took some pictures. We came back to Paris to wind up the story, and met in the offices at Gallimard, where I was supposed to have my picture taken with Jean Giono.

Time magazine sent a reporter out to interview Giono on what he thought about me, and that got into the American press by accident. He said, "I give you all of Hemingway, Dos Passos, and Fitzgerald for this Chester Himes." *Time* never printed it, but someone else got hold of it, and it was printed in other newspapers in New York. The American public hadn't thought about me for a long time. I was completely finished, as far as they were concerned.

MF: Which one of your detective stories do you like best?

CH: Let me think . . .

MF: Maybe it's too difficult for you to choose. Perhaps they get mixed up.

CH: No, they're not like Balzac's, not quite. *La Reine des pommes* is undoubtedly the best of the books from a story point of view, because in the other detective stories I did different things. It's a remarkable story even for me.

MF: I think that *Blind Man With A Pistol* is richer than most of our detective stories. You have infused into it reflections about the state of race relations in America, the way you did in *The Primitive*.

CH: Yes, that was my intention. It took a long time to write *Blind Man With A Pistol*. I worked off and on for about three years because I didn't want to write just another detective story. I wanted to write a sociological story about race relations.

MF: What kind of reception have your books gotten in the other countries where you've been published? Weren't they translated into German, Italian, and Spanish?

CH: The books in the *Série noire* have been published in most of the countries of the western world; all the countries of Europe, the Scandinavian countries, Denmark, Sweden, Norway, and Holland, Germany, Italy, and Belgium.

MF: Did you have the same kind of success there as you had in France?

CH: No, not everywhere. Some countries are just beginning to read them. My greatest success with this series has been in France, and then in England and America.

MF: Could you tell whether they were read in Harlem?

CH: Yes, they were. Harlem was quite receptive to them. The book that had the greatest appeal in Harlem was *Pinktoes*. It got quite a bit of good publicity there.

MF: What about *Une Affaire de viol*? Has it been published in English?

CH: No, my agent is trying to arrange its publication in America now.

MF: You presented *Une Affaire de viol* as an inquest, as a case. This was different from your detective stories. Were you experimenting with something?

CH: I was experimenting with form, and intended to write a very long novel. This is a synopsis of the novel I intended to write. I wanted to show that in cases where a black man is accused of rape—guilty or not—the whole affair is politicized. It doesn't matter whether he's guilty or not. Just the idea of a black man being accused of rape in a white society is political.

MF: If you look back on your favorite works, do you find a line of conscious development?

CH: Yes, the line moves with the stages of my life. I wrote straight protest novels when I lived in America. When I left America, I began thinking about other things. The transition between the protest fiction and what I'm doing now is *The Primitive*. After that, I got into writing the detective stories.

When I wrote *Pinktoes*, I was in a different stage. While I wrote it, it became extremely funny. It became ridiculous, and the serious things I wanted to write about, I began to see in an absurd light.

MF: Was that change parallel with a change in the way you considered literature in relation to politics, for instance?

CH: I suppose, but it wasn't a conscious process. It was spontaneous.

MF: Now, you believe literature is incapable of influencing politics, correct?

CH: I don't believe writers have any affect on politics.

MF: What about the therapeutic role of writing? I'm thinking of Wright, who said, ''I had to write it out of my system.''

CH: Well, at the beginning of my career, I don't think I was using it as therapy the way Wright was. My approach to literature is different. Even now my writing isn't therapeutic. It's just an attempt on my part to illustrate the absurdities of life.

MF: An ironic comment on the absurdity of the social situation?

CH: Yes, a kind of philosophical approach. I think that writing should be a force in the world, I just don't believe it is. It seems incapable of changing things. You know, if I'm not mistaken, one of the things Flaubert said was that the thing he liked best about politics was the violence. Violence, because politics didn't make any sense, especially in America.

MF: What about your autobiography? Is your autobiographical writing a different kind of literary experience than writing novels?

CH: I began writing it some time ago, because I thought I should leave a record that Chester Himes passed through the world.

MF: You left a record with your other writings.

CH: Yes, but I thought I'd explain why I did certain things to people who might be curious, such as why I left America, what I thought about certain things, how I got to be the kind of person I am. I think there are people in America who want to know. I owe an explanation to black people of why I left the black community, and went to live by myself in a strange white world. This is seldom done by a black man.

MF: By yourself? Don't you see friends, people like Frank Yerby, in Spain?

CH: What I mean is that most American black people have kept to ghettos for many reasons, but mainly to hide from the prejudice and the arrogance of white people, and because they wanted to be to-gether, for protection, and togetherness. I didn't do this, and this is part of the reason why I have to explain myself.

MF: Did you make friends with French writers while you were in Paris? Or with your translators?

CH: Well, Yves Malartic and I were, and are, very good friends, and Marcel Duhamel, too. But the major reason I didn't make more friendships with French writers is because of the language barrier.

MF: Well, you understand French pretty well, don't you?

CH: No, I don't.

MF: When did you leave for Spain?

CH: I left Paris five years ago. First I went to Denmark, and then I came back to spend a summer in the South of France, and then I went to Amsterdam. I've been away from Paris since 1965.

Because I couldn't speak the language, I've remained a stranger. This isn't the fault of the French, either. I remember when I first came to Paris I was invited several times to meetings of the French Writing Society, but they were speaking a language I didn't know. I ended up just standing there, and although I'd liked to have talked with them, I couldn't. I made several attempts to try to learn French, because I was desperate to communicate, but I never mastered enough to speak it well.

When I first arrived, I had been studying French in America for about three months. I remember when I met my translator in front of the Deux Magots at Saint-Germain-des-Près, I said, "Je suisse tres contents de vous voir," I think. Does that make any sense? He looked at me, and he said, "Himes, I'm afraid I don't understand." I didn't try to speak French again that night. I attempted to speak French again on several occasions, but never found anyone who understood me. I have a speech defect anyway, a slight lisp, which causes my voice to become blurred. At times, people find it difficult to understand my English.

I made one more attempt to learn French at l'Alliance Francais, but I decided I was just wasting my time. Of course, by then I was writing the detective stories, and didn't have the time to study French.

MF: I have the impression that Afro-American writers who came to Paris between the two World Wars had a very positive image of France, perhaps due to the cordial treatment of black troops during the first World War. The second generation, which was yours, Wright's, and Baldwin's, saw it as a kind of refuge. But the latest group—I am thinking of people like William M. Kelley, seem to view it only as a port of call. They're more interested in Africa and the possibilities of meeting Africans that Paris offers. What do you think?

CH: I never saw any relationship between me and Africa, and I doubt modern Africans feel any kinship to American Negroes. I find nothing in Africa to attract me. I know a number of Africans, and have become friends with them, but those friendships didn't come about because I am the descendant of African slaves.

Kelley was interested in Africa. Many people of his generation are,

such as LeRoi Jones. These people like to talk about cultural nationalism, and feel there's some kind of cultural bond between black
Africans and black Americans. I agree that there may be some
historical and cultural bonds, but I'm a writer of contemporary fiction.
My thoughts are centered on contemporary realities. What takes
place in America today is far more important to me than what
happened in the past. If I was a scholar, I might think differently.

MF: Does that mean that you restrict yourself, as a writer, to the
lives and problems of poor Harlemites, or perhaps the black bourgeoisie?

CH: No, it isn't that I restrict myself, but more that my concerns as
a writer are for the individual, rather than the whole of society. Of
course, I read about it in the papers, and listen to radio and watch
television. I'm vitally interested in what's going on in Vietnam and in
America. I think America is destroying itself, even while it tries
to survive.

When I sit down to write, though, it's different. It's difficult for me
to write about life on a grand scale; I don't understand life that way. I
don't think I'd be effective if I tried to write that way.

Take the example of Richard Wright. Wright was writing from his
own limited perspective when he wrote his short stories, *Native Son*
and *Black Boy*, but in his own way he was a genius. But when he
began trying to enlarge the scope of his writing, such as in *Pagan
Spain* and his book about the Bandung Conference, I think he lost his
effectiveness as a writer. I began to doubt he would ever again create
something of importance. I tend to dismiss that period of his work as
unimportant and best forgotten. But when he turned to the material
he wrote about in *The Long Dream*, that's when he began to be a
writer again. I think if I tried to do what he did, step onto a larger
stage, the same thing would happen to me.

MF: Talking about this, I'm reminded of the piece you wrote about
Harlem for *Présence Africaine*.

CH: That was straight reportage, and I was writing about something
I knew very well. Harlem is part of my world.

MF: What do you think about Melvin Van Peebles's adaptation of
La Reine des pommes in *Hara-Kiri*?

CH: I thought the cartoons were atrocious, but they paid me more

for the permission to do that book than I earned from Gallimard when
I originally sold it to them.

MF: When you describe a scene in Harlem, you have a kind of
rabelaisian approach. You write about people making love, eating,
fighting, playing games, running. This kind of picturesque description
seems to make caricatures of people, so don't you think you invited
this kind of treatment [in *Hara-Kiri*]?

CH: There's some truth in that, but my way of creating a scene is
to describe enough things in order to make an entire picture. Take for
an example the scene from *La Reine des pommes*, where Jackson is
driving away in his stolen hearse, with the boy in the coffin, and so
on. All those details make the scene complete. You know, if you get a
police report about an incident, and get all the statements from the
witnesses, you tend to get a rather jumbled and confused picture. In
a way, that's another form of reality. I think that's the kind of reality
that you find in Harlem. You not only have the actual reality of the
incident, but also the individual realities of each person who tries to
remember it. Probably the nature of life in Harlem is such that the
eyewitness accounts of any given event will be conflicting. I try to
present things in such a way that the reader can understand this
phenomenon.

MF: So what you're saying is that you try to stress the degree
of contrast.

CH: Yes.

MF: You never take the side of any of the characters, do you?
There are no good guys or bad guys in your Harlem.

CH: Well, isn't that the way people really are, neither all good, nor
all bad?

MF: Yet many writers tend to simplify, don't they?

CH: Sure, because it's easier, but this isn't the way it exists in life.
Everybody has different facets. It depends on when you see him, and
what the circumstances of the meeting are. I think a writer should
make that clear.

MF: What about the Black Muslims? Do they think they're being
treated unfairly in *Blind Man*?

CH: If they read the book, they might think they are, but I doubt
any Black Muslim reads my books. However, I do know that people
who are sympathetic to Black Muslims read my books. I have a good

friend who is the proprietor of a book store in Harlem, and who is sympathetic to them, but he and I think alike on this point. But this doesn't change his sympathies for the Muslims.

I want to make a point about something. There was a recent review of *Blind Man With A Pistol* in the *New York Times* in which the reviewer closed the review with the remark, "I must sadly say that Chester Himes is anti-Negro," or something like that. What is interesting is the number of letters that the *Times* received from black people, essentially saying, "why can't Chester Himes write about his people and make them funny? Philip Roth writes that way about Jews." The *Times* published some of these. The black community gave me a lot of support for this story. They don't resent what I did at all. They have a sense of humor about it. Black readers in America have reached a certain point where they want more than just the facts. It isn't enough to say that black people are suffering. It doesn't help them much.

MF: A film is being made of *Cotton Comes to Harlem*. What's the latest news about it?

CH: We were discussing that downstairs. It's been released, and I got some news about it. It's promising to be a great success. The film made a house record from the income, but we're having difficulties with Plon about the rights in the contract. They insist they own a percentage of the rights, and are settling that with the lawyers from United Artists. Gallimard, who owned all the first rights, signed a release, and are trying to come up with a way of taking *Cotton Comes to Harlem* away from Plon, and putting it in the Gallimard series. It's the only one of my detective stories not in the *Série noire*.

MF: What do you think of the possibilities of revolutionary nationalism in the U.S.?

CH: There were a lot of riots breaking out in the U. S. a few years ago. Then, during the spring of 1968, Martin Luther King was killed, and that was the end of the riots. After that there were a number of Black Panther clashes with the police all over America. That's about the time I realized that all this disorganized violence was like a blind man with a pistol. That's how my last book got its title.

I was trying to make a statement. Disorganized violence isn't effective, and it doesn't do a thing but make black people more vulnerable. If there must be violence, I believe it should be organized violence. They should organize an effort like the people in North Vietnam have. If the Viet Cong weren't so well organized, there's no way a group of peasants could put up such an effective resistance. They've fought America to a standstill. If American blacks could put up an organized resistance, America would find them as difficult to deal with as the Viet Cong. If they can't get organized, then they ought to find another way to achieve equality.

When I realized all this, that's when I really began to get this book together. The point I was trying to make became obvious. I realized nothing but violence will ever improve the position of American Negroes. It wouldn't have to be anything cataclysmic, but if it were organized, that might be enough.

MF: When you wrote *Lonely Crusade*, you were quite critical of the white trade unions and working classes. Do you think there has been any great change in the attitudes?

CH: The situation I described was how things were during the Second World War. All that has changed now. The political statements I made in *Lonely Crusade* are no longer valid. The only value that book has now is the picture of human relationships I portrayed.

Profile of Chester Himes
David Jenkins / 1971

Nova (January 1971), pp. 50–52.

Chester Himes is variously described as the greatest find in American crime fiction since Raymond Chandler, a bloody nihilist, a grizzled old pro, and probably the best contemporary American practitioner of the lost art of narration. He is self-described as being 'motivated with an extraordinary, unimaginable violence of the mind.' His series of eight Harlem thrillers amputate and disembowel the Black Experience. His goodies are usually more violent even than his baddies. In his youth he smashed up more segregationist restaurants than you've had hot dinners. Among his hundreds of former domiciles is the Ohio State Penitentiary, accommodation enforced after a gun-point robbery of a couple of rich whites in Cleveland.

The recurrent theme in his reported conversation is that of the coming black revolution resulting in the whites turning on themselves, razing cities with the whites, blacks and rats still inside. His novel on this theme has been abandoned, partly because, he has said, he was shocked himself by its violence.

You are therefore unprepared for the gentle old man with sad preoccupied eyes, who favours weak Pastis, and whose nearest approach to crime these days is the ruminative clipping of his neighbour's geraniums to help along the scrubby garden around the new bungalow he and his English wife, Lesley, have built in the village of Moraira, between Alicante and Valencia on the Costa Blanca.

Although Himes has been self-exiled in Europe for 17 years, his writing still has the reek and grotesque humour of Harlem running through it. There is little moral blandishment, no attractiveness, in the heroes. The famous pair of black detectives, Coffin Ed and Grave Digger Jones, 'with their identical big, hard-shooting, head-whipping pistols, had always looked like two hog farmers on a weekend in the Big Town.' Coffin Ed, his face badly scarred by acid, is nothing more nor less than a psychopath.

Himes insists that he is barely exaggerating the violent facts of life

95

in his thrillers. The violence is chronicled with a dispassionate care
that is part violently repellent, part violently funny. The daily reports
coming into the precinct station are themselves savage vignettes of
Harlem living: 'Man kills his wife with an axe for burning his breakfast
chop . . . woman stabs man in stomach 14 times, no reason given . . .
man arrested for threatening to blow up subway train because he
entered wrong station and couldn't get his token back . . . man
dressed as Cherokee Indian splits white barman's skull with homemade tomahawk . . . man arrested on Seventh Avenue for hunting cats
with hound dog and shotgun . . . 25 men arrested for trying to chase
all the white people out of Harlem . . .'

As Grave Digger says: 'We got the highest crime rate on earth
among the coloured people in Harlem. And there ain't but three things
to do about it: make the criminals pay for it–you don't want to do
that; pay the people enough to live decently–you ain't going to do
that; so all that's left is let 'em eat one another up.'

It is impossible to think of a rhythm of life so different from
Harlem's as that of Moraira. The Siamese cat, Griot–after whom the
house has been named–follows the sun round the Moorish terrace
with slow padding inevitability. The only disturbing sounds are those
of the water-sprinklers on the garden, the coming and going of the
curé across the road–'Here comes de Pope'–and the rocket that is
sent up at 10 o'clock in the evening by the cinema down in the village
to announce that the main film is about to start. The population of the
house is completed with a lizard called O. Henry, who lives in a rafter
on the terrace, and another lizard called Pinktoes–named after
Himes's satirical novel about liberal New York politics–who seems to
be inveigled out from his stony home by the music of Lester Young.

Chester Himes seldom goes out. When he does, it is usually in his
beige Mark X Jaguar, which seems to be wider than most of the roads
there-abouts. His speech is soft, as if spent of spleen. It is punctuated
with rare but tremendous laughs. Himes was amazed to learn that
Morning Glory seeds were supposed to be hallucinogenic. 'OK,' he
said. 'There's a Morning Glory plant, let's get some seeds.' We sat
for a while in silence, munching a seed apiece. Simultaneously,
Lesley's face, his face and my face wrinkled in disgust. 'That's
terrible,' he said, collapsing in shoulder-shaking, eye-streaming laugh-

ter. But within seconds his face is recomposed into a slightly misan-
thropic glare.

His anger, similarly, is short lived. His car parked awkwardly at the
side of the road, we started to get out. 'Stay in the car,' he shouted.
The subject is returned to in fury several times in a few minutes, then
is completely forgotten.

Despite the soporific nature of his present life, his past is most vivid
in his mind, perhaps because of its contrast.

Himes was born at almost the exact geographical centre of the
United States, Jefferson City, Missouri, in 1909. His accent is a
curious mixture of succotash Southern and Harlem. 'The last tahm
Ah was in the States, somebody stole all my goddam shoits.' His
father was a teacher of blacksmithing and wheelwrighting at the
Lincoln Institute, a college formed by black infantrymen who fought
for the North in the Civil War. Himes's youth was a peregrination of
the campuses of Agricultural and Mechanical Colleges around the
South, Missouri, Mississippi, Arkansas, and Georgia. During his late
teens, his family moved North, to Cleveland, Ohio.

His childhood, he says, was more or less happy. Home-taught by
his mother, he was comparatively insulated from the excesses of
Southern prejudice. 'The main thing I remember was that my father
had one of the first automobiles owned by a black person in the South.
It used to rattle along those roads, scaring the mule teams driven by
whites. Those whites used to get out their rifles and start shooting at
us. So my mother took to carrying a pistol with her.'

Himes was the youngest of three sons. One of his brothers, blinded
in youth by a school laboratory explosion, was the academic, and is
now a sociology teacher in North Carolina. The other was a waiter in
New York. He became an official in the waiters' union, and is, says
Himes, probably the most famous of the three in Harlem itself. It was
in Cleveland that Himes's problems really began. When he left high
school, he took a job in a chichi hotel as a room-service bus-boy.
Collecting a tray of dishes one day from an upstairs room, he fell
down an elevator shaft, breaking three vertebrae, his left arm, his
chin, and all his teeth. He was in hospital for six months, after which
he drew a state pension for 10 years. The pension was not grand–75
dollars a month–but for a black boy of 16 it was considerably more
than his contemporaries had.

His career in petty (and not so petty) crime began at about this time. 'I got to running around with some underworld characters, prostitutes and gamblers, and show people who used to hang around. I forged some cheques, stole some guns and automobiles. I used to gamble, you know; dice and cards. Some of the games were really big. There could be as much as 15,000 dollars on the table, which was really big money for black people in the Depression.'

One of the characters Himes met was a hoodlum from Seattle called Gus Smith, nicknamed Bunch Boy. Bunch Boy had operated a Policy racket in Chicago. (Policy was an elaborate lottery game much loved in the ghettoes.) His greatest claim to fame was that while in Chicago he had been kidnapped by the Al Capone mob and held to ransom for 80,000 dollars. 'Bunch Boy took a liking to me because of my age, and he let me run a game from time to time.

'The servants of the rich whites of Cleveland used to come into Bunch Boy's place and talk about their employers. One of these people was the chauffeur of a couple of rich whites in the very rich area of Cleveland Heights. He told me where their money was kept–on a top shelf in the bedroom–and one night, actually it was Thanksgiving Eve–I went out there and robbed them.

'I watched the couple come back from some place, and go in. I followed them in through the garage. They were in evening dress and were just having cocktails, I remember. I waved my gun at them–it was a .44–and locked them up. I took the jewellery, which was insured for 28,000 dollars, and a big stack of $100 bills, straight from the bank. I got outside and took the Cadillac coupé they had driven up in. As I was driving away, the cops were just outside. They started shooting at me, so I drove at 85, maybe 90 mph. It was snowing like hell, so I lost them. But about five or six miles out of town, the car left the road. I was unhurt this time, so I stepped out of the car, walked back to Cleveland, and took the train to Chicago.

'I knew of a fence in Chicago called Jew Sam. I reckoned that by pawning the jewellery I would get enough to get to Mexico. What I didn't know was that a white woman had been robbed in the Blackstone Hotel two nights before, and had said that she had seen a black man making off with her jewels. So, as soon as I went in Jew Sam's place, he was on to the police. I was arrested, and in the detective bureau, this woman identified the jewellery I had as hers. I believe that this woman later admitted having faked the robbery to fool her husband. She had actually pawned it. Anyway, while I was at the detective bureau, the cops got a reader on the robbery in Cleveland, and that was that.'

The sentencing judge informed Himes that he had taken 10 years off the life of each of his victims, so he was sentenced to 20 to 25 years in the State Penitentiary. He entered the prison on December 27, 1928.

'In the dormitories were long tables running down the middle. The first man up in the morning spread a blanket on the table and set his game up there. I organised this, with the help of the guards, ran a gambling syndicate and became chief banker for the black convicts. My pension kept coming in, and I started making considerable amounts of money from the gambling, probably more than the rest of my family put together during the Depression.'

On Easter Monday, 1930, a group of convicts tried to organise a break-out. They planned to start a fire as a diversion during the change-over of the guard. The fire burned too slowly, however, and by the time it really started giving off the right amount of smoke, the guard had changed, and there was nobody around with enough authority to order the gates opened. So over 300 convicts died in the resulting conflagration. Shortly after this, the Ohio law was changed, and the lower limits of long-term sentences no longer left to the discretion of the sentencing judge. So Himes actually only served seven years and seven months of his sentence.

After the fire, Himes bought a Remington typewriter and taught himself to type. He started contributing stories to magazines in 1931. His greatest influence was–and still is–Dashiell Hammett. 'I was reading these stories in magazines, and I thought I could do about as well. But Hammett had the genius that none of them ever reached. *The Maltese Falcon* made a great impression on me. It was the first story in which a woman got sent to prison.'

In 1934, he had a story published in *Esquire*, then another, this one about the fire, called "To What Red Hell." While he was in prison, he contributed more stories to *Esquire*, his by-line always accompanied by his prison number.

By the time he came out of prison in 1936, his parents were divorced. 'I think I was probably the biggest cause of their break-up.

My father was softer on me because of my accident, and my mother
wanted me to have more discipline, and this caused some bitterness.'
Finding work was difficult. Finding a publisher even more difficult.
He worked for a while in Cleveland on the Works Progress Administration–founded by President Roosevelt to give jobs to the unemployed–
writing his history of Cleveland for a guide book. He also wrote 100-
word prose poems for the *Cleveland Evening News*, for which he
received one dollar per piece.

In 1940 he went to Hollywood, where he worked with the Communist Party collecting clothes and money for Spanish Civil War exiles.
He was never a member of the Party–indeed has never been a member
of any party–and remembers: 'We used to go round the homes of
Hollywood sympathisers. They would invite you in for a drink, but
you would never get past the kitchen.' His experiences with the Party
were recorded in *Lonely Crusade*, soundly hammered by American
Communists, but acclaimed by the French Communist press. Most of
the war, up to 1944, he spent working in the shipyards and factories
of the West Coast, building, among other things, Liberty ships at
great speed. In 1944 he was awarded a grant by the Rosenwald
Foundation to finish his novel about the shipyards, *If He Hollers Let
Him Go*, and went to New York.

Between 1944 and 1953, when he shipped out, he lived in and
around New York, on the fringes of liberal politics–which inspired
Pinktoes–and in Harlem itself, the basis of most of his subsequent
detective stories. 'I had lost interest in America long before, before
even the robbery, but I could never find enough money to leave.'
Eventually, he sold a novel to New American Library for 5,000
dollars, and went to Paris.

Around Europe, he says, 'I carried Harlem with me. I have lived in
most European countries now, and I have never found one that was
really more *simpatico* to me. I'm not disappointed, because that was
never what I was looking for. I never had enough to give to any of the
communities I was living in, so I never got anything out. I think the
most stimulating time for me was in Paris, when I was with a whole
lot of expatriate blacks. With the only exception of Harlem, my
location doesn't appear to make any difference to me. One book I
wrote in Paris, the next in Copenhagen, the next in Kitzbühel, the
next in Paris and so on.'

His first detective story, *La Reine des pommes*, translated as *A Rage in Harlem*, was published in the *Série noire* in Paris by Marcel Duhamel. It was written in two months in 1957. For it, Himes was paid $1,000. 'I certainly didn't realise I had written the best of my detective stories, and I didn't ever take it seriously. I did it simply for the money, sitting up nights, over Christmas and New Year, with a bottle of St. James's rum. Most of the detective stories were written in a month or two each, and always when I needed the money.' The stories were immediately successful in France–'I guess because of that French cynicism'–and he was awarded the Grand Prix Policiere. Cocteau described *La Reine des pommes* as a masterpiece. Two new anti-heroes, Coffin Ed and Grave Digger had been born.

Himes never set out to produce sociological works, but he has, in fact, produced a body of social reporting of a very high order indeed. 'If I had wanted to express my own revulsion for violence then I would have made the violence even more repellent, really repellent. I am simply creating stories that have a setting I know very well. I remember the ghettoes of Cleveland when it was certainly not unusual to find in the morning two or three black guys dead in the side of the road.

'For the blacks there is no police in the ghetto. I have created two black detectives who are acting out in fiction what should be happening in reality. The courts in New York never seem to convict a black man for killing another black man. There is no way of defending black people from each other. They have always been the victims of predators, of confidence tricksters. I remember a great confidence trick called The Blow, in which a guy would claim that he would be able to convert a $10 bill into a $100 bill by putting it into a stove. Countless people were taken in by this.'

'There is more danger in the ghetto for me than for a white person. Even the black community has accepted that my stories are realistic. The feeling of revulsion at violence is completely beside the point. It exists. A black person doesn't get protection from the courts if his property is violated.'

But the experience is also absurd, and very funny. In one book, a large black woman, keeping her purse between her legs, is robbed as she is kneeling in church by a man carefully cutting away the back of her skirt with a razor. A man with his head shot off is repugnant, but is also absurd. 'The Spanish don't publish my books because they wouldn't sell. They like their tragedy undiluted by humour. I saw a play on television the other night in which a whole family is poisoned by the soup. I think that's very funny, but the Spanish don't.'

Himes is not a bitter person. He has taken instant revenge on the aggravations in his life, violently and usually in writing. Significantly, his best book, a beautiful novel called *The Primitive*, points to the uselessness of racial resentment.

A black revolution, says Himes, is highly possible, though unlikely at present. 'All the so-called leaders of the black people in the United States are effectively neutralised by publicity. I have never fully endorsed the black movements, although I have supported both the Black Muslims–I was a friend of Malcolm X–and the Panthers. I don't think they will succeed because they are too used to publicity, and a successful revolution must be planned with secrecy, security.

'Yet there is no reason why 100,000 blacks armed with automatic rifles couldn't literally go underground, into the subways and basements of Manhattan–and take over. The basements of those skyscrapers are the strongest part of the building. There would be no way, there is no weapon, to get them out. You could bomb Manhattan and all, and still not reach underground. This was the novel I was writing, and I don't know if I have the energy or determination to finish it.'

Himes has never used a European locale for his post-1953 stories, except for two novelettes set in Paris to be published soon in America.

'I guess the only place I am at home, really at home, is in Harlem, but I could never possibly live there. My mind is shattered by the injustice of it. The cops, of course, are just stupid. When my shirts were stolen, the cop said in all seriousness, if you see someone wearing one, let us know. The whites are going to have to back down, and I don't know if they can bear to do that. I believe in organised revolution with violence as the only way for the blacks to instil enough fear into the whites to make them back down.'

He looks out over another astonishing sunset on the hills towards Benidorm and makes such a mild gesture with his hand that it is difficult to believe it is he who has just said that. 'The white people of America have left them (the blacks) nothing to believe in,' Chester Himes has written. Except one thing, says Himes.

A Kind of Uncle Tom

Helmut M. Braem / 1971

Stuttgarter Zeitung 38 (August 1971). All rights reserved. Translation copyright by Michel Fabre. Printed with his permission.

The interviewer met Himes when the latter participated in a panel on black American literature with James Baldwin at the U. S. Army base in Stuttgart.

HB: Mr. Himes, why did you leave the United States twenty-five years ago to settle in Europe?

CH: I was thirty then. I'd heard from friends how cheap life was in Paris.

HB: Did you ever return to the United States?

CH: I briefly returned to the United States in the hope of earning money, and of reestablishing contact with people back there. But I got an opportunity to make a living in Paris, using Harlem as a locale for some detective novels. I just did it to make a living, but ultimately realized that my work had become a kind of classic in the field, because it dealt with American Negroes. Afterwards, I travelled a good deal around Europe and finally settled in Alicante, mostly because of the mild climate.

HB: Is your autobiography the last step in your writing career?

CH: Not at all. When I think of all the material I still have to work with, it's hard to see an end to it. If anything stops me, it might be heart trouble, though.

HB: Do you think literature can have a positive influence on the world?

CH: I've always distrusted that outlook. I've never believed literature could change anything.

HB: Yet some books have brought about reforms. Would you deny the impact of a book like Zola's *Germinal*?

CH: That's true, but any process that literature helps to start is a long, drawn out one.

HB: The people you depict in your domestic novels don't seem to

103

be conscious of the discrimination they suffer. Are you saying that their situation is hopeless?

CH: It isn't true that none of them understand their situation, just that they have no way of changing it. Most of them lack the intellectual background to even understand that things could be any different.

HB: Have you met any real-life models for your detectives, Coffin Ed Johnson and Grave Digger Jones?

CH: Oh, yes. I thought especially of a couple of black lieutenants in Chicago. They were notoriously violent, and killed many people.[1]

HB: In your autobiography it says that you were sentenced to a prison term for theft and burglary when you were a youngster. Malcolm X and Eldridge Cleaver, who also served prison terms, suggest that time in prison can be used to develop self awareness. Was this true in your case?

CH: Most certainly, if only because I started writing while I was in the penitentiary. However, the political and social scene in America was very different from the time in which Malcolm X and Eldridge Cleaver lived.

HB: Where do you stand on today's Negro movements?

CH: The extremist groups, like the Black Panther Party, have no interest in me, of course. They probably consider me a kind of Uncle Tom. I don't have any special interest in them, either. Most of them are only looking to feather their own nests.

HB: Mr. Himes, are you going to stay here any longer?

CH: Unfortunately, that's impossible, because Griot, our cat, would certainly destroy my studio back home and chew up all my books if I did.

---

[1] Elsewhere Himes suggests his inspiration came from two detectives he knew of in Los Angeles.

Chester Himes
Michael Mok / 1972

From *Publishers Weekly* 201 (April 3, 1972), pp. 21–21. Reprinted by permission of Cahners Publishing Company.

Chester Himes, ex-convict, jewel thief, bedroom athlete, busboy,
porter, expatriate, but above all writer, talks about himself—
something he does with verve and brilliance—in the first volume of
his autobiography, *The Quality of Hurt* (Doubleday), and in conversation with *PW*:

"I was speaking to a black studies class at Hunter College," he told
PW, "and the young professor, who was black, kept quoting from an
article in the Sunday *Times' Book Review* (which I hadn't read) that
said I wasn't a true spokesman for the black race, that the Harlem of
my books was not the real Harlem. . . .

"Well, I explained that I had created a Harlem of my mind; that I
have never attempted to be the spokesman for any segment of the
black community. I take my stories from the Black Experience as I
have undergone it.

"Before long, the kids were on *my* side. Young people don't want
to confuse stories in books with their own reality. They resent books
that claim to show the interior of their minds. They aren't looking for
any 'spokemen.' They can speak for themselves. The best a black
writer can do is to deal with subjects which are personal; so he can
tell how it was for him."

This is what Himes has done in *The Quality of Hurt*. Doubleday
will also bring out a collection of Himes's short stories this fall titled
Black on Black. The second volume of his autobiography, the working
title of which is "Writing for Life," is scheduled for some time next
year. That title has a double meaning for Himes: He says, "I am a
writer and no one can take that away. A writer writes and a fighter
fights." The title of the second volume of autobiography also refers to
the fact that he was stony-broke in the period of which he writes in
the book, and literally was writing to live.

Speaking of the title of the first volume of his autobiography, Himes says "The quality of hurt that most black people feel is reflected in many ways; the man with the machine gun is logical enough, but so is the quality of pity. The quality of hurt caused me to feel tenderness and pity towards this white woman (their affair takes up much of the first volume) and I wanted to record it because it was true. But the fact that a black man might feel pity for a white woman is—especially to certain black people—totally unacceptable."

Part of *The Quality of Hurt* is devoted to the seven and a half years Himes spent as a young man in the Ohio Penitentiary and the fire there in 1930 that left 332 convicts dead and made him a professional writer. His searing account of the tragedy was published in *Esquire* in 1932 as "To What Red Hell."

". . . The prison was burning out of control when would-be help arrived and the keys to the cells were lost in the panic. Rescuers, led by black convicts with sledge hammers, threw themselves into the flames and smashed off the locks so they could drag out the prisoners, who were roasting alive. . . ."

Details of the disaster went 'round the world, as did stories of the heroism of the convicts, many of whom were black. The ensuing clamor for reform resulted in a modification of the penal code and parole system and ultimately led to Himes's release (he had originally been sentenced to 20–25 years.) "I suddenly found that I had hope."

Referring to the revolutionary spirit abroad in U.S. prisons today, he says. "At the rate that black prisoners are going in and white prisoners are coming out, it's only a question of time before there will be only blacks in the jails. The revolution inside the walls is taking place because the white establishment is sending some of our best minds to prison. . . ."

On revolution in general, he told *PW*: "I have always believed in a black revolution by violent force. Such a revolution would fail (that is to say, the establishment would win the war through massive lethal strength) and numberless brothers would die. . . . But the enormous sympathy the failed revolution would generate could exert such savage pressure on the American political and economic system that the white establishment in panicky desperation would give blacks whatever they wanted.

"But this revolution would mean more than lecturing on lecture platforms; it would mean going out and getting killed. . . ."

Himes is best known to the young people of Europe (his stories are immensely popular in France, Germany and England) and in the United States as the author of such chillers as *Blind Man With A Pistol* (Morrow) and *Cotton Comes to Harlem* (Putnam), which was turned into a runaway smash movie by Sam Goldwyn.

"The two cops, Coffin Ed Johnson and Grave Digger Jones, are roughly based on a black lieutenant and his sergeant partner who worked the Central Avenue ghetto in L.A. back in the 1940s. My cops are just as tough, but somewhat more humane. The original pair were pitiless bastards. (Ultimately one of them killed his partner in a gunfight over a woman and was himself forced into early retirement.)

"As I said before, many of my brothers resent that I have created a Harlem of my own, the fact that many foreigners and sometimes even Americans mistake my Harlem for the real thing. But these same people loved the film. They will see wild distortions in the movies and think they're great, but when they spot the smallest distortion in my books, they pounce."

Himes feels that his crime stories perform a service to the blacks of America by acquainting outsiders with the poverty and deprivation under which they live. "You'll also notice that the characters in my detective stories, in order to remain credible, had to grow with the passage of time and as they did so, they developed a greater race consciousness," he says.

Sadly enough, Himes, who lives in Alicante, Spain, sold the rights to *Cotton* outright, but if Hollywood brings out a series like the Bond fantasy (which is the intention) he will be in Fat City. "Just tell people I'm not there yet," he says.

Portrait of a Man Reading
Michael J. Bandler / 1972

Washington Post Book World (April 9, 1972), p. 2. Copyright 1972, *Washington Post* Writers Group. Reprinted with permission.

What's your earliest reading recollection?

I remember reading many collections of Roman and Greek mythology: the Golden Fleece, Horatio at the Bridge, and so on—but I don't remember the actual titles. My mother, who didn't like the schools for black children, taught us at home. So all my early reading came from books she suggested. I do remember vividly, though, my reading in prison, which was cheap American fiction, that is, fiction published by slick paper magazines. I read a number of classic detective stories in a pulp magazine called *Black Mask* in the early 1930s. I read the early stories of Dashiell Hammett and Raymond Chandler before they became known to the world. *The Maltese Falcon* by Hammett was one that appeared in serial form in *Black Mask* before it became a book. I read *Lady in the Lake* and the other Philip Marlowe stories of Chandler, but I think that was later.

When did you first become aware of the presence of a black writer of note in America?

As the son of a black schoolteacher in the South, I was aware from the time I was born—almost—of the presence of black writers. Every black schoolchild knew the poetry of Paul Laurence Dunbar, which was recited in school. Then, of course, there were Frederick Douglass and Booker T. Washington. Later on, I read the work of Langston Hughes and the early books of Richard Wright: *Black Boy*, *Native Son*, *Uncle Tom's Children*, and *The Outsider*. And I remember an autobiography by Langston Hughes, *The Big Sea*. Actually, most of the early books I read about blacks were written by whites: *Kingsblood Royal* by Sinclair Lewis, Margaret Mitchell's *Gone With the Wind*, and *Strange Fruit* by Lillian E. Smith.

Who were your literary models?

I would suppose that, if I was influenced by any writer, it was the early William Faulkner and Dashiell Hammett. I read all of Faulkner: *Sanctuary*, *Light in August*, *The Sound and the Fury*, *As I Lay Dying*, and the rest, but I remember reading *The Mosquitoes* early on. Later I was influenced by the verisimilitude of Raymond Chandler, who could do many things with words that I had great admiration for, although I always felt his essential character, his detective Philip Marlowe, was asinine. But his imagery and phraseology impressed me greatly.

If you had to assemble a packet of books for a ghetto kid in Cleveland, let's say, which books would you choose?

That's the hardest question you've asked. It's very difficult for me to say. I could name *Native Son*, by Richard Wright, but I'm not sure I'd want a ghetto kid to read it. It's a revolutionary book, and I think a great book. But I don't know if it would affect a ghetto kid's mind in the right way.

Why not?

I think it would have an adverse effect. If the problems of the ghetto can't be solved by inspirational writings, then they can only be solved by outright revolutionary books. *Native Son* isn't in either category; it's somewhere in between. I think Maya Angelou's *I Know Why the Caged Bird Sings* and John A. Williams's *The Man Who Cried I Am* would be valuable books for a ghetto kid to read, much more so than any of Dick's books, although I would choose *Black Boy* in preference to *Native Son*. *Black Boy* is an autobiography that a ghetto kid could understand without any injurious mental effect, and it would make him understand himself better.

How about a book by a white writer for a ghetto kid?

Well, certainly I'd include my favorite Faulkner book, *Light in August*, because overall it makes the whole business of racism quite absurd; the confusion, shouting, and wrangling is all for nothing. And if it would make the ghetto kid see it as absurd, it would also cause him to react beneficially.

Which other books by whites have impressed you?

For a long time I was reading the great Russian novels of Tolstoy, Dostoevsky, and Gogol. *The Brothers Karamazov* is one of my favorite stories. Of course, it has a very simple detective story theme.

The mystery element carries the whole book. I've enjoyed W. Somerset Maugham, especially *Of Human Bondage* and some of his short stories. I read many of Louis Bromfield's books in the past: *The Rains Came*, *Twenty-four Hours*, and others. I worked on Malabar Farm for a while a number of years ago. Then there were the Ernest Hemingway stories, D.H. Lawrence's *Sons and Lovers*, and later John Updike's *Rabbit Run*. And I read Mario Puzo's *The Godfather*, like everyone else.

Are there any Continental authors you've grown to appreciate during your years of living abroad?

Well, I never learned to read in a foreign language. But in translation I've read the works of Maupassant and Emile Zola. Zola's *La Terre [The Soil]* and his book about the French miners, *Germinal*, were the most important ones for me.

Have you kept up with the flood of black American writers of today?

It's hard to find works by blacks in Europe. But recently, I've read a number of books by young black writers, including Ronald Fair's *We Can't Breathe* and *Many Thousand Gone*, *Yellow Back Radio Broke Down* by Ishmael Reed, and Cecil Brown's *The Life and Loves of Mr. Jiveass Nigger*. Brown's book is very accurate. I've spoken to people who know the scene, who've lived the expatriate life for 35 years, and who know Copenhagen and Stockholm and they've praised its authenticity. I've read hardly any black poetry; as for plays, I've read LeRoi Jones's *The Slave*, *Dutchman*, and *The Toilet*. And I hate to admit this, but the only piece of James Baldwin's I've ever read was *The Fire Next Time*, which I read in *The New Yorker*.

What's been your most satisfying reading experience?

Well, I was greatly taken by Maya Angelou's *I Know Why the Caged Bird Sings*, but I must confess, I sound naive, that I was most impressed by a book that is unknown, but not at all inconsequential, Melvin Van Peebles's book on the making of his film, *A Bear for the F.B.I.* He wrote about its conception, its filming and editing, and you felt that he was thinking—throughout his earlier tribulations—that even with his financial difficulties he would not accept any help from the white establishment. This paperback is one of the most inspiring books on black accomplishment available.

What are you reading right now?

A book by Carl Van Doren on the writing of the Constitution, *The Great Rehearsal.* I had read *John Paul Jones: A Sailor's Biography,* by Samuel Eliot Morison, and I became fascinated with the individuals who lived at the time of independence, and the particular feelings that surfaced later during the time the Constitution was written.

Is there any book you've wanted to read, but haven't?

Yes, I'd like to read Claude Brown's *Manchild in the Promised Land.*

Who's the blackest white writer you know?

You mean the one who understands the black people best? Well, I always felt that Faulkner was able to capture the mentality of blacks in the South better than any other white writer I've read. He exaggerated sometimes, but he has some very sharp portraits of black people in the South in his works. Lots of blacks and whites dislike him for being a so-called black white writer, though.

Don Chester Himes: Evening with an Exile

Charles Wright / 1972

From *The Village Voice* (June 1, 1972), p. 24.

Early evening: rain and sleet. Darkness blossoms like a field of daisies. On such an evening, a man might etch intrigue, love, or despair. And the venerable Chelsea Hotel is a place where a man might wait for the countdown or enjoy the spoils of victory. Emerging from the elevator, I encountered Marjorie Morningstar. She carried a Vuitton tote bag and was worthy of James Bond. But Chester Himes (author of *Cotton Comes to Harlem*) was doing his thing, which was accepting a goodbye, cheek kiss from the pretty, purple-coated girl from publicity. There was another striking female in the room: Ms. Himes, Blond, English, she completed her phone call, kissed her legal lover of seven years, and departed.

I am not very good at interviewing people, even people I admire. But Chester Himes is warm and very real. We made small talk about the magnificent Edward Hopper window view, then sat down in easy chairs, facing each other. I had finished reading the recently published first volume of Mr. Himes's autobiography, *The Quality of Hurt*. Questions, questions—cluttered the wine red foyer of my mind. Griot, the 17-year-old Siamese cat who always travels with Mr. and Ms. Himes, bolted over and inspected my boots. Himes said: "Griot is named after the magicians in the courts of West African kings." He looked over at Griot and continued: "I visited my brother in Greensboro, North Carolina, and attended an integrated party. This was unheard of years ago. But everyone seemed to know each other. This isn't true of New York."

Chester Himes looks like an elegant sportsman, a man of distinction, and—with his beard—bears an uncanny resemblance to Ernest Hemingway. However, Himes is black and basic. "You know there is only one black writer. Just as soon as he makes it, they tear him down. We black writers have got to stop fighting each other. Whitey has always pitted one black against the other. The field slaves and the house slaves. Their motto has always been divide and conquer."

Divide and conquer would come up time and again in our hour-and-a-half conversation. After all, Himes was "advocating black revolution in the '40s." He admires young black writers, militants, and said: "I've come to believe that the only way the American black will ever be able to participate in the American way of life is by a series of acts of violence. It's tragic, but true. Martin Luther King couldn't make a dent on the American conscience until he was killed." Himes, who spent seven and a half years in prison, follows the American prison revolt with great interest. And he remembers the prison of his youth: "It was a stinking place, hardly changed since the Civil War. Cells were over-crowded. Conditions were bad. On Easter Sunday, 1931, some scaffolding caught fire and 321 convicts were burned to death. The National Guard was called in. There was a bloody riot."

Chester Himes's emotions are not colored by the eight violent novels he wrote about the Harlem ghetto. (These detective novels were written very fast, read extremely well, and, as Himes told me: "They worked. They jelled.") He accepts violence as he accepts the cold, rainy afternoon: with interest and amused detachment. If he's bitter about his struggling literary years, he's cool. His emotions reside behind the barricade and he crosses his legs, laughs warmly, recounting double-dealing publishers, sketching fine vignettes of James Baldwin, Richard Wright, Ralph Ellison, and Robert Graves. Listening to him, one would not think he has lived in the underworld where crime is the main course. Certainly Chester Himes is not a heterosexual Jean Genet. Middle-class America framed the background of the gentleman from Missouri; the underworld provided the paella for the detective stories, including the celebrated *Pinktoes*. The Grave Digger-Coffin Ed novels are behind him. A few years ago in Mexico, Himes suffered a stroke and wrote the last detective story. Besides, he doesn't take too kindly to the motion picture version of *Cotton Comes to Harlem*.

Now, giant columns of lights glow in the distance. The sky is a deep blue. The clamor of rush hour seems far away. Griot is sleeping on the floral-covered bed. An unopened tin of Tabby cat food is at the foot of the bed. And everything is going well. This is not so much an interview as a conversation between two black writers. Chester Himes

might have been my father who had been away at war, away at sea, or
in prison for a decade. I like the man who is also a writer. We do not
have to go through the generation gap bit. You see, Himes sided with
James Baldwin during his famous feud with Richard Wright. "The
sons must slay their fathers," Baldwin said. Himes remembers, pays
affectionate tribute. Earlier, we had mentioned the literary Jewish
mafia. Perhaps our black moment was just over the hill.

Certainly, Himes is optimistic. In fact, he's optimistic about almost
every Goddamn thing. A benevolent patriarch, he carries misery as
one would carry a basket of eggs or fly a kite. Occasionally, briefly,
he seemed to stiffen in his easy chair and his warm eyes would express
discomfort. Then there was the thing with his hands. His taut hands
moved rapidly across the arms of the chair as if testing their quality,
strength. Suddenly, I remembered a Moroccan friend with a cancer-
ous foot who counted wooden beads (the size and color of coffee
beans) to axe pain. I do not know if it was painful for Don Himes to
listen to some of my remarks. But I do know when the moment
arrived for me. It moved swiftly and ever so precise to the outhouse
of my mind. But in the beginning it was a Fat City scene. Two dudes
discussing the crown jewels of the planet: women. The mood of our
conversation was not: if she's ugly, put a paper bag over her head or
all broads are alike in the dark. Our conversation would not have
offended women's lib. All I know is that black women wouldn't cotton
to it.

Chester Himes began by praising Cecil Brown's *The Life and Loves
of Mr. Jiveass Nigger*, a good, funny, put-down novel. "I've lived in
Denmark," Himes said, "and I know the scene. I thought at last that
someone was telling it like it is between black men and white women."

In *The Quality of Hurt*, Himes wrote: "Emotions between black
men and white women are erratic, like a brush fire in a high wind."
Now he was quoting the line to me. But that wasn't what I wanted to
hear. I began by telling him it's a new world over here, that black
women have suffered the loss of their men for centuries and I believed
that now it was time for black men to reassure black women. There's
a hell of a novel about black and white sexual relationships. It hasn't
been written. Himes, with his talent, and with more than two decades
of female goy experience, just might be the writer.

Once more, Chester Himes seemed to relax and laughed warmly.

He mentioned a long short story he has written in Paris titled *A Case of Rape*. The plot is delicious and I hope he writes the novel.

By the time you read this, Himes will have returned to his small estate in Spain, to complete volume two of his autobiography. He loves Spain and the Spanish people and even approves of Franco's government. His reasons are logical and hilarious and I refuse to divulge them.

You see, it was basically a good, black evening. I had begun to like the naturalistic black writer who will never live in his native land. Pollution, violence, and the douche bag of American problems have something to do with it. But Chester Himes believes that he would "die within a year if I returned to the States." The majority of us are familiar with The Living and Breathing American Death. Earlier I said Himes carries misery like a basket of eggs or like a man flying a kite. I might add: like a proud man with a battered flag. Hadn't he said: "I am willing to pay everything in cost."

Racism Impetus behind
Author's Career
Flontina Miller / 1973

The Greensboro (NC) Record (December 27, 1973), p. A–8.

The behavior of black people in America's ghettos has been made absurd by the abounding absurd racism in the country, believes black author Chester Himes.

The 64-year-old Himes is the product of a generation in which the nation's black people were more or less complacent with their subordinate status, he said. But Himes, an exception to the rule, said racism has "affected me all my life." It was this despised racism which he said helped launch him to world renown as a writer.

Himes and his attractive British-born wife are in Greensboro this week where they are spending the holidays with Dr. and Mrs. Joseph Himes of 1110 Moody Rd. Dr. Himes, Excellence Fund Professor of sociology at the University of North Carolina at Greensboro, is brother of the writer.

In an interview yesterday, Himes who lives in Spain, talked to the *Record* about his work and philosophy and modern-day black writing and films.

Himes is probably remembered most often among today's young blacks for two of a series of nine detective stories about Harlem, *Cotton Comes to Harlem* and *Come Back Charleston Blue*, the basis of two black movies which packed theaters. He is critical of how the film producers altered his stories and of the black movie boom in general.

"In neither of these stories did they (producers) follow the story I wrote entirely," he said. "In *Cotton Comes to Harlem*, for instance, as a take off on Marcus Garvey's back-to-Africa movement, I used the back-to-southland movement and played a white character against a black character. But the producers removed the white character entirely and dropped the whole idea of the back-to-south movement."

Decrying the violence of the popular modern black film, Himes said: "I believe in the course of time black movies will destroy all good and creative writing in America. I don't say they are all bad, because they put the black man in the theater where people can become accustomed to seeing him. But I think sadistic films are a bad idea and will do more harm than good."

The writer added that he does not consider his detective stories to be the "blood and thunder stories" the movie industry has made them.

Himes said his earlier works were "protest novels" or the classic Negro novels, in which a black protagonist protested after being a victim of severe racism. All his later works are traced with the theme, "the absurdity of racism," which he adopted after writing *The Primitive*, a satire on American racism and *Pinktoes*, a gentle satire about interracial couples in New York.

He said his philosophy in writing changed around 1955 when he realized the protest novel no longer could accomplish anything as a black literary work.

"It had accomplished as much as it could during the life of Richard Wright and I felt a new approach was needed," he commented.

Himes said the people who for years promoted racism in America knew it was absurd and hence were able to abandon it in a considerably short period of time.

"I can remember when Governor of Alabama George Wallace was a very staunch racist, when he stood on the steps at the University of Alabama and barred black students from entering," he said. "But in recent months even George Wallace has agreed racism is absurd. This proves the people who were doing this knew it was absurd all along.

"The absurd racism of which blacks in the ghettos have been victims has caused them to behave absurdly," Himes added.

Himes feels white Southerners can abandon racism faster than white Northerners because of the large population of foreigners in the North, who in attempt to acquire the habits of Americans, cannot understand how absurd racism is.

Himes said back in his youth he had the desire to get away from racist America. This longing cost him a seven-year stay in an Ohio prison.

Himes said he grew tired of life in a Cleveland ghetto at 18 and decided to rob an elderly white couple in a "restricted" white middle class neighborhood for money to escape to Mexico.

"I was arrested in Chicago, trying to leave the country, charged with first degree highway robbery, and sentenced 20 to 25 years," he recalled.

Himes said he has kept up with black writing in America and views it as being mainly opportunistic.

"Black writers at present are writing on a wave of recognition and opportunism," he said. "They are writing everything from protest stories of a sort to text books but see it as a way to make money. Most of the writing, I think is quite good, but whether good or bad, almost all is commercial."

Himes said he and his wife of 14 years moved to Spain from Paris, France five years ago. This is his first trip back to the United States since the early 1950s when he visited his brother in Durham.

"The South looks altogether different today than it did in the early 50s. I can't say if things are sincere or not, but they look sincere," he said.

Among Himes' works are *If He Hollers, Let Him Go* (1945), *Lonely Crusade* (1947), *The Third Generation*, an autobiographical novel (1953), and *Cast the First Stone*, a novel about prison life, (1952).

His last novel was *Blind Man With A Pistol*, the final book in his detective story series. He also has written a book of five short stories which will be published in the spring.

While living in the U.S., Himes, a native of Jefferson City, Mo., said in addition to Ohio, he lived a while in the South and for several years in Harlem.

Conversation with Chester Himes

Jean Miotte / 1977

Adapted from *Miotte-Himes* (Paris: SMI/L'art se reconte, 1977), pp. 7–16. Reprinted by permission of Lesley Himes.

French abstract painter Jean Miotte first met Himes at the Old Navy Cafe in Paris. In fact, he found the Himeses an apartment in his house on rue Bourbon-le-Chateau in 1964. They became friends and later kept up a correspondence. When, in 1975, Miotte visited Himes in Moraira, they had a long conversation about art and writing, about Europe and the United States, etc. which led Miotte to edit and incorporate this exchange into a book of paintings he was preparing. Following his visit, Himes sent him additional comments, leaving Miotte free to use this material the way he liked. Miotte wished to have a balanced exchange in which each man's position would be presented equally in the book, and did not make use of all the material Himes sent him.

The text for this interview was prepared by Fabre from slightly edited texts and carbons of letters in Himes's papers, and from material Miotte recorded earlier. Miotte's part of the dialogue has been condensed for publication.

Miotte begins by asking Himes how he can manage to live in Moraira, far away from the big city. In his mind, Himes is always connected with Harlem or Paris, and he, himself, could not paint if he were not stimulated by the busy life of city streets.

Himes: I can live anywhere. I imagine a street, and it comes alive in my imagination. So do the streets and people of Harlem. The memory of a woman comes alive in a lover's mind, and that's what makes him a good lover. It's the ability to imagine that makes people successful at whatever they do. Memory is the most essential thing for any creative person.

Miotte says that he loves the big trees on his estate at Pignons, but today's painting is 'abstraction'—abstraction being the expression of another reality. "Do you think I should paint a tree, a nude body?"

Himes: No, no, your painting takes the place of a tree or a body. To me, your paintings are more natural than a real tree, or even a painting

119

from nature. But you can't compare your paintings with nature. They're a thing apart from life. They're an inspiration, and they have their own meaning to those who respond to them.

I think your paintings would be foreign to the life of Harlem. The people there lack the intellectual experience to understand your paintings. Your paintings are abstract designs that have meaning, but not to people without the education or training to appreciate them.

Miotte then discusses how important it is for the masses to be able to understand the meaning of a work of art or literature. His main criterion for a successful work is not technical excellence, but rather the intensity of its emotional and spiritual impact.

Himes: Yes, I understand, but there are more Europeans than people in Harlem who could understand your paintings. Fewer than one percent of the people there could understand your work because they lack the education. The very young in Harlem might react favorably, not that they would understand them, but they would like them. They would react to the colors and respond to the life in them.

I was reading a story about a famous ballet teacher who came to Harlem to teach ballet. The tuition was free, and he was very encouraged by his young students. Ballet appeals to the intellect, it appeals to your emotions. But 99 percent of the people in Harlem don't understand it at all, even the people who had the money to go and watch it. Of course, only one in one thousand had the money to go, anyway.

When you were in Harlem, did you ever go to a bar called the Red Rooster? It's very near a place called Small's, just up the street.

Miotte recalls visiting such places in Harlem in 1961 and 1973, and remembers the fugitive, transcendent feeling that is so much alive in black rhythms.

Himes: Well, you know, almost all black Americans can dance. If you think of dance, you think of black Americans.

Have you been to Harlem lately?

Himes: No. I don't even write to my brother who has lived in Harlem during the last seven years. Of course, Harlem used to be Small's, the Apollo Theater, and so on. But Harlem is a ghetto now. There's only one black man in Harlem who owns a business.

A generation ago black people discovered that Jews owned most of Harlem, and about 1950 they attempted to do something about it.

They picketed the Jewish owner of the Apollo Theater and other places on 125th Street. The only black business owner on the street owned a cheap restaurant.

The best pictures we have of Harlem, to my mind, are from some of the television programs, like *Kojak*. The atmosphere on that show is excellent. *Kojak* lets you see what Harlem people do out on the streets. You can see the small rackets, the prostitution, and so on. It might cause you to look at Harlem with disgust.

But Harlem keeps changing. Blacks have been pushed aside by the Puerto Ricans. Puerto Ricans are more progressive, and better educated. They get better jobs. Very few blacks have gotten ahead. Harlem is dreadful, and there's nothing funny about it. My poor brother lives there in fear and misery. Many blacks moved down toward Central Park, and over towards Fifth Avenue during the 1970s.

Miotte talks about the inspiration he derives from New York City. To him, Paris seems more like a village, while New York is a city. Paris is more stuffy and provincial, while New York embraces anything new. What does Himes think about the two cities?

Himes: You and I feel absolutely differently about New York. New York was my greatest antagonist because I was a writer. It did everything it could to stop me from writing. I was asked recently [by Michel Fabre] to write a few pages on what France meant to me. Let me quote from them:

"France was an escape from racial prejudice in the publishing industry. I believe that America allows only one black man at a time to become successful from writing, and I don't think this has changed. France seemed to be a place where my talent would make me as successful as Alexandre Dumas.

"In Paris I learned to survive on the scraps from the markets, such as stale bread and spoiled wine. France didn't support me, but it kept me alive and strong enough to concentrate on my writing. For two years I didn't receive a penny from the United States. Hotel proprietors let me have shelter until I could afford to pay them. Every franc I earned during those years I earned from French publishers. In other words, Paris allowed me to live and get ahead. Nobody refused me anything because I was poor."

Knowing all that, it should be easy to understand why I disagree with you about New York. I can see how New York might seem to white foreigners, so I can agree with you up to a point. It's too bad I could never experience that while I lived there. It's ironic that I had to come to France in order to experience life in New York.

However, I understand what you mean in everything you have said, in your basic comparison between New York and Paris. You are a modern Frenchman with a modern talent, and your approach to this talent makes you different from French artists born fifty years ago. This is what makes you like New York. You understand it, you draw strength from it, you're fed by it—the kind of food that agrees with you and nourishes you. You see it as a city while Paris seems to be a village. This is all understandable, and I think this is partly due to your age. If you were older and had spent more of your life in France, you might think differently. You admire New York's positive aspects without realizing that these same things might be undesirable to somebody who is older. You don't even consider people of my race, like any white American. You don't feel this way about me because you like me and admire me. But white Americans do.

You have rare intelligence, even foresight, and you seem to think that New York could replace Paris as the center of new art and ideas. But this doesn't make me happy, rather it disgusts me.

I don't have two separate lives, one in Europe and the other in the United States. The only life I have left to me is here, in Europe. I'm sorry. The United States offers me nothing anymore, except money.

What will your next book be?

Himes: My new book is *My Life of Absurdity*. It deals with my life in Europe, beginning with the time I arrived in Paris, then covering the rest of my travels. Even here. I was living here [in Spain] when I finished the book. It doesn't deal with my life in the States. I've only visited there two or three times.

I like Spain when it's warm. This has been a very agreeable month. Next month will be another good month, and then the one after that starts getting cold. It sometimes gets very cold for Spain. Since the houses here are not very well heated, it sometimes feels colder than it is.

I don't really have to go anywhere. The city I most like in the world is Paris. I don't need Spain for my work. I hate Spain. I hate almost every place I have ever lived, except for the place I have created, either to knock it down or build it up. I'm sorry I must write these disappointing [things]. I have enjoyed talking to you tremendously, but I can't feel toward the United States as you do.

The comedy and anger in Himes's personality tends to underscore the tragedy in his books. Himes's seems to be an aesthetic of exaggeration and burlesque, not very different from a painter's approach.

Himes: The comedy and uproar of my characters' actions are all created in my mind. All my work comes out of my imagination.

I don't think sexual frustration is the wellspring of my imagination. When you read my autobiography, you can understand this. I have a lot of sex in my books because my stories require it. Sex moves Harlem. The only release blacks have is sex. What is there to believe in? They don't have any money; they don't have any recreational activities, no place to go. Sex is the last motivation and the most forceful.

I write on the principle of the "straw man." No situation, no criminal, no crime, no person is as bad as I present it in my writing. I exaggerate in order to knock it down or change it for the better. Crimes are more flagrant. Everything must be exaggerated so the good work of the cops is better understood.

Sometimes I believe they aren't real, but then I begin to think that they are, and that they can do the things I want them to do. They are no longer "straw men," but real men in the world of the living. Yes, my two cops are a symbol for me. They are larger than life.

In *The Primitive*, Jesse Robinson is what Americans call "a primitive" until he kills Kriss. But by killing her, he somehow becomes a human being. Human beings kill more people in America than the plague, "law abiding" humans, that is. But white Americans don't see the humanity of a black American, not until he kills a white person.

Moitte insists that an artist should always be conscious of world events and concerned about suffering and oppression.

Himes: Most of the great artists of the world are moved by oppression and cruelty. Artists are made by their feelings for other people, by the hurt they absorb from strangers. This is because they love people, and want civilization to go forward. Artists accept the problems of the oppressed as their own. I join the artists of the world in seeking to free my black people from oppression.

You have been close to many painters, too.

Himes: I have been very close friends with artists, both in America and Paris, and much of my inspiration comes from knowing them. It seems like we live the same kinds of lives and are moved by the same things. We are brothers and sisters, and black artists more so, because we suffer the same kind of misfortunes.

Moitte thinks that the appeal of his painting is not different from that of jazz. He wonders whether Himes believes it is essentially different.

Himes: Jazz musicians reach only a certain percentage of the people. As a rule, jazz appeals to the lower class, the poor, the uneducated, and not the middle class.

I think a lot of people would enjoy your paintings in Harlem. They might not understand them, but they would like them. They probably wouldn't interest the middle class, but the Harlem people that live the night life, that sing and dance, will like them. A lot of those people have what is called "soul." They live freely enough to enjoy such things without being troubled.

No, I don't think [the appeal of music and art are essentially different]. The appeal is to the same line of thought and emotion as the jazz musicians have, and as the free dancers in Harlem have. And the dancers and musicians understand one another, you know.

My writing is very close to the improvisation of jazz. The jazz musician thinks, he feels, he rehearses, he performs, he scores, he improvises until he gets a beat. With it, he is playing jazz. That is what we all have in common. Good jazz is pure art, just like your paintings.

It is through a formal understanding of certain definite values that the jazz musician has conceived, organized, and developed his art; the same is with me and with you. It is a literal transformation; inherited conventions have actually been restated, recognized, and ultimately reconstructed as a new expression. This is the way it is with us.

Chester Himes Direct
Michel Fabre / 1983

From *Hard-Boiled Dicks* Nos. 8–9 (December 1983), pp. 5–21.*

MF: When did you actually begin to write short stories? Did you begin when you started college, or only in the 1930s when you first began to be published?

CH: No, I began writing short stories in the penitentiary. At first, it was a way of escaping from the environment I was living in, although I often wrote about the everyday experiences of the prisoners whose lives I shared.

In my early prison stories, I wrote about white characters. It made publication possible, or at least easier, in big magazines like *Esquire*. When I started writing in the U.S. in the early thirties, a black writer had a hard time getting published. For a long time no one realized that I was a Negro. I wrote about white men because their problems were the problems of convicts, no matter what color they were. They experienced the same emotions, whether they were black or white. I rendered the prison environment faithfully, something critics acknowledged years later.

MF: Did you write exclusively about convicts?

CH: No, I wrote a story about a football player, and another one about two detectives. It was only after I was released from prison that I started writing about other kinds of lives. You know, I didn't deliberately choose to write about Negro life. The war was a tremendous shock, psychologically, and its effect on combatants, civilians, even wives, became a theme for my stories.

MF: In "Two Soldiers," you show how the growth of a relationship between a black American and a white American results in a triumph of the spirit in the midst of battle.

CH: Yes. I must confess it was a clumsy attempt at propaganda. But I needed the reconciliation between the two soldiers, even though it may've been too trite.

During the war, tragedy was an everyday experience, and the

heightened emotions sometimes changed a person's feelings about things. The protagonist of "So Softly Smiling" wonders about the role Negroes might play in the war, about the possibility of national unity. The Negro ultimately realizes that his part is as important as that of a white American.

MF: Was it to escape from the racial climate that you decided to move to Europe in 1953?

CH: My desire to leave America probably resulted from a terrible humiliation I suffered in 1947. I had been invited to sign my novel, *Lonely Crusade*, and to be interviewed on the radio. At the last moment, everything was canceled without my being told. In this particular novel, I attempted to describe the constant, long-standing fear that lurks in the minds of American Negroes, along with the impact of Communism, of industrialization, of the war, of white women on black men, and the plight of black couples. There wasn't a single event in the story that hadn't actually happened. My characters were real people, living in familiar situations, but no one liked that novel. I ran into a wall of hatred. I wasn't able to leave the country at once, but promised myself I would as soon as I had enough money— which took another six years. I finally sailed to Europe in 1953.

MF: How did you manage to live in Europe?

CH: I had to move about during the first couple of years, while working on *The Primitive*. I went back to New York City for a while, but couldn't remain there. I left for Paris again in 1956.

I started writing detective novels in Paris, and *For Love of Imabelle* was published there in 1957. These novels were later published in the U.S. My earlier work was sociological fiction, generally autobiographical. It was called "protest fiction" by the critics. I had only handled the detective genre in a few stories.

MF: In your thrillers, the black characters seem surprisingly unaware of social and racial problems.

CH: When I describe life in Harlem, the people live in poverty and moral misery, but retain a capacity to enjoy every moment. Most of the characters are petty criminals or victims, and many of them have only a hazy perception of the oppression they suffer, or any understanding of the link between racism and economic exploitation. Of course, all of this is part of the fabric of their lives, and they aren't thinking about it. They're far too busy surviving.

MF: Yet this isn't the case in all your novels and stories.

CH: There are some differences. My domestic novels rarely deal with racism explicitly, except *Blind Man With A Pistol*. These books are really about ghetto hustlers getting around the law to make a living. They show how you can beat the law in ghetto situations, and the solutions are pretty simple, even mathematical.

But the stories portray an increasing number of ordinary characters who appear alongside the criminals and detectives, and those characters help fashion a kind of human comedy, a picture of ghetto people and the circumstances of their lives.

There are many different characters in the short stories: a decent black couple in "One Night in New Jersey," delinquents and murderers in the prison stories. Each one has his own emotional makeup, his own past, his own worries. At the same time, the action in a short story focuses upon a central consciousness.

The realism is mostly emotional, and what matters is how the evolution of a character within a situation makes him more violent because his environment is so unpredictable.

MF: Do you think your personality changed because of your living in Europe?

CH: Of course. Here a Negro becomes a human being. There's nothing grotesque about a black man meeting a white woman here. There's nothing unnatural about it. This isn't the case in the United States.

Racism became a big problem for me in 1940, when I found I was barred from most of the employment I could find. Segregation hadn't really affected me until then, but it became tangible. I felt I could actually see racism. It colored everything. My first wife was a beautiful black woman, but I was never able to provide the kind of life for her I wanted because we were only Negroes. We separated after fourteen years.

MF: The stories you wrote around that time often deal with characters who have identity problems. I'm thinking particularly of "Dirty Deceivers."

CH: White society has always wanted black people to feel uncomfortable. There's nothing strange about a Negro whose features and color are close to the white man's trying to pass for white, even if it drives him insane. At the same time, Negroes used to living in constant fear have always found solace in drug addiction.

MF: Has your living in France played an important role in your career?

CH: Only to some extent. I was known in the United States before I left in 1953, and *If He Hollers* had sold well. But I remained a "Negro writer;" in other words something marginal in the mind of the public; a not quite respectable writer for reasons that had nothing to do with morals. The only Negro writer at the time who enjoyed any status as an "American writer" was Richard Wright. He was recognized as such, but I wasn't, nor were many others.

Later, my detective stories sold well in the United States, but they weren't considered important enough to be reviewed.

MF: Don't you think this is a question of literary genre?

CH: Possibly, but to be a black man, and a writer of detective fiction, amounted to a double handicap in America when I started writing in that genre.

Things have changed now. Detective fiction is being taught in universities. I was glad that Professor Edward Margolies wrote about my novels, along with those of Raymond Chandler and Dashiell Hammett [in *Which Way Did He Go: The Private Eye in Dashiell Hammett, Raymond Chandler, Chester Himes, and Ross MacDonald.* New York: Holmes and Meier, 1982]. This is where they belong. Blacks are now treated equally with whites, just like detective fiction is being treated equally with so-called legitimate fiction. Dostoyevsky and Agatha Christie have each written about crime in their own ways.

MF: You seem to enjoy writing about the most unbridled kind of violence in your thrillers. Don't you also like to depict thieves, quacks, con men, and such?

CH: Of course I do. That's why there're so many black pimps, religious quacks, con men who deceive white people lusting for black bodies, and petty thieves in my Harlem novels. Especially in *For Love of Imabelle* and *Back to Africa [Cotton Comes to Harlem]*. I deal with religious charlatans, fake sisters of mercy, nuns in disguise, with the lost souls who join the Muslims or the supporters of Daddy Grace and Father Divine. Charlatans are found mostly in religion, or in the pseudo-political "Back to Africa" movements.

MF: Did you live in Harlem for very long?

CH: No, I didn't. Only a few months at a time. Just long enough to absorb its atmosphere, although it keeps changing, mostly in terms of fashion, slang, and what is or isn't hip.

I've sometimes been reproached for providing an exaggerated picture, revelling in the depiction of cults and con men, for instance. You only have to go there to realize that reality is often stranger than fiction. At any rate, I don't try to paint an exaggerated, exotic picture.

I really became familiar with the Harlem underworld in the mid-fifties, when I was broke and alone in New York City. I got to know its geography, its secret places. What I learned about the black bourgeoisie, I learned in the forties when I was staying with cousins of mine, whose lifestyle I depicted in *Pinktoes*.

I put the slang, the daily routine, and complex human relationships of Harlem into my detective novels, which I prefer to call "domestic novels" for that reason. This is a world of pimps and prostitutes who don't worry about racism, injustice, or social equality. They're just concerned with survival. It may have been because my head was buzzing with so many problems that I enjoyed their company so much.

MF: Did you write at all when you were living in Harlem?

CH: No, I don't remember what I did. I was really staying at the Albert Hotel in Greenwich Village, not residing in Harlem.

MF: Have you written most of your work outside the United States?

CH: A lot. I kept writing wherever I was staying because I had to publish in order to survive after I left the United States. I began "Spanish Gin" in a little Spanish fishing harbor called Puerto Pollensa, on the island of Mallorca where I lived in the fifties. At the time, I drank heavily, and this may explain the madness of that weird, fantastic story. I've even written in Mexico. I revised *Back to Africa* in the little village of Sisal, where the natives were still living much as they had three centuries ago. There were no comforts there, except a single telephone, and not a single automobile in the village.

MF: I am surprised you're so concerned with comfort.

CH: Nowadays, at my ripe age, I need some comfort, or what everyone else in Europe considers indispensable: electricity, heating, running water, a clean house.

MF: Did you really stop writing after the second volume of your autobiography?

CH: Yes, for all practical purposes. Because of my health.

MF: Do you usually write a story a long time after the incidents or events which inspired it, or do you make use of recent occurrences in your life?

CH: In the fifties, I wrote quickly to make a living, and any topic or theme was fair game. I wrote three stories, "The Snake," "A Night in New Jersey," and "Spanish Gin" during that time, and only the last one was based on recent events. The other two were based on events that had taken place in the mid-forties.

MF: When is writing the easiest for you?

CH: It's hard to tell. Sometimes I write with greater ease because I'm boiling with outrage at something. Writing helps me to settle accounts at times like that. Other times I write best when I'm most hard-pressed, when I have to make money quickly. That's the way I wrote the first five detective novels for *Série noire*. What I was writing seemed to mirror my mood. I was continually looking for a place I could call home, and a kind of life that would suit me. When I found the right place, and some happiness, as I did in the sixties near Aix-en-Provence, I found it more difficult to write for some reason.

MF: What's your writing routine?

CH: I like to get up early, have a big breakfast, and work at one stretch until it's time for lunch. If the mail is good, I generally go on with my writing. If it's bad, my mind is disturbed for the rest of the day. I have nearly always typed my manuscripts, without consulting any reference books or dictionaries. In my hotel room in Paris I only needed cigarettes, a bottle of scotch, and occasionally a good dish of meat and vegetables cooking on the burner behind me. Writing's always whetted my appetite.

MF: How much realism do you put in your stories, and how much is imagination?

CH: I hardly remember myself. I wouldn't be able to tell you whether such-and-such a character in my prison novel really existed, but I distinctly remember details, atmosphere, a railing and a gate, a street corner, a section of sky seen from a barred window, or the jingling of the warden's keys. It becomes blurred as the years go by. My characters are mostly composites. I borrow a detail here, a detail there, using a chance encounter or something that impressed me. For instance, in *A Case of Rape*, the black painter who walked the streets of Paris with a snow-white Borzoi dog is real, as is the same man painting his hotel room white, except for black footprints reaching up to the ceiling. He was called Bertel.

MF: Did you imagine the bizarre episodes of "Spanish Gin"?

CH: This story seems utterly fantastic and crazy, but it had its origin in a party that actually took place in Puerto de Pollensa in 1955. Willa and I had been invited by a homosexual couple, who lived in a superb villa with a terrace overlooking the bay. Bob was born to a wealthy Boston family, and Mog was a fair-haired German boy, a fitting aryan type, whose opinions had caused him to be fired from his job at the U.S. Embassy, where he was teaching literature. We were at the end of a long literary discussion which had just turned sour. I went out to the restroom, and upon my return I found Bob lying on the floor. Mog had accused him of flirting with Willa, and had knocked him out. Of course, we'd been drinking a lot of Tom Collinses with cheap Spanish gin. So much so I passed out myself, for part of the afternoon.

Then we tried to play Monopoly. By nightfall, I became totally engrossed in the bosom of a guest who was feeding our host's cat caviar, while Willa cast angry glances at me. Things didn't go any further because Willa and I went back to our place, soused and wet because we accidentally walked into the ocean.

I don't know why I decided to cook kidneys in the kitchen when we came home. I was doing this when I heard a great crash in the bathroom. I found Willa lying on the tile floor. She'd broken her collarbone and, as she fell, hit her temple on the bathtub. She was so drunk that she'd tried to step out of her dress and her foot had gotten caught in it. She had a black eye for a long time, and people thought I'd hit her. We were so drunk, and it was all so crazy, that I didn't have to exaggerate much to create an utterly crazy story.

MF: What about your prison stories?

CH: Just open *Cast the First Stone* and you'll realize what kind of material I found in the penitentiary. This is one of my most autobiographical novels, although the publishers cut a lot out of it. But most of the events I used happened to the tough guys I found in jail, rather than to myself.

MF: Did you live in the South for a long time? You describe it well in "The Snake."

CH: That story isn't set in the South. I explain in my autobiography how I spent a couple of months on a ranch belonging to my brother-in-law in California near the Nevada border. I was then working on *Lonely Crusade*. The ranch had little in the way of comforts, and the area was almost deserted. We had to fight an invasion of rats first, and then rattlesnakes came out in the spring. I shot the first one as it came across the yard.

A neighbor told me that we had to burn its body, otherwise the female would come in search of her mate, so I did. That very evening another snake came by, and it crept beneath Jean's naked legs as she was resting in the hammock. It seemed to me that it took forever to crawl by. I struck it with a spade as it was reaching the tool shed. It stood up and bit the handle with such violence that it made a dent in it and broke a fang. I struck it dead, hitting like mad, cutting it into small fragments. Later I shot half a dozen other snakes. From then on, every time we left the house, I felt compelled to search it for fear a snake would be in there.

MF: Has actual experience ever matched the power of your imagination?

CH: One particular case is the fire that destroyed part of the Ohio penitentiary and claimed 360 victims. I used it as the basis for "To What Red Hell."

The only other case I remember concerns a character in the story, "Strictly Business." My hero was a gangster, a tall, blonde bodyguard of Swedish origin. I met him when I was looking for work in the 1940s, and asked Frank Bucino, a little one-eyed Italian, for work. He always went around with this tall, blonde, Swede bodyguard.

Bucino had transformed a training camp for the German American Bund into a summer camp, with cottages and trailers. My wife and I worked there, and we lived in the old Bund tavern, on the first floor, with three dogs. We had a Mack truck that I drove at breakneck speed. I wrote about all this in the story, " A Night in New Jersey."

MF: Which is your favorite character, among all you've created?

CH: It's certainly Jesse Robinson, in *The Primitive*. I put a lot of myself into him. I probably said everything I wanted to say in that novel, but it caused a great deal of trouble between me and the publisher. I had to intervene repeatedly with my editors to restore things they'd cut out. They found the novel too daring, too risky, too obscene, and cut quite a bit out of it without my permission. The

French translation is closer to the original because Yves Malartic made it from the original typescript.

MF: What did you attempt to prove in *The Primitive*?

CH: This was an attempt, and I believe a successful one, to depict the repressive influences in our time, and our attempt to reconcile the community values of Christian religion with the economic ethics of capitalism. We cling to moral conceptions that don't fit the circumstances of our lives.

It was the same in France a hundred years ago. Zola's *Nana* said more, in my opinion, about the sexual frustration and impotence of the ruling class in France, than about the desires of a prostitute. Zola was dealing with the national stupidity of his time.

In *The Primitive*, I put a sexually-frustrated American woman and a racially-frustrated black American male together for a weekend in a New York apartment, and allowed them to soak in American bourbon. I got the result I was looking for: a nightmare of drunkenness, unbridled sexuality, and in the end, tragedy.

What I wanted to show is that American society has produced two radically new human types. One is the black American male. Although powerless and small in numbers, he can serve as a political catalyst. The other type, the white American woman, has developed into something beyond our imagination.

MF: Why?

CH: She's better educated, better off financially, and enjoys more freedom than women have at any other period in history. Yet she's the most unhappy, and sexually incomplete creature ever produced, because she isn't loved or cared for. In *The Primitive*, I exaggerated the situation slightly, and showed how modern woman is the victim of a dangerous delusion that every person of color is a primitive. In fact, the new Negro is a psychological hybrid, the result of the vulgar and depraved compulsions of our culture. The white woman doesn't appreciate how dangerous this has made him.

MF: Your novels very often deal with the black man-white woman relationship. Is this a personal obsession?

CH: I think this is related to one of Western culture's strongest themes. In our culture, the white male both places the white woman on a pedestal and victimizes her. Just the way the black man is victimized. This makes them natural allies. Their mutual attraction derives, in part, from a subconscious wish to break taboos. The black man, also wants to possess the white woman sexually as a form of revenge against his white oppressor. In spite of this, the black man is capable of giving the white woman a kind of love she can find nowhere else. This is what I attempted to show in *A Case of Rape* and *The Primitive*.

MF: *The Primitive* is indeed one of the best depictions I know of sexual psychology.

CH: I may have been a pioneer in this kind of exploration. Whether or not I wrote it as a personal catharsis is irrelevant. There's a lot of violence in this novel, and a frightening struggle between sexes and races, but I also incorporated tremendous compassion for the anguish these two characters suffer.

The novel shows a white woman's desperate quest for love among those she believes are primitives. She's looking for the kind of admiration that twentieth-century American culture denies her, but she fails to understand that the man she seeks it from is an extremely complex personality, which is why the affair ends so tragically.

MF: Yes. Jesse Robinson can't help gradually coming to hate her. What do you hate most yourself?

CH: Racism and what it has done to me. The paranoid delusion that I've been placed on earth simply to be the victim of humiliation.

MF: Do you read many treatises on psychology, psychoanalysis, or sociology?

CH: I never do that, nor do I suggest psychoanalytical motivations for the crimes committed in my domestic novels. The motives for crime are simple: money, fear, hatred, jealousy—motives I know from personal experience.

MF: Does a life of crime ever appeal to you?

CH: Real crime sickens me. I think criminals deserve to be punished.

MF: Why are there so few female criminals in your novels?

CH: I never really thought about it, but it's probably because I have a different image of women. I know there are real female murderers, but I don't like writing about violent women. There's only one female murderer in my detective novels, and that's Iris in *Back to Africa* *[Cotton Comes to Harlem]*. Billie only kills to help the detectives in *For Love of Imabelle*. There are women who experience violent emotions in my other books, such as Kriss in *The Primitive*, who'd like to kill Jesse, but none of these characters is what you'd think of as a professional killer.

MF: What do you think of the political use of violence? Have you ever read Franz Fanon?

CH: No, I never read him, but I was told he alluded to some of my work in his book, *Black Skin, White Masks*. I've often spoken about political violence, but I merely acknowledge that it exists, I don't tell people to go out and do it.

You know what I see out there in the real world? Instead of organizing a well-structured political movement capable of efficient action, the Black Panthers waste their time playing "cops and robbers." And the American press, which likes nothing more than to titillate its readers with stories about crime, has undercut the Panthers' revolutionary potential. If the black masses ever thought that the Panthers might improve their lives, they know better now. The opportunists of both races are manipulating the Panthers for their own purposes.

MF: Is that what you intended to show in *Blind Man With A Pistol*?

CH: Yes, the Panthers, and other nationalist movements like the Black Muslims. I started another thriller, called *Plan B*, which is about a large-scale black rebellion led by a black subversive organization, but I didn't quite finish it. In it, the man who secretly sends weapons to blacks finds his plan wrecked because black people don't have the political maturity needed to band together into an effective force. Instead of waiting for an organization to form, each one of them begins shooting white people for his own personal reasons.

MF: This is because of a lack of solidarity?

CH: Yes, a lack of black solidarity.

MF: When did you work on this novel?

CH: In 1967, when I was living in the South of France and here in Alicante. It grew out of a story called "Tang," but I became uncomfortable with it after a while, because the story became too exaggerated. I originally envisioned a general conflict between the races, but in the final scene Coffin Ed and Grave Digger, shoot at each other. One of them takes the side of his race brothers, while the other one chooses to uphold law and order, not because he feels any loyalty to whites, but because the political and social implications of the rebellion are too much for him.

MF: Why did you kill them off? Was this a literary consideration, or did it reflect some ideological position?

CH: Well, it shocked me to discover that I'd inadvertently ended the careers of Coffin Ed and Grave Digger, because it amounted to a kind of literary suicide. Maybe this is the reason I couldn't complete the book, although I did write a synopsis for an ending. At the time, I had nearly completed all the books that my original contract with Duhamel called for, and I suppose I wanted to turn my attention to autobiographical writing.

Then I became fascinated by a story Phil Lomax told me about a blind man shooting a pistol in the subway. It sounded so completely absurd, a blind man killing people at random, or perhaps according to a choice governed by his blindness. That story resulted in *Blind Man With A Pistol*.

MF: In which of your characters do you most see a reflection of yourself?

CH: Personally, I never felt any attraction to violence. Besides, black violence against whites has never been as important as the American press pretends to believe. It was obvious to me that blacks had no chance in an armed confrontation, the odds being one to ten. It's through acting upon white guilt, and by knowing how far to carry their threats, that Negroes might achieve the greatest results.

MF: Do you think there's any difference between the novels published by Gallimard in the *Du Monde Entier* series, and those published in the *Série noire*?

CH: Marcel Duhamel asked me to write for the *Série noire*, but my previous novels had appeared in such prestigious series as Nadeau's *Le Chemin de la vie* with Corréa, and *Feux croisés* with Plon. Before that, Gallimard had accepted *The Primitive* for their *Du Monde Entier* series, although it is in many respects a crime novel. I liked that very much. In writing for *Série noire*, I was limited by a formula, but this didn't prevent me from saying whatever I wanted. At the same time, my "mainstream" novels are set in a world that is just as violent and obscene as the world of my domestic thrillers. It's the media, the press, the critics who decide how to categorize you. They're the ones who really define literature.

MF: Have you ever had any trouble with the French media?

CH: On several occasions, articles that dealt with my work or career, and that had already been planned for publication, didn't appear. One example is a *Paris-Match* interview done in 1958, and another is an article on Harlem that I had written at the request of Pierre Lazareff. It was turned down, but was later published in *Présence Africaine*. I gave *Candide* magazine a piece in which I compared racism in Algeria with racism in Alabama. *Candide* printed it, but French friends warned me about reprisals by the Organisation de l'armee secrete. I was worried for a while, but nothing happened.

MF: You wrote somewhere "Writing had become my *raison d'etre*, something that couldn't be taken away from me. I had become a writer." What is, in your opinion, the particular function of writing?

CH: In the penitentiary, the simple fact of being able to write a story, to type it on the typewriter, gave a man a particular status. Other convicts respected you for it.

Writing was also a way to escape, because it meant connecting with the novelists I admired, like Dostoyevsky. I admired him, and found an affinity with what he did in *The Brothers Karamazov*. I became part of a peer group apart from that of convicts.

MF: Which writers do you admire the most?

CH: Among American writers, Faulkner comes first. Some of his less important novels display a terrific sense of humor. You might remember that *The Reivers* delighted me when you and John [A. Williams] brought it to me while I was in the hospital in April of 1963. Well, I think Faulkner is the greatest. I admire Hemingway's short stories, too.

MF: You often spoke of Faulkner as the master.

CH: I did. He was, to me, the greatest writer in the world until he died. I read all his early works, and it's the early Faulkner who influenced me most, together with Hammett. *Sanctuary, Light in August, Mosquitoes*—Faulkner can plumb the depths of a soul better than anyone else.

His portrayal of black people is also masterful. More than anyone else, he managed to define and express the mind of the South, both black or white. He was prone to exaggeration, but his picture of Negroes in the South is lively and acute, in spite of the fact that he's occasionally been accused of racism. My favorite book by Faulkner is *Light in August*, because it shows the absurdity of racism, and the confusion and suffering it causes.

MF: Which American writers do you like nowadays?

CH: You must realize that any educated black American is aware of different literary traditions than those you found in white schools, at least until recently. My mother had a good education, and she made a point of telling us about the poetry of Paul Laurence Dunbar, which we would recite at school. There were nineteenth-century figures like Frederick Douglass, and later, there was the poetry of Langston Hughes. His autobiography made you want to travel to Europe and Africa, and meet all kinds of people.

These books weren't best-sellers, however, and most of the successful books dealing with black people were written by whites, such as Sinclair Lewis or Margaret Mitchell.

MF: What relationship have you had with black novelists?

CH: I've known most of them over the years, like Richard Wright, James Baldwin, Ralph Ellison, and I've long been the friend of John A. Williams. His novels—*The Man Who Cried I Am* and *Sissie* especially—are excellent. His work is unknown in Europe, and much neglected in the United States. But those writers weren't my influences, they're my friends.

MF: Yet you're sometimes impatient with them in your autobiography, and when you depict Wright in *A Case of Rape*.

CH: That book is pure fiction. I didn't use Dick Wright or William Gardner Smith as characters, although I had them in mind when I created my characters. I know Dick believed he was Roger Garrison. He believed he was the only black American writer in the world, and that everyone was against him. It wasn't true.

I wrote *A Case of Rape* in order to show the prejudice and humiliation American blacks endured in France during the Algerian War, not to expose any antagonism that may have existed between black American writers and artists in France. I loved Dick more than you can imagine.

MF: What about Richard Wright as a best seller?

CH: *Native Son* rocked the nation like a bomb, like the great revolutionary novel it was. But *Uncle Tom's Children* had already given a remarkable picture of the living conditions of Negroes in the South.

MF: You were a great admirer of Wright. Do you think you belong to the "Wright school" as has sometimes been claimed?

CH: When you write about the same time as a great writer, and explore similar topics, critics tend to dump you into that same category. There was no school, no circle, but rather a friendly association. I greatly admire the writer in Wright. I didn't always agree with him, but he opened the way for us. He wrote in a strikingly original way.

In *The Man Who Cried I Am*, John A. Williams has written very accurately, I think, about the Wright who lived in Paris, grappling with complex problems and unethical people. I sometimes wonder why that novel has never been translated into French. I know very few contemporary American novelists, but I think Ishmael Reed is among the best that I have read.

MF: Did you associate with black writers other than Wright in France?

CH: There was a young man who wanted to make films, and who became a writer for that reason—Melvin Van Peebles. He adapted the text for the cartoon series Wolinski created from *For Love of Imabelle* in *Hara-Kiri* magazine. Van Peebles made good money from that. Since then, he's enjoyed considerable success with *Sweet Sweetback's Baaadasss Song* and *Don't Play Us Cheap*.

MF: Which novelists have made a strong or lasting impression on you?

CH: Among those I'd mention detective story writers—but they are far more than that—such as Dashiell Hammett and Chandler. Also Dostoyevsky, Maupassant, Flaubert. I also think of Zola's *Germinal* and *The Soil*. I've known French writers like Jean Cocteau, Jean Genet, Jean Giono, and the British writer, Robert Graves, who was my neighbor in Mallorca, but those were superficial acquaintanceships, rather than literary influences.

Now, Flaubert explores the French society of his century better than anyone else, including Balzac. He's fascinated by politics and violence, which may explain why I am attracted, not by his style alone, but by the attitudes he expresses.

MF: Are you violent, or sensitive?

CH: You can't have one without the other. The more sensitive you

are, the more easily wounded you can be, and the more likely you are
to burst into violence.

MF: Have you got a strong sense of humor?

CH: I'm not the one to answer that question. I think my readers
have found a lot of humor in my detective novels, in my depiction of
Harlem, and even in some of the dramatic scenes of *The Primitive*.

You need to make a distinction between caricature and humor. I
don't think I'm a caricaturist. I provide the details of a scene or a
character, and never exaggerate without a good reason for it. By
rendering all the details of a scene, you can create a more balanced
picture. Through exaggeration, you can sometimes reveal a reality
not otherwise apparent, but you must use caution.

MF: You've sometimes been called a "surrealist" writer. Do you
think that's accurate?

CH: I didn't become acquainted with that term until the fifties, and
French friends had to explain it. I have no literary relationship with
what is called the surrealist school. It just so happens that in the lives
of black people, there are so many absurd situations, made that way
by racism, that black life could sometimes be described as surrealistic.
The best expression of surrealism by black people, themselves, is
probably achieved by blues musicians.

MF: What do you think of spirituals?

CH: Blues, spirituals, jazz, is the music of my people, my people's
greatest cultural contribution to civilization.

MF: Are you still very fond of the blues?

CH: At my age, music is one of the few pleasures left, as long as
you retain some hearing. When I was a teenager, I was fond of black
musical comedies in the theatres of Cleveland and Columbus, Ohio. I
remember hearing Ethel Waters sing in *Running Wild*. I remember
singers whose voices were so sensuous, they were even more erotic
than the naked bodies of dancers. I never cared much for classical
music, but jazz is something else.

MF: Could you mention the names of a few musicians you like?

CH: Plenty of them. But some are no longer known today, like
Budd Jenkins, whereas others have become legends, such as Louis
Armstrong. Budd Jenkins is the one who made me love the trumpet.
Also Buck Clayton and Cootie Williams. Duke Ellington even wrote
a splendid "Concerto for Cootie." Among sax players, Lester Young

remains my favorite, even though I love Miles Davis, Roland Kirk, and the unforgettable Coltrane.

The musicians I've known personally always seemed to me to be exceptional characters, not in the sense of being gods, but ordinary men who had a talent that raised them up and doomed them at the same time. Most of them were ruined by drinking and drug addiction. Budd Powell was the heaviest drinker I've ever known. He was usually drunk when he played. He had to be in order to play the way he did.

MF: What musicians' records have you bought recently?

CH: No really recent ones. There's Archie Shepp, Cecil Taylor, and Pharaoh Sanders.

MF: What about jazz singers?

CH: There was Bessie Smith, the great Bessie. And Lady Day was a queen. Stubborn as a mule, completely indomitable, but with a lot of class. She was beautiful.

MF: Have you ever been tempted by show business?

CH: I loved it when I was a teenager, but writing got hold of me while I was in the penitentiary. It captivated me from the day I read Dashiell Hammett's *The Maltese Falcon*, which was serialized in *Black Mask* magazine. He had an extraordinary gift for telling stories, while describing at the same time his milieu, and the corruption of American society.

MF: What about your own autobiography? Do you see it as the message of a witness to our times?

CH: The acclaim of *The Quality of Hurt* was one of the marks of my success with the American audience. When I went back to New York City in 1972, they gave receptions for me, and I was asked to speak on the radio and television with other writers. Since then, I've gone back to the West Coast, to the home of my friend Ishmael Reed. But I have sometimes lost contact with a lot of what is happening in the U.S. Not so much with political developments, but with everyday things that are always changing.

MF: Which black autobiographies moved you the most?

CH: *Black Boy* and *The Autobiography of Malcolm X*. You know, Malcolm had read one of my novels as a young man. And I found Maya Angelou's autobiography [*I Know Why the Caged Birds Sings*]

very moving. She's full of life and talent, and has a lively sense
of language.

MF: How do you feel about *Regrets sans repentir*, the condensed
version of your memoirs in French translation?

CH: I trust Yves [Malartic's] choice. He retained what was important to French readers. Of course, the French title doesn't correspond
to the titles of the two American volumes. I originally conceived of
my autobiography as a sort of chronicle, not as a work of art. I wanted
to bear witness to my era, and about the way I looked at it.

MF: *The Quality of Hurt* and *My Life of Absurdity* are very
pessimistic titles, aren't they? Do you still feel the same way about
your past?

CH: I've known some hard times in my life. I worked at all kinds of
jobs, spent a long time in jail, lived in many places. I've suffered, and
my life has often been absurd. But I've also known joy and love, and,
at last, I've begun to enjoy some celebrity. I have the satisfaction of
having done what I wanted to do without compromise, although I
often paid a high price for it. Now I am old and sick. I can see things
in a different light, and the little things have really become unimportant.

*This is the English version of interviews Fabre made in the 1970s and published in
French as a montage, "Chester Himes en direct . . ." in *Hard-Boiled Dicks,* Nos. 8–9
(December 1983), pp. 5–21. It included "Chester Himes: 'J'écris, c'est ma couleur.' "
(*Les Nouvelles Littéraires,* December 7, 1978, p. 8); material supplied to Michel
Grisolia for his "Chester Himes: de la souffrance à l'absurdité" (*L'Express,* September 24, 1983, pp. 47–51); also interview material supplied to Jean-Paul Kaufmann for
his "Chester Himes: la tentation de la violence" (*Le Matin,* October 27, 1993, pp.
26–27) and his "Chester Himes: Un nègre au paradis" (*Le Matin,* November 14,
1984). Copyright Michel Fabre. Printed with his permission.

Chester Himes's Crusade:
An Interview

Maurice Cullaz / 1985

Jazz Hot (June 1985), p. 50. Reprinted with permission of Maurice Cullaz. Translation copyrighted by Michel Fabre.

MC: There are many young people among your French readers.

CH: I'm really happy to hear that. Indeed, I really admire young people and write mostly for them. I believe young people are our only hope for meaningful change in this world. I hope that, sooner or later, they'll be able to control the future. It would be wonderful, wouldn't it?

Of course, young people also like music, especially jazz, rhythm and blues, spirituals—all of which is very important to my people.

MC: Did you know any black policemen who inspired the creation of Coffin Ed and Grave Digger?

CH: Yes, there were two Negro policemen I knew when I was living in Los Angeles. I used them as models for Coffin Ed and Grave Digger. They were a captain and a lieutenant who worked in an area mostly populated with black people, the Los Angeles ghetto. This was long before Watts developed into a sort of black city within the city. At the time, most of Watts was still just a big field where cattle grazed. Can you imagine that? These two policemen supervised this district located around what has since become Central Avenue.

MC: Why do you like France, and Paris?

CH: First of all, my books were very successful in France. In fact, I started writing detective novels at the request of Marcel Duhamel. He asked me to write my first thriller, and advised me on the structure of a detective novel, the importance of dialogue, and suggested how I should develop the plot, characters, general atmosphere, and suspense. As a result, I wrote exclusively for the *Série noire*. My novels first came out in French translation, then the English versions followed in the United States and Britain. Finally they were translated into several other languages. But they initially appeared in France, and the catalyst was Marcel Duhamel.

MC: Do you consider yourself specifically a writer of detective novels?

CH: No. I consider myself a writer first and foremost. I wrote novels and short stories before I ever thought of writing thrillers. As I told you, it was Marcel Duhamel who was responsible for my writing them. Before then, I had written five or six novels that had nothing to do with detective fiction. Duhamel had read them and liked my style, my "voice," the atmosphere I conjured up, and the characters I created. It's Duhamel who created Himes, the writer of detective fiction. Besides, I continue to write regular fiction.

MC: Is *If He Hollers Let Him Go* an autobiographical novel?

CH: This was my first novel. It wasn't really autobiographical, although it takes place, as you know, in a shipyard. I worked in shipyards myself. By the way, Marcel Duhamel selected, accepted, and translated that book for Albin Michel in 1948.

It isn't really autobiographical, although I always strive to develop a story within an environment I can recreate from my own personal experience. These are the reasons, I believe, why a novel such as *If He Hollers Let Him Go* has such a ring of truth.

MC: Many among your readers discovered the atmosphere of Harlem only through your descriptions.

CH: Yes, I wanted to locate all my detective stories in Harlem, where I lived for a time, and which I knew thoroughly. It's a very unusual setting, where people live fast. Harlem is a swinging place.

I once set a story in Harlem that has no connection with crime. This novel, *Pinktoes*, is based on fact, although I made it more colorful, and I changed the names and setting. But the incidents and characters are based on fact. I'm a character, myself, although a very minor one. I'm writing about a period of my life in *Pinktoes*.

Have you ever read the extraordinary autobiography of Malcolm X? He describes Harlem with absolute authenticity. I attempted to do the same thing. What makes me happy is that the people of Harlem can recognize each spot in their city, and see themselves mirrored in one character or another in my books.

MC: Can you tell us something about the novel you call *A Case of Rape*?

CH: In that novel, one of the first I wrote while living in Paris, I tried to show how prejudice and discrimination can dramatically affect a court case. It can distort the whole judicial process.

There, too, I based my protagonists on real people, but changed their names and so forth. Still, some of them might recognize themselves and hate me for it. In some cases, I didn't even bother to change names or disguise major characters. In *For Love of Imabelle*, for example, all the characters are readily identifiable. If you went to Harlem, you could quickly recognize the streets, the stores, and the people I depicted.

MC: In several of your books, you say, in effect, "Anything can happen in Harlem."

CH: You can take that literally. Every facet of life is represented in Harlem. It's a microcosm in which we can study all the reasons that make people do things or not do them, show off or lie low. Prostitution, vice, gambling, drug addiction, and violence are right out in the open. Any poor, jobless sucker can get forty or fifty thousand dollars to buy "snow" by stealing it, borrowing it, or collecting it through some kind of con game. The trouble is, anybody can play the game, but everybody can't win. The losers try to cut their losses any way they can.

MC: Which musicians did you get to know and like personally?

CH: I loved to listen to Lester Young, "Prez." I like all the records he cut. He was really talented, and his conversation was dazzling. I remember the duets, the duels, the contests between Prez and Hersal Evans in Count Basie's orchestra, and the jam sessions with Prez in different nightclubs. I knew Billie Holliday quite well. Lady Day was as fascinating when she talked as when she sang. She was a splendid woman, a true queen, an indomitable character.

But how can I describe the way Prez used to play and the way Lady Day used to sing? Those who have their records can get some idea of it, just like those who are kind enough to read my books can get some notion of Harlem and the people who live there.

Index